Michael Wood is a freelance journalist and proofreader living in Newcastle. As a journalist he covered many crime stories throughout Sheffield, gaining first-hand knowledge of police procedure. He also reviews books for CrimeSquad, a website dedicated to crime fiction.

twitter.com/MichaelHWood
facebook.com/MichaelWoodBooks

Also by Michael Wood

DCI Matilda Darke Thriller Series

BELOW GROUND

DCI Matilda Darke
Book 11

MICHAEL WOOD

One More Chapter
a division of HarperCollins*Publishers*
1 London Bridge Street
London SE1 9GF
www.harpercollins.co.uk
HarperCollins*Publishers*
Macken House, 39/40 Mayor Street Upper,
Dublin 1, D01 C9W8, Ireland

This paperback edition 2023
1
First published in Great Britain in ebook format
by HarperCollins*Publishers* 2023

A catalogue record of this book
is available from the British Library

ISBN: 978-0-00-853563-6

This novel is entirely a work of fiction.
The names, characters and incidents portrayed in it are
the work of the author's imagination. Any resemblance to
actual persons, living or dead, events or localities is
entirely coincidental.

Printed and bound in the UK using 100% Renewable Electricity
by CPI Group (UK) Ltd

For Maxwell
26-10-2010 – 26-03-2023

Prologue

From *The Hangman's Hold* by Lionel Miller

Chapter 6: Nemesis

Before my first meeting with Steve Harrison, I made two lists. The first consisted of the things I thought were important to discover about *him. The second was full of things I thought were important to* him.

I'd read a great deal of news reports about Steve so knew of his past, his route into joining South Yorkshire Police and his fall from grace, the murders he committed in 2017, and his role in the atrocity in Sheffield in 2019 which left dozens of innocent people dead. There was one person who was the centre of both of those acts, and I wanted to know how important Detective Chief Inspector Matilda Darke was to Steve Harrison.

However, I didn't want to bring her up straightaway. I wanted to allow her to linger in the background while I got an essence of Steve and his make-up. I didn't have to wait long before Matilda's name was mentioned. Steve spoke it within five minutes of our first meeting. I didn't ask him to elucidate and continued with my own set of questions to discover the information I've mentioned in the first few chapters of this book. I kept Matilda firmly on the back burner, all the time, making a mental note of the number of times Steve referenced her. She has played an enormous part in his life despite the fact I doubt they've spent more than half an hour in each other's company and exchanged more than a dozen words. What is it about this woman that has had such a deeply disturbing and profound effect on him?

I went into our fifth meeting with the sole purpose of spending the hour talking about Matilda Darke and when I sat down, I looked up at his blank face. Steve is a very difficult person to read. He's mastered the art of deception. This blank canvas is perfect for spotting the tell-tale signs of interest. I looked Steve in the eye and said, 'I'd like to talk to you about Matilda Darke.'

This was the moment Steve allowed his guard to slip. It was only the briefest of slips and he soon returned to the stoic, calm, almost laissez-faire attitude he'd become skilled at, but in those few seconds I saw Steve's pupils dilate, I saw the twitch at the corner of his left eye, I saw him lick his lips and swallow. He was excited.

'When did you first meet Matilda Darke?'

'I knew Matilda Darke before I met her.'

'How?'

'Her name was well known around the station. She was an exceptional detective. She was in charge of an elite unit. She was given all the best cases to solve, and she had a very high success rate.'

'You wanted to be on this team?'

'Absolutely.'

'Did you want to be Matilda Darke?'

I don't think Steve was expecting me to ask this question and it was a while before he replied.

'Eventually. I was prepared to pay my dues and work my way up the ranks from a lowly PC. It was the route Matilda had taken.'

'So, you wanted to follow her journey?'

'Yes. I'm not afraid of hard work.'

'Can you remember when you first set eyes on Matilda Darke?'

'Oh yes. Absolutely,' he said with a surreptitious smile. 'It was at a murder scene at a house in Greystones. I was standing in front of a cordoned-off area to keep the braying public at bay and Matilda arrived. She showed me her ID and I made a note of her name and rank, lifted the crime scene tape for her and she thanked me and headed for the house.'

'That was the first time you saw and spoke to her?'

'Yes.'

'What did you think of her?'

'I thought she was wonderful.'

'What was wonderful about her?'

'Her mind. Her attitude. Her rank. Her demeanour. She was the face of violent crime within South Yorkshire Police. She was respected.'

'Did you ever work alongside her?'

'Many times,' he said with a wistful smile.

'Can you tell me about them?'

'I attended a 999 call. A body had been found in Graves Park and I was the first officer on the scene. I knew Matilda and her team would get the case, so I hung around. She spoke to me when she arrived; told me I'd done a good job at securing the scene.'

'How did that make you feel?'

'Like I'd been noticed.'

'And had you?'

The smile dropped. 'No.'

3

'She didn't remember you?'

'No. I was just a uniform to her.'

'What was your ambition at that stage?'

'I wanted to be on her team. I wanted to be a DC.'

'Couldn't you have applied for that role?'

'There was no room on her team for a new DC. She had Rory Fleming, Scott Andrews and Faith Easter. Three people who had no right being on her team.'

I detected a hint of venom in his voice.

'Why not?'

'Well, I believe Scott is now a DS. He's obviously a late developer so I'll give him credit. Rory, well, he reminded me of a puppy. He'd be excited to be among the action, but he was soon distracted. He wasn't fully committed to being a detective, certainly not one on such a prestigious team.'

'And Faith Easter?'

'Faith was scared of her own shadow.'

'But you liked Faith?'

Steve thought about answering. He opened his mouth a couple of times, but instead gave his answer in the form of a shrug.

'You entered into a relationship with her.'

'I'd started killing by then. I wanted to know how close Matilda was to catching me. Faith was easy to win over.'

'Why did you start killing?'

'Because Matilda knew I was a threat.'

'In what way were you a threat?'

'She knew of the potential I had. She knew I could easily climb the ranks. She knew I'd usurp her.'

'How did she know that if she didn't know who you were?'

'Ah, but she did know who I was. Don't you see? Her just seeing a uniform and supposedly forgetting my name was a ruse.'

'Was it?'

4

'Yes. She wanted me to think I was insignificant, but I cottoned on to her straightaway. I didn't fail my sergeant's exam. She sabotaged the results. She made sure I was marshalling Sheffield Wednesday crowds at their home games and walking the streets of West Street and Devonshire Street on busy Saturday nights. She didn't want me anywhere near CID and major crimes.'

'Because she knew you were a threat to her leadership?'

'Exactly.'

It was at this point that I decided to change tack. There is no evidence whatsoever that Matilda Darke ever tried to stifle Steve Harrison's ambition. I've spoken to his former sergeant at South Yorkshire Police. I've seen his record, and I've seen his exam papers. He took the sergeant's exam four times and failed by a significant margin each time. There was no sabotage. I don't put this to Steve at this time as I want to understand his perception of events from his first kill up until his capture. However, he seems to enjoy talking about Matilda Darke. I can see a sparkle dancing in his dark eyes when he says her name. There is something more, deeply buried, regarding his feelings for Matilda.

'Do you hate Matilda Darke?'

'No.' His answer comes quickly.

'Do you love Matilda Darke?'

'No.' There was a pause before his answer.

'There is a fine line between love and hate,' I say. 'Both are extreme emotions. I get the impression you're standing on that fine line, and you're wavering and could fall into any category at any time.'

He smiles. It's the famous smile we've all come to know from his picture being slapped all over the front pages.

'I don't love or hate Matilda Darke,' he says, his voice much lower and slower than before. 'My feelings for her are strong but they cannot be labelled.'

It's at this point I can feel the hairs on the back of my neck stand to attention. He licks his lips slowly. He is savouring the moment. He wants to shock me.

'I want to fucking destroy Matilda Darke. And one day, one day soon, I will.'

Chapter One

Tuesday 19th January 2021

Donal Youngblood hated winter. This one seemed to be dragging, and it was only January. He arrived at work in the dark, left in the dark, and worked below ground level in rooms with no windows. The only time he saw daylight was when he could snatch a spare five minutes at lunchtime to pop out and grab a sandwich.

Donal was a technical assistant to a Home Office pathologist and with deaths in South Yorkshire on the increase due to the Covid-19 pandemic, they'd never been busier. Today alone he'd assisted in four autopsies, registered eight new bodies brought into the post-mortem suite, chased up two suppliers who hadn't delivered, filed five reports, replied to countless emails from the coroner's office and the police and grieving relatives and endured a painful call from his mother back in Dublin chastising him for not calling since Christmas. On top of all that, it was still only bloody Tuesday. He had it all to come again tomorrow, and he was scheduled to work this coming weekend, too, just like he'd worked last weekend, and the one before.

During his laughably short lunch break, a call had come through from South Yorkshire Police, and pathologist Dr Adele Kean had been called out to Wigtwizzle as bones had been found. He returned to the empty suite to find a hastily written Post-it note stuck to the screen of his computer. She told him to finish tidying up the lab, prepare the case notes for review at the meeting tomorrow, chase up the suppliers again, and have an early finish.

Was that a joke? There was no such thing as an early finish. By the time he'd put his coat on and turned off the lights in the office it was gone half past six. He dragged his feet across the car park. He was shattered. He wanted nothing more than to fall into bed and sleep until April at the earliest.

The engine of his ancient VW Polo started on the fifth attempt. He crunched the gears and headed for home. He drove with the windows down so the harsh easterly wind hit him in the face. He needed something to keep him awake for the journey. The irony of crashing and ending up in one of the fridges in the mortuary he'd just left was not lost on him.

He pulled up outside the block of flats he lived in at Brightside, grabbed his bag from the front passenger seat and headed for the stairs. He didn't even bother to check if the lift was working; it hadn't done since he'd moved in a year ago. He took long strides, two steps at a time, and tried his hardest not to inhale the stench of piss on the stairs.

'Donal!'

He heard his name being called as he stood outside his front door, key already in the lock. He recognised the thick Yorkshire accent of his neighbour, Mrs Simms. She was a kindly old lady, and she made an amazing banana bread, but he really wasn't in the mood for her right now.

He turned to her and gave her his best placatory smile.

'Good grief, Donal, you look like you've spent a week on the lash.'

'If only.'

'Is everything all right?'

'Fine. Just ... very busy at work.'

'I thought I hadn't seen you much lately. Anyway, I'll not keep you. This arrived for you this afternoon. I had to sign for it.'

She held out a small grey plastic bag. His eyes lit up. He knew what it was straightaway.

'Thank you,' he said, taking it from her. It felt light in his hands, but what was inside weighed a tonne.

'I see that's cheered you up.'

'It has. It really has. Thank you so much, Mrs Simms.'

He turned on his heel and ran back to the stairwell. Who needed sleep?

Donal had been dating Detective Sergeant Scott Andrews since the early days of the pandemic. It wasn't a normal romance, and their early dates weren't easy to arrange and were often socially distanced and masked up. However, the attraction between the two was instant. Scott had been through a great deal of trauma over the past couple of years. His boyfriend – his first boyfriend – Chris Kean had been a teacher who was shot and killed while shielding his students during a dark day in Sheffield's history just over two years ago. Scott had struggled to come to terms with the loss and still felt like he was cheating on Chris by being with Donal. They'd had a few long chats over recent weeks where they'd opened their hearts to each other. Scott wanted to settle down. He wanted normality and stability, but he was frightened of losing Donal the same way he lost Chris.

It was understandable. But Donal felt exactly the same way about Scott and knew that if the relationship was going to progress, he would have to take the lead.

Once back in the car, Donal tore into the package, pulled out the small box and looked at the engagement ring. His smile grew.

His heart skipped a beat. Now, he was nervous. He hoped Scott would say yes.

Donal set off and headed for Ringinglow where Scott lived in an apartment above the garage of his boss, DCI Matilda Darke. Just before Christmas, she'd told Scott he no longer needed to pay rent and should save the money to put towards a deposit should Scott and Donal wish to move in together. Along with the ring, Donal was going to tell Scott he also had some savings he'd been squirreling away and, crazy house prices depending, they could start looking for somewhere now.

He stopped at a red light, pulled down the visor, lifted the little flap and checked out his appearance in the small vanity mirror. He looked shocking. His black hair was flat to his head, his skin was dry, his eyes were half-closed and there were dark lines beneath them. He'd been working sixteen-hour days since Christmas and hadn't had a single day off yet. He really needed some sunshine.

He turned off Ringinglow Road and down the once boneshaker of a driveway to get to Matilda's impressive former farmhouse. Fortunately, it had recently been tarmacked and he and his knackered Polo were thankful.

There was a Vauxhall Astra, which Donal recognised as being a pool car from South Yorkshire Police, parked outside Matilda's house. He knew Scott would already be home.

He parked and climbed out, pulling his coat tight around him as the single-digit temperature plummeted below zero as darkness fell. He went to Scott's flat above the garage, looking up as he did to see it was in darkness. He rang the bell and knocked on the door, standing back to look up once more at the window to the living room. It remained dark.

Wondering if Scott was in the house, he ran over to the main building, knocked on the door and pressed the bell a few times. He hopped from one foot to the other to keep warm. He waited impatiently. He rang the bell again. Nobody came to the door.

He went over to the living-room window, cupped his hands around his eyes and leaned in for a look. There was nobody in there and the fire wasn't lit. It appeared as if there was nobody home.

Digging his mobile out of his coat pocket, he found Scott's number and called it. While waiting for the call to connect, he placed a hand on the bonnet of the pool car. It was cold. Whoever was inside had been home for a while.

He heard ringing.

It was coming from inside the house. Scott was definitely inside. Or his phone was, at least.

He ended the call and bent down, lifting the letterbox and having a nosy inside. All he could see was blackness.

He turned on the torch app on his phone and shone it inside. What he saw made him fall backwards in horror.

Donal's medical training kicked in. He jumped up, tried the

handle, but the door was secure. He elbowed it a few times, but it wouldn't budge.

He looked around him for something he could use as some kind of battering ram. He found a few loose rocks towards the side of the house, picked one up and hurled it at the living-room window. The sound of breaking glass echoed around the quiet night. Scraping away the shards of glass with the sleeve of his thick coat, he climbed inside.

With panic etched on his face, he ran through the room, opened the door leading to the hallway and looked down at the stricken body of the man he was hoping to ask to marry him.

Chapter Two

Detective Sergeant Sian Robison had only recently returned to work at South Yorkshire Police after taking time out to re-evaluate what she wanted out of life. After discovering her husband of more than twenty-five years was a serial killer, she felt her time as a detective was at an end. How could she possibly work for the police when she had no idea what her husband was doing for all those years? However, Sian was a born detective. She was at her happiest when investigating murder and violent crime. It was where she belonged, and she fell back into the role with ease.

The working day was coming to an end and she and DI Christian Brady were wrapping things up for the day. DC Zofia Nowak was still at her desk.

'Zofia, why don't you get yourself off home?' Sian said.

'My dad's picking me up tonight. I always go to my parents for tea on Tuesday night. It's the only way I could get my mum to stop fussing over me – by having a timetabled schedule of visits.'

Zofia was confined to a wheelchair following an incident in which she was pinned between a Land Rover and a tree during the pursuit of a killer. The driver of the car had been Sian's husband, Stuart. There wasn't a day went by when Sian didn't feel guilty about that, and she had wondered how their working relationship would cope, but they'd sat down, had a good long chat, tears had been shed, and they were fine with each other.

'What's on the menu tonight?' Christian asked.

'Home-made beef wellington,' Zofia said with a hint of a smile. 'My mum may be a worrier, and, yes, she does get on my nerves occasionally, but she really is the best cook in the world. Nobody leaves her house with a rumbling tummy.'

'I haven't had beef wellington for years,' Christian said.

'Me neither. I could just eat something filling,' Sian agreed.

'I'll see if I can sneak out a doggy bag,' Zofia said. She looked at the bank of monitors on her desk and her eyes widened. 'Oh my God! A 999 call has just come through from Donal Youngblood. He's at Matilda's house. He's asked for police and an ambulance.'

Sian had jumped up from her seat. 'What's happened?'

'I don't know.' Zofia's eyes darted left and right as she rapidly read the screen. 'He says there's been some kind of a disturbance. Oh my God! Scott's been stabbed.'

'Jesus!'

Christian grabbed his jacket and his car keys. 'Zofia, find out what you can, send it through to Sian's phone.'

Sian was frozen. Fear had gripped her. This team had been through hell over the past few years. They couldn't endure more.

'Sian! Come on!' Christian called out.

She snapped out of her dark reverie, grabbed her coat and

ran out after him. In the doorway, she turned back and made eye contact with Zofia. They both had fear imprinted on their faces.

Christian drove at speed out of the police station car park and headed for Ringinglow. He was hit by rush-hour traffic almost straight away. He turned the siren on and took the pavement to get past a queue of stationary vehicles going nowhere.

Sian grabbed the handrail above her and tried to navigate her phone with one hand. She selected Donal's number and rang him. He answered almost straightaway.

'Donal. It's Sian. What's going on?'

'Sian, I don't know what to do,' he said, clearly in tears. 'I've called for an ambulance twice. There's a delay. There's so much blood and Scott's unconscious.'

Sian had put the phone on speaker. She and Christian exchanged worried glances.

'Shit,' Sian said. 'Okay, Donal. You know all about stemming blood flow. You've had medical training. Apply pressure.'

'I am doing. I've got my jumper pressed over his wound and my coat wrapped around him to keep him warm. There's nothing else I can do. His pulse is barely registering. I'm losing him, Sian,' he cried.

Christian shook his head. He was ploughing through the busy streets, ignoring the beeps from other road users, and fumbled in his jacket pocket for his own phone.

Sian wiped her eyes. She swallowed her emotion.

'Donal, where's Matilda?'

'I … I don't know,' he stumbled. 'There was no one else here when I got here. The house was all dark.'

'Okay. Donal, we're on our way. Just … just do everything you can to keep Scott warm. I'm going to see what I can do about hurrying up an ambulance.'

She ended the call and turned to Christian. 'Where's Matilda?'

'Call her,' he said, his phone to his ear. 'This is Detective Inspector Christian Brady from South Yorkshire Police. I need an ambulance urgently. I have an officer with serious injuries,' he said.

With shaking fingers, Sian selected Matilda's number and called.

'Jesus Christ! How long?' Christian almost screamed. He ended the call. 'There's a shortage of ambulances and staff. He's on a waiting list. It could be another hour.'

'I doubt he'll last that long,' Sian said. She looked at her phone. 'Matilda's phone is going straight to voicemail.'

'Shit.'

Christian drove at speed past the Botanical Gardens and almost collided with a taxi on Hunter's Bar roundabout. Sian closed her eyes tightly shut and didn't open them again until the beeping from irate drivers stopped.

Christian turned from Ecclesall Road South onto Knowle Lane, and the traffic opened up. He was able to pick up speed as he shot the lights at Bents Green and, just ahead, an ambulance with flashing lights turned off Ringinglow Road and down Matilda's driveway.

'Oh. Thank God!' Sian exclaimed.

By the time Christian and Sian pulled up outside Matilda's house, the back doors to the ambulance were open and so was the front door to Matilda's home.

'Donal!' Sian called out. She jumped out of the car before it had come to a stop.

She ran to the house and Donal stepped out. His eyes were red with tears.

'What happened?'

'I don't know. I just ... I really don't know.'

Christian joined them. He looked at the house and saw a broken window in the living room.

Donal followed his gaze. 'It was the only way I could get in. I couldn't break the door down.'

'That's okay. Don't worry about it.'

'He's been stabbed. More than once. He's lost so much blood.'

They all turned and looked inside the house at the vast hallway. A crew of two paramedics were at work trying to stabilise Scott's vital signs before they moved him to the ambulance and took him to hospital.

'What happened? Did Scott call you?' Sian asked.

'No. I wasn't due to come over tonight. I just decided to surprise him. Nobody answered the door. I rang Scott and heard his phone ringing inside. I looked through the letterbox and ... oh my God!' He collapsed with emotion.

Sian leaped forward and put her arms around him. She tried to comfort him, but she was almost a foot shorter than him.

'Donal, Scott has got everything going for him. He's young. He's fit. He'll be fine. I know it.'

'Donal, did you hear Matilda's phone ringing? Sian's been calling it?' Christian asked, jumping straight into detective mode.

'No,' he answered, not taking his eyes from the open doorway of the house.

'Was there anyone else in the house?'

'No. I don't think so.'

'Any sign of a break-in?'

'I don't know,' he said, raising his voice. 'I haven't been any further than the hall.'

'It's okay, Donal. Don't worry. We'll have a good sweep of the house when we can get in,' Sian said, stepping in front of the two of them. 'Where's Adele this evening, Donal?'

He shook his head. 'I haven't seen her since lunchtime. She's out at Wigtwizzle. Bones have been found or something.'

'I'll give her a call.'

Sian took her phone out of her pocket and stepped away for some privacy.

The paramedics began to wheel the stretcher out of the house. Scott was securely strapped to it, a mask over his nose and mouth, his eyes closed. Blood spatter on his face.

'Can I go with him?' Donal asked.

'Are you family?'

'He's as good as,' Christian answered for him.

'Thank you,' Donal said, before climbing into the back of the ambulance.

The door slammed closed and less than a minute later, the ambulance began to pull away, lights flashing, sirens cutting into the cold night.

Sian stepped towards Christian. She had her phone in her hand. 'Adele's not answering either. I've tried calling Matilda again and it's switched off.'

'I really don't like the sound of this, Sian.'

'Something's happened to her, hasn't it?'

A set of headlights turned the corner and bathed Christian and Sian in a glow of harsh white. They turned and saw a crime scene investigator's vehicle stop in front of the garage.

'I asked Zofia to send a team out,' Christian said by way of an explanation. 'Matilda's house is a crime scene.'

They turned to look at the beautiful eighteenth-century building Matilda had made her home and were both thinking the same thing. They hoped they didn't find Matilda dead in there somewhere.

Chapter Three

C hristian and Sian shivered in the doorway of Matilda's home. It seemed strange to be here without Matilda inviting them in, offering them a cuppa and making them feel at home. Where the hell was she?

It was dark outside, and the mid-January temperature was well below freezing. If she was out in this, exposed to the elements, it did not look good.

Sian held her arms around herself tightly to stave off the cold. She was shaking. She didn't know whether it was fear of the unknown or the weather causing her to shake. She looked down at the mess of dried blood in the hallway. A large pool sat where Scott had lain, waiting for help. Paramedics had stepped in it and bloody footprints led off further along the vast hall. Now, white-suited forensic officers had put down metal footplates and were going about their business to look for signs of a break-in or a disturbance, anything that would give them a hint as to Matilda's whereabouts.

'I've called someone to come out and board up the living-room window,' Christian said. 'I've also called Ridley and he wants us back at the station right now.'

'What's happening here, Christian? What aren't we seeing?'

'What do you mean?'

'There's no obvious sign of a break-in. We know that Matilda and Scott left the station together. He drives her home every night, for crying out loud. He's here, in a locked house, lying on the floor, bleeding out, and Matilda's nowhere to be found. What does that say to you?'

Christian took a deep breath. He shook his head. 'I don't know, Sian. I really do not know. We need Scott to pull through so we can talk to him.'

'Should I phone Matilda's mum and sister? They might have heard from her.'

Christian didn't get a chance to answer as Sian's phone rang in her hand, making her jump. She looked at the screen. Adele was calling. She held it up to show Christian. She swiped to answer.

'Sian, what's going on? I've had about a thousand missed calls from you.'

'Adele, where are you?'

'I'm in the car right now. I've been out at Wigtwizzle all afternoon. We got a call from someone in CID telling us a car had been found abandoned in woodland and a body was in the boot. Haven't you been told?'

'Yes. I had heard. Listen, is Matilda with you?'

'No. I haven't seen her since this morning. Hang on a minute, some dick in an Audi's up my arse. I bloody hate sales reps. Yes, and the same to you,' she called out. 'Sorry, Sian, you were saying.'

'Adele, are you on your way back to the house?'

'Yes. I don't know if you've noticed, but it's pitch-dark, and there's a bottle of vodka in the freezer with my name on it.'

Christian shook his head.

'Adele, could you detour and meet us at the station?'

'The station? Why?'

'I don't want to go into details while you're driving, but there's been an incident at your house.'

'What kind of an incident?'

'I'd rather tell you in person.'

'Sian, you're scaring me now. What's happened?'

Sian took a deep breath. 'Scott's been stabbed.'

'Oh my God! Is he all right?'

'He's gone to hospital. Donal came round and found him. We don't know anything more yet.'

'And Matilda?'

Sian bit her bottom lip. She had no idea what to say.

'Sian. What about Matilda?'

'We don't know,' Sian said, choking back her tears.

'What do you mean, you don't know?'

'We can't find her, and her phone is switched off.'

'Her phone is never switched off.'

'I know.'

There was a long silence. Sian could hear the sound of traffic in the background.

'Are you still there?' she asked.

'I'll … I'll meet you at the station,' Adele said. Her voice was quiet and heavy. The call ended.

'Does she know where Matilda is?' Christian asked, hopeful.

'She hasn't seen her since first thing this morning.'

'Jesus! I don't like the sound of this.'

'Which one of you is DI Brady?' the Crime Scene Manager asked.

'I am,' Christian said.

The man pushed back the hood of his white forensic suit to reveal a shock of white blond hair. 'We've done a full sweep of the downstairs and there is no evidence of a break-in. All the doors to the property are secure and so are the windows, apart from the one in the living room that I've been told you know all about.'

'That's right.'

'The electrics were off at the mains. However, it wasn't a power cut or a surge or anything. It simply looks like a switch was flicked on the circuit board.'

'How, if there's no evidence of a break-in?' Sian asked.

'Your guess is as good as mine,' the man shrugged.

'Have you found any prints or trace evidence?' Christian asked. 'Scott would have put up a struggle.'

'We've found nothing yet. We've got a few good sets of prints from the kitchen. We need to check them against the occupants of the house. I've sent someone to the hospital as well to get DS Andrews's clothing and they'll take a scraping from under his nails for skin samples. If he did struggle, we'll get something.'

'Thanks ... erm—'

'Felix. Felix Lerego. I started yesterday.'

'Welcome to the force.'

'Thank you,' he smiled. 'It's been a busy day. Bones at Wigtwizzle, now this. Why did I think a move to Yorkshire was going to be quiet?' he asked with an excited grin.

He didn't wait for an answer but turned on his heel and returned to the kitchen to join his team.

'She's dead, isn't she?' Sian said, looking through the living-room door at the pool of blood in the hallway.

'Sian, don't,' Christian said.

'If they managed to overpower Scott, they can do anything.'

'If they've killed her, why not leave her here? Why hide the body?'

Sian stormed out of the room. She carefully stepped on the steel plates and went into the kitchen. Christian followed. She went into the conservatory, pulled open the doors and practically fell out into the freezing cold night. The external lights came on, but Matilda's back garden was expansive, and the light didn't reach all the way to the end.

'She's out there somewhere,' she said, looking into the darkness. 'Beyond the garden it's just woodland and farmland. I bet they've just dumped her there to die on her own.'

'Sian, don't do this to yourself,' Christian said.

'We're going to find her there, I know it.' She turned to Christian, tears in her eyes. 'She's dead. I can feel it.'

Chapter Four

The Homicide and Major Crime Unit suite was lifeless. The lights were on and the whole room was reflected in the windows. It was pitch-dark outside, yet it wasn't even eight o'clock. It was going to be a long night.

Detective Constable Finn Cotton had been at home when Zofia had called him to let him know Scott had been stabbed and Matilda Darke was nowhere to be found. He told his wife he had to go back to work, and she'd given him that look she always had when she was worried about him. He reassured her, but his words fell on deaf ears. A police officer had been severely injured and was currently undergoing emergency surgery, and another was missing. Of course she was scared.

When Finn arrived back at work, he found Sian sitting at her desk, head in her hands, and Zofia gave him a blank look. He went over to her and asked for the latest, but there was no more news on Scott or Matilda.

'Christian's sent Tom to the hospital to wait with Donal. As soon as there's any news, he's going to let us know,' Zofia said, her voice barely above a whisper.

Her mobile lit up.

'Is that anything?'

She looked at the screen. 'It's my mum. I've cancelled going round to hers for tea and she's got it into her head I'm making up an excuse not to see her. Bloody parents.'

'What about Matilda? Have you been trying her phone?'

'It's switched off. I've run a trace and it was last pinged at a cell mast on Ringinglow Road close to where she lives. She was definitely in the car with Scott on the way home, it would seem.'

'So, we need to know what happened between getting out of the car at the house and Scott getting stabbed.'

'The only person who can tell us that is currently unconscious, being operated on.'

'How serious is it?'

Zofia looked past Finn to Sian. She hadn't moved. She lowered her voice further. 'According to Felix, there was a great deal of blood in Matilda's hallway and, apparently, Scott was cold and unresponsive. It doesn't look good.'

'Jesus!' Finn said. 'Who's Felix?'

'New CSM. Started yesterday.'

'Oh.' He turned around and looked at Sian. He went over to her and squatted beside her desk. He placed a comforting arm around her. 'Sian, is there anything I can get you?' he asked in his softest voice.

She lifted her head. Her eyes were red from crying. 'No. Thank you.'

'When did you last eat anything?' he asked, noticing her hands shaking.

She thought. 'I'm not sure.'

He opened Sian's bottom drawer, her famous snack drawer, filled with bars of chocolate, packets of crisps and nuts and biscuits. He pulled out a Mars bar and handed it to her. 'I'll make you a tea.'

'I couldn't stomach it.'

'It'll help. Trust me.'

He went over to the drinks station and flicked the kettle on.

The atmosphere in the room was dark. There were only three people in the huge space, but it seemed claustrophobic and oppressive. He made Sian a mug of tea and took it over to her. The Mars bar was untouched.

She took the mug from him and wrapped her cold hands firmly around it. She blew on it and took a sip, immediately pulling a face.

'You've put sugar in it.'

'You're shaking. You're in shock. It'll help.'

'It tastes revolting.'

'Then that means it's helping,' he smiled.

'What's happening here, Finn? Where's Matilda?'

He let out a heavy sigh. He glanced back at Zofia. She didn't have an answer. 'I really don't know, Sian.'

'There was no sign of a forced entry. Neither Matilda nor Scott are the type of people to let a random stranger come into the house. They must have known who it was.'

'Scott was found in the hallway,' Zofia began. 'Maybe they were caught unawares when they arrived home. Felix said the power had been cut. Maybe ...' she trailed off, not wanting to think the worst.

'This isn't random, is it?' Sian asked. She took another drink of the hot, sweet tea and pulled another face. 'This is a targeted attack against the police, against Matilda.'

'Sian, we can't think that until we know the facts. We won't be any use to anyone if we start guessing,' Finn said.

She nodded. She knew he was right, but it didn't stop her flights of fancy.

The doors to the suite opened and ACC Benjamin Ridley walked in. His jacket was off, his sleeves rolled up and tie askew.

'Any news on DS Andrews?' Ridley asked.

'Still in theatre, sir,' Finn said.

'And DCI Darke?'

'We don't know where she is, sir. Nobody's been able to reach her.'

'Are you all right, Sian?' Ridley asked, taking in the look of horror etched on Sian's face.

'No. I'm not.' She took another sip of her tea, pulled a face and handed it back to Finn. 'I can't drink that.'

DI Christian Brady pulled open the door and came in. He looked shattered. His shirt was untucked from his trousers and his eyes were drawn.

'Anything?' Sian asked, hopefully.

'No.'

'Someone must have been lying in wait,' Sian said. 'They cut the power to the house, obviously assumed Matilda would be on her own, and Scott got in the way, so was stabbed.'

'But if this was someone targeting Matilda who had been keeping an eye on her, they would know she's unable to drive at the moment, so Scott takes her home,' Zofia said.

'Okay,' Sian mused. 'So, they want to get at Matilda, and they bring a knife along with them to get Scott out of the way quickly. They open the front door, go inside, and whoever is lying in wait jumps Scott and stabs him.'

Ridley cleared his throat. 'There is one other theory,' he said, not making eye contact with anyone. 'Is it possible Matilda is the one who stabbed Scott and fled?'

The room descended into a painful silence as they all took in Ridley's words. Christian looked down at the floor. Finn removed his glasses and began polishing the lenses on his tie. Zofia studied her nails.

Sian swallowed hard. 'If you really knew Matilda, you wouldn't even think that, let alone say it.' Her voice was low and heavy. She wiped away a tear.

'I'm looking at it from every conceivable angle. I don't believe for a moment Matilda would stab DS Andrews, but we'd be thinking that if it were two different people.'

'This angle shouldn't even be part of the discussion,' Sian said. Her words were slow and powerful. 'Matilda would never, ever, stab Scott, or anyone else.'

'There's still a question mark over whether Laurence Dodds jumped or was pushed from the roof of the Arts Tower last year,' Ridley said.

'Matilda Darke is not a killer,' Sian stated. 'If you think she is, why reinstate the unit? Why give her her job back?'

'I'm simply playing devil's advocate.'

'No. You're not. You're planting unhelpful seeds of doubt and clouding people's judgement with nonsense.' Sian was red with anger, her voice almost a shout.

'Sian, calm down,' Christian said.

The door was pushed open and knocked into Christian, almost sending him flying. Adele Kean stood in the doorway. She was red-faced, out of breath, and her coat was hanging off her shoulders. Everyone turned to look at her. As soon as Sian saw her, she crumpled and burst into tears once again.

'Someone needs to explain to me what the hell is going on,' Adele said.

She looked over to Sian who was being comforted by Finn.

'Scott was found stabbed at the house this evening. There's no sign of Matilda anywhere,' Christian said.

'I don't … I …' She paused and took a breath to compose herself. 'Is he all right?'

'He's in surgery.'

'But … Matilda's … hang on … I don't understand any of this. You said you can't find Matilda anywhere.' Adele looked around the room, taking in the grim faces looking back at her. 'Oh my God,' she said, realisation dawning. She pulled out a chair and sat down before her legs gave way from under her. 'I don't know how much of this she's told you. Ever since the shooting two years ago, she's received silent phone calls and cards with threatening messages. We always assumed they've been from a sick fan of Steve Harrison. Matilda hasn't received any for a while, but, on Christmas Day, a woman came to the house. Matilda's mother looked through the window and saw someone walking away from the house. When Matilda went outside to have a look, the wreath on the door had been replaced by a hangman's noose.'

'I remember,' Christian said. 'You called me, and I called Wakefield Prison to make sure Steve was still locked up.'

'And is he?' Ridley asked.

'Yes. He's in the Supermax wing. All his mail is checked before it's handed to him, and all outgoing mail is checked before it's sent. He hasn't had any visitors for over two years.'

'Why start again now, then?' Ridley asked, hitching up his trousers and perching on the edge of a desk.

'I don't know,' Adele said.

'This is connected to Steve, isn't it?' Sian asked. She shook herself out of Finn's embrace and wiped her eyes. 'Someone, some sick, twisted freak, has been writing to Steve and he's managed, somehow, to get them to hurt Matilda. He's always blamed her for him being sent to prison. That's why he manipulated his brother Jake into committing the shootings. This is all his doing.'

'We don't know that for sure,' Ridley said.

'Oh, for goodness' sake, of course it is,' she almost snapped. 'This has got Steve's name all over it.'

'Sian,' Christian said, putting his hands up and warning her to calm down. 'We need to speak to Scott. Only he knows what happened. We have to wait until he comes round and is able to talk to us.'

'Christian's right,' Ridley said.

'In the meantime, God knows who could be doing God knows what to Matilda,' Sian cried through her tears. 'The longer we wait, the more chance there is of finding her dead.'

'Oh, God.' Adele bowed her head to her chest.

'We have no other choice but to wait,' Ridley said. 'I know how you all feel about this. I know how close you all are. That's why you're such a good unit. But we have very little information to go on here. The only possible choice is to wait until Scott can talk to us.'

'I'll give Tom another ring,' Finn said, taking out his mobile.

Sian stood up quickly, sending her chair skidding back to the wall. 'We could go to Wakefield Prison. We could strip Steve's cell. We lock him in a room and tell him to tell us everything he knows.'

'We don't have any reason to do that right now, Sian,' Christian said. 'Besides, if Steve saw us in a panic, desperate for information, he'd clam up and enjoy the show. You know he would.'

Reluctantly, Sian nodded. She knew Christian was right. She sat back down.

Ridley cleared his throat again. 'Christian, I want you to lead this investigation. The second DS Andrews is awake, we need his statement. In the meantime, double-check with Wakefield Prison that Steve is still safely locked up and get a list of all his registered visitors and regular people he gets mail from.'

'Will do.'

'Get a record of Matilda's mobile phone, go through it, and identify any calls she's had in the last twenty-four hours. If they come up clean, extend the time frame. Do the same with her computer and check her emails.'

'Do you want me to go and talk to her mother?' Sian asked.

'No. I don't want you on this case,' Ridley said.

'What?' she snapped.

'You're too emotionally involved. You need to take a step back from this.'

'Christian's known Matilda just as long as I have.'

'But he's not in tears and screaming accusations. I'm sorry, Sian, I cannot allow you to go tearing into Wakefield Prison. If Steve sees how attached you are to this, he'll get a kick out of it.'

'He's right,' Christian agreed.

'I can't just sit here and do nothing.'

'You can work with DI Sharp on the investigation into the body found out at Wigtwizzle today.'

'What? But we don't even know if that's a murder enquiry yet.'

'A body was found in the boot of a car, DS Robinson. I very much doubt they put themselves there.'

'But ...'

'No. This is non-negotiable. DI Brady leads the investigation into the stabbing of DS Andrews and the whereabouts of DCI Darke.' He turned to Christian. 'Report directly to me and nobody else.'

'Yes, sir.'

'I suggest you all go home and try and get some rest. I know it won't be easy, but I get the feeling tomorrow is going to be an incredibly long day.'

He looked around at everyone then left the room with his head down.

'What an absolute cock!' Sian spat. 'I cannot believe he's just thrown me out like that.'

'Sian, calm down,' Christian said. 'I'm going to need all your help in finding Matilda. Don't worry. I'm not going to freeze you out.'

She gave him a weak smile.

'Am I going to be allowed to go home?' Adele asked.

'I'm afraid not. The house is a crime scene,' Christian said. 'I can take you to get a few things, but you won't be able to stay there tonight.'

'I'd offer to put you up at mine, but I'm literally full to the rafters,' Sian said.

'It's okay. I'll give Pat Campbell a ring.'

Finn ended his call and put his mobile back in his pocket.

'Anything?' Christian asked.

'No. He said he can't talk right now. Scott's mum and dad are there. He's going to call me when he can get away.'

The room fell silent. Nobody knew what to do next or what to say.

'So,' Zofia began. 'Where do we go from here?'

'If I knew the answer to that, Zofia, I'd be doing it,' Christian said.

Chapter Five

Wait. That's all they could do. Go home and wait until tomorrow. DCI Matilda Darke was missing. She could be in urgent need of medical attention. She could be lying dead in a ditch somewhere, but all her colleagues, friends and family could do was wait.

Were they expected to go home, enjoy a lovely meal, sit in front of the TV and watch *Holby City* with a glass of wine, go to bed with a good book and have a solid eight hours of uninterrupted sleep and wake up feeling fresh and revitalised to start the day anew? How was any of that possible?

Christian drove Adele to her house for her to collect a bag of clothes for tomorrow and any toiletries and personal items she might need. The forensic team had finished. The house was in darkness. When Christian unlocked the front door and they stepped into the vast hallway, they both felt the sense of loss, of the change that had occurred.

Adele turned on the lights. They looked down and saw the mess of dried blood on the solid wood floor.

'Is it wrong that all I can think about is how the floor is going to need sanding and restaining?' Adele asked.

Christian snorted a laugh. 'No. I thought the same. I think the carpet in the living room will need replacing, too.'

Adele went over to the living room and pushed the door further open. 'I remember going with Matilda to choose the carpet. She took bloody ages to find the colour she wanted.' She looked at the boarded-up window and turned back to Christian. Tears were pricking her eyes. 'What the hell happened here, Christian?'

He chewed on his bottom lip. 'I really don't know. Scott is our best answer. We just have to wait until he comes round.'

'How can we wait?' Adele wrapped her arms tightly around her. She looked to be in physical pain at the distress of Matilda's disappearance.

'I've no idea. Go and pack a few things. I'll drive you round to Pat's.'

Adele made her way to the stairs, taking care not to walk in the blood. Halfway up, she turned back. 'The electricity. It wasn't a simple power cut, was it?'

Christian shook his head. 'It was deliberately turned off.'

'This is a targeted attack. Isn't it?'

'It would appear so.'

Adele studied Christian's face for any sign of what he was thinking. 'You think she's been kidnapped, don't you?' He gave her a single nod. 'So why haven't whoever's taken her made contact?'

'I don't know.'

'You do, but you don't want to tell me, do you?'

'It's just a theory. One of many I have running around my mind,' he said. The look of hurt on his face was almost painful.

Adele was on the verge of tears once again. 'Why aren't we doing anything?'

'There's nothing we can do until we're able to speak to Scott and get the full story.'

'What if Scott doesn't wake up?' Adele asked, a catch in her throat.

'Adele.'

'I'm serious. Look at all that blood. And don't give me that crap about him being young and healthy. I'm a doctor. That kind of talk won't wash with me.'

Christian took a breath. 'Zofia is checking CCTV and ANPR cameras on the route from the police station to here. We're going through Matilda's phone records and emails. We're doing everything we'd normally be doing, Adele.'

'So, I'm just expected to sit and do nothing while you trawl CCTV footage?'

'There's nothing for you to do at the moment. I know it's not easy, but we just have to wait.'

'It's going to be a bloody long night.'

DS Sian Robinson had an email on her way home from work telling her the offer she'd put in on a five-bedroom house in Whirlow had been accepted. She should be over the moon. Finally, the family could move out of the impossibly tiny three-bedroom terraced house in Woodseats and she could take her furniture out of storage. She read the email and put her phone back into her pocket. She didn't care.

Life continued around her. She sat on the sofa, staring into space. She'd texted Anthony, her eldest, telling him to make tea for his sister and brothers and make sure Danny and Gregory had done their homework and not to spend too long on the PlayStation when they went to bed. When she eventually arrived home, it was almost midnight. She was drained and slumped onto the sofa without even taking her coat off.

Her youngest two kids were already in bed. Anthony and Belinda had waited up for her.

'Any news?' Belinda asked, sitting next to her mother on the sofa.

Sian shook her head. 'Scott's still in theatre. There's no sign of Matilda anywhere.'

'She can't have just disappeared.'

'I'm aware of that, Belinda,' Sian answered, sharply.

'Mum, have you eaten?' Anthony asked, standing by the door to the kitchen.

'No. I'm not hungry. Did you feed the kids?' she asked, suddenly remembering.

'Yes. I did a tuna pasta bake thing. I've got leftovers. I can warm you some up in the microwave.'

Sian gave a warm smile. 'Thank you. I'd love a cup of tea.'

Anthony smiled back and disappeared into the kitchen.

'Mum,' Belinda began. 'Does this have anything to do with what happened at Christmas?'

Just before New Year, Matilda and the team had been hunting a serial killer who murdered young women. He'd latched onto Matilda, followed the investigation and kidnapped Belinda. On the roof of the Arts Tower, one of Sheffield's tallest buildings, there was a standoff between the killer and Matilda, Belinda having escaped. The killer had fallen, but there was gossip surrounding his actual demise. Did he fall or was he pushed? Ever since, Matilda had been quiet and distant.

'I don't know, Belinda. I really don't,' Sian said.

'I know she'd felt ... bad about how it all ended,' Belinda said. 'It's obviously been preying on her mind. You don't think she's let it get to her, do you, and ... I don't know ... maybe decided to ...' She left the sentence hanging in the air.

Sian turned to her. 'To what? Do a runner? She wouldn't do that. And how do you explain Scott being stabbed? You think she stabbed him, too?' Her voice had an icy edge to it.

'No. I don't. I don't think that at all. I'm just saying she's not in the best place right now, mentally. Maybe she's decided she needs a break.'

'And Scott tried to stop her, so she stabbed him.'

'No. I didn't ... I don't ... Mum, I'm sorry. I didn't mean to ...' Belinda stood up, wiped a tear away and went into the kitchen to join her brother.

Sian remained on the sofa. They'd all been talking at the station about whether Laurence Dodds fell, jumped or was pushed. Sian didn't care. He'd threatened to kill her daughter. She was glad the man was dead. But if Matilda had pushed him, who knows what the shock of turning into a killer would do to a person as morally upstanding as Matilda.

Pat Campbell was a retired detective whom Matilda often used as a sounding board when investigating particularly disturbing cases. Pat had spent Christmas with Matilda and Adele following the death of her husband from Covid last summer. Adele had phoned her, explained what had happened, and Pat immediately told her to come over.

Christian dropped Adele off at the detached house in Bradway and Pat pulled her into a tight embrace as soon as the front door was closed behind them.

They were sitting in the silent living room. The TV was off and the clock on the mantelpiece was the loudest thing in the whole house.

'I've been thinking,' Pat began. She took a sip from the mug of tea in her hands and pulled a face. It had gone cold while they'd both been sitting and musing over the whole nightmare situation. 'From what we know, Scott and Matilda left the police station and headed for home. We can assume they arrived as Matilda's phone pinged at the closest cell mast and Scott was found in the hallway. So, the obvious scenario is that Matilda has been kidnapped. What we have to work out is by whom and why.'

'How do we do that?' Adele looked up. Her eyes were heavy.

'By looking at the people who have a grudge against Matilda.'

'I can only think of Steve Harrison.'

'There'll be others. Matilda is an exemplary detective with an impressive track record. She's put away dozens of killers in her career, and, thanks to our pathetic justice system, some of them will be back on the streets. I'll have a word with Christian in the morning. He needs to look at all the cases she's worked on and find out where all the killers she's put away currently are.'

'Finn and Zofia are doing that,' Adele said. 'Christian said on the way over in the car that they're going to be pulling all the recent cases and going through them. He's sent Sian home. She's a mess.'

'She's bound to be. They've been through a lot together.'

'You're a former detective, Pat. What do you think? Is it connected to a case Matilda's been working on?'

'I don't know. Matilda doesn't have much of a personal life, so it's not as if she's got a jealous ex-boyfriend in the shadows. All she does is work. I'd definitely be looking at her caseload.'

'But why now?' Adele asked, wiping away a tear. 'Is it someone recent she's come into contact with, or does it go way back? If so, how far back?'

'You've known Matilda the longest. Who's disliked her so much they're willing to kidnap her and stab Scott in the process?'

Adele adjusted herself on the sofa as she thought. It didn't matter how she sat; she couldn't get comfortable. 'Steve Harrison, definitely.' A heavy frown appeared on her forehead as she tried to think. 'I don't know. Sian's husband, maybe. But he admitted his crimes, so maybe not. If Ben Hales was still alive, I'd include him. I really don't know, Pat.'

'There is an alternative angle to consider.'

'Go on.'

'It's strange. I was only reading about this the other day. You know how I like to read psychology journals and true crime books. There was a criminologist in America who said that when a crime occurs, we look at the victims to hunt for the perpetrator, but law enforcement officials should also consider who else would be hurt, on a psychological level, by what has happened to the victim.'

'What do you mean?'

'Who would suffer the most from Matilda's disappearance?'

Adele's frown deepened as she thought. Her eyes widened in shock as she worked out what Pat was getting at. 'Me?'

Pat leaned forward. 'Matilda is missing. Your technical assistant, Lucy Dauman, has been missing for more than a year. You connect them both.'

'You think this is about me?'

'I'm saying it's another angle to look at. Is there anyone who has a grudge against *you*? Someone *you've* upset recently?'

'No,' she half-laughed, incredulously. 'I'm a pathologist. I see very few living people in my line of work.'

'What about your ex-husband?'

'Robson? Oh, come on, Pat. I haven't seen him since Chris's funeral. Before that it was … well, I can't remember when. We're not involved in each other's lives.'

'What's he up to these days? Is he a success? Happy? Married?'

'I've no idea.'

'Maybe he isn't. Maybe he's failed at everything he's tried. Maybe he's seen you driving around in your Porsche, seen the big house you live in, and he's jealous that you've done so much with your life, and he hasn't.'

'I … No. It … it can't be Robson,' she said, not quite believing her own words.

'I'm not trying to scare you, Adele. I'm simply saying, it's another angle to look at.'

'Thanks for that, Pat. That's me not sleeping tonight,' she huffed, slumping back in her seat and folding her arms.

'I've got the perfect solution for a sleepless night.' She stood up and went over to the sideboard. She held up a bottle. 'A prescription from Dr Glenfiddich.'

Chapter Six

After dropping Adele off at Pat's home in Bradway, Christian called Harriet, Matilda's sister, and asked if he could come over and see her. She didn't live far from Pat's house, a semi-detached in Greenhill. Fortunately, her mother, Penny, was there, too.

Christian pulled up outside the house and looked at it. Lights were on in every room. It was a picture of normalcy. A mother and two teenage boys were going about their lives, sharing an evening meal before going their separate ways. The boys would probably retreat to their bedrooms and play whatever game they were currently immersed in while Harriet and Penny most likely shared a bottle of wine and surfed the channels for something decent to watch on television. Christian was about to destroy all that as soon as he knocked on the door.

He climbed out of the car into the cold, dark night and shivered as he pulled his coat closed around him. His breath formed in front of him, and he walked slowly up the garden path to the green front door. He hesitated, rang the bell and stepped back. This was worse than delivering the death message.

It was a long few seconds before the door was opened and Harriet stood, framed in the doorway, a glass of wine in hand. She was shrouded in a warm glow from within. She was dressed in blue jeans and a cream sweater. She didn't look much like Matilda and took more after their mother – a fuller figure, as Penny put it. Big hips, big shoulders, big bones and big ... other attributes, too.

Harriet smiled. 'Hello, Christian. How are you?'

'I'm okay, thanks,' he lied. 'Could I come in for a quick word?'

'Sure.' She stepped back, still smiling. She held up her glass. 'Would you indulge me in a fantasy of asking a detective if he'd like a drink and him saying, "No thanks, I'm on duty"?' She laughed.

He gave her a weak smile. 'Maybe some other time.'

Her smile dropped. 'Oh my God! Something's happened to Matilda, hasn't it?'

Penny came out of the living room. 'What is it? What's happened to Matilda?' Penny looked like an older version of Harriet, but wore more make-up, had much more hair, dyed a reddish-brown, and wore an ankle-length skirt and black sweater.

Christian's mouth dried. He swallowed hard. 'I just ... there's something I need to tell you. Can we sit down?'

Harriet led the way back into the living room. She had to grab her mother by the elbow and coax her in. They all sat down. Harriet and Penny shared a sofa and held hands. Christian sat on a sofa opposite. The room was tastefully decorated in neutral colours. It was bright and airy, warm and homely.

'You both know DS Scott Andrews, don't you?' Christian asked.

'Of course,' Harriet answered.

'He was found stabbed this evening. He's currently in theatre undergoing emergency surgery.'

'Oh no,' Harriet said.

'The poor boy,' Penny said, a hand going up to her mouth. 'What happened?'

'We don't know. The thing is, he was stabbed at Matilda's house.'

'What?' Harriet exclaimed.

'And we can't seem to find Matilda anywhere. We know she left the station with Scott. We know they headed for home, but Matilda seems to have disappeared. Her phone is switched off.'

'Matilda's phone is never switched off,' Harriet said.

Tears streamed down Penny's face. She gripped hold of her daughter tighter.

'She's missing? My daughter's missing?'

Christian didn't reply and the silence grew.

'Is she?' Harriet asked. 'Is Matilda missing?'

Christian nodded. 'Something happened at the house. The electricity was deliberately turned off, from what we can gather. The only person who can tell us anything is Scott and until he pulls through ...' he said, tapering off.

'And will he pull through?' Harriet asked, concern etched on her face.

'I don't know,' he said, wiping a tear away before it had a chance to fall.

'What are you doing about finding Matilda?' Harriet again. Penny seemed to have fallen into a trance. Her face was blank, and she stared somewhere into the distance.

'Literally everything we can think of. We're working through the night. I've got Finn and Zofia going through the cases Matilda's working on. Forensics are checking Matilda's emails and computer. And I've got a search team heading for Matilda's house right now to trawl the woods at the back.' He didn't tell them he'd had to call in every favour he had to get the search started now rather than wait until daylight.

Penny stood up and went over to the window. The curtains were closed, and she made no attempt to pull one back.

'I knew something like this would happen one day,' she said, barely above a whisper. 'I hate her working for the police. From day one, I said it was the wrong job for her.'

'Mum ...' Harriet began but didn't know what else to say.

'It's a dangerous world out there. There are some seriously sick people, and they're getting worse. Kids are killing each other over a row on social media. Look at knife crime. It's out of control in some cities. There was a shooting in Burngreave a few months ago. Guns in Sheffield! It's getting worse than America.'

'Mum, please,' Harriet said, her voice breaking with emotion.

Penny turned her back on the window and looked at Christian. Her eyes wide. 'Is this to do with Steve Harrison? There was that noose on Matilda's door on Christmas Day. She tried to play it down, but we all saw it in her eyes. She was scared. Is he behind this?'

'I honestly don't know, Penny,' Christian said. 'We're going over everything. I've been on to Wakefield Prison, and nothing has changed in Steve's status. Obviously, we're going to have to look further into it. Is there anything you can think of that might help us? Has anything happened recently that Matilda's told you about?'

'She doesn't tell me anything,' Penny said, turning back to the window.

Harriet shook her head. 'I ask her about work when I see her. She always says everything's fine. She's ... well, I've thought she's looked tired recently, almost as if she's got something on her mind. I saw her at the weekend. I asked if she's getting enough sleep and she said no more than usual. But there was something she wasn't telling me. Something is on her mind. I know it.'

Christian cleared his throat and adjusted his position on the sofa. He was clearly uncomfortable. 'Has Matilda mentioned anything about Laurence Dodds?'

Penny turned back from the window. 'He was the man who was killing those young women last year, wasn't he? He jumped from the Arts Tower.'

Christian nodded.

'What's he got to do with this? He's dead.'

'I was just wondering if Matilda had said anything about him.'

Penny and Harriet exchanged a glance. Christian picked up on the sudden change of atmosphere.

'We're all on the same side, here. You can tell me anything,' Christian said.

The silence grew between them all once more.

'Harriet.' Christian turned to her. 'What do you know about Laurence Dodds that I don't? What's Matilda said?'

'Nothing. It's just ... Matilda took the case to heart, didn't she? It's left her feeling a bit low.'

Christian looked to Penny and back to Harriet. This went deeper than either of them was prepared to say.

'You're not telling me everything, are you?' Christian asked Harriet.

'Christian.' Penny eventually spoke up. 'Please, find Matilda. I don't care what you have to do, just find her. Bring her home.'

He nodded. 'I will. But I can only do that if—'

She cut him off. 'I mean it, Christian. *Whatever* you have to do,' Penny stated firmly.

Chapter Seven

DC Tom Simpson pressed down the handle on the door to the relatives' room with his elbow and pushed it open with his bum. He was precariously holding four plastic cups of tea in his hands.

'Oh. Where's ...?'

'They've gone out to get some air,' Donal said, looking up with wet eyes.

Scott's parents had rushed straight to the hospital as soon as Donal ended the call to them. The second his mother stepped into the room and saw the distressed look on Donal's face, the tears came, and they wouldn't stop.

During the mass shooting in 2019, many officers had lost their lives. Scott had witnessed the horror at first hand. He'd watched his boyfriend Chris Kean gunned down in cold blood. He'd stood next to his best friend and colleague, DC Rory Fleming, as he was shot at point-blank range. He was showered in blood and brain matter. In the immediate aftermath, Scott had had to be taken to the hospital where he was sedated and treated for shock.

Although Scott wasn't physically hurt, the psychological torment was palpable and his mother, on more than one occasion, pleaded with him to rethink his career. However, Scott was more determined than ever to be a detective. Chris and Rory would have haunted him forever if he'd given up and walked away.

Now, fate seemed to have caught up with Scott, and he had been injured in the line of duty. The medical staff had said the right placatory words, but the fear in their eyes spoke volumes. Scott had lost a great deal of blood. His chances were not good.

Tom put the cups of orange tea down on the chipboard coffee table. He sat down on a vinyl chair. 'I've never known anyone cry so much,' he said, speaking about Scott's mother.

'She's a very emotional woman. The first time Scott introduced me to her, she held my hands, said what a lovely-looking young man I was and burst into tears.'

Tom stifled a laugh. 'Does that mean she likes you or not?'

'I'm not sure.' Donal gave a pained smile then looked at his watch.

'Has anyone been in?'

'No. Surely he's out of theatre now. It's gone midnight.'

'Do you want me to go and find someone?'

'Would you?'

'Sure. I'll be right back,' Tom said, standing up and walking quickly to the door. He'd spent the best part of five hours sitting in this cramped room with two overly emotional parents and a dazed-looking Donal. He was trying to put a brave face on for them all, be the strong and confident one, but he was in just as much distress at the stabbing of a colleague.

He left the relatives' room and immediately felt the relief wash over him. His shoulders relaxed. He was away from the tension. For now.

The corridor was empty, though there was a constant background noise of life in a hospital continuing as usual. Even in the dead of night, a hospital wasn't silent. There was always something happening behind one of these doors.

He turned a corner and saw a young nurse behind a reception desk.

'Excuse me,' Tom said. 'Can you check on a patient for me, please?' He held up his warrant card.

'Sure,' the young man said. 'I've literally just come on shift. If you'll give me a moment to log on.'

Tom watched as the nurse pulled a chair up and sat down. He didn't seem old enough to be a qualified nurse. He was short, slim, fresh-faced and looked as if he hadn't even started shaving yet.

'Name?'

'Scott Andrews. He's a detective sergeant with South Yorkshire Police. He was stabbed earlier this evening. Or late yesterday evening.' Tom gave a wry smile.

The nurse looked up. 'A detective was stabbed? That's horrible.'

'Yes.'

'Do you know him?'

'Yes. We're in the same unit.'

'Oh my God.' He looked back down at the screen. 'Well, he's out of theatre and in recovery. That's a good sign. I tell you what, I'll have a word with Tracey, she's one of the theatre nurses, get the lowdown, and I'll come and find you. Give me about ten minutes.'

'That's great. Thank you.'

'What's your name?'

'Tom Simpson.'

The nurse smiled and nodded. Tom smiled back, turned,

and headed back to the relatives' room and the rancid tea that was waiting for him.

The nurse watched until Tom was out of sight before digging his mobile out of his pocket, scrolling through his contacts and making a call.

It was a while before it was answered, but then, it was gone midnight.

'Hello,' a groggy voice said.

'It's Jason Fleet from the Northern General. We've got a detective in surgery following a stabbing. I thought you'd like to know.'

There were a few long seconds of dead air before there was a reply.

'Name?'

'Scott Andrews. He's a detective sergeant. Do you know him?'

'Yes, I do. How bad is he?'

'He's in recovery, but it was touch and go. I don't know all the details yet.'

'When did this happen?'

'Hang on.' The nurse went back to the computer screen. 'He was brought in about eight o'clock last night.'

'I checked the scanner before I went to bed at eleven. There was no mention of an officer being stabbed.'

'Well, I've got a DC Tom Simpson hanging around asking questions about him, so something's going on.'

'Why are they covering it up?' he asked himself. 'Jason, you're a star. Thank you. Have you still got the same bank account?'

'Yes.'

'I'll send you some money across. Cheers for this.'

'No problem. I'll keep you informed.'

Danny Hanson ended the call. Yesterday had been a long day and he couldn't wait to get to bed. As always, he checked the press line from South Yorkshire Police to see if there was anything interesting going on, made a note of a few potential follow-ups, then went to bed. He'd been asleep for less than an hour before the call from the hospital woke him up, and now he was buzzing.

Danny was a freelance journalist and reporter who had a semi-regular job with BBC News, presenting, occasionally, from the newsroom in London, but mostly out and about in the field reporting on the big stories that could make headlines. He also kept his hand in with print journalism, where his career started, and he'd delivered many front-page leads to the *Guardian* over the years. The uncovering of historical sexual abuse and its cover-up among South Yorkshire Police last year was a major coup and he was currently in the process of going through the final draft of his exposé book, which was due to be published towards the end of the year.

Most of his stories had come from DCI Matilda Darke. He'd latched onto her early in his career and spotted straightaway that she would provide him with great copy. He'd been right, too. The Carl Meagan saga, DI Ben Hales turning rogue, the wedding-day horror at Dore, PC Steve Harrison becoming a serial killer, the shooting in which Matilda herself had been a victim, then, only last year, Stuart Mills, the husband of a detective sergeant, turning out to be a killer of sex workers. Matilda really was the gift that kept on giving. Now, one of Matilda's own had been injured, yet South Yorkshire Police seemed to be sitting on it. Why? Was he stabbed in the line of duty, or was this a personal attack?

He looked at the clock. It was half-past midnight. Matilda was bound to be still awake and working if one of her team had been stabbed. He scrolled through his phone until he found her number and called. It didn't ring and went straight to voicemail. That could only mean one thing, the phone was switched off.

Danny frowned. Matilda never switched her phone off. He decided against leaving a message.

Something was very wrong.

He leaned back in bed and pulled the duvet up around him. It was another cold night and the shiver that ran up his spine was partly from the cold and partly because of the electric excitement of a potentially huge story falling into his lap. He couldn't help but smile.

Chapter Eight

Are you awake?

Sian's phone lit up silently on the bedside table next to her. She picked it up and read the message. She didn't bother replying to Christian's text. He obviously wanted to talk so she rang him.

'I didn't wake you, did I?' he asked by way of a greeting.

'I haven't been to sleep yet,' she said.

'Me neither. I went to bed, but I was just tossing and turning. I was keeping Jessica awake so I decided to get up. I'm sat in the living room with the dog fast asleep on my lap.'

Sian gave a weak smile. 'At least you've got company. I'm on my own in a single bed in a tiny box room trying to make shapes out of the damp patches on the ceiling.'

'No news on that house you put an offer in for?'

'Oh. Yes. I got an email from the estate agent on my way home. My offer's been accepted.'

'That's good news,' he said, his voice lacking cheer.

'Is this conversation as painful for you as it is for me?' she asked.

'Jesus Christ, Sian, I've been going over everything in my mind all night and I can't think of anyone who would have done this.'

'I just keep coming back to Steve Harrison,' Sian said, wiping her eyes with the back of her hand. 'I know detectives make enemies, but Steve's really the only one who's physically wanted Matilda dead.'

'I know.'

'It has to be him, Christian. It can't be anyone else.'

'I've been on to Wakefield Prison, Sian. His status hasn't changed since he was moved to the Supermax wing. There is no way he could have orchestrated this.'

'You know what he's like,' she said, raising her voice slightly. 'He's a devious, manipulative bastard. He's got fans all over the world writing to him. He'll have got one of them to do his dirty work for him.'

'We can't get fixated on Steve, Sian. What if it's not him?'

'Who else?'

There was a long silence before Christian answered. 'I don't know. We're going to have to go through every case Matilda's worked on recently.'

'Could it have something to do with the sexual abuse scandal?' Sian asked. 'Uncovering all that abuse going back thirty years upset a lot of people, and cases are still going to court. That bloke who read the news on *Calendar* in the '90s, he was sentenced only last month. Then there was that retired councillor. Did you hear what he said when he was found guilty? He said it was a witch-hunt and he'd do everything he could to clear his name.'

'We need to make a list, Sian. We need to go back and make

a list of every single person we've come into contact with who could have the slightest grudge against Matilda and follow them up.'

'That's going to take time, Christian. We don't have time,' Sian said, struggling to hold back the tears. 'I mean, if they've killed her, why not leave her at the house? Whoever's doing this, they've taken her for a reason. If it was a ransom thing, surely they would have made contact by now. All I keep thinking is that they've taken her to ... oh God,' she said, not able to say the words.

'Sian, I know it's not easy, but you need to try and keep a level head. We need to remain rational. That's the only way we're going to find her.'

'She's been so good to me over the years, more so since everything happened with Stuart. I've got to find her, Christian.'

'We will.'

'I can't believe I'm sitting here in bed trying to get to sleep. I should be out there looking for her.'

'And where would you look?'

'I don't know, but ... I just feel so ... AARGHH!' she screamed, releasing some pent-up anger.

'That's precisely why you need to get some rest, Sian. You're no good to anyone right now. Finn and Zofia are working on the past cases. Forensics are out at Matilda's house doing a sweep of the woods. Hopefully, by the time morning comes around we'll have a definite lead we can work with.'

Sian didn't say anything. All Christian could hear was the sound of crying.

'Sian, do you want me to come round?'

'No. It's not fair, leaving your wife and kids. I'll be fine.'

'I know it's not going to be easy but try and get some sleep.

We're going to be working flat out tomorrow. We're going to need all our energy.'

'You'll let me work on the case, won't you? I can't not be involved.'

'Leave it with me.'

There was a knock on Sian's bedroom door.

'Shit, I think I've woken everyone up.'

'I'll see you in the morning, Sian.'

Sian ended the call and told whoever was on the other side of her bedroom door to come in.

The door opened and Belinda stood in the doorway, dressing gown hanging off her shoulders, hair standing up in all directions and heavy eyelids.

'I heard you screaming. What's up?'

Sian wiped her eyes. 'I just needed to let out some emotions, sweetheart. I'm fine. Honest.' She gave her the best smile she could muster.

Belinda came into the room and sat on the edge of Sian's bed.

'Is Matilda missing, as in she's just decided to have a break from life for a few days, or is it more serious?'

'It's more serious. We think she might have been kidnapped.'

'Oh God. Who by?'

Sian shrugged. 'We don't know.'

'You'll find her though, won't you?'

'We'll do everything we can. I promise.'

'I really like Matilda,' Belinda said, putting her arm around her mother. 'She's like a second mum to us all.'

'She drove me to the hospital when I was in labour with you,' she said with a smile.

'Did she? You never mentioned that before.'

'I can't remember why she came over. I'd only just gone on maternity leave. I kept pushing the date back and practically had to be forced out of the station. I was in the kitchen making us a cuppa and my waters broke. You should have seen the look on Matilda's face.' She laughed at the memory. 'She was with me all through the birth, too. I can't remember where your dad was.'

'You should have called me Matilda, after her.'

'I wanted to. It was your dad who chose Belinda.'

Belinda squeezed her mum tighter to her. 'You'll find her, Mum. I know you will.'

'I hope so, sweetheart.'

'Do you want me to stay with you?'

'Yes, please.'

Sian moved up on the single bed to allow her only daughter some room. They lay on the bed together, Belinda's arms around her, in silence, shrouded by darkness and the unknown.

Chapter Nine

Wednesday 20th January 2021

Adele hadn't slept. It was difficult to sleep in a comfortable bed, in a warm, safe house, while the whereabouts of Matilda were unknown. Was she currently chained up in a damp and draughty basement somewhere? Had she, like Scott, been stabbed and was lying in agony somewhere? Or – and this was the thought that caused the tears and the outbreak of emotion in the early hours – was Matilda Darke dead? There was no chance Adele would be able to sleep now, picturing her best friend in a ditch somewhere, exposed to the elements, the local wildlife doing what they needed to do to survive when they came across a free meal.

Also vying for attention in Adele's mind was what Pat had said. Was she the real target in all this? Her technical assistant, Lucy Dauman, had been missing for just over a year. She disappeared without a trace in December 2019, two weeks before her wedding. Her car was found abandoned a few days later. Her mobile was switched off and her bank account hadn't been touched. Now, Matilda had suffered a similar fate. Would she ever be found? Were the people closest to her going to disappear one by one?

At five o'clock, Adele abandoned all hope of trying to sleep and got up. She might as well do something useful rather than torment herself with the dark thoughts racing around her mind.

She dressed and decided to head into work. She left a note for Pat next to the kettle in the kitchen, thanking her for giving her a bed for the night. She promised to be in touch and to let her know the moment she heard anything about Matilda.

Adele drove through the dark, cold, silent streets of Sheffield to Watery Street, where she worked. It was lucky the roads were empty as she had no idea how she managed to get there. She remembered easing out of Pat's drive, then pulling into her designated parking space, but had no memory of the drive in between.

She headed for her small office in the Medico-Legal Centre, pulled out a chair and sat down. She looked around her at the chaos of her desk, a mixture of reports pending, reports overdue and reports to be queried. She and Simon Browes had a book due out in March, a definitive guide to the post-mortem process and the minute detail of what happens to a body when the heart stops beating, and she needed to approve the cover and check the proofs of the chapters she'd written. Simon had already done all the work he needed to do on his share of the book, and everyone was waiting for Adele to sign off on her half.

She opened the email from her editor and looked at the cover design. Simon's reply was included. He'd gushed over seeing his name on an actual book. He'd written articles in journals for years, and his name was well known in academic circles, but this was to be his first book. He could pop into any branch of Waterstones or WHSmith or Blackwells and see his name on a shelf. Whenever he spoke about it, his eyes lit up. Adele's love for the project had begun to wane long ago. As she looked at the proposed cover on the screen, saw her name in big red letters, there wasn't even a flicker of elation on her face. She no longer cared. She hit reply, gave her approval and closed down the email.

There was a Post-it note attached to her landline. Written neatly in Simon Browes' handwriting, it reminded Adele that she had to choose who she wanted to dedicate the book to.

Tears pricked at Adele's eyes. Her first book was dedicated to the memory of her son, who was killed in a school shooting in 2019, saving pupils in his care. She had planned to dedicate this book to her best friend and saviour, Matilda Darke. Would this need to be dedicated to her memory, too?

She screwed up the Post-it and lobbed it into the bin. She couldn't handle this right now. It was too much.

———————

'Blimey, you're in early. Usually, I'm the first one in,' Claire Alexander said as she shook out of her coat.

Claire was a radiologist who oversaw the 3D autopsies. In recent years, Sheffield had become one of the leading cities in the country in the advancement of post-mortem technology, and it was all thanks to Claire's hard work.

'Mind you, I was tempted to stay in bed,' Claire continued. She'd spotted Adele in her office, door open, head down, but hadn't taken in the tear tracks down her face. 'At this time of year, when the alarm goes off and I see it's still pitch-black outside, I just want to pull the duvet up over my head and go back to sleep. I reckon bears have got it spot on. We should hibernate until the spring. Minus three according to my car this morning. And how long is this month going to drag on for? The twenty-first, apparently. I'm sure it should be March by now. Adele?' she asked as she stopped in the doorway to Adele's office.

Adele looked up. Tears were running down her face.

'What's happened?' Claire asked.

———————

Over a mug of tea, Adele filled Claire in on everything that had happened since yesterday afternoon. It hadn't even been twenty-four hours since Donal went round and found Scott slumped on the hallway floor in a pool of his own blood. It seemed longer.

'You don't think … no.' Claire stopped herself.

'What?'

She cleared her throat. 'I know Matilda's been through a bad patch since she was shot. Then her unit was closed down and she was made redundant. I mean, all that is bound to influence a person, isn't it? I just … is it possible she's decided to walk away from it all?' Claire asked, her voice soft and quiet.

'You mean run away?'

'Yes. It does happen. People reach breaking point and just go. They don't think of the consequences. It's like they just shut down.'

'How does that account for Scott being stabbed?'

'Ah.' Claire frowned. 'I don't know about that.'

Adele shook her head. 'Matilda would not run away like

that. After the shooting, when she was back at work and I was struggling with Chris's death, we sat down, we had a good long talk and promised to be there for each other. It didn't matter what the issue was or how embarrassing it might be, we'd share everything. And we have done. Matilda would not leave. Something has happened to her. I know it,' she said, her voice breaking.

'Well, I'm guessing Christian and everyone will be doing everything they can. They go above and beyond when something happens to one of their own. They'll find her, Adele,' Claire said, placing a warm hand on top of hers. 'I know it.'

'So do I. I'm just worried about what state she'll be in when they do.'

'Look, why don't you go home? Take the day off.'

'I can't. I'd only spend the day fretting. Besides, my house is still a crime scene. I'm better off here.'

Claire turned at the sound of a door being slammed. Staff were arriving. The working day was about to begin.

'I'm here if you ever want to talk, Adele,' she said.

'Thanks.'

'I'd better get started.'

She went out of the office, leaving Adele on her own. Adele closed her eyes and tried to muster a single ounce of strength to help her get through the day. She had no idea how she was going to do it, but she had to remain strong. Submission was not an option.

It was another hour before they started work. Simon Browes had arrived and all three of them were wedged into the anteroom Claire spent most of her day in, overlooking the digital autopsy suite. There was a bank of three large monitors in front of her. On a scanner in the main suite, the body found in the back of a car in woodland yesterday was secured in a body bag. It was light and no trouble at all to lift.

Claire keyed in the relevant instructions, and the CT scanner began its work. The body was scanned in a spiral, like a slinky, moving around the body from top to toe. Claire set the thickness of the spirals to the smallest possible setting, 0.6mm. She wanted as much detail from the scan as possible, considering the condition the body was in. In less than ten minutes, a full body scan was sent to Claire's computer, taken front to back, top to bottom and side to side. Using her computer, she would now be able to view the body in a number of images, in photographic form, or as an X-ray. She would even be able to turn the body over and look at it from any angle, while not physically touching it, and preserving any forensic information that might be helpful to the police investigation.

Self-confessed Luddite, Simon Browes was not a fan of 3D autopsies and was more at home when he was scrubbed up and had a scalpel in his hand. However, he'd been forced to admit over the years that information from the scans had been useful when it came to performing his own invasive post-mortems.

Claire studied an X-ray image. 'Well, we've no organs to see if any were punctured with a knife or bullet and there are no nicks and grazes on any of the bones that I can make out.' She zoomed in on the neck. 'Ah, the hyoid bone is broken.'

'Strangled,' Adele said.

'Possibly.' Claire changed the image to a photographic one.

'She's practically skeletonised, I can't get any images of bruising.'

'She?' Adele asked.

'A guess. I'm going on the size of the body. We could be looking at a woman or a young male who hasn't reached puberty. We're going to need an anthropologist to determine sex and age. The teeth are intact. Hopefully, there'll be a dentist somewhere with a record. And you could get DNA from the femur. Fingers crossed they have a criminal record and it's on file.'

'So, it's definitely murder then?' Adele, again.

'I'm not a detective, obviously, but I've never known a body being found in the boot of a car being suicide.' Claire turned to Adele and gave her a wan smile.

'You're quiet, Simon,' Adele said.

'Sorry?' he asked, his eyes locked on the computer screen.

'I said you're quiet.'

'I just ... I can never get my head around what technology can do these days.'

'You're getting closer to coming over to the dark side, Simon,' Claire said. 'You'll be ditching the Betamax in no time.' She winked.

Adele chuckled.

Simon grunted. 'Bring the body through when you're ready.' He left the small room, closing the door carefully behind him.

'He hates it when I take the mickey,' Claire said, a cruel smile on her lips. 'How are things with you two?'

'We're taking things slowly,' Adele pulled out a chair and sat down next to Claire. 'It's weird. I mean, I've known Simon for years then all of a sudden, we're dating.'

Claire looked over Adele's shoulder and through the

window to make sure Simon wasn't within hearing distance. 'What's he like when he's not being all stuffed-shirt pathologist?'

'You know, he's actually very sweet,' Adele said, a hint of a smile breaking out on her face. Her hand went unconsciously to the necklace he'd bought her for Christmas. 'He's incredibly shy. Painfully so. But I don't know, he's just … he's lovely to be around.'

'Lovely?'

'What's wrong with lovely?'

'Nothing. Cushions are lovely. Dressing gowns are lovely. I'd never describe a man as lovely.'

'Well, Simon is lovely.' A sadness swept over Adele. 'Right now, I think lovely is what I need.' She sighed. 'Jesus Christ, Claire, where the bloody hell is Matilda?'

Chapter Ten

Members of the Homicide and Major Crime Unit were assembled in the suite. DI Christian Brady stood at the top of the room and looked out at the grave faces of DS Sian Robinson and DCs Finn Cotton, Zofia Nowak and Tom Simpson. The room was much quieter without Scott and Matilda.

'The forensic team have finished at Matilda's house,' Christian began. 'They've done a full sweep of the woodland at the back and haven't found anything useful. Back at the house, there is no evidence of a break-in, but we have established the electricity was purposely shut off. The only prints found in the house belong to Matilda, Adele, Scott and Pat Campbell, who stayed there over Christmas and New Year. Last night I spoke to Matilda's mother and sister. Harriet was the last to have contact with her, at the weekend. They exchanged texts two evenings back. I've read the conversation and it's a perfectly normal chat between sisters.

'Now, Chief Constable Ridley has put me in charge of the

investigation, and this is what we're going to concentrate on. However, there was also a body discovered in the boot of a car at Wigtwizzle yesterday.' He indicated the board behind him with various close-up shots of the body in the boot. 'Ridley wants Sian to work alongside DI Sharp from CID, and that's what's going to happen, on the surface. However, judging by the condition of the body, it's been there for some time. A few more days won't matter. We're all going to concentrate on finding Matilda. Now, our best bet is waiting until Scott wakes up.'

'I stayed at the hospital all night,' Tom began. His eyelids were heavy with fatigue. 'I went home about two o'clock, once we heard Scott was out of theatre and in recovery. I called Donal up first thing and Scott's been moved out of ICU. It seems the operation was successful.'

'Oh, thank goodness for that,' Sian said, visibly relaxing in her seat.

Zofia wiped her eyes. 'I've hardly slept, thinking about him.'

'Any chance of being able to speak to him today?' Christian asked.

'Donal said he'll call me as soon as he wakes up.'

'Until we can speak to Scott,' Christian continued, 'we have to assume the obvious: that someone targeted Matilda and has kidnapped her. The question is, who?' He looked at the blank faces looking back at him. 'The obvious suspect is this man, Steve Harrison.' From a folder, Christian took out an old photograph of former PC Steve Harrison and placed it on the murder board.

'Steve Harrison is a legend in his own right and I'm sure you all know the story, but I'm going to tell you it anyway, so you hear it from someone who witnessed everything he did rather than from the rumour mill. Sian and Finn, you were in the midst of it, but Zofia and Tom, pin your ears back.

'In 2017, Steve Harrison was a PC at this station. He tried to pass his sergeant's exams, but failed, on more than one occasion. He lacked discipline and thought he was being suppressed by his superiors. He found people throughout Sheffield who were given what he considered to be lenient sentences for crimes they'd committed, and hanged them. He obviously thought that if he couldn't be a great detective then he'd be a great murderer. He fixated on Matilda, inveigled himself into our team, a team he believed he should have been a part of, and tried to destroy it. He faked a relationship with DC Faith Easter, got all the information he needed from her, and when he'd finished with her, he hanged her, in front of Matilda.'

Christian paused and took a sip from a plastic cup of water. All these years later, and it was still difficult to talk about what had happened.

'Steve was sentenced to life in prison, but he taunted Matilda from his cell. He even manipulated his own brother, Jake, in enacting his revenge, and in January 2019, Jake opened fire and killed several officers from this station. From this team alone we lost Rory Fleming, Ranjeet Deshwani and our ACC, Valerie Masterson. Matilda was shot twice and managed to survive, but Jake went to the hospital to try to finish her off. He didn't succeed, but he did kill her father in the attempt.'

The atmosphere in the room plunged and a heavy silence took hold. Christian's words were slow and quiet, thick with emotion.

He continued. 'From January 2019, Steve Harrison has been

living in the Supermax wing of Wakefield Prison, which is basically a prison within a prison. He's in his single cell for twenty-three hours every day. All his mail is monitored before it's given to him, and any outgoing mail is checked before being sent out. He's received no visitors since the beginning of 2019. However, he does receive a great deal of mail from fans around the world.

'In the aftermath of the shooting, Matilda began receiving silent phone calls and cards, taunting her. We believed this was from a fan of Steve's, someone who blames Matilda for him being incarcerated. We've never been able to track the person down. However, they had stopped in recent months. On Christmas Day, Matilda's mum saw a woman walking down Matilda's driveway. When Matilda went out to see who it was, she found the Christmas wreath on the front door had been replaced by a hangman's noose. I called Wakefield Prison to check that Steve was still there and his status hadn't changed. It hadn't. When Matilda was … well, whatever happened to Matilda last night happened, I called them again. He's still in the Supermax wing and he's still receiving no visitors.'

'Could this be someone else?' Tom asked. 'Detectives make enemies all the time. Has she put anyone else away who's vowed to get revenge once released?'

'Good question,' Christian said, looking to Sian. 'That's what we need to do. We need to look back at Matilda's career, discover who else could have wanted revenge.'

'I've made a list,' Sian said, flicking through her notebook. 'I hardly slept last night, and I've been going over some of the people we've come into contact with recently, particularly people who've denied their crimes. There are a lot from the sexual abuse case. There's a retired bloke from Sheffield City

Council, Raymond Lassiter. He was sentenced only last month. According to reports in the media, he says he's innocent and blames the police, South Yorkshire Police in particular, for leading a witch-hunt.'

Zofia, sitting at her desk, pen poised over a notepad, scribbled down the details when Sian was talking. 'I'll look him up and his close acquaintances. Sian, if you want to give me your pad, I'll work through all the names. I've already got some here that I was working on last night. I'll cross-reference.'

'Are you sure? It's a lot of names.'

'You don't want to know the programs I've got installed on my computer. I can track people down in no time,' she said with the hint of a smile.

Sian went over to her desk. 'I've missed people off, I know I have. It's just people who came into my head.'

'Don't worry, Sian, we'll go over everything,' Christian said.

'What about outside of work?' Finn asked. 'Is there anyone she's upset or angered? Or maybe a relative of someone she's put away?'

'Again, something else to work on. We need to interview those who know Matilda personally. That means you, Sian. It also means Adele, Pat Campbell, Matilda's mother Penny and her sister Harriet,' Christian said.

'Are we getting the press involved?' Zofia asked.

'No.' Christian replied firmly. 'Not at the moment. We need to keep this between ourselves. At least until we've been able to interview Steve Harrison. If he is behind this, I don't want him thinking he has the upper hand.'

'But if he knows Matilda's been kidnapped, he will have the upper hand,' Zofia said.

'She's right,' Sian agreed.

'I've spoken to the Chief Constable and the governor of Wakefield Prison. We're going to move Steve Harrison out of his cell then go in and check everything he's got. If he's involved, there'll be something there pointing us in the right direction. Does anyone have anything else to add?' Christian seemed to have aged ten years overnight. He looked grey. He had dark circles beneath his eyes, and he was wearing yesterday's shirt.

'I was just thinking,' Tom began. 'The victims of Steve's original killings were all hanged and then a noose was left on DCI Darke's door on Christmas Day. Is it possible whatever happened last night has something to do with them? A police officer killed them. Maybe the relatives of those killed blame the police in some way. I know it sounds far-fetched, but it is possible.'

Christian thought for a brief moment. 'True. Zofia, can you get a list of all the victims and track down their nearest relatives?'

'Will do.'

'Sian, I want you to go to Watery Street and get the PM results from our body in the car ...'

'Hang on,' she interrupted. 'I know I have to ...'

Christian held up a hand to silence her. 'Let me finish. Get the results of the PM, do everything we need to in order to try to identify the body, then go along to the Northern General and, fingers crossed, Scott will be awake and able to tell us something.'

She smiled and mouthed, 'Thank you.'

'Finn, get your coat and a pool car. We're going to Wakefield Prison.'

'Really? I've literally had two hours' sleep.'
'I'll treat you to a Nero and we'll open a window.'
'Who's our union rep?' Finn asked Zofia as an aside.
'I am,' Sian said.
'I'll go and get a car.'

Chapter Eleven

M atilda Darke opened her eyes. For a few seconds, she had no memory of who she was or where she was. Then, reality dawned. Her first thoughts were about Scott. The last she'd seen of him was him on the floor of her hallway, his face contorted in agony, blood seeping out of a stab wound to the stomach. *How long ago was that?* She hoped he was all right. He was just getting his life back on track after losing his boyfriend in the shooting. He deserved all the happiness in the world.

Matilda tried to sit up. She felt groggy like she usually did on a Saturday morning after a Friday night spent on the sofa with Adele, drinking wine and having a Marvel movie marathon. There was nothing for Matilda's eyes to adjust to. No chink of light coming from under a door or through a gap in the curtains. She was in total darkness.

She stood up and held her arms out in front of her like a zombie in a cheap horror film. She took a few tentative steps forward before she hit a wall. It was cold and damp to the touch. The brick was rough. She ran her hands along it, walking slowly, fearful of what she might touch, might step in. She soon reached the end of the wall, turned and walked along the adjacent wall. It was such a small room, no bigger than a box room, no bigger than a … prison cell. A dark thought came to her. Is this where she was? But what kind of a cell didn't have a door or a window?

A little further along and she came to a door. It was solid and the handle, once she'd located it in the dark, was stiff. She grabbed and pulled it, but it wouldn't open. She banged on it hard with clenched fists, but no sound came from the other side. She placed her ear to it, listened intently for any sign of life. Nothing. She'd been locked in here and left. Abandoned. Why?

Carefully, Matilda made her way back to the single bed. It was an old iron frame with a thin mattress. As she sat down, the springs groaned under her weight. There was no duvet, no blankets, nothing to keep her warm. There was no food, no water, nothing to keep her alive. She wiped away a tear. She'd been brought here to die.

What could have happened last night? She remembered coming home from work. Scott was driving. Human remains had been found in woodland in a funnily named place, so Adele would be late home. The house was silent and in darkness. She'd asked Scott if he wanted to come in for a drink.

Why?

She couldn't remember. She'd turned on the light in the hallway. Nothing happened. There'd been a power cut. Scott said something.

What did he say?

Matilda's head ached as she tried to recall. Everything was so fuzzy. Nothing made sense.

She went into the kitchen. The fuse box was in the utility room. As she made her way there, she heard a sound that made her jump. It was a cry of pain. She was holding her mobile in her hand, using the torch function to light the way. She went running back into the hall and saw Scott on the floor. Blood was pouring from his stomach. She tried to run to him but was stopped.

Who by?

'I don't know,' she said quietly to herself.

It was dark. There was a figure standing in the doorway.

Think, Matilda. For fuck's sake, think.

It was a woman. She was tall. She had dark hair, and it was in a severe bob. She'd seen her before but couldn't think where. She said something.

'You just won't die, will you, Matilda? Who do you think you are, Sidney fucking Prescott?'

Of course.

A few days before Christmas, she and Scott were in a pool car when a car shot out of a side road. Scott slammed on the brakes and they'd both lunged forward in their seats. The seatbelt had yanked Matilda back and left her bruised on her shoulder. The driver of the car looked at them. There was something strange about her face. She looked … Matilda couldn't think. She didn't look scared or relieved at a near-miss. She looked … horrified.

Matilda didn't give it another thought. A random event. A few days later, while she was speeding to the Arts Tower, a car shot out and ploughed into the car in front of her, driven by DC Finn Cotton. Finn was fine. A slight concussion, a splitting headache and slightly shaken-up, but he was back at work within a few days. The woman who was driving the car that had crashed into Finn remained seated in her car, another strange look on her face. Matilda recognised her, eventually, as the woman who'd almost collided with her. It was the same haircut, the severe bob, and it was the same expression she saw when they made eye contact. Matilda had begun to think that she was petrified, but not because of what might have been; it was because she'd failed.

Who was she?

The figure in the shadows stepped forward. She stepped over Scott's writhing body. From her bag she took out a taser and fired it at Matilda. Matilda dropped to the floor. She'd never known such pain before as fifty thousand volts of electricity coursed through her body.

The woman leaned over her. There was a smile on her face. She had a syringe in her hands. She said something before Matilda lost consciousness. What was it?

Matilda gasped. Her memory returned. She remembered what the woman said to her before she was injected and plunged into a state of unconsciousness.

'Steve Harrison says hello.'

Chapter Twelve

D S Sian Robinson pulled into a visitor's space at the Medico-Legal Centre on Watery Street and turned off the engine. She didn't get out of the car. She sat behind the wheel and tried to marshal her thoughts. Where the bloody hell was Matilda?

Over the past couple of years, Sian had been through great torment. First, the shooting in which so many of her friends and colleagues had died. Then, the investigation into the missing sex workers. Eight were dead, murdered, three were still missing. The killer, when identified, had shocked everyone on the Homicide and Major Crime Unit, by being Sian's husband, Stuart. They'd been married for more than twenty-five years, and from her coming home, saying how her day had been, talking about the cases she'd worked on, Stuart had been storing all the information so he could use it to commit murders without appearing on the police's radar. Sian's life had crumbled. If it hadn't been for her kids, and Matilda, she had no idea where she would be right now; possibly in one of the fridges in Adele's post-mortem suite.

Sian took a deep breath and let out a heavy sigh. She'd be no use to anyone sitting and allowing her thoughts to take over. She pushed open the door and stepped out into the cold January air.

It was warmer in the autopsy suite, but not much, so Sian kept her coat on. Adele made her a mug of tea and she stood by the gurney with her hands wrapped around it to keep the blood circulating in her fingers.

Adele pulled back the white sheet covering the body found in the boot of the car in Wigtwizzle.

Sian pulled a face. 'I've been in this job so long, seen so much, yet I'm always amazed at what happens to our bodies when they're simply left to the elements. It's like on those nature programmes where you see a zebra carcass in the Serengeti after the lions have finished with the meat. You don't realise that's what happens to us, too.'

Simon Browes stepped forward. He had recently changed into clean scrubs. A strong smell of soap emanated from him. 'The human body is made up of about sixty per cent water. When the heart stops pumping and life is extinct, everything breaks down. The brain and muscles are seventy-five per cent water. Once all that has seeped away, there's very little left.'

A phone rang in Adele's office. She went off to answer it.

'Does the body tell you anything?' Sian asked Simon. 'Do you know the sex at least?'

'We've been saying "she" simply because of the height – we estimate her to be about five foot three or thereabouts – and the make-up of the pelvis. The pelvis is the go-to bone for visual identification of a skeleton. There's an anthropologist coming over from the university this afternoon.'

'There was nothing on her then, no ID?' she asked.

'No.'

'What about in the car?'

'I don't know about that,' Simon said, covering the body. 'It's still out there at Wigtwizzle. Apparently, it's very thick undergrowth. They're going to have to clear away a few bushes and trees before they can get a low loader in.'

'How did the car get there in the first place then?' Sian asked, thinking aloud. She knew it wasn't a question anyone could answer.

'Beats me,' Simon shrugged. 'However, we don't know how long the body, or the car, has been there. There's every chance the surrounding area was once more accessible, and nature has been allowed to grow around the car.'

'Are we talking years here for this body?' Sian asked, nodding towards the skeleton.

'Tests are ongoing,' he said with a hint of a smile.

'Can you tell how she died?' Sian asked, taking a sip of her tea.

'The hyoid bone is broken, so we're assuming she was strangled. We did manage to get DNA from her, though.'

'How?'

'I was able to extract it from the femur,' he said, almost matter-of-factly.

'Why there?'

'There have been many studies conducted to see which bones in the human body retain their DNA the longest and the femur produced the best results, followed by the ribs, then the pelvis. One particular study by the US Armed Forces DNA Identification Laboratory revealed that the dense cortical regions of long, weight-bearing bones, such as the femur, tend to retain their DNA longer than bones with a larger percentage of trabecular tissue, such as the skull.'

'No offence, Simon, but that was just noise to me,' Sian said.

'It's all to do with the density of the bones. However, a particularly informative study was done using the bones of pigs, and although the pigs were adults, they were still relatively young. The femur of a twenty-year-old male may be comparatively different to one of a seventy-year-old male. There are innumerable contributory factors to take into account. I wrote a chapter on this in the book I'm writing with Adele.'

Sian gave a pained smile. She doubted the book would be fighting Ian Rankin for the top spot in the bestseller charts. 'I look forward to reading it. So, you said you were able to extract DNA. Let's hope she's on the database. I noticed the teeth were intact – could they be a help, too?'

'Absolutely. She has a couple of missing molars and she's had both upper wisdom teeth extracted and there are a number of fillings. There'll be a record of that somewhere.'

Sian leaned down to get a closer look at the dental work. 'Is there any way of guessing how old the fillings are from the type of filling used?'

'We can do a breakdown of composite material, but we may as well wait for DNA results first. Failing that, we'll take an impression of her teeth.'

'Poor woman,' Sian said, not taking her eyes off her. 'I haven't looked at the missing persons register for a while. I'll give Zofia a ring and ask her to see if anything matches the description. Not that we've much to go on.'

'I've hit the jackpot,' Adele said, coming back into the suite. 'Our body here is indeed female. She's on the National DNA Database.'

'Really?' Simon asked.

'Twenty-seven-year-old Jackie Barclay has been missing since April 2018,' Adele said.

Sian dropped her mug. It shattered as it hit the tiled floor and tea splattered everywhere.

'I'm so sorry,' Sian apologised once Adele had led her into her office and closed the door behind her.

'You've no need to apologise. The tea is terrible here,' she smiled.

Sian tried to smile back, but a grimace appeared on her face.

'I'm guessing you know this Jackie Barclay?' Adele said, pulling up a chair and sitting opposite her.

'No. Well, sort of. Not really.'

'Okay, we're not getting much further here, are we?'

'I had her file on my desk for a long time. She worked the streets as a sex worker. She was among the eleven we were investigating when …' She swallowed hard. She had a bitter taste in her mouth. 'When it turned out Stuart was the killer. He admitted to killing eight of them. Jackie and two others were never found. Stuart didn't admit to killing them.'

'Oh, bloody hell, Sian,' Adele said. 'Look, I hate to say this, but these women, they're in a job that is highly dangerous. She could have been killed by someone else. This doesn't have to be Stuart.'

'It just brought it all back. I mean, it never goes away. There are times when I don't think about it for days and I'm happily walking along and all of a sudden it's like a light is switched on in my head and I'm remembering the dead women, the state of their bodies, what he'd done to them, and the fact I shared a bed with that bastard for twenty-five years.' Her words were lost to tears.

Adele grabbed a box of tissues from a shelf and handed them to her. She stood back and watched as Sian wiped her eyes and blew her nose.

'I don't know what to say to you, Sian.'

'Why did this have to happen now? Why did she have to be found now, when we've got Matilda missing to concentrate on?'

'Look, speak to Christian. He's like a substitute Matilda. He'll know what to do for the best.'

She nodded. 'You're right.' She stood up and took a few deep breaths. 'Is there any way to tell if she was raped?'

'The body's too far decomposed for that.'

'I really was married to a monster, wasn't I?'

'There was no way you could have known what he was up to. Besides, this may not have anything to do with Stuart. I'm here if you need me, Sian. You know that.'

'Thank you.' She smiled wearily. 'I'd better be getting back.'

'Okay. You'll ring me if you hear anything about Matilda, won't you?'

'Of course. I've got a dark feeling about this, Adele. Something's going to happen over the next few days, and it's not going to have a happy ending.' Sian opened the door and left the small office, heading for the exit of the mortuary suite with her head down, dragging her feet on the floor.

Adele watched her leave. She suddenly felt a deep sense of foreboding wash over her. Sian was right. Everything seemed to be falling apart.

She selected a number on her mobile and dialled. It went straight to voicemail, so she left a message. 'Christian, it's Adele Kean. We've identified the body found in the boot of the car at Wigtwizzle yesterday. She's Jackie Barclay. She was a sex worker who went missing in April 2018. When Stuart Mills admitted his murders of eight women, there were three others still missing that he denied killing. I'm wondering if the area where this one was found might also be where the remaining two are buried. Forensics are out there today clearing the area to get a low loader in so they can bring the car back for testing. You might want to give them a call, warn them of what they may find. Give me a ring if you need any more information. Talk to you later.'

She ended the call and sat back in her seat, a perplexed look on her face. Sian's prophetic words ran around her mind. Nothing had been the same since the shooting in 2019. Everything was dark and bleak. Matilda, Adele, Sian, Christian, Scott, they'd all been through so much heartache and horror. Surely things couldn't get much worse.

Chapter Thirteen

D anny Hanson had barely slept. As soon as he ended the call with his contact at the Northern General Hospital, he called the automated press line at South Yorkshire Police but there was no mention of a stabbing incident. After a few hours' sleep, his alarm waking him at seven o'clock, the first thing he did was try the press line once more to see if it was updated. Nothing. While waiting for his toast to pop up for breakfast, he tried Matilda's mobile again. It went straight to voicemail. There was something very wrong. Matilda often avoided his calls, but the phone always rang before the voicemail kicked in. Her phone was switched off. The question was, why?

He chewed his granary toast with a heavy frown on his forehead. If there had been a major incident, he would have known about it. He had contacts all over the city who would have alerted him. The fact his phone was silent spoke volumes. There was a media blackout. His eyes lit up at that realisation. Something big was happening within South Yorkshire Police and they didn't want the press finding out. This was where

Danny Hanson thrived. He was a dogged journalist. He would get to the bottom of it. Another front-page exclusive for one of the quality papers. Another leading story on the BBC News bulletins with live handovers to 'our chief crime correspondent'. Maybe a second Press Award to go with his Specialist Journalist of the Year award for his coverage of the Sheffield shooting.

A grin on his smooth face, he practically leapt from the kitchen table and ran into his bedroom and into the en suite. A quick shower, taking extra time on his hair as it was one of the things his followers on social media commented on whenever he was on TV, and then back into the bedroom to choose from the array of check shirts in his wardrobe.

While dressing, he made a call, putting the phone on loudspeaker so he could style his dark, curly hair into an unkempt, messy look that took an age to perfect.

'DI Brady,' the call answered.

'Christian, good morning. It's Danny Hanson. How are you?' he asked in his best cheery tone.

There was a sigh and a slight delay before Christian replied.

'I'm very well, thank you,' came the non-committal answer.

'And I'm well, too. Thanks for asking.'

'What do you want?' There was an edge to Christian's tone.

'I'm trying to get through to Matilda Darke. I've been trying since yesterday afternoon, actually. Her phone seems to be switched off. Is there something wrong?'

'No. Nothing's wrong,' he said, too quickly for Danny's liking.

'Is there a reason her phone is turned off?'

'It isn't. As far as I'm aware.'

'Really? When was the last time you spoke to her?'

'Danny, what is it you want? I'm very busy.'

'It's Matilda I want to speak to. I'm working on a couple of stories at the moment, and I've uncovered something that ... well, let's just say, the police should know about it.'

'You can tell me.'

'Thank you. No offence, Christian, but Matilda and I have an understanding.'

'You do?'

'Yes. Since the sex abuse story, we've grown to respect each other's professions.'

'I'm not sure what to say to that,' Christian said after a beat of silence. 'I tell you what, I'll tell Matilda you've called and *if* she wants to get in touch with you, she'll do so.'

'So, Matilda's fine?'

'She is.'

'And DS Andrews?'

Another lengthy silence.

'Are you still there, DI Brady?' Danny asked.

'Yes. I'm here. I'm very busy, Danny. Are we really going to go through every member of the team while you enquire after their health?'

'Only the ones who've been stabbed.'

'Where did you hear that?'

Danny looked at his reflection in the mirror, took in his thick, dark hair, his twinkling eyes, his strong jawline. He smiled to himself.

'So, it's true?'

'No. I just wanted to know where you'd heard such a thing.'

'I'd tell you if I could, but I can't. So, there is no truth in DS Scott Andrews being stabbed?'

'I'm afraid I have to go now, Danny. I'll pass on your message to DCI Darke. Goodbye.'

The call ended.

Danny's smile grew. Christian hadn't answered his question because to do so would have revealed something was happening within South Yorkshire that the police didn't want the press and the public to know about.

'Sorry, Christian,' Danny said as he grabbed his phone and laptop from the bed. 'But you're a public servant. And the public want to know *exactly* what you're up to. And I'm going to tell them.'

Danny drove his new-to-him silver Peugeot from his rented flat in Hillsborough to Ringinglow, a short distance away, where Matilda Darke lived.

It was another cold morning and the streets were full of people going to work and school, well wrapped up against the elements in thick winter coats, hats and gloves. Faces were red where the zero-degree temperature, seeming colder in the stiff easterly breeze, nipped at bare skin. He shivered just looking at them and cranked up the heating in the car.

He slowed down on Ringinglow Road, much to the annoyance of the driver of the Audi behind him, who undertook and gave him the finger as he passed. Finding the entrance to the narrow track, Danny turned right.

When Matilda first moved into the old farmhouse, the track was uneven and full of potholes and cracks, the trees overgrown on each side. She really was going for the solitary lifestyle and didn't encourage visitors. Since her best friend Adele had moved in and treated herself to a very sleek Porsche 911, the track had been tarmacked, the trees cut back, and the drive up to Matilda's front door was smooth and welcoming.

Danny smiled to himself. He'd bet a month's wages Matilda hated the fact people could drive up to her home and she wouldn't know about it until the bell rang.

The first thing Danny noticed when he pulled up was the sheet of chipboard covering the living-room window. Something had definitely happened here. He was at the beginning of a huge drama. He felt his journalistic senses tingling.

Danny climbed out of the car, buttoned his waist-length peacoat and raised the collar. He took out his phone and snapped a photo of the house, then a second, zooming in on the boarded-up window. He looked around him as he approached the house. There were no cars about, but that meant nothing; they could be in the garage. The flat above the garage and even Matilda's home were both in darkness. He assumed Matilda and Adele would be at work. Scott, despite what Christian said, was obviously in hospital. He looked at his watch. It was a little after eight o'clock. He knew detectives started work early, especially if there was a major incident, but surely Adele, a pathologist, didn't need to leave the warmth of the house this early.

He rang the doorbell and stepped back, looking up at the huge house. He'd kill for somewhere like this. Not that he could afford it. His book about the investigation into the historical child sex abuse was due out later this year, and he'd received a sizeable advance from a top publisher. He'd already spent the first payment on the second-hand car and a whole new wardrobe. Hopefully, the next two payments and whatever he made from appearances on news programmes and at events to publicise the book would help with a mortgage on a decent house in a decent area.

There was no answer, so he rang the doorbell again and

knocked loudly. He leaned into the door and tried to make out any sound from within. He couldn't hear anything and put that down to the thickness of the wood rather than an empty house.

He went over to the living-room windows and took in the shininess of the nails in the wood and the shavings on the windowsill. It had obviously been placed over the window recently, which meant this was a very active investigation. He cupped his hands around his eyes and leant into the second window. The living room was empty; the fire unlit, the television off, magazines and books neatly arranged on the coffee table, no used mugs and plates. It was neat and tidy.

Danny went back to the front door and rang the bell a few more times. He squatted to the ground, lifted the letterbox and using the torch from his phone, looked inside. He almost fell backwards when he saw the pool of dried blood on the hallway floor.

Chapter Fourteen

As Sian struggled to find a parking space in the rabbit warren known as the Northern General Hospital, her phone began to ring. She answered using handsfree, without looking at the display.

'DS Robinson,' she said as she leaned forward in the driver's seat, nose almost touching the steering wheel as she scanned the car park for a space.

'Sian, it's Donal. Are you free at all this morning?'

'I can be. What do you need?'

'Scott's woken up. He's a bit groggy, obviously, but he really needs to speak to you.'

'Funnily enough, I'm at the Northern now trying to find a … got one,' she said, swinging the car urgently to the left and grabbing the last available space. 'Give me a few minutes and I'll be right with you.'

Sian needed to keep busy. If she allowed herself a few moments to sit and think, she was in danger of losing it completely. Matilda was missing. She could help. She would do everything in her power to help the investigation. Jackie Barclay had been found. That was a good news story, especially for her family, who had been searching for answers for the past three years. However, was it Sian's husband who had killed her? He was currently serving a life sentence in Wakefield Prison for killing eight sex workers and a witness, and almost killing her. Was there going to be another victim to his tally? That was what she couldn't allow herself to focus on. If she thought about her husband, the twenty-five years of lies, deceit and duplicity, then the tears would flow, and she doubted they would stop. She needed to be strong.

She headed for the main entrance to the hospital, taking long strides and with her head held high. Gone were the days when people stared at her, instantly recognisable as the woman who was married to a serial killer. She buttoned her coat against the cold and tucked her shoulder-length red hair behind her ears. She could fake being confident. She'd had a good teacher in Matilda.

It took a while, and the instructions from the woman on reception hadn't been accurate, but she soon found where Scott was recovering. She washed her hands with sanitiser from the machine on the wall by the door and made sure her face mask was covering her nose and mouth before entering.

She knocked lightly and went in.

Scott was sitting up in bed. He looked pale, but then he always did. Tall, and incredibly fit thanks to an obsession with running and training, he had blond hair and blue eyes. He looked younger than his thirty years, despite the red circles around his eyes and the heavy lids from the anaesthetic. He smiled when he saw Sian, but he looked as if he was suffering from the world's worst hangover.

Sitting by the bed, Donal's face was full of concern and worry. He looked as if he hadn't slept at all last night.

'How are you feeling?' Sian asked, her voice quiet and motherly.

'I'm fine,' Scott said with a dopey smile.

'He's just been dosed up with painkillers,' Donal said.

Sian went around to the far side of the bed and sat down. She took Scott's clammy hand in hers. 'We were so worried about you,' she sniffled.

'Tough as old boots, me,' he said, his voice slightly slurred. 'How's Matilda?'

'What have you told him?' Sian asked Donal.

'Nothing.'

She took a breath and increased her grip on Scott's hands. 'Scott, what happened when you and Matilda got home?'

He looked to Donal and back to Sian. 'Where's Matilda? Has something happened?'

'She's missing.'

'What?' he asked. 'How? I mean, where is she?'

'We don't know. We're hoping you can tell us what happened.'

'Donal, can I have a drink of water, please?'

Donal got him a plastic beaker of water from the bedside locker. Scott's hands were shaking as he took a few long sips.

'We got to the house, but it was in darkness. Matilda turned on the lights, but they didn't come on. We thought it was a power cut. I went to get a torch from the car. I opened the front door and there was someone standing there. She had a knife.'

'She?' Sian asked. 'It was definitely a woman?'

'Definitely. I didn't have time to think or say anything. She just lunged forward and stabbed me. I tried … I … I just dropped to the floor.' His hand went straight to his stomach.

'What happened next?'

Scott squeezed his eyes closed as he searched his memory. 'I heard her talking. She said … I don't know.' He frowned and looked to be in great pain.

'Think, Scott. Matilda is missing,' Sian urged.

'She said something about Sidney Prescott,' he said, perplexed as to its meaning.

'Who's she?'

'She's a character from the *Scream* films,' Donal added, a frown on his face too. 'Scott, are you sure? We were just watching *Scream 4* the other night. Are you remembering everything right?'

'Of course I am,' he replied, annoyed. He turned back to Sian. 'She used a taser,' Scott said. 'I saw Matilda … she dropped to the floor, and she was shaking.'

'A taser?'

'Oh my God,' Scott said, his eyes widened. 'I've remembered. She took a roll of tape from her bag. She put a strip over Matilda's mouth, and she injected her with something. Before she did, she said that Steve Harrison says hello.'

'Steve …' Sian began. 'Oh, Jesus Christ!' She leaned back in her seat and visibly paled. 'Scott, is there anything else you remember?'

'She was dragging Matilda across the hallway. I tried to move but every time I did, more blood came out. I didn't see anything after that. I think I must have passed out.'

'That's okay. The woman, Scott. Did you recognise her?'

He nodded. 'She did look familiar. I can't place her.'

'You need to think, Scott,' Sian said, her voice heavy with urgency.

'You need to give him time, Sian. He's been through a lot,' Donal said.

'We don't have time.' She raised her voice. 'It's been almost twenty-four hours since Matilda went missing and if Steve Harrison is involved, which is looking likely, then God only knows what's happening to her.'

Scott shook his head. He looked to be in physical pain as he tried to think. 'I can't. I'm sorry. I know I recognise her from somewhere, but I can't think where. It won't come to me.'

'Look, maybe if you rest,' Donal said. 'Close your eyes for a bit. It might help to relax.'

'I need to phone Christian,' Sian said, standing up and scrabbling for her phone in her pocket. 'He's on his way to Wakefield Prison. He can talk to Steve. Scott, please, I'm begging you ...' She didn't need to finish the sentence.

'I will try. I promise,' he said. His eyes were wide and filled with tears.

'I know. I'll be back in a bit.' She left the room and as she turned from the door, she bumped into a nurse coming her way. 'I'm so sorry.'

'That's okay.' He smiled back. 'Are you a relative of Mr Andrews?'

'No. I'm ... I'm a colleague, and a very close friend.'

'It's only relatives at the moment, I'm afraid. Mr Andrews needs to rest.'

'Of course, I'm sorry. It's just ...'

'Are you a detective, too?' the nurse asked, lowering his voice.

'Yes. I am.'

'Then I guess it'll be all right,' he said, giving his best smile.

'I don't suppose I could see some identification, could I? I mean, for all I know, you could be a reporter. We know what they're like, don't we?'

Sian smiled. 'Absolutely.' She fished in her pocket for her ID and showed it to him.

'Detective Sergeant Sian Robinson,' he read. 'Lovely photo.'

She looked back at it. 'You think? I've aged quite a bit since it was taken a couple of years ago.'

'Haven't we all?' he said with a smile before walking away.

Jason Fleet looked back over his shoulder to make sure he wasn't being watched by the red-headed detective before taking his mobile out of his pocket and firing off a quick text to Danny Hanson. Fingers crossed he'd add an extra twenty quid to what he was paying him. Every little helped.

Chapter Fifteen

Finn Cotton was driving the pool car with Christian Brady in the front passenger seat. He was getting emails all the time from various departments and officers who were checking Matilda's mobile phone and emails. She'd received no communications that couldn't be followed up and corroborated in the past forty-eight hours. Her mother and sister were being interviewed again and they couldn't think of anything that had happened recently to raise concern. A voicemail from Pat Campbell mentioning the disappearance of Lucy Dauman and wondering if Adele could be the target of the kidnapper was a different angle Christian hadn't thought of. In the message, Pat mentioned Adele's ex-husband, Robson. He would need tracking down.

Christian selected Zofia's number and called her. She answered before the first ring finished.

'Zofia, I need you to locate Robson Kean for me.'

'Robson Green?'

'No. Kean.'

'Who's he?'

'He's Adele's husband. Well, ex-husband, actually.'

'Why?'

'Now I come to think about it, I think Kean might be Adele's maiden name. Actually, I'm not even sure if they married or not. Jesus, I can't think straight. Look, try and find out if Adele and Robson were ever married and track him down.'

'O...K. What am I supposed to do when I find him?'

'Ask him for his alibi for yesterday.'

'You think Adele's ex-whatever-he-is has kidnapped Matilda?' she asked, incredulity clear in her voice.

'I … no. I don't know,' Christian gabbled. 'Just find him for me. Also, double-check with the forensic team and make sure they've definitely finished at Matilda's house. If so, contact a crime scene cleaning company and have them sent out to clean up the blood. I'm guessing Adele will want to go back home tonight.'

'No problem. I know a good one. Anything else?'

'Sian's ringing,' Finn said, looking at his phone.

'No,' Christian said, ending the call.

Finn swiped to answer and put his phone on loudspeaker.

'Hi Sian,' Finn called out.

'Steve Harrison's got her,' Sian said. There was no time for greetings.

'What?' Christian asked.

'I've been speaking to Scott. He said that she was kidnapped by a woman whom he vaguely recognises but can't remember from where. He said that she used a taser and then injected Matilda with something, but before she did, she said, "Steve Harrison says hello."'

'Oh my God!' Christian said, running a hand over his buzzcut.

'You need to interview Steve.'

'I know. But we both know what he's like. He'll love the attention and keep his mouth shut. I've been speaking to the governor of Wakefield Prison and he's using a random security check of cells to get Steve out of the way so we can go through all his stuff. If that doesn't give us any leads, then we'll speak to him.'

'Christian, there's something else,' Sian said, her voice dropping an octave. 'Adele's identified the body in the car at Wigtwizzle as Jackie Barclay.'

'Name sounds familiar.'

'She was a sex worker who disappeared around the same time as all the others – the ones Stuart killed.'

'You think he's responsible?'

'Who else could it be?'

'Jesus! Sian, are you all right?'

'No. I'm not. Look, he's in Wakefield, too. Can you talk to him while you're there?'

'I'll see what I can do. Send me through any information you've got on Jackie Barclay.'

'Will do.'

A silence developed between them.

'Sian,' Christian began, clearing his throat. 'If I do get to speak to Stuart, is there anything you want me to say to him?'

It was a long, deathly silent moment, before Sian replied. 'No. Nothing.' She ended the call.

The silence in the car grew as Christian and Finn took in the conversation with Sian. They'd both suffered at the hands of Steve Harrison and his evil actions. Deep down, they knew prison wouldn't stop him from creating more havoc. The team was still suffering the effects of the shooting. None of them were ready for more carnage.

'What are you thinking?' Finn broke the silence.

It was a while before Christian answered. 'I'm not sure.'

They were in the fast lane of the M1, almost coming to the end of their journey.

'Steve Harrison is behind all this, isn't he?'

'It's beginning to look that way.'

'He's tried twice before to kill Matilda and failed. He won't want to fail a third time. He'll give the order to kill her, won't he?'

Christian swallowed hard. 'I'm afraid so.'

Chapter Sixteen

W akefield Prison, a category A prison, is home to the most dangerous and violent men in Britain. Dubbed Monster Mansion, it has housed infamous killers such as Ian Huntley, Harold Shipman and Colin Ireland and currently has Jeremy Bamber, Ian Watkins and Mark Bridger among its inmates. The formidable building, opened in 1594, radiated a malevolent atmosphere. Behind these thick, high walls lie the most depraved, disturbed and destructive men in the country. Simply looking at the monolith sends a chill down the spine.

Finn found a parking space close to the main entrance and pulled in. As he turned off the engine, he leaned down to look at the prison through the windscreen. As a young detective and a student of criminology, he was fascinated by the diseased minds within these walls. As a person, he was scared to death to meet them. He swallowed hard.

'Did you know the nursery rhyme "Here We Go Round the Mulberry Bush" comes from Wakefield Prison?'

'Does it?' Christian frowned. He was taking off his seatbelt and almost opening the door when he stopped, intrigued by Finn's statement.

'Yes. The inmates who were mothers – obviously this is going back many hundreds of years – would walk around the mulberry bush to exercise.'

'Huh. I never knew that,' Christian said, climbing out of the car.

Finn joined him. 'I'm pretty sure the mulberry died though – not that long ago, if memory serves. So there isn't one there now.'

'You're a mine of pointless information, aren't you?'

'You never know what questions might come up on the sergeant's exam,' Finn smiled.

'When do you go in for it?'

'I haven't got a date through yet. Hopefully it won't be long.'

'Will you stay on at South Yorkshire?' Christian asked. They were walking slowly towards the prison, almost as if they wanted to delay their arrival.

'I'd like to. It all depends if there's a place for me. With Sian back and Scott a DS, Matilda won't need three of us on the team.'

They were buzzed into the building. Christian showed his warrant card and explained the reason for their visit while Finn stood in wonder and took in the depressing atmosphere. In the office, he was fine, the merest hint of butterflies in his stomach, but he knew, once he was shown through the gates and into the main part of the prison itself, he would be within touching distance of evil.

Christian and Finn turned off their mobiles and handed them over to security and walked through the scanners. Finn had his bag emptied and thoroughly searched. A beeping noise meant that he had to walk through again, minus his belt and glasses. He passed the second time.

'That's a shame. I was hoping you'd be pierced somewhere intimate, and we'd all have a good laugh,' the prison officer said.

Finn gave a nervous smile.

The governor, Jeremy Fields, an imposing man on the cusp of retirement, met Christian and Finn and led the way to Steve Harrison's cell in the Supermax wing of the prison, an officer bringing up the rear, sandwiching the two detectives in.

Fields had worked in the prison service his whole life. There was nothing he hadn't seen and he had given up being shocked decades ago. He towered over them both, standing at six foot five, and although he was lean and lacked muscle, he radiated an aura of a man not to be messed with.

'On the whole, Steve Harrison is a model prisoner,' Fields said as he took huge strides, his heavy shoes echoing around the walls. 'Having said that, he's in his cell for twenty-three hours a day and receives no visitors. There's very little trouble he can cause.'

'He gets a lot of mail, I've been told,' Christian said.

'He's our most popular inmate. There was a true crime documentary on Netflix just before Christmas about him. Did you see it?'

'No,' Christian said.

'Yes,' Finn said.

'His post almost doubled overnight. It's still coming through even now. He gets letters and cards from women the world over. Marriage proposals, requests for visits, requests for a sample of his sperm so they can have his baby, padded envelopes with silky underwear in them. You wouldn't believe what some of these women want him to do for them. Or to them.'

'But he's a psychopath,' Finn said.

'That's part of the attraction.'

'Surely that's just feeding his ego, though.'

'He doesn't receive them,' Fields said, looking back at Finn over his shoulder. 'Part of his restrictions is that he only personally receives mail from a verified list of people. Everything else is destroyed.'

'Can we see that list?' Christian asked.

'Of course. It's more of a Post-it note, really.'

'So, where is Steve now?'

'In the library. We can keep him there for an hour before he starts to get suspicious, so you don't have long. He did moan about a random check of his cell as he had one less than a month ago. However, that's what the word "random" means, in my book.'

They were led through a series of doors and gates, each of them slammed closed and locked behind them. With every door passed, the further they went into the heart of the prison. By the time they reached Harrison's cell, even Christian was starting to feel nervous about being here.

'Does Steve send mail out?' Finn asked, his eyes darting around him.

'Hardly ever.'

'When was the last time he sent a letter out?'

Fields was silent for a long time while he thought. 'About a year ago.'

Christian and Finn exchanged glances. They were sure Steve Harrison was behind Matilda's kidnapping, Scott had confirmed that, but how had Steve communicated with the kidnapper if they hadn't exchanged mail?

'Does Steve make many phone calls?' Christian asked.

'Occasionally. He's supervised when he does, though.'

'Do you know who he calls?'

'Absolutely. Again, it'll fill a Post-it note.'

'Are there any members of staff who spend more time than they should with Steve?'

'No. They're rotated on a regular basis. Staff don't work on the Supermax wing for long before they're posted to another wing. It's very random.'

They reached the cell, stood in the doorway and looked at the small room Steve Harrison called home. It was no bigger than a boxroom. A single window, sealed shut, an en-suite toilet and a single bed. A built-in chest of drawers on which a small TV stood. There was a shelf with a few well-thumbed paperbacks and on the walls, posters, newspaper cuttings and photos looked down on them.

'Finn, go through everything as quick as you can. Anything interesting, take a photo.'

Christian took the governor to one side and asked him about the possibility of having a quick word with Stuart Mills once they'd finished.

'I'll check to see if he's in,' Fields said with a wink. 'Henry here will bring you back to the front office when you've finished.' He looked at his watch. 'You've got about fifty minutes.'

Christian walked into the cell and found Finn standing in the middle, staring at a wall, his eyes wide and mouth open.

'What is it?'

'Look. He's got photos of Matilda.'

Christian stepped closer. On the wall by the bedside table, next to where Steve laid his head, were a number of small photos of Matilda. A couple had obviously been cut from newspapers or printed from the net, but two were actual photos, taken with a camera and printed on photo paper. One showed Matilda in the car park of South Yorkshire Police HQ and in the other she was standing outside her own front door.

'Jesus Christ!' Christian said.

'He's obsessed,' Finn said, his voice quiet. He was fixed to the spot, his eyes glued on the photos.

'Get your camera out, Finn. Take pictures of everything in this room, starting with those.' He pointed to the photographs.

Finn put his bag on Steve's bed and with shaking fingers unzipped it and took out the Nikon he'd signed out of the station's storeroom. His eyes kept glancing to the pillow. That was where Steve laid his head at night. He probably had a solid eight hours' sleep and wasn't disturbed once by nightmares and a dark past trauma. Something so innocent and innocuous as a pillow made Finn feel sick. He always thought something could be learned from a man as evil as Steve, to understand the workings of a devious and malevolent mind, but now he was so close to him, to the ordinariness of his life, Finn felt nothing but repulsion. There was an argument that people like Steve Harrison should be destroyed.

'Finn!' Christian hissed. 'Shake a leg, mate.'

'Sorry,' Finn said, and began snapping photos of the pictures of Matilda. He dreaded to think how the photos would turn out. He couldn't keep his hands still.

Christian went over to the bookshelves and flicked through the pages to see if anything was hiding between them.

Finn cleared his throat. 'I suppose Steve thought he belonged on an elite unit. He has an entitled view of himself and I'm guessing he assumed he should be among the best in the police force. Matilda was in charge of such a unit and had the final say over who joined her team. When he wasn't picked, he'll have taken it as a personal attack.' He crouched and began going through the drawers of the bedside cabinet.

'Possibly.'

'When Steve's brother shot Rory, Scott told me that he mentioned them both being on the HMET, as it was then called. Steve thought he was better than Scott and Rory and deserved a place on the unit over them.'

'Then why not shoot them both?'

'According to Scott, Jake said he was only to kill one of them, so the other could suffer.'

'Scott told you that?' Christian asked, stopping in his task.

Finn nodded. 'He truly is pure evil, isn't he?'

'You're the one with the criminology degree. You tell me.'

'I'm not qualified yet. I'm in my final year. I'll let you know once I pass. But, yes, he is the embodiment of evil.'

Finn turned his attention to the bed. He lifted the mattress but there was nothing there. He looked under the bed and pulled out a battered paperback copy of *The Hangman's Hold* by Lionel Miller. The spine was heavily broken and the pages well thumbed. Steve had obviously spent many hours reading the book written about himself. He truly was a narcissist, revelling in his own sick achievements. Christian flicked through the pages to see if there was anything hidden inside. Nothing. When he reached the end of the book, he stopped and took a closer look at the end pages, purposely left blank. There was something written on them in incredibly small writing.

'Bloody hell,' Christian said to himself.

'What is it?' Finn asked, turning around.

'Listen to this: blah, blah, blah … "*the serial killer gene does exist. It's been proved to be real, and I've asked for my brain to be scanned to see if I've got it, but the governor has said no on more than one occasion. It's called MOAO and it's commonly known as the warrior gene, and it plays an important role in breaking down neurotransmitters such as serotonin. People with a defected MOAO have a low dopamine turnover rate and that has increased their aggression levels than people who don't have the defect. But then that brings up the argument of nature versus nurture. If I have a defected gene then I was obviously born with it, so was I born to kill? Was I singled out as being a mass murderer from the second I was born and no matter what I tried to do with my life, whether it was raise millions of pounds for charity or invent a cure for cancer, I was also going to kill people at some point in my life? On the other hand, where did I get this gene defect from? I'm made up of DNA from my mother and father. Did one of them have the gene defect? If so, why didn't they kill anyone? Or was the defect in the make-up of the mashed DNA from the two that went on to make me ..."'*

Christian stopped and looked up, his eyes wide. 'What's he talking about?' he asked, a deep frown on his face.

'For a start, he's got it wrong. It's not MOAO, it's MAOA and stands for Monoamine Oxidase A.'

'You've heard of it?'

'Yes.'

'What is it?'

'Well, you know the subject always comes up about whether serial killers are born or created by society? There's been all kinds of research into whether there's a killer gene that can detect a killer before they strike. I can't remember who came up with this MAOA theory but there was a test done with violent criminals in Finland and a high percentage of murderers had a defective MAOA gene.'

'So Steve thinks that's what he's got, too? He's trying to justify his actions.'

'Possibly. There's a counter-argument that some people also have a defective MAOA gene and they've never committed murder. Like Steve says, it's called the warrior gene and it's found in the X chromosome and goes back to the whole masculinity thing: men being warriors, fighters and saving damsels in distress.'

'There's loads of this here,' Christian said, flicking through the book. 'He's written in impossibly tiny handwriting to fit everything in.'

'What else is he saying?'

Christian squinted as he went back to the book and angled it towards the weak light coming through the small window. 'It's rambling. He's going on about this killer gene and how it will answer so many unanswered questions he's got.' Christian turned the page, and another. 'Oh my God … Listen to this: *"There will come a time when the law will have to catch up with science and see that killers are a product of genetics rather than society and when someone is arrested for murder, mass murder, and even if they admit it, the law should not jail them for life when it was an act they couldn't help. I'm assuming a landmark case like this will happen in America first, but I will try my hardest to be the first killer in Britain to be pardoned for committing an act over which I had no control."* Jesus Christ, he's going to try and get out of prison on a genetic technicality.'

'That will never happen.'

'How do you know?'

'For a start, human rights groups won't stand for it,' Finn said. 'Also, hypothetically, if this gene is proven to be linked to people being murderers, and it hasn't been, then people who have it can't live in open society. They'd have to be placed somewhere to protect innocent people. We're in the realms of science fiction here, where people are locked up in a secure environment before they've even committed a crime. That will never happen. At least, not in our lifetime, and certainly not in Steve Harrison's lifetime.'

'He sounds convincing.'

'Of course he does. He's trying to convince himself more than anything. Don't forget, he spends twenty-three hours a day in this room. He's got to do something to stop himself from going mad – or going any madder than he already is.'

Christian handed the book to Finn. 'Photograph all the pages. I'm giving myself a headache reading his small writing. We'll print them off and have a good look back at the station.'

'Is it going to be any use to us in finding Matilda, though?'

'I don't know. But this is our one and only chance of being in here. I want to know exactly what's going on in his diseased mind.'

'Can't we just take this with us?'

'Steve cannot know we've been here until we have the evidence to confront him with, or to get an official warrant to search this cell. All this is evidence of so far is a bloke who's completely cuckoo bananas.'

'Maybe he's trying to get himself committed and into a cushy institute rather than a prison.'

Christian gave Finn a severe look. 'Over my fucking dead body,' he spat, angrily.

'I'm afraid that's time up, fellas,' Henry, the prison officer, said from outside. 'We can't keep him away from his cell for long without him kicking off.'

'Have we got everything we need?' Christian asked Finn.

Finn looked around him. 'I think so. I just really want to get out of here.'

'It gives you goosebumps, doesn't it?' Henry said with a hint of a smile.

'I don't think I'll ever understand how someone can be so violent and evil and get such enjoyment from it,' Finn said, his face pale.

'I don't think we're supposed to. The best thing to do with people like Steve is to act like they don't make any difference to the world. Steve's a narcissist. He's a psychopath. And he craves attention. The only way to treat him is by not giving him any. Do you have a therapist on site?' Christian asked the prison officer.

'Really? You want therapy already? You've only been here an hour,' Henry smiled.

'I meant, do you have someone whom the prisoners can talk to?'

'We've got a counsellor who comes in on a regular basis to talk to the prisoners. It's entirely up to them if they want to.'

'Does Steve?'

'You kidding? A counsellor is a captive audience. Steve sees her every visit.'

'I'm going to need to talk to her.'

'She's not in today, but I can get you her contact details.'

'Thanks.'

As he was leaving, Christian took one last look over his shoulder. His eyes landed on the photos of Matilda by Steve's pillow.

'I've got a feeling in the pit of my stomach that Steve Harrison is laughing at us. He knew we'd come here and search his cell. He's planted something here for us.'

'What? We haven't found anything.'

'Maybe we have.'

When Steve Harrison first joined the police force, he received a great deal of attention simply because of how he looked in his uniform. He was of average height and build but his black hair, piercing eyes and amazing smile won over countless admirers. He was an incredibly good-looking man. The problem was, he knew it, and he used his looks to get what he wanted. Even once he was convicted of his crimes and sent to prison, he latched onto his fellow inmates, who would delight in watching him taking longer in the shower in exchange for some home comforts for his cell.

It was his good looks that caught the attention of people the world over. The number of serial killers was on the wane. There was a peak in the 1970s and 1980s, most of them being in America. Nowadays, with the advances in technology and CCTV cameras, killers could swiftly be identified and caught. The popularity of programmes such as *CSI* and *Silent Witness* informed people of the basics of forensics and they knew what the police looked for at a crime scene. It wasn't easy for a multiple killer to survive for long in a savvy world, and when one did, he made the headlines.

Steve Harrison's handsome face adorned the front pages of newspapers and magazines for months, and his orchestration of the shooting in Sheffield in January 2019 and the infamous day of terror that would go down in history gave him more coverage. Books were written about him. He appeared in features, psychological journals, documentaries on ITV and Netflix. There had even been a drama in development, but that had gone quiet recently, following the outcry from several families of Steve's victims. There was no shortage of publicity for Steve Harrison, and so the letters, cards, poems, underwear and marriage proposals kept on coming.

Three weeks ago, when his cell was randomly searched, Steve thought it was a ploy. The timing was perfect for him putting the final pieces in place for Matilda's capture. However, here he was again, in the library, for another random security check. He knew this was a ruse to search his cell for evidence to locate Matilda. Not that they'd find anything. Still, let them go through the motions.

Steve sat in the library, his new books chosen, and smiled. The twinkle in the eye that had won him so many admirers over the years had long since disappeared thanks to the harsh life inside a maximum-security prison. His soft skin and shiny hair had dulled, too, but the smile remained. Some said it was the smile of a confident man. Some said it was the smile of contentment. Some said it was the smile of evil.

The library was empty apart from three people: Steve Harrison, prison officer Ray Clarke, standing by the door, and the librarian, Stuart Mills.

'Any chance of going back to my cell now, Mr Clarke?' Steve asked.

'Not yet.'

'Oh. Is there a problem?' he asked, his voice dripping with faux innocence. 'Only I've chosen my books so, you know, I'm just killing time here.'

'Don't worry, as soon as you're allowed back, I'll let you know.'

'My cell was only searched three weeks ago. Nothing has changed in that time. All my mail is checked before it's given to me. I don't have visitors so nothing can be passed to me. I don't mix with other prisoners. In fact, the only other prisoner I do see on a regular basis is Stuart here. Isn't it, Stuart?'

Stuart looked up at the mention of his name. His blank expression didn't change, and he soon went back to his work.

The prison officer didn't say anything either.

'Bloody hell, you two are fantastic company. Stuart, have you received any interesting post recently?'

Stuart didn't acknowledge him.

'Anything from your kids?'

Still nothing.

'I bet they've disowned you, haven't they? It can't be easy for four kids in their teenage years coping with the fact their father was a serial killer. How many was it you killed again?'

Steve delighted in watching Stuart's jaw clench and the muscles and tendons in his face tighten. His face flushed, he swallowed hard and gripped his cheap biro tighter.

'Does Sian write to you?' Steve asked.

Stuart slammed his pen down.

'That'll do, Steve,' Ray Clarke said.

'What? I'm only making conversation. I've got to do something while you lot are stripping my cell searching for … well, you know what.' He smiled at Ray and maintained eye contact until the prison officer looked away.

Steve turned his attention back to Stuart. 'Sian Mills. Oh, no, she's gone back to her maiden name now, hasn't she? Sian Robinson. That must really hurt, Stuart. Does it? Does it hurt?'

'I'm not talking to you, Steve,' Stuart said without looking up.

Steve laughed. He loved getting under people's skin. He stood up and walked over to the window that looked out on the open space of the prison below. He watched prisoners coming out of their cells, sitting in the communal area, chatting, reading, playing a game of pool. He wasn't allowed to do any of that. He missed it. But he didn't let the officers see it bothered him. The loneliness of isolation had taken some getting used to.

Something caught his eye. He recognised one of the men being led along a corridor. If he wasn't mistaken, that was Detective Inspector Christian Brady from South Yorkshire Police. He'd put on a bit of weight since he'd last seen him, and his hair had disappeared, too. The stress of police work had taken its toll on him. Still, it confirmed his suspicions of this so-called random security check. She must have gone through with it and kidnapped Matilda. His plan had worked, and the police were looking to him as the mastermind behind it all. This was going to be so much fun.

Steve turned back to the prison officer by the door. He smiled. 'I do believe I should be able to go back to my cell now, Ray.'

Chapter Seventeen

I n the office at the front of the prison, Finn began to relax.
There were several secured doors between him and the
violent prisoners, and Steve Harrison, hopefully, was now back
in his cell, with the door firmly locked behind him. Finn sat
staring into space while he tried to get his mind around what
Steve had written in that book. He wouldn't be surprised if
some fame-seeking, money-hungry shyster of a solicitor tried to
take Steve's case to the High Court to prove the killer gene
existed and Steve shouldn't languish in a prison cell, but be in a
more secure unit, a gated complex with luxurious surroundings.

Finn released a heavy sigh. How some people could live
with themselves, he had no idea. The world was going crazy,
and it was getting crazier by the day.

'Can I use this phone?' Finn asked one of the office staff.

'Sure. Press nine for an outside line.'

Finn called Zofia back in Sheffield and asked her to email a
photograph of Jackie Barclay to the prison so they could print
it off and show Stuart Mills. He hung up the phone and sat

down at one of the desks. His energy seemed to have been sapped by the dark atmosphere of the prison.

'You look like you want to vomit,' Henry said to him. 'First time in a maximum security prison?'

'Actually, no,' Finn said. 'I've just never been able to get used it. How do you do it? I've had a headache since I pulled into the car park, and it's gotten worse all the time I've been here.'

The officer smiled. He was only young, probably the same age as Finn, not even thirty yet, but his eyes had a hard stare.

'It's a job,' he shrugged. 'You have to keep reminding yourself that the people in here are serial killers, rapists, child abusers, the lowest of the low, but they're also great manipulators, too. Anything they tell you could be a trap or a ruse or a lie to get what they want. You cannot let your guard drop for a single second. And don't let them get under your skin.'

'Don't you find that scary?'

'I learned very quickly not to be scared.'

'How?'

Henry pulled out a chair and sat down next to Finn. 'You know about the trick with the sugar in a kettle of boiling water, where you throw the water in someone's face and the sugar sticks to the skin, causing harsher burns?'

Finn nodded.

'I saw that happen on my fifth day here. The victim was a fellow officer and while I was helping to administer first aid, all I could hear was laughing in the background. I must have aged twenty years that day.'

'Jesus Christ! What did you do?' Finn asked.

Jeremy Fields slapped a hand down on Finn's shoulder,

making him jump out of his seat. 'I see Henry here is telling you the delights of our profession.'

'Yes. I very much doubt I'll be sleeping for the next few nights.'

Fields smiled, revealing a set of stained teeth. 'Here's the information you wanted – the people Steve Harrison is allowed to have contact with.' He handed Finn a bright pink square Post-it note.

'Is this it?'

'I told you it could fill a Post-it note.'

'There are only three names on here.'

'What were you expecting?'

Finn thought for a moment. 'I'm not sure.'

'Serial killers are not as popular as they'd like you to believe,' Fields said, leaning against a wall and folding his arms. 'Yes, Steve is getting fan mail from around the world, but he won't see them, and when these women – because they are mostly women – don't get a reply, they won't write a second letter. They'll forget all about him and move on with their lives. The problem with this country is, murder is sexy. It's entertainment. Crime shows are on TV almost every night, viewing figures for soaps increase when they have a murder, and you can't flick through the channels without some killer from history being analysed. However, although Steve Harrison is infamous, as soon as that Netflix documentary drops from the top spot, people forget all about him.'

'Until the next documentary.'

Fields shrugged. 'It's a vicious circle. One that is never-ending.'

'So, why are you here?' Henry asked. 'What's Steve done this time?'

'This time?'

'Last time the police showed an interest, it was because his brother decided to shoot half of Sheffield. Something like that happened again?'

'No. It's … it's complicated,' Finn said.

'It usually is with Steve.'

'What's he like? Finn asked. 'Do you talk to him?'

'I've had a few conversations with him,' Henry said, sitting back in his seat and crossing his legs. 'The thing you have to remember about Steve is a lot of what he says is an act. It's put on to shock you. I'm no longer easily shocked, so Steve can say what he likes, and it just washes over me. When he's not acting up, when he's chatting about anything in general, a book he's reading or a favourite film, he's actually a friendly, chatty bloke. You can almost forget what he's done.'

'I'll never forget what he's done,' Finn said, forlorn.

'Were you there? On the day of the shooting?' Henry asked.

Finn nodded. 'I lost some good friends that day. I'll never forget. I'll never forgive. I shouldn't say this, but the Steve Harrisons of this world should be locked up and ignored. Leave them to rot.'

'Shouldn't a police officer believe in rehabilitation?' Henry asked, a slight smile on his lips.

'For some people, there's no such thing as redemption,' Finn said quietly. He looked around him. 'I can't stand it here,' he said, swallowing the bile in his throat.

The door to the small office was opened and Christian stepped inside, having used the bathroom.

'Why does my DC look so pale?' Christian asked.

'We're telling him all about the delights of the prison service,' Fields said with a smile.

'Bloody hell, Finn, with everything you've seen over the past few years, you should be hardened by now.'

'I don't think we should be hardened. There's a fine line between desensitised and being stone-bloody-cold.'

Christian looked at Finn, studied his soft features, the look of pain in his eyes. They needed to get out of this place as quickly as possible.

'Is Stuart Mills ready for a visit?' Christian asked.

'I'll take you through,' Fields replied.

They walked along the narrow corridor in silence to a specially created interview room where prisoners could have time in private with their solicitor. Stuart was already in the room, sitting at a table screwed to the floor. Christian and Finn took a seat opposite. There was a toughened glass screen dividing the two.

The last time Christian saw Stuart, it was as he was taking his statement in South Yorkshire Police HQ, when Stuart admitted killing nine people. That was fifteen months ago in October 2019. Then, Stuart Mills was an imposing figure, a tall man with a rugby player's build. Sian often referred to him as a gentle giant, a big cuddly teddy bear. How wrong she was. How wrong everyone was. The man was leading a double life as a cold-hearted killer.

Christian couldn't take his eyes from Stuart. He didn't look like the same man. Prison had aged him terribly. He had a grey pallor about him, dark circles beneath his eyes, and he radiated an air of sadness. He'd lost weight, and it wasn't a good look for him.

'Stuart, thank you for agreeing to see us,' Christian said. He attempted to sound hard and unaffected by Stuart's appearance, but he genuinely was shocked by the transformation. 'How are you?'

A glint appeared in Stuart's eyes. It was probably the first time since he'd been locked up that someone was asking how he was. He gave a hint of a smile. 'I'm fine. Thank you. You?'

'I'm good.'

'The family?'

'They're doing okay.'

Stuart swallowed. 'Sian?'

'She's … she's fine.'

Stuart's bottom lip wobbled. 'My kids?'

'They're fine. They're … they're doing really well, Stuart.'

He smiled. 'Good. I'm glad.'

Christian looked to Finn and gave him the nod to get the printed photo of Jackie Barclay out of his pocket.

'Stuart,' Christian began. 'When you were arrested, we questioned you about the whereabouts of eleven women who were sex workers. Eight of whom had been found dead and you admitted to killing them. The other three were still missing and you denied having anything to do with their disappearance.'

'That's right.'

'The body of Jackie Barclay was found dumped in the back of a car in woodland at Wigtwizzle the other day. She was strangled and had been there for some time, possibly not long after she disappeared in 2018.'

Finn pressed the sheet of paper to the glass for Stuart to have a good look at the photo.

'This picture was taken a year before she went missing,' Christian said. 'Do you recognise her?'

Stuart glared at the photo. His expression remained unchanged. He didn't say anything.

'Her body is severely decomposed but we're trying to get samples from her and if there is anything of you on her, we will find it. However, you could save us a lot of time if you tell us whether you killed her or not.'

Stuart remained silent.

'Stuart, please,' Christian said.

'I'll tell you. But I want to talk to Sian first.'

Chapter Eighteen

D S Sian Robinson's mind was a miasma of darkness. She was sitting behind the wheel of the unfamiliar pool car with the windows down, despite it being a cold day, airing the car of its rancid smell of stale body odour and whatever street food whoever had used it last had eaten in here. There was a hint of curry, but something else, something stomach-churning.

Sian didn't know what to do next. She wanted to help in the hunt for Matilda Darke, but knew she wasn't allowed. She wanted to discover why Jackie Barclay had ended up in the boot of a car in the middle of nowhere but knew that as soon as CC Ridley found out who the body belonged to, and the fact that her ex-husband might be the killer, she would be taken off this case too.

'*Might* be the killer,' she said to herself. As if she was in any doubt. Of course Stuart was responsible.

Eleven women had gone missing over a five-year period. Eight had been found dead and three remained missing. Now, one of the three had been found. Where were the other two?

Was it possible a second killer was out there stalking sex workers at the same time as her husband? Yes, it was possible, but highly unlikely.

Once the press discovered news of another dead sex worker, they'd swarm on the city like the vultures they were, making nuisances of themselves, tearing the meat off any hint of scandal they could get their hands on and eking it out until there was nothing left. They'd come straight for Sian. They'd hunt her down, bang on her door day and night, wanting to know if Stuart was the killer, if she really knew what he was up to, if she'd been to visit him in prison. It would be back to the dark days once again when Stuart's crimes were first uncovered. She couldn't put her kids through all that again.

Somehow, they'd survived. They'd all survived the onslaught. Their lives were fragile. Would they survive another battering? Anthony and Belinda were fine. They were old enough to take it on the chin, realise the journalists were simply scum doing their job and brush it off. Gregory and Danny were at a difficult age. They both had exams coming up, pandemic permitting. The rest of their lives hinged on the next year or two. The last thing they needed was the added pressure of being hounded by the media again and talked about by their peers.

Sian's phone rang. She saw it was DI Sharp calling and swiped to answer.

'Sian, can you do me a mahoosive favour?' she asked. There was something about her playful tone that made her smile.

'It depends what it is.'

'I'm outside Jackie Barclay's sister's house. I'm just about to go in and talk to her and I've had Felix on the phone at Wigtwizzle. The council have turned up and they're kicking off about the car in the woods causing an obstruction or something. Are you free to pop out there and kick him between the legs or something?'

Sian smiled. 'Leave it with me.'

'Cheers, Sian, you're a sweetheart,' she said, ending the call.

Sian started the car and pulled out into traffic. She'd been sitting in the car park of the Northern General Hospital for far too long while she tried to marshal her thoughts, but wallowing in a car park surrounded by illness and death was not doing anyone any good. She needed to be proactive. She needed to show her boss, and the world, that it didn't matter what was thrown at her, she'd be ready with a huge baseball bat to swing and smash it out of the park. Fuck Stuart. Fuck the press.

———————

Sian had been driving for five minutes when she realised she had no idea where Wigtwizzle was. She hadn't even heard of it until yesterday when told about the body being found. It sounded like a made-up name, like something out of a children's television series. *Today, boys and girls, let's see what Mr Wibble and Mrs Wobble are up to in Wigtwizzle.*

According to her satnav, it was in the middle of nowhere, and could very well have been a made-up fairyland. It was in the parish of Bradfield, which she had heard of, six miles south of Penistone, twelve miles northwest of central Sheffield, and a million miles away from reality. Once the satnav had programmed a route, she found she was heading in the wrong direction. She performed an illegal U-turn, stuck two fingers up to the dick in the Mercedes who called her a stupid bitch, and headed for the back of beyond.

One of the things Sian loved about Sheffield was that it was so close to the countryside. There were so many beautiful walks to explore, and breathtaking scenery, and all within a few minutes' drive from the city centre. Although, since the outbreak of Covid-19, the city centre was a veritable ghost town and shops were closing down at an alarming rate. Who'd have thought Debenham's would close?

It wasn't long before the shops and houses became scarcer, the roads became wider, the view opened up and she was surrounded by fields and wide-open spaces. She opened the windows and, despite the single-digit temperature blasting her face and chilling her bones, she found herself smiling, and her shoulders relaxing.

She passed the calm waters of Broomhead Reservoir, turned off Yewtrees Lane onto Allas Lane and then took a left onto Lee Lane. She was following the satnav while also looking out for any sign that there was an active crime scene around here somewhere. She passed a farmhouse and thought how lucky the residents were to live in such picturesque surroundings. She could smell the countryside, the earthy, peaty smell. She turned a corner and slammed on the brakes. Dead ahead was the blue and white crime scene tape alerting locals and passers-by that something terrible had happened here. Murder was not restricted to the towns and the cities; it visited the countryside, too.

She turned off the engine and climbed out of the car. She looked towards the scene ahead but couldn't see much from the road. From the boot of the car, she took her walking boots out of her backpack and slipped off her sensible flat shoes. She zipped up her coat, pulled a beanie hat from the pocket and pulled it down over her ears to stave off the cold and headed for the freezing and bored-looking PC standing guard.

'DS Sian Robinson.' She flashed him her warrant card. 'Anything happening down there?' She squinted through the gaps in the trees but couldn't see anything.

The PC stood tall and looked down at Sian. He was pale and shivering, his teeth chattering with cold.

'Nothing. For the past hour the CSM has been wrangling with someone from the council about clearing out some of these trees to get a low-loader in to get the car out. The council are kicking off.'

'That's rich coming from them. I thought Sheffield City Council loved nothing more than cutting down trees unnecessarily.'

'That's what I said.'

She looked at him with a smile. 'Really?'

'Yes. That's how I ended up being posted on here freezing my balls off.'

She handed him the keys to her car. 'Here, I doubt anything is going to be happening for the next half an hour or so. Go and warm up in my car. And I'm feeling generous, so you can have the KitKat in the glove box.'

'Thank you, ma'am,' he said with a smile, grabbing the keys and heading for the car.

Sian made her way through the thicket of trees. She could hear the loud discussion before she saw anyone. A few CSIs were dotted around in their familiar white oversuits.

'Good afternoon,' she said loudly over the heated chatter. 'DS Sian Robinson. I thought I'd come and see how everything's going.'

The CSM turned to her, opened his mouth to speak, but the anorak from the council got in there first.

'Finally, someone official from the police. I have called, but nobody seemed interested. Bob Waterhouse from the Parks Department.' He held out his hand for Sian to shake. She was glad they were both wearing gloves.

Bob was the embodiment of average. Average height, weight and looks. There was nothing special to stand out. His trousers were navy, his anorak was beige, his head was bald, and his eyes were dull.

'Is there a problem?' Sian asked.

'I am aware you have a dead body, and this is a crime scene and you're hoping to get forensic detail from the surrounding area. I'm cognisant of that. I don't want to stand in the way of the police doing their work, but when it comes to the wilful destruction of our beautiful countryside, I take issue.'

Sian looked to the CSM who raised an eyebrow. She looked to the car then back to Bob Waterhouse.

'I'm guessing the car was driven here, so it was somehow able to bypass all these trees. I'm sure if we find out how it got here it'll be possible to remove it without cutting any trees down.'

Bob's jaw almost fell to the floor. 'There will be no cutting down of these trees,' he said, his voice echoing around the woodland.

'I'm guessing you wouldn't be protesting if I were the CEO of a large construction company with a blank cheque in my hand.'

'Are you suggesting—?'

Sian cut him off. 'I'm suggesting nothing. Now, if you'll pop that vein back in your head, and let me talk to my Crime Scene Manager in private for five minutes, I'm sure we'll come up with a solution that will please us all.'

Reluctantly, Bob stepped away. He fished out his mobile and began making a call.

'I can't stand clipboard warriors,' Sian said.

The CSM laughed. 'I don't believe we've been properly introduced. Felix Lerego,' he said, hand held out.

'Sian Robinson,' she smiled. 'Nice to meet you.'

'You too.'

They headed for the black Toyota Corolla, which had seen better days. It had succumbed to the elements and was more rust and bird shit than paint. Three of the tyres were flat and another had long since perished. Sian bent down and read the number plate: T41 CKK.

'Have we run the number through the PNC?'

'Yes. Someone from your team forwarded me an email.' Felix took his phone out and scrolled through his emails. 'It was last registered to a Barbara Short who lives in Gleadless – am I saying that right?' Sian nodded. 'In 2016, she was involved in a car crash and the car was written off. You can see the damage around the other side. It was scrapped and was listed as such by the scrap dealers with the DVLA. To all intents and purposes, this car no longer exists.'

'So how did it end up here?'

'That's a question for you to answer. All I do is manage the crime scene.'

'And how's that working out?'

'Shall we move on?'

Sian smiled and followed as he made his way over uneven ground to the other side of the car.

It was colder in the woods than it was out. The sun could not penetrate the thickness of the trees and Sian shivered, pulling up the collar of her coat.

'Can't we tow the car out somehow? It's not far to the road.

I'm sure you'd be able to get a pick-up to winch it up through the trees. It might be a bit of a squeeze, but, like I said, it had to get here somehow.'

'I'm guessing it's been here a few years and the woodland has thickened out over time. We might have to slightly damage some undergrowth.'

'Well, trees bounce back. Give it a couple of years and you won't know a car has even been here.'

'Do you want to say that to Bob or shall I?'

'It's your crime scene. You manage it,' she grinned.

He gave her a 'thanks for nothing' smile, rolled his eyes and headed for the man from the council, tripping on an exposed tree root as he went.

Sian headed for the group of CSIs. 'Have you found anything from the car?'

'Well, without getting too gruesome, the body had decomposed inside so all we've been able to get are samples from the carpet still remaining and whatever had leaked through to the woodland beneath.'

'Fingerprints?'

'None.'

'Samples of clothing?'

'Only from what the body was wearing.'

'How about from the front of the car? Anything from the driver's side?'

'Nothing, I'm afraid.'

'I don't know why they're having this argument, then. Why not just take the thing apart and get rid of the scraps?'

'That's what I said. You know what men are like, though.'

'Bloody useless.'

'Precisely.'

Sian turned around to inspect the woodland. She had never

been out here before, and it wasn't the kind of place she'd come to on her own, but it was a beautiful place for a hike. In summer you could bring a picnic. Not that she had anyone to picnic with.

She let out a heavy sigh and trundled on, kicking at the undergrowth. Her mind went back to Matilda. It was going dark. She'd been gone for almost twenty-four hours. The longer time went on without anyone knowing where she was, the less chance of her being found alive. That was a thought that tugged at the heartstrings. She and Matilda had been through so much together. She couldn't imagine her life without Matilda in it.

Sian tripped on something and fell to the ground. She immediately looked around to see if anyone had seen her fall and was now laughing at her. Fortunately, she'd walked far from the crime scene, and they were all busy. She leaned back against a tree and looked at what she'd tripped over. A branch had fallen at some point and was sticking out from behind a tree. She grabbed it with her gloved hands and pulled. It took some yanking to pull it free, but it would save others the embarrassment of falling arse over tit. It would be her good deed for the day. When the branch came free, she tossed it behind her and headed back to the crime scene.

A few steps on, she stopped. She'd seen something among the detritus of decaying leaves and exposed dirt. She turned back and saw the grimace of a skull staring back at her.

Another body. A second body. There were three women, three sex workers still missing. One had been found in a car not ten feet from where she was standing and now she'd found another. Was this two of three? Was the third close by?

'Jesus Christ, Stuart. What the fuck have you done?' she said to herself.

Chapter Nineteen

The printer in the Homicide and Major Crime Unit spat out page after page. Finn had uploaded to his laptop the photographs he'd taken of the prison cell and of the pages in the paperback book Steve Harrison had used to write his ramblings. Now he was printing them all off and trying to put them into some kind of order.

'Finn, you were here at the time of Steve's original killings, weren't you?' DC Tom Simpson asked.

'Yes. I was in uniform, though.'

'The thing is, I've had two people burst into tears on the phone to me and one of them called me a bastard and slammed the phone down.'

'Who was that?'

Tom rifled through his notepad. 'The ex-wife of Brian Appleby.'

'I'm not surprised,' Finn said. 'Brian Appleby was a paedophile. He moved to Sheffield after he was released from prison. His son was at university here and, for a while, the son – can't remember his name – was a suspect for the killings as he had no alibi. He ended up killing himself. I'm guessing his wife blames her ex-husband for the death of her son, too. Or possibly us.' ,

'Wow. Anyway, she's in France now. She's remarried and changed her name. She took some tracking down. The only person I can't find a next of kin for is Gordon Berry. Even Zofia has hit a brick wall,' Tom said.

Since Zofia's accident in 2019 which left her permanently needing a wheelchair, she had changed her focus from being a detective who chased criminals on foot to becoming invaluable when it came to anything connected to computers. She could hack her way into anyone's social media accounts and had a program on her laptop – which might not be a hundred per cent legal – to find personal information about someone that only a central governmental department should have access to.

'Gordon Berry was practically a loner,' Zofia said. 'He had very few friends and family. The ones I found are either distant cousins or acquaintances he worked with.'

'In that case, we have to say he has no one in his life who would want to avenge his death,' Finn said as he took more printed pages from the tray and shuffled them so they were neat.

'Can I ask a more personal question while it's just us three here?' Tom asked.

'Go on,' Finn prompted.

'I've been reading over the case notes and there was a Detective Inspector Ben Hales who was hanged around that time. It turned out he committed suicide, but for a while everyone thought he was another victim of the Hangman. It's a bit suspect, isn't it?'

'DI Hales *definitely* killed himself,' Finn said.

'But actually in DCI Darke's house? That's really cold.'

Finn looked at the door to make sure no one was coming in. He walked over to Tom and Zofia's desk and spoke in a hushed voice.

'There was a huge history between DI Hales and DCI Darke. He thought he should have had her job and was very bitter about it when she was given promotion. It's a long story.'

'Sounds quite similar to Steve Harrison,' Tom said. 'A man angry at Matilda for heading an elite unit. I'm beginning to think working here is jinxed.'

'But why did this DI Hales kill himself in Matilda's house?' Zofia asked.

Finn checked the door once again before he continued. 'The house Matilda lived in was built by her husband. She loved it. She cherished it. It was all she had left of him, and she said she could feel his presence in every room. DI Hales wanted to destroy that. And he did. She ended up selling. It broke her heart.'

'Bloody hell. Definitely no love lost between those two then?' Tom asked.

'None at all.'

'But don't go spreading this all around. Sian told me this in the strictest confidence. Speaking of Sian, how are you getting on with her list, Zofia?'

'I've got through about half. I spent ages talking to Raymond Lassiter's daughter. She's convinced her father is innocent and he's being used as a scapegoat.'

'Did she mention DCI Darke?' Finn asked.

'Not by name. She mentioned South Yorkshire Police as a whole and Richard Ashton's iron-grip hold over prominent people. She's very bitter about it.'

'Does she have an alibi for Tuesday evening?'

'Yes. She was moving all her things into a new house in Stafford so she could be near her father, who has just arrived to spend his jail term in HMP Stafford.'

'Wow. Okay, keep going through the list and if anything crops up, let me know.'

'I will,' she said, a look of concern on her face.

'Are you all right?'

'No. I'm really worried,' Zofia said. She glanced out of the window. 'It's getting dark. It's almost a full day since Matilda went missing and we haven't had a word from anyone. What if—'

'Don't,' Finn interrupted. 'Don't start speculating. It'll do your head in. It's best to keep busy. Speaking of which, I've printed off all these pages from Steve Harrison's book. I've read a few of the pages and, well, I'm really not sure what to make of them. Are they the ramblings of a serial-killing psychopath? Are they written for our benefit so we think he's completely bonkers or does he genuinely believe all this stuff? Also, hopefully, there'll be some mention of who he's using in the outside world to communicate with. I want you to read them, see what you think. Maybe together we can, I don't know, work out what he's thinking.'

'I'm not sure I want to know what Steve Harrison is thinking.' Zofia shuddered.

'Everyone will tell you never to get inside the head of a serial killer because it will just screw you up. Unfortunately, that's exactly what we've got to do here in order to find Matilda,' Finn said.

'I hope South Yorkshire Police are going to pay for the therapist when we're finished,' Tom said with a smile.

'And for all the wine I'm going to be drinking,' Zofia added.

In Chief Constable Ridley's office, Christian Brady was sitting on a rigid chair, a bottle of water in hand. He'd have preferred a coffee but Ridley had given up caffeine.

Benjamin Ridley was standing at his floor-to-ceiling window, which gave a panoramic view of the steel city. He was looking out, watching as a crane swung over an apartment block being built in the city centre. It was starting to go dark, and it wasn't even four o'clock yet. There were no clouds in the sky. It was going to be another bitterly cold night.

'Have you been into town recently?' Ridley asked out of nowhere.

'I can't say I have, no,' Christian replied, taking a sip of water.

'There are so many closed shops. I'm not sure if it's people changing how they shop, Brexit or the Covid pandemic which is killing off the high street.'

'Maybe a combination of all three.'

'Debenham's has gone. That's a big building to be empty. I can't believe John Lewis won't reopen either. It was only last year they signed a twenty-year contract with the council to remain in Sheffield.'

'I don't think anyone saw a pandemic coming.'

'No,' Ridley said, wistfully. 'It makes you wonder what's happening to society, doesn't it? Everything's changing. And so quickly, too.'

'Sir,' Christian began, raising his voice, trying to get his attention back on topic. 'What do you want to do about Stuart Mills?'

Ridley sighed and bowed his head. He turned his back on the view and returned to his seat. He sat, knitted his fingers together and leaned forward on the desk. His brow was furrowed and his skin looked dull and tired.

'You know Sian better than I do. Do you think she'll go and see him?'

'No,' Christian answered quickly.

'Have forensics come up with anything from the body in the boot?'

'Jackie Barclay. No, they haven't. She's too decomposed. There's no trace of anything that could tell us who her killer is.'

'Okay. Well, if Matilda were here, I'd ask her to have a succinct chat with Sian and try to persuade her to visit her husband. Unfortunately, that task now falls to you. We can't force her, obviously, but we need to give it a go. It's in the interest of this investigation. Surely Sian will see that, and common sense will prevail.'

'And if she won't?'

Ridley inhaled deeply. 'Well, I don't like doing deals with prisoners, but if that's what we have to do, then we'll do it.'

Christian nodded. He stood up and headed for the door.

'Any news on Matilda?' Ridley asked.

Christian turned back. 'No, sir. Not yet.'

'Nobody's been in touch to say they've got her?'

'No.'

'So, it's not a kidnapping for ransom?'

'It would appear not. If Steve Harrison is involved, and it's looking very likely, we believe his order will have been to kill Matilda.'

'But what satisfaction would he get from that if he's not the one doing the killing?'

'I don't know. It all depends on who is doing the killing, their connection to Steve, and what Steve has ordered to be done.' Christian swallowed hard. 'I hate to say this, but it's been at the back of my mind all day. I have a feeling Matilda may never be found. That is something Steve Harrison will get a great deal of pleasure from.'

Ridley didn't say anything. There was nothing to say. The atmosphere thickened.

'I'll go and see where we are with both investigations. I'll keep you informed.'

Ridley didn't look up. He seemed to be deep in thought.

Slowly, Christian turned and left the office. His head was down, and he was deep in thought too. He closed the door firmly behind him and leaned back against it. He released a breath he hadn't realised he'd been holding. The urge to cry was too much right now.

Chapter Twenty

Getting a signal on her phone in Wigtwizzle was not easy and Sian had to drive for more than a mile before a bar appeared on her screen. She pulled over, grabbed her phone from the bracket on the dashboard and was about to call Matilda, the one person she relied on most, until she remembered Matilda was missing. How could she have forgotten? Emotion swept over her, and she wiped away a tear while she dialled Christian.

'Sian? Where have you been?' Christian asked by way of a greeting. 'I've been trying to phone you for over an hour.'

'Sorry. I was out at Wigtwizzle. You can't get a signal among all those trees.' She took a breath. 'Christian, another body's been found.'

'Oh my God.'

'What if it's another of the sex workers? What if this was Stuart's burial place?'

'Okay, Sian, calm down.' He could sense the rising emotion in her voice. 'Sian, come back to the station. I need to talk to you.'

'What's going on? Has Matilda been found?'

'No. Nothing like that. But we need to talk. Just drive slowly and carefully.'

There was a long silence while Sian composed herself. 'Christian, what the hell is happening here?'

'I really don't know, Sian. Look, forget about coming back to the station. We can't talk properly here,' he said. 'Go straight to my house.'

'Are you sure?'

'Yes. Jennifer got me a subscription from a wine company for Christmas. You can have a taste of an Israeli Rosé.'

'I didn't realise Israel made wine.'

'No. I was surprised, too,' he said, a chuckle in his voice.

'I'll be about twenty minutes.'

Christian's home life looked like something from a 1980s sitcom. He was happily married to Jennifer and had two beautiful young children and a Dalmatian puppy, who seemed to have made himself the centre of attention in the short time he'd been with them. Despite a concern over the Covid pandemic and Christian's chilling childhood coming back to haunt him last year, the family were once more happy and relaxed. A dog in the house had certainly improved everyone's mental health.

The doorbell rang and Christian answered, holding the puppy in his arms. He found Sian on the doorstep looking cold, drawn, tired and on the verge of tears. He invited her into the warmth and closed the door behind her.

'It's quiet in here. Where are the kids?'

'Jennifer's taken them upstairs. She's allowing them an extra hour on the PlayStation as long as they're quiet.'

Sian smiled. She sat in the middle of the sofa and looked around her. It had been a while since she'd been to Christian's house. It was warm and comfortable. Messy, with the usual detritus that comes with having two children under the age of ten. The mantelpiece was full of photos of the kids taken at school in their uniforms and the coffee table littered with magazines, colouring books, school textbooks and abandoned toys.

The electric fire was blazing, the radiators on high and Sian felt herself beginning to thaw.

Christian placed the puppy on the floor, and he made a fuss of Sian for a few minutes until he returned to his bed and curled up in front of the fire.

'You've got him well trained,' Sian said.

'The kids wear him out, bless him. As soon as they go up to bed, I think he's thankful for some peace at last.'

'I'm glad I didn't go back to the station,' she said. 'For some reason, I couldn't face it.'

'I know what you mean. There's a heavy atmosphere about the place.'

'There's been no word from Matilda?'

'None at all.'

'Where the hell is she, Christian?' Sian asked, tears filling her eyes.

'I wish I knew. Do you want a drink?'

'Yes, please.'

'I can give you a glass of wine or something to warm you up.'

'I'm actually quite keen to try an Israeli wine,' she smiled.

'It turns out that bottle was empty. I've opened a Mongolian red that's breathing in the kitchen.'

Sian laughed. 'Oh. That sounds ...' She couldn't finish the sentence.

She followed him into the bright kitchen and pulled out a chair at the table while he poured two glasses. He handed one to her and sat opposite. They each examined their glass and took a sniff at the contents.

'That's a strong smell,' Sian said, stifling a cough.

They raised their glasses in a silent 'Cheers' and took a sip, both recoiling at the taste.

'My goodness, that's awful,' Christian spat.

'It tastes like cough medicine,' Sian said.

Christian pushed his glass away. 'I think I might send this one back to Mongolia.'

'You might want to hang onto it. This could be a vaccine for Covid.'

'I'll get us something else.' Christian picked up the glasses and poured the contents down the sink. 'Maybe I shouldn't have done that. It might dissolve the pipework. I've got a Shiraz, unless you want to be daring and try another from my round-the-world collection.'

'I think I can die happy knowing I've not tried Vanuatu Rosé. Any chance of a coffee?'

'Sure. Are you hungry? I can make you something.'

'I'm not. I missed lunch, but I'm not even hungry.'

'You should eat, Sian.'

'I know. I'll have something with the kids when I get home.'

'How are they all?' Christian asked as he set about filling the machine with a Brazilian blend that gave the kitchen an aroma much more pleasant than the bitter-smelling wine.

'They're fine. Anthony's taken over the dog-walking business while the university decides what to do next for lectures while Covid is still rife.'

'And Belinda?'

'Christian, don't get me wrong, it's lovely having a chat with you, but you've got a sour look on your face that isn't just from the wine. Something's happened that you need to tell me about and you're worried how I'm going to react.' She took a deep breath. 'Matilda's dead, isn't she?'

'No, she isn't,' he quickly answered. He brought the coffees over to the table and sat down again. He took a slow, lingering sip. 'Finn and I went out to Wakefield Prison this morning. We searched Steve's cell. We found ... well, we can't really make sense of what we found yet.'

'Did you speak to Steve?'

'No. Ridley doesn't want us to yet. Not until we have something concrete we can say to him.' He cleared his throat and adjusted his position on the wooden seat, clearly uncomfortable. 'The thing is, we also saw Stuart.'

Sian's face was blank at the mention of the man she was married to for more than twenty-five years.

'We asked him about Jackie Barclay.'

'And?'

'He wouldn't say.'

Sian frowned. 'Wouldn't or couldn't?'

'Wouldn't. He said he'll answer our questions, but he wants to see you.'

Sian's mouth dropped open. 'What? No. Absolutely not.'

'Sian, calm down. I'm not going to make you do anything you don't want to do. In your position, I wouldn't want to see him either. But you've just found a second body out at

Wigtwizzle. What if she's one of the missing sex workers, too? If she's as badly decomposed as Jackie Barclay ...'

'She is,' Sian interrupted. 'She's just a skeleton.'

'Then we'll have nothing to work on to find out who killed her. Look, Sian.' Christian reached across the table and placed his hands over hers. 'Don't make a rash decision. Go home. Talk to your kids about it. Talk to someone impartial like Pat Campbell. But, please, give this some serious thought.'

Sian pulled her hands away. She looked down and when she looked back up, tears were rolling down her face. 'I'm never going to be free of the man, am I?'

'There is a way you can have the upper hand here.'

'How?'

'If you went to see him, walked in there with your head high, your shoulders back, confident, looking amazing and happy, and showed him that you're getting on with your life. Stuart has lost weight. He looks drawn and tired. Prison life isn't suiting him at all, by the look of it. If you went in looking like life was a party, it would show him that you're not letting him, or his crimes, get to you.'

'But I don't look amazing. And I'm certainly not happy and confident.'

'Not yet. But you'll get there, especially when you move into your new house. In the meantime, you can fake it.'

Sian thought for a beat. 'I really don't want to see him. I promised myself I'd never see him again.'

'I know. Promise *me* you'll think about it, though.'

She nodded.

'Take all the time in the world. You don't have to decide right away.'

'I'll talk about it with Belinda and Anthony.'

'Is there anything I can do?'

She leaned forward and placed a hand on top of his. She looked directly into the centre of his eyes. 'Promise *me* one thing,' she said, succinctly.

'Anything.'

'Never invite me over for a glass of wine ever again.'

They both laughed.

Sian picked up her coffee, took a sip and looked at Christian over the top of her cup. She could see his eyes darting back and forth. He had something else on his mind. 'There's something else, isn't there?' she asked.

'I had a call this morning. And I've just had a call tonight, too. And one from the press office. Danny Hanson's been in touch.'

'Vulture.'

'He's tried calling Matilda about something – he won't tell me what – and her phone is switched off. I tried to put him off, but I'm no actor. I think he could tell I was covering. He went out to Matilda's house, lifted the letterbox and saw all the blood. He knows Scott's been stabbed and he wants to know why there's a media blackout.'

'What have you told him?'

'Nothing. I'm ignoring his calls.'

'He won't give up.'

'I know. I got off the phone to Ridley just before you arrived. We've come up with an idea, but it involves you.'

'Why do I get the feeling I'm not going to like this?'

'We need to keep Matilda's disappearance out of the news. We can't allow Steve to know we're panicking and scratching our heads wondering where the hell she is. Ridley's idea is to inform Danny Hanson of the bodies found at Wigtwizzle and let him in on what we uncover in the investigation,' he said, refusing to look up from his coffee cup while he said the last part.

'You mean, give him to me to deal with?'

'Technically, it's DI Sharp's case. She'll have to put up with him, but once he knows you're on the case as well, well ...' He let the sentence hang in the air.

'I'm really beginning to regret coming back to work,' she said, looking down into her coffee cup. Her face was gaunt, and her shoulders sagged.

'It gets him off the main scent of Matilda going missing.'

'No, it won't. You know what Danny's like when it comes to Matilda. He'll ask me about the blood in the hallway. He'll ask about Scott being stabbed. He won't give a toss about the bodies in the woods.'

'He will if we play it the right way.'

'And what is the right way?'

Christian stared at Sian. He hoped she'd work it out for herself so he wouldn't have to say it. Sian's eyes widened. The penny dropped.

'You want me to give Danny Hanson the inside story on what life was like being married to a serial killer?' she asked, her voice calm, but she was seething behind the words.

'No. *I* don't. It was Ridley's idea.'

'And if I say no?'

'I don't know,' he shrugged.

She stood up and went over to the double doors leading out into the back garden. It was pitch-dark outside and all she could see was her reflection looking back at her. She didn't like what she saw and quickly turned away.

'Less than three weeks ago, on New Year's Eve, me, Belinda and Anthony raised a glass of Prosecco and said this year would be amazing, that we'd make 2021 the best year in a long time. How can it all have turned to shit so quickly?'

Christian didn't reply. He couldn't.

Sian turned back to face him. 'I don't have any choice, do I?'

'Yes. You do. And whatever you decide to do – with Stuart and with Danny – I'll be with you every step of the way. You're not on your own here. I'll support you no matter what. I promise. We've been through so much together over the last few years. I'm always here for you, Sian. I'll not let you go through anything on your own.'

Sian closed her eyes and took a deep breath as she thought. Eventually, she opened them again. 'I'll take Danny off your hands. I can handle him. He's not the confident tosser he likes the world to think he is. As for Stuart, I'm sorry, but I'm not setting foot in that prison to visit him. We do this the way we've always done it by following the evidence.'

'You're a good woman, Sian,' Christian said, smiling. He held out a hand to her. She took it and came back to the kitchen table.

'Now I know what that goat felt like in *Jurassic Park*.'

Chapter Twenty-One

Adele Kean pulled up outside the house she shared with Matilda in her silver Porsche 911. She turned off the engine and sat back, looking up at the house shrouded in darkness. She looked around her. There was nothing but silence. This would be the first time she spent the night alone here, and she didn't like it.

She climbed out of the car and studied her surroundings. In the background, she could hear the distant hum of traffic from Ringinglow Road, but that was all. It was dark so there were no birds in the trees singing and there was no breeze to knock the bare branches together. All was quiet, eerie, frightening.

She opened the front door, entered quickly and slammed it closed behind her, locking it with the bolts at the top and bottom. She looked down at the floor. The blood had gone. There was a strong odour in the air of powerful cleaning materials. It made her sneeze. Suddenly, she wished she'd booked into a hotel room for the night. She was heading for the kitchen where the alcohol would be chilling nicely in the fridge when her phone rang. She dug it out of her coat pocket and looked at the display. Robson was calling. She swiped to answer.

'Hello, Robson,' she said. She wasn't in the mood to talk to him. The last time they'd spoken was at their son Chris's funeral two years ago.

'Adele, is everything all right?'

'Fine, thanks,' she lied, hoping she sounded breezy enough for it to sound convincing. She walked into the kitchen, turned on the light with her elbow and went straight to the freezer. She didn't fancy a glass of wine; she wanted vodka, neat.

'I had a phone call today from someone at South Yorkshire Police,' he said. 'A Detective Constable Sophia Novak, I think she said.'

'Zofia Nowak,' she corrected him.

'Whatever. Anyway, she was asking all kinds of questions about where I was yesterday evening and when the last time was we spoke. What's going on?'

Adele put the phone on speaker while she poured a large measure of vodka into a glass. She sat down at the kitchen table with a thud and took several gulps before answering.

'There's been an incident. Something's happened and the police are asking routine questions.'

'But why me?'

Typical. Always making it about him.

'It's got nothing to do with you, Robson. It's about me.'

'Oh.'

'I'm fine, by the way,' she said, her words dripping with sarcasm.

'Are you … are you sure? Is there, you know, anything I can do?' he asked. It was obvious he was asking merely out of politeness rather than wanting to arrange a flight from

Scotland to Sheffield to help a woman he abandoned with their baby once university was over all those years ago.

'No, Robson. There's nothing you can do.'

'Well, if there's … I mean, you'll look after yourself, won't you?' There was the tiniest hint of genuine concern there.

'I've been looking after myself my whole life, Robson. I'll be fine.'

'Look, Adele, I know …' There was a pause. He was obviously moving to a quieter room, away from his wife and children. 'I know I was a shit to you. I can't excuse my behaviour. I was a bastard, a coward, for leaving you and Chris like that. There isn't a day goes by when I don't think about him, about you, and what I did. You were a great mum. Chris turned out amazing and it's all down to you. I really do think a lot about you, Adele.'

Adele looked down into her empty vodka glass and poured another large measure. She felt drained with everything that had happened over the past twenty-four hours. If Matilda wasn't there to offer comfort, then she'd want her son, Chris, to put his arms around her and tell her everything was going to be all right. But he was dead. Murdered. She had no one. Tears were welling up inside her.

'Promise me you'll call me if there's anything you need,' Robson continued.

Adele wiped her eyes with the backs of her hands. They came away wet. She didn't want him to hear the emotion in her voice. She cleared her throat. 'Robson,' she began. 'We haven't spoken to each other since Chris's funeral. Before that it was … well, it was so long ago, I can't even remember. We've moved on.'

'We spent a very important part of our lives together. We had a son together.'

'Chris is dead, Robson.' She raised her voice. 'We have nothing left.' She ended the call.

She drained the glass of vodka and slumped onto the table. The tears flowed and she wailed in torment. She'd cried for her son many times over the years. The painful grief had faded and when she thought of him now, it was with fondness, and with a hesitant smile. However, Matilda going missing had brought everything back. It wasn't just Chris's murder, it was an accumulation of things – Lucy disappearing, Pat's husband dying from Covid and her not being able to be with him in his final moments, Sian's happy family life being destroyed by Stuart murdering sex workers. And on top of all that, there was her day-to-day job of cutting up people to discover how they died. It had never encroached on her life before, but lately, in the past couple of years, she kept them with her. The sex workers, eight of them, all young women in their twenties, all of them failed by a broken society. The victims of the terrorist attacks she'd attended in Manchester and London. The young children murdered by their parents, some of them just toddlers. How can performing a post-mortem on an eight-month-old baby simply be all in a day's work?

Adele sat back in the chair, looked up to the ceiling, opened her mouth and let out a painful cry. She'd been holding onto so much emotion in recent years, and it was too much. She needed to let it go. Tears were streaming down her face, and they wouldn't stop.

An hour later, the sound of the doorbell ringing woke her up. Adele had literally cried herself into an exhausted sleep. She jumped up and it took a few long seconds for her to recognise her surroundings. She ached, having been slumped over a table with her forearm as a pillow. The doorbell rang again.

She staggered into the hallway and looked down. It was the first time since coming home that she'd noticed the difference in the flooring where the professional cleaning company had cleaned up all the blood. Maybe the whole of the hall would need sanding and staining again to get it all to match. Or maybe the wood should be ripped up and a new floor laid.

She looked through the spyhole in the door and was surprised to see Simon Browes standing on the doorstep. She opened the door and shivered as the chill from outside enveloped her.

'Hello,' he said with a wan smile. He looked awkward, his eyes darting all over the place. He stood tall in an ill-fitting beige coat and walking boots. He was playing with his fingers and opened and closed his mouth several times, rejecting the words he was searching for, no confidence in what he wanted to say. 'I … I … I thought that maybe you wouldn't want to be on your own tonight after, well, you know, after everything that's … with Matilda. I mean, I don't know if you are on your own, obviously. I mean, your car's here and there aren't any others, but … I can go if you want me to.'

Adele smiled. She stepped back from the doorway. 'Come in.'

'Are you sure? I don't want to intrude or anything.'

'You're very welcome.'

'You've been crying,' he said as he entered the house.

'Yes.'

'Are you … you know … are you all … well, I mean, I know you're not, but are you …?'

'Will you hold me?' she asked him.

'Hold you?'

'Yes. I know you find emotions difficult to deal with, but I really need a strong pair of arms around me right now.'

'I'm not exactly strong.'

Adele sighed. She held out a hand, grabbed his and headed for the stairs, pulling him behind her. 'Simon, I want you to hold me. Then I want you to help me try and forget everything that's happened for a while.'

'How do I do that?'

She smiled. 'I'll show you.'

Chapter Twenty-Two

Matilda Darke woke up. She'd been dozing on and off for most of the day, despite being cold and uncomfortable. She put it down to the effects of whatever she'd been injected with.

She wished she knew what time it was. She was sitting in perpetual darkness. There was a nasty smell of damp in the air. A cold chill was blowing in from somewhere and she had nothing to keep her warm except the clothes she was wearing.

How long have I been here?

She stood up and stretched. Her joints ached. Her bones ached. Even her aches had aches. She held out her arms and took tiny steps forward like Frankenstein's monster. She kicked something and stopped. There was something on the floor that hadn't been there before.

She bent down and fumbled in the darkness. It was a tray. On it was a plastic bottle of water that was cold to the touch and a sandwich in a cardboard box. Someone had been in here while she'd been sleeping and left it for her.

With shaking fingers, Matilda unscrewed the cap on the

bottle and took long swigs of water. She almost emptied the bottle before realising this might be the only drink she'd be given for a while and she would have to ration it. She tore open the sandwich and took ravenous bites. It was cheese and pickle on white bread. It wasn't fresh – the bread was stale and the cheese was rubbery – but she didn't care. It was food. It was fuel. It would give her energy.

Sitting back on her haunches, she thought about what this meant. Whoever had taken her was prepared to feed her, so keeping her alive was paramount. That meant they had a use for her. But what? Was she a bargaining chip for something? Had her kidnappers made contact with South Yorkshire Police and demanded a ransom, or that someone be let out of prison in exchange for her safe release?

Steve Harrison says hello.

Was that Steve's game? He knew he was in prison for the rest of his life. He was on the never-never list. Was he hoping to gain his freedom by having Matilda kidnapped and forcing the police, the Home Office, into action to release him, or Matilda would never be seen again?

Matilda wiped a tear away from her cheek. She suddenly thought of her mother, Penny. She'd been through so much over the past couple of years with the death of her husband and moving house. The last thing she needed was the worry of her daughter being kidnapped. She'd always hated Matilda being in the police. Her mind always went to the dark side and expected the worst. This would be hell for her right now.

'It's no picnic for me, either, Mum,' Matilda said to herself.

She stood up and went to the door. She raised her fist to bang on it, but, in mid-air, her hand caught on something. She fumbled around, waving her hands in the air as if swatting away a bee. She caught it, ran her fingers over the rough texture. It was rope. Towards the bottom, she felt the thickness and the twists and then the loop.

Matilda knew exactly what it was. The kidnapper had no intention of keeping her alive, but they didn't want her dying through malnutrition or dehydration. They wanted her to hang herself. In her hands, Matilda was holding a hangman's noose.

Chapter Twenty-Three

I t was the first full day of Matilda Darke being missing, and the second night. There had been no word of her. It was as if she'd simply vanished.

Christian Brady was in bed, and despite stifling many a yawn while his wife Jennifer watched something with subtitles on BBC4, he was unable to sleep. He lay with eyes wide open, mind whirring and not settling on a single thought. He turned and looked out of the window – he always slept with the curtains open – and looked at the brightness of the full moon shining down on Sheffield. There wasn't a cloud in the sky and an infinite number of stars were twinkling. As he'd gone around the house, checking the doors were locked and making sure his kids were asleep, he'd gazed out of the window and seen a harsh layer of frost on the cars lining the street. It was another night of sub-zero temperatures. If Matilda was out in this, exposed to the elements, there would be no way she could survive a second night.

'Christian, you need to try and get some sleep,' Jennifer

said. She snuggled up next to him, placing a warm hand on his chest.

'I know,' he said without looking at her. 'I just ... I can't stop thinking about where ...' He trailed off.

'Look, you said you think Steve Harrison is behind all this, so why don't you go to the prison tomorrow, slam him up against a wall and get him to tell you what he knows?'

A hint of a smile spread across his lips. 'Because this isn't *Life on Mars* and I'm not Gene Hunt. Besides, if Steve saw that I was rattled, he'd play to it.'

'Then send someone else. He doesn't know Finn or ... what's the new guy called?'

'Tom.'

'Tom. So, send those two. You've raved about Finn, and Tom must be good or Matilda wouldn't have him on the unit. If Steve is presented with two blokes he doesn't know, he won't be able to read them. He won't have the upper hand.'

Christian frowned as he thought. He turned to his wife and smiled. 'Do you fancy a job on our team?'

'And have you as my boss? I don't think so. I bet you're a tyrant,' she smiled.

He wrapped his arms around her and pulled her closer to him. He could feel her warmth against his body. For the first time since Matilda went missing, Christian could feel himself relaxing. He had an idea for tomorrow, and it was a good one.

'I can't see this having a happy ending,' he eventually said.

Jennifer took a deep breath. She gripped her husband tighter. She opened her mouth to say something but decided against it.

Chapter Twenty-Four

Thursday 21st January 2021

I am not a disturbed psychopath. Dr Sofia Marks doesn't have a clue about me. She's never met me. She's never tried to approach me for an interview yet, for some reason, she felt qualified to talk about me on The Hangman's Hold *on Netflix. They should have got Dr Olivia Winter on the documentary. Now, she listened. She understood me. I hope she'll write a book about me one day. All Sofia Marks knew about me was what she's read in the papers and searched for online. How can anything you read on Wikipedia be taken as gospel? And we all know what the press are like. They're liars. Journalism is a business. It's all about selling papers, getting viewing figures and clicks on websites. They don't give a toss about the truth. They only care about money. Like everyone else in this world. So, what is the truth? Well, for a start, if I was a disturbed psychopath, I'd be hell bent on destruction. My sole preoccupation in life would be to kill, maim, and obliterate people and their lives and the lives of those they hold dear. And I'm not. I've committed murder. Mass murder. I'm aware of that. I accept my label as a serial killer and a manipulator. I understand all that. If I was a disturbed psychopath, would I be able to understand it? I doubt it. Since being transferred to the Supermax wing in 2019, I haven't killed anyone. I haven't attacked anyone. There have been plenty of opportunities and when I was alone in that room for five minutes with Wesley Green, I could have done all sorts to him. I could have stuck my thumbs into his eye sockets and blinded him. I could have kicked him to death. I could easily have overpowered him and raped him. I didn't. What did we do in those five minutes? We chatted. He told me about his son passing his A-Levels and getting into his first choice of university to study biodiversity. We joked that neither of us quite knew what biodiversity was and tried to work it out. Then the power came back on, the automatic lock kicked in and the door was open. Back to normal life. I'm not a disturbed psychopath. I'm a killer. And I'm a killer because I had no choice in the matter. In 2017, my eyes were opened, and I realised life was a game and in order to win you had to know the right people. I didn't. However, like everyone else, I don't like to lose, so I had to adapt and create my own rules to the game. I used the tools I had to hand. The fact I was a police officer gave me access to records the public at large don't have. So, I found people who had committed crimes and been given pathetic sentences, and I made them pay. I was doing a service. Yet, every game needs to have an element to stop you from winning in order to add a sense of danger and excitement. The first game little children play is Snakes and Ladders. You go up the ladder, but if you land on a snake, down you go, and try again. My snake was called Matilda Darke. I needed to defeat her to win. Now, I'll hold my hands up here and say she bested me. I couldn't win and I was caught. Fair enough. So, I tried again. I tried a newer tactic and roped in my brother. Jake knew his task, but he was preoccupied with his own demons and he, too, failed to beat the enemy and win. Bloody snakes. I'm defeated. I accept that.*

I tried to beat Matilda Darke and I failed. She's won the game we were playing, and I have to accept the result. But the thing about playing a game is that you can have more than one go. Look at chess and the many different moves you can make to win. Just because you lose one game doesn't mean you should give up. You play again and again. You continue to play, and you might lose the next game and the one after and the next fifty games, but eventually, you'll win because you'll make the right move at the right time. It takes patience, skill, determination, and belief to win. I have all that in spades. I simply have to adapt my game plan. The rules have changed. I'm locked up in a Supermax wing for a start. I need more than a double-six to get me out and I don't have someone to give up a crystal to secure my release. It's just me. On my own. A single player.

'I can't read any more of this.' DC Finn Cotton slapped the sheets of paper down on his untidy desk.

He, Zofia and Tom had pledged to stay as long as it took at the station to go through the printed photos he had taken of the end pages of *The Hangman's Hold*. However, Harrison's handwriting was so small that it had taken further copying and enlarging just to make it legible. At around midnight, Zofia was flagging, despite the triple-shot espresso Tom had fetched them all from a nearby Costa. Finn told them both to go home and they didn't need telling twice. Finn promised to stay for another hour, but he'd fallen asleep at his desk long before then and woke up at six when one of the cleaners made a racket bringing a Henry vacuum cleaner through the glass doors. He'd gone home, showered, shaved, changed his clothes, chatted to his wife for ten minutes and wolfed down a bowl of Crunchy Nut cornflakes, before heading back to the office.

An hour later, Tom and Zofia came back into the suite, arriving at the same time. Tom was even wearing the same clothes as yesterday. The rumour mill was running, but there was no time for innuendo.

'How are you getting on?' Zofia asked as she made Finn a coffee after enquiring how long he'd been at the station.

That's when he told her he couldn't read any more.

'He's trying to justify his actions from the very beginning. A lot of it is waffle about why he's a killer and what made him do it. He's keen for us to know he's not a psychopath and that he's in control, but ... I don't know,' he said with a frown, scratching his head. 'He contradicts himself all the time. On one page he's blaming a defective gene, on another he's blaming Matilda, later on he's blaming society. I just ... he's doing my bloody head in.'

'Do you think the fact he wrote all this in a book about himself might be significant?' Zofia asked.

'I don't know. There's no rationale to any of it,' Finn said, running a hand through his hair.

'What other books did he have in his cell?' Tom asked.

'I've got a photo here somewhere.' Finn woke his computer up and selected the images he was looking for.

He projected them onto the whiteboard at the end of the room and zoomed in on the paperbacks. There were six books, all well-thumbed, stood neatly on the shelf. *Wire in the Blood* by Val McDermid, *Messiah* by Boris Starling, *The Killer Inside Me* by Jim Thompson, *Darkly Dreaming Dexter* by Jeff Lindsay, *The Poet* by Michael Connelly, and *Red Dragon* by Thomas Harris.

'All books about serial killers,' Zofia said.

'Yes, but *The Hangman's Hold* book wasn't on the shelf with the others. It was under his mattress as if he was keeping it close to him for some reason,' Finn said.

'Maybe he was writing in it the night before,' Tom added.

'Possibly.'

'Egotistical?' Tom asked.

'Most definitely.'

'I don't know Steve Harrison, obviously,' Zofia began. 'But is it possible he left this book apart from the others so you'd find it?'

'But he didn't know we were going.'

'But if he is behind Matilda's kidnapping, and it's obvious he is, then he knew you'd come at some point.'

'And if he knew the police were coming, he'd leave something for us,' Tom finished her thought.

'Do you know what I really think?' Finn said, sitting back and picking up his coffee cup in both hands.

'What?' Zofia asked.

'I think all of this is a set-up. Yes, he's behind Matilda going missing and he knew we'd want to speak to him but first we'd want to know what he was up to. He's placed those books there on his shelf to make us think he loves reading about serial killers. He placed *The Hangman's Hold* under his mattress so we'd find it. And he wrote all that crap in the back so we'd think he had some kind of amazing insight into the human mind.'

'Is there any way of finding out how long he had those books in his cell?' Tom asked.

'I'm not sure. I'll give the prison another ring and ask.'

'So, we can't read anything from these photos? We can't get any clue as to where Matilda is from all this?' Zofia asked.

'I don't think we can. I felt strange the moment I walked into Steve's cell,' Finn said. 'I thought it was simply because it was a prison cell of a killer, but the more I think about it, the more I realise it's because the whole cell was designed for us to read more into what was there than we should do.'

'So, is Steve still having serial killer tendencies or is he living his life getting his kicks from reading gory fiction?'

'I don't know. Both. Probably,' Finn said, taking off his glasses and rubbing his eyes.

'Where do we go from here?' Tom asked.

Finn didn't answer. He couldn't. Tom and Zofia exchanged a glance and Tom looked back to the photo of Steve's cell on the whiteboard.

'He really does have a fixation on Matilda, doesn't he?' he said, staring at the photos of Matilda by Steve's bed.

'That's an understatement,' Zofia said.

'But he's been in prison since 2017. To spend all that time constantly thinking about one person, blaming them for everything, that's ... well, that's not normal.'

'Who said Steve was normal?'

'Reading what he wrote in *The Hangman's Hold*, he thinks he's very normal.'

Zofia wheeled herself over to Finn's desk and picked up a printed page from the back of the book. She cast her eye over it, a heavy frown on her face.

'There is a technique to find out when something was written. It's all about indentations on the page and analysing the ink.'

'We'd need the original for that,' Finn said.

'Then we get it. Scott said the woman who injected Matilda mentioned Steve's name. That's more than enough grounds to get a warrant and strip Steve's cell. We leave him with nothing. He'll hate that,' Zofia said. 'Also, if we can prove this has been written recently, then it was written purposely to throw us off the scent. It's confirmation that Steve knows exactly what's going on, who's taken Matilda, and possibly where. Then we go in with all guns blazing, slap him in solitary confinement, pull his fingernails out with pliers if necessary.'

Tom smiled. 'It's a shame you're not in charge of the Home Office, Zof. You'd have the crime rate down in no time.'

'Oh no. I want to be Justice Secretary. I'd love to sort out sentencing and prison reforms. I'd rip out their TVs and en suite toilets. No winter duvets and yoga classes for them.'

'Slopping out at 7 a.m. and sewing mail bags for twelve hours a day,' Tom added.

Finn wasn't listening. He tuned them out while he thought more about what Zofia had said. This was a game to Steve Harrison. The problem with putting people in prison for life without the chance of release was that they had nothing to aim for. Why should they follow the rules of the prison when no further punishment could add to the time they'd been given? Steve knew he'd never be released so he had no qualms about playing mind games with the authorities. He would sit back and watch the destruction of society with a smile on his face. The worst thing the police could do right now was put Steve centre stage. Unfortunately, they were going to have to play into his hands to try to extract information from him. Unless there was another way.

A small smile spread across Finn's lips. There was another way.

Chapter Twenty-Five

C hristian pulled into his parking space and turned off the engine. He whipped off his seatbelt and climbed out of the car. He'd just managed to warm up on the drive from home and now, stepping out into the freezing January morning, a blast of cold air made him wrap his coat around him and head for the door at speed.

He stopped halfway to the entrance when something caught the corner of his eye. He turned and saw Sian sitting in the driver's seat of her car. The engine was off. She was staring into space, a blank expression on her face.

Christian went over slowly, bent down and looked through the passenger window. He didn't want to knock loudly and make her jump, but despite the shadow he was casting over her, she didn't seem to notice his presence. He cleared his throat. Nothing. He exaggerated a cough. Still nothing. In the end, he rapped loudly on the glass and Sian almost jumped through the sunroof. She lowered the passenger window.

'Bloody hell, Christian, what are you trying to do to me?' she asked, a hand over her heart.

'I've been stood here aiming coughs at you for the best part of three hours,' he said, a smile on his cold face.

'Sorry. I was ... just thinking.'

'Penny for your thoughts?'

'My thoughts are more expensive than that.'

He shivered. 'Mind if I get in? I've just heard a thud and I think one of my balls has dropped off.'

She stifled a smile and unlocked the door for him.

He climbed in, slammed the door behind him and placed his hands in front of the heater. 'My goodness, it's a cold one this morning. I really didn't want to get out of bed when the alarm went off. Not that I slept much.'

'Me neither,' Sian said, quietly.

'Did you speak to your kids about ... everything?'

She nodded. 'Do you know, I didn't realise how grown-up they all were until last night.'

'What do you mean?'

'I sat Anthony and Belinda down and told them about the bodies found at Wigtwizzle and they were so sensible about the whole thing. They didn't cry at Stuart being plunged back into our lives again, or the fact that there may be more victims to add to his tally. They both looked at the whole situation with an open mind.'

'That's good, isn't it?'

'It really is,' she said, looking at him with a smile.

'Do they think you should go and see him?'

'They said it was up to me, obviously. Only I can make the decision and they'd stand by what I decided to do. But, in the interests of the investigation, they said I should visit him.'

'Wow. They sound more grown-up than we do,' he laughed. 'What have you decided?'

'I'm still not going.'

He was not expecting that. 'Oh. Why not?'

She took a deep breath. 'Whenever I think of Stuart, I think of what he did. All those years he spent visiting sex workers and killing them, and I knew nothing about it. And I should have done. It reminds me of what a self-centred person I was.'

'How can you say that?'

'I was. I was perfectly happy in my own little world – a nice home, a happy marriage, four kids, a good job. I had the blinkers on and didn't once think to look around me at the true picture.'

'Is that really what you think?'

'Yes.'

'Sian, I hate to say this, but Stuart was a master manipulator. He fooled us all. None of us could have seen that coming. Not even Matilda. He played the parts of two different people exceptionally well. Nobody is to blame for not seeing his true colours.'

She looked at him. There were tears in her eyes. 'I am.'

'But if you are, then so are your kids. They should have seen a change in their father, especially Anthony and Belinda, being the oldest. If you're blaming yourself, you need to blame them, too.'

Sian wiped a tear away before it had a chance to fall. She looked through the windscreen, her eyes gazing far into the distance.

'I'm trained to spot killers. They're not.'

'But they didn't notice a change in their father, a man they saw every single day. For all I know, Jennifer could be off killing men and be so good at it, I haven't realised. But if she did turn out to be a multiple murderer, I wouldn't blame myself. I'd blame her.'

'You wouldn't blame yourself for not seeing the signs?'

'Of course not. Jennifer's a grown woman. She's to blame for her own actions. Not me. Now, can we stop turning my wife into Myra Hindley, as I'm going to really freak out when I go home tonight and I see her spatchcocking a chicken.'

Sian laughed out loud. 'You started it.'

'I know. And I'm finishing it, too. Come on, let's get into the warmth and see what Huey, Dewey and Louie have been up to.'

Christian got out of the car and closed the door. He buttoned up his coat and waited for Sian to join him. As they headed for the rear entrance to the station, Sian linked arms with her DI.

'Thanks for what you said, Christian,' she whispered.

'You're welcome. I know I speak a lot of bollocks, but occasionally I make sense.'

'Have you been here all night?'

Christian and Sian were in Christian's office. Standing in front of his desk was DC Finn Cotton, the printed pages from the back of *The Hangman's Hold* in his hands.

'I went home about … I can't remember what time it was … for a shower and a change of clothes.'

Sian looked over her shoulder out into the main suite. 'It looks like Tom was here all night. He's wearing the same clothes as yesterday.'

Finn cleared his throat. 'Erm, no. Tom and Zofia went home around midnight. I think Tom stayed at Zofia's.'

'Really?' Sian asked. 'Stayed over, as in stayed over?'

'Is there any other kind?' Finn replied.

'Maybe he slept on her sofa as it was so late,' Christian said.

Sian and Finn looked at him.

'Don't be so naïve,' Sian said. She looked back out into the suite and saw Tom and Zofia talking and looking at the same computer screen. They were a tad too close to each other for mere colleagues. 'I'm glad. Zofia's had a bad few years since the accident and everything. It's good to see there's happiness in her life once again. And Tom seems like a nice lad. I think they'll be good for each other.'

'Hmm,' Christian said.

'What does that mean?'

'I'm just worried about the fallout if they split up.'

'That's it, Christian, positive thinking,' Sian smiled. 'Now, Finn, Steve's notes. Any clues on his involvement with Matilda?'

Finn sat down on the spare seat. 'None. I've been looking at the photos we took of his cell and reading through this in every way I can, and I think the whole thing is a set-up. I have had an idea, though.'

'Go on.'

'Well, it's safe to say that Steve Harrison is definitely involved because of what the kidnapper said to Matilda before she injected her. We need to talk to Steve, but if we go and ask for his help, he's going to smile and enjoy the show. However, if we go and tell him that an attempt was made to kidnap Matilda but was unsuccessful, we might be able to get him to reveal who was involved. He's not going to want to be seen to be complicit in a failure where he can't gloat, so he'd put the blame solely on whoever kidnapped Matilda.'

Christian leaned back in his seat and thought for a moment. He looked over to Sian, who gave him a brief nod, agreeing with Finn's idea.

'You might be on to something there, Finn. We need to play

this bastard at his own game. I've also had an idea of my own. Actually, it was Jennifer's.'

'Using her criminal mind, was she?' Sian said, a chuckle in her voice.

Christian gave her a faux-daggered look. 'If I went to see Steve, or even if Sian went, he'd clam up. He wouldn't help us at all. Even if we remained poker-faced, he knows us and would be able to see he's getting to us. If we send a couple of detectives he doesn't know, then he won't be able to read you.'

'Me?' Finn asked.

'Yes.'

'I'm just a lowly DC.'

'You're also doing a degree in criminology and you're practically a DS,' Sian said. 'When are your exams, by the way?'

'Some time in March, I've been told.'

Christian leaned forward. 'Go to the prison as Acting Detective Sergeant Finn Cotton. You've got a DC with you. Tell him about the attempt made to kidnap Matilda. It failed. The woman who did it scarpered, but she mentioned Steve's name before she fled. That bit is true at least. If he doesn't tell you who she is, the blame will be solely his and any privileges he's got will be taken away.'

'I like that plan,' Sian said.

Finn remained quiet, his legs together, his hands tucked beneath them.

'You need to be confident, Finn. You need to be a ball-busting bastard of a sergeant. Like Sian,' Christian said, tipping Sian a wink.

'Right. Okay,' he said, clearly nervous. 'I'll go and have a word with Tom.' He stood up and made his way over to the door.

'Finn, before you go. I know you've had a lot of work on, but did you manage to go through that list of people who regularly contact Steve?'

'Yes. I did. Hang on.' He dashed out of the room for his notebook.

'Do you think he'll be all right?' Sian asked. 'He knows the practical side of being a detective very well, but do you think he has what it takes to go up against someone like Steve Harrison?'

'Well, this will be his test. The problem is, he's the only person who can do this. You, me, Scott, Steve knows us. Finn is the only other detective I can trust for this.'

'That's true. There's a lot riding on him, isn't there?'

Before Christian could answer, Finn came back into the office with his notebook. 'Right, as you know, there were three people on the list of contacts Steve can get letters from. There's Janet Crowther, Linda Bellamy and Amy Monroe. Now, Janet Crowther—'

'Is his aunt,' Sian interrupted. 'When Jake Harrison went on the shooting spree he started with his mother and father. Janet's sister and brother-in-law. It was Janet who found them. Why would she be writing to Steve?'

'I've no idea,' Christian said. 'Fancy popping along to see her?'

'I didn't think I was allowed to work on this case.'

'You're not. You're just having a friendly chat. Find out what they've been saying in their letters and if he's given any hint about what he's been planning.'

'Wouldn't the prison have kept copies?' Sian asked. 'We could just ask them.'

'It would be nice to hear it from Janet's point of view. Who else is on the list, Finn?'

'Linda Bellamy. I've looked her up and she's a psychotherapist. She works at the prison on a freelance basis. I've been on to the prison and every time she's there, Steve makes an appointment to see her.'

'Would you like me to go and talk to her, too?' Sian asked.

'You can do. I think we know what her answers to all your questions will be.'

'"I can't break patient/client confidentiality",' Sian said with a smirk.

'Precisely. Who's the last person?'

'Amy Monroe.'

'Who's she?'

'According to the prison, she's Steve's cousin. She's not on the PNC and I've no contact details for her. There's a mobile phone number but it just keeps ringing out.'

'Something else to ask the auntie,' Sian said.

There was a tap on the glass door. They all looked up and saw Tom in the doorway.

'Scott's back.'

None of them could get out of the room fast enough. They were surprised to find Scott back at his desk. He looked shattered, though his hair was neatly combed, he was freshly shaved and his suit fitted perfectly, as always.

'What are you doing here?' Christian asked, hands on hips.

'I work here.'

'Shouldn't you still be in hospital?' Sian asked.

'I discharged myself.'

'That was a bloody stupid thing to do,' Christian said.

'The doctor came round and gave me a clean bill of health. I've been stitched up and there's no internal damage. I'm fine. Besides, they needed the bed.'

'But shouldn't you be at home resting?' Sian asked.

'I'd go out of my mind at home. Besides, I need to be here. Any word on Matilda?'

'Not yet.'

'Any leads?'

'Only from what you were able to tell us,' Sian said.

'You'll need to give us a full statement, Scott,' Christian said.

'I know. I will. The thing is, on the way over here, I remembered where I'd seen the woman from, the one who took Matilda.'

'Where?' Sian asked, pulling up a chair.

'Remember when me and Matilda were driving from the Children's Hospital just before Christmas and that car almost ran into us? And then on the way to the Arts Tower, that car crashed into Finn's car?'

'Yes. So?'

'The woman driving was the woman who kidnapped Matilda and stabbed me.'

'Are you sure?' Christian asked.

'One hundred per cent.'

'Did you get a good look at her?'

'I did,' Finn said. 'When I eventually came round, she stayed with us until the ambulance came. Then she just disappeared, didn't she, Scott?'

'Yes. To be honest, I was so worried about Finn that I didn't think to get her details from her. I asked her a few questions, but she was in a daze herself from the crash. I put it down to her being in shock. Looking back, I think she was probably pissed off for hitting the wrong car. She was deliberately aiming for Matilda.'

'So, when she couldn't kill her like that, she contacted Steve and asked how she could be more creative,' Sian said.

'It looks like it.'

'So, who is she?' Zofia asked.

'That's the million-dollar question,' Sian said.

'Right, you two,' Christian began, pointing at Finn and Scott. 'I want detailed statements from you both about the crash. Anything you can remember; we need to know about it. Scott, I want your statement from when Matilda was taken. Then I'm going to get an artist in here and you're going to put together an image of what this woman looks like. Matilda has now been missing for almost forty-eight hours. We need to find her fast. The kidnapper obviously has a mission, and we have to stop her from completing it.'

Tom cleared his throat to get their attention. 'I hate to be a wet blanket here, but if this woman tried to kill Matilda by crashing into her, then she's not thinking of her own safety. The speed she was driving when she crashed into Finn, she's lucky she wasn't seriously injured. She sounds like a loose cannon and if she failed to get Matilda that way, she's bound to make sure she doesn't fail again.'

The room fell silent as they took in Tom's destructive words. He was right. The woman, whoever she was, obviously didn't care what happened to her if she was willing to kill herself in a car crash, as long as she took Matilda with her. This could very well end up as a case of murder/suicide.

Chapter Twenty-Six

C hief Constable Benjamin Ridley looked as if he hadn't slept much last night. He probably hadn't. One of his most high-profile detectives was missing, kidnapped, with no leads to her whereabouts, and a hungry journalist was only a few steps behind and catching up fast. Sticking to a heart-healthy diet was all well and good, but in times of stress, it took more than an apple and a glass of prune juice to relax him. He'd asked his secretary to get him a sausage sandwich and a large latte. All that was left of the sandwich was the smell of fried meat in the air. It was delicious while he was eating it, but it was lying heavy in his stomach, and while Christian and Sian were helping themselves to tiny bottles of water from his mini fridge, he was rummaging around in his desk drawers for a box of Gaviscon tablets.

'Is there any update on Matilda?' Ridley asked, rubbing his stomach hard to try and force up a trapped belch.

'No,' Christian said. 'There's no CCTV from around Matilda's house. She doesn't have any neighbours so we can't go knocking on doors, and the forensics haven't given us anything from the house. Also, we've been through her mobile, her laptop, her tablet and all her emails and nothing stands out. Hopefully, once Scott and Finn have sat down with an artist we might get something we can approach the media with.'

'I really don't want the media involved in this. This force may be out of special measures, but we still have a watchful eye hanging over us.'

'None of this is the force's fault,' Sian said.

'No. But one of us is missing. It was allowed to happen. And if we don't find her soon, how will it look to the public at large if we fail our own officers?'

'I've had two voicemails from Danny Hanson already this morning asking for Matilda,' Christian said.

'I hope you didn't reply to them,' Ridley said, looking up from rummaging in his desk drawer.

'No.'

'Good. Screw it,' he said, slamming the drawer closed, his search fruitless. He looked to Sian. 'Now, Sian, we're going to give Danny the story of the bones found at Wigtwizzle. He's meeting someone here from media liaison who's going to tell him that now we're out of special measures, we're aiming more towards transparency so something like the sex abuse scandal can never happen again. We want to work with the press rather than keep them at arm's length.' He burped and apologised but looked better for it. 'It's all bollocks, I know. We hate the press, and they hate us. We don't trust them and the same in reverse. However, the media are well known for being sneaky and underhand, so it will be nice to play them at their own game. At least until Matilda is found.'

'Danny isn't a fool,' Sian said. 'He saw the blood in

Matilda's house. He knows Scott was stabbed. He knows I'm close to Matilda and he'll question me.'

Ridley gave a quick glance to Christian, then back to Sian. He burped a second time. 'Once Danny Hanson knows the identity of the victims at Wigtwizzle, I'm hoping that will be enough of a distraction for him.'

'I really don't like being used as bait,' Sian said.

'We can't have the press finding out about Steve Harrison once again being able to manipulate people from his cell and arrange the kidnapping of a high-ranking detective.'

'What do you think Danny's going to say once he finds out you've been blindsiding him? He's not stupid, you know.'

Ridley looked at them in turn again.

The penny dropped. 'You're hoping I'm going to spill my guts to Danny, aren't you? You're hoping I'm going to sit down with him and talk about what life was like married to one of Britain's most prolific serial killers. I am not airing my dirty laundry in public just so you don't have to answer a few questions from the press. I'm sorry. I'm not doing it,' Sian said, defiantly sitting back and folding her arms.

'I'd never ask you to do that, Sian,' Christian said.

'No. You're not,' she said, staring daggers at Ridley, indicating who was asking her.

'I'm looking at the bigger picture, Sian. This force has been under so much scrutiny over the past few years. We cannot take any more. We just need to stave off Danny for a few days, until we know what's going on with Matilda.'

'I refuse to turn my life into a soap opera,' she said.

'Look, Sian, you're a good detective,' Ridley began after calming himself down with a few deep breaths. 'You're also an excellent people person. I know you'll be able to keep Danny off the scent of Matilda's disappearance. Now, I don't care how you do it, what you tell him, as long as he doesn't smear this force in the press.'

Nobody said anything. Sian sat, unmoved, a sour look on her face.

'This is for Matilda, Sian,' Christian said, leaning over and placing his hand on hers. 'I know it's easy for me to say but I'd definitely do it if it was Jennifer who'd put her spatchcocking skills to more sinister use.'

Sian struggled to hide her smile. She bit her bottom lip hard.

———

Danny Hanson was waiting in an interview room and as soon as the door opened and Sian stepped in, he stood up and flashed her his winning smile that gained him so much attention on social media whenever he appeared on television.

Sian's heart sank as soon as she saw him. He was useful and she had warmed to him, slightly, after she saw a more sensitive side to him during the historical sex abuse case, but, at the end of the day, he was still a journalist, still a reptile. In her head, she counted to ten and listened to the sound of her heart thumping loudly.

She smiled. It felt false. 'Good morning, Danny.'

'DS Robinson, it's lovely to see you.' He held out his fist for her to bump, the post-Covid greeting.

'I've never done a fist bump,' she said, acquiescing. She pulled out a chair opposite and sat down.

'Before we get down to business,' Danny began, 'can we lay our cards on the table?'

'Of course.'

'I know something's going on. I saw all that blood in

Matilda's house. I know Scott's been stabbed and I know it's not been released to the media. I'm guessing it's some kind of a domestic incident between Scott and his boyfriend, and I perfectly understand why you want to keep it quiet. That's fine. However, why is Matilda's phone switched off? It's never switched off.'

'It's not,' she lied, hoping her face didn't give her away.

'It is,' he said. He fished around in his satchel and pulled out his phone. 'I've called her three times this morning and voicemail kicks in straight away.'

'Ah,' Sian said. 'I'm guessing she hasn't given you her new number.' She had no idea where that came from.

'She has a new number?'

'Yes. We have a work phone and a personal phone, obviously, and Matilda never has. She's always just used the one phone. It's finally caught up with her and she's had a slap on the wrist and been given a new number.'

'Oh. Can I …?'

'No,' she interrupted. 'I'm not allowed to give you her new number. Only she can do that.'

'Right. Well. I suppose … right,' he said, looking slightly bewildered.

Sian was relieved. It was a blatant lie, but it had a ring of truth about it. Danny had accepted it and was disappointed there wasn't anything more sinister going on.

'And the business with the blood at Matilda's house?'

'Like you said, it's a personal matter.'

'But Scott is all right?'

'Yes. Back at work and moaning about a ruined Paul Smith shirt,' she smiled.

'Oh.' Again, he looked disappointed.

'So, you've been informed of our new transparency policy

where we're inviting members of the press to shadow us on select cases.'

'Yes,' Danny said, the frown still deep on his forehead. 'To be honest, I did think it sounded more like a cover-up, like you're trying to get me off the scent of something bigger.'

'You need to be very careful about that paranoia, Danny,' Sian said with a smile. 'It can eat away at you, and you'll start seeing men in macs and fedoras in the shadows.'

'Yes. You're probably right,' he said, still looking dejected that his suspicions had all seemingly had innocuous stories behind them.

'Anyway, moving on,' Sian said, feeling elated at having bested a reporter. 'We've found two bodies out at Wigtwizzle in the countryside. One of whom has been identified. Now, obviously, you can't be with me until crime scenes have been processed or in the mortuary, but I can let you in on the groundwork, so to speak.'

'Yes.' His face lit up at the hint of a juicy story. He dug back into his satchel and pulled out a hardback A5 notebook. He flicked through the pages, most of them full of notes in his neat handwriting. 'I've been given the name of Jackie Barclay as the first victim. Now, she was a sex worker who went missing around the time your husband was killing sex workers. Is that right?'

'Ex-husband. And, yes, that is right.'

'Have you identified the second body yet?'

'No.'

'Have you interviewed your husband? Ex-husband, sorry,' he quickly corrected himself.

'I haven't, no,' she said. Beneath the table, her hands curled up into tight fists, her fingernails digging into her palms.

'Do you think Stuart is responsible for these murders, too?'

'We don't know that yet. We'll see where the evidence takes us.' She could feel her flesh crawling at simply hearing the name of the man she slept with for more than twenty-five years and the lies upon lies he told her and her children. She hoped Danny was useless at reading body language. She was pretty sure she was displaying a great deal of rage and antagonism right now.

'Sian,' he said, pen poised. 'This is obviously bringing back horrific memories for you from the time you found out your husband of more than a quarter of a century was a serial killer. How do you feel now?'

She shrugged. 'Fine. Actually, I'm feeling a little hungry. Shall we make our way out to Wigtwizzle and pass a MacDonalds drive-thru on the way?' she said, standing and preparing to leave the room.

In the doorway, Sian stole a glance at Danny as he packed his satchel. The frown was back. He was confused by Sian's laissez-faire attitude. She smiled to herself. Police–1. Press–0.

Chapter Twenty-Seven

The forensic team were back at Wigtwizzle at first light to begin excavation of the bones Sian had discovered the previous day. A skull, an ulna and several ribs were found before bad light stopped play. It was evident the bones had been there for some time and wildlife had found them at some point and had their fun. Whether there was any meat left on the bones when they clawed at them was something Adele and Simon Browes would have to take a closer look at back at Watery Street. The main task today was to carefully pack up what they'd found and see what else lay in the undergrowth of this picturesque and seemingly quiet corner of South Yorkshire.

Crime Scene Manager Felix Lerego was making sure nothing would stop them today and had ordered arc lights to give the searchers maximum light beneath the canopy of trees. There were crime scene tents and cadaver dogs on standby.

Lerego was new to South Yorkshire Police. Originally from Brighton, he'd excelled at college and university, graduating eighteen months ahead of his peers. His parents wanted him to pursue a career in law, but he was fascinated by the beginnings of a crime rather than what happened once a perpetrator was caught. He wanted to be at the gruesome end of the murder, without actually being the one to plunge in the knife. Because of his great intelligence and enthusiasm for forensics, he volunteered in a postgraduate programme that saw him travel the world and attend the aftermath of natural disasters to search for survivors and recover the dead. During his work in America he made contact with the FBI, and made sure they recognised his name for future events. It wasn't long before he was asked to attend major crime scenes. His first sight of a dead body in situ was in the immediate aftermath of a school shooting in Texas. He walked into the primary school, suited up, and carefully stepped around dead bodies of five-, six-, and seven-year-olds. Tragic? Yes. Terrifying? Yes. Fascinating? Abso-bloody-lutely. This was his calling.

Upon returning to Brighton, eager to set down roots somewhere after his shock at turning thirty so quickly, he applied for his first job in crime scene management. He was off to Sheffield.

Standing at the entrance to the woods at Wigtwizzle, he watched as white-suited CSIs began their work. His attention was rapt. He didn't think of the suffering people would be going through at the loss of their loved ones, he just hoped these innocuous-looking woods led to the uncovering of a mass grave site. He'd love to be in the thick of a massive murder investigation for his first job at South Yorkshire Police.

A CSI walked out of the scene carrying a large green plastic tray. She was heading for a van when he stopped her to take a look at the latest findings. More ribs, a second ulna, a pelvis – on the small side, Felix thought, probably from a female. This second body was another woman. He knew about the three missing sex workers South Yorkshire Police had on their books. Was this the second one? Was there a third out there somewhere? He waved the woman off to properly store and document the bones.

'Is there anything you want, Felix?' Cathy, one of the more junior CSIs, asked him as he was sitting on the edge of the boot of his Range Rover, pulling on a white forensic suit.

'Yes. I'd like a map of the woodland, and get on to Charlie and see if he can get someone with a drone out here. I'd like an aerial view to see if we can uncover any walkways seen from above. I'd also like boundary lines drawn, and get a ground-penetrating radar unit on standby.'

'Right. I actually meant tea or coffee?'

'Oh. No time for that, Cathy. Come on, chop-chop.'

He knew others within his team saw him as something of a workaholic and a ghoul, but he couldn't help it. His fascination with all things dead and undiscovered was electric. He was at his happiest when at a crime scene.

He entered the woods, watching as a fingertip search began of the area where the ribs had been found – three metres away from the skull, evidence of a disturbed scene, and of animals' enjoyment of playing with the dead. There were plenty more ribs to be found. Other bones, too.

'Felix!' He heard his name being called, but where it was coming from wasn't evident. He eventually found someone waving at him.

He squeezed his way past a small group of CSIs squatted over what, at first glance, appeared to be a femur. He almost stopped. Were they teeth marks? He stepped over rugged undergrowth and almost tripped over an exposed root.

'What are you doing so far over here?' he asked.

'I was over there with the others. I looked up and ... I don't know … being at ground level, you see things more clearly, don't you?' Jacob Grimes asked. 'Something about this section didn't look right. The ground was raised. I thought I'd have a quick look, and, well …' He didn't finish but looked down at the woodland floor.

Felix followed his gaze. More exposed bones. His excitement grew.

He bent down and dusted away the soil. An exposed femur still attached to the complete pelvic girdle. The coccyx and sacrum were still there. The ischium was badly damaged, and Felix could just make out the fifth lumbar vertebra before the rest of the spinal column disappeared underground. He didn't pull away more of the earth. This needed to be photographed before more excavation could be done.

'She was dragged a long way, by the look of it,' Jacob said.

'You think this belongs to the same body, do you?'

'Yes. We've found one femur. This is obviously the other.'

'Tell me, Jacob, how many pelvises are usually found in the human body?'

'Well, one.'

'And as we've already found one, this can't be from the same body, can it?'

'We've found a third?' He asked the unnecessary question.

Felix bent lower for a closer look. 'And unless I'm very much mistaken, this pelvis belongs to a man.'

'Bloody hell!' Jacob exclaimed. 'How many more bodies are buried around here?'

'My thoughts exactly.' Felix turned away. He didn't want a junior officer to see the excitement in his eyes. His first case as a CSM and it was one of, potentially, mass murder.

Chapter Twenty-Eight

S ian and Danny took separate cars and parked next to each other in the MacDonalds car park. She wasn't overly hungry and the thought of more of her ex-husband's victims being discovered made her feel sick. However, she needed to put on a brave face for Danny and not allow him to think she was bothered by all this. She sipped at her coffee and nibbled at the Big Mac.

'Can I ask you something, off the record?' Danny asked. He was sitting in Sian's front passenger seat, shovelling huge handfuls of fries into his mouth.

'Really off the record?'

'Yes. I won't write about this, it's just something I want to know.'

'Go on.'

'How do you carry on? When you found out about Stuart, it must have seemed like the end of the world. Your whole family was torn apart. How do you get over something like that?'

Sian looked at him. He did seem genuinely interested. She

took a deep breath. 'I don't know. You're right. It did seem like the end of everything. I was numb to all of it. It was unbelievable. How could I not know the man I was married to all that time, the man I had four children with, was a serial killer? It didn't make sense. Sometimes, even now, when I think about it all, it seems like it's happened to someone else and not me. To be perfectly truthful with you, Danny, if it wasn't for my kids, I think I'd have killed myself. That's how bad it was.' Sian surprised herself by how truthful she was being.

'Have you ever been to see Stuart?'

'No,' she answered quickly.

'Don't you want to? Don't you want to ask him questions? Your head must be full of them.'

She thought for a long moment. She really did want to ask him questions. She wanted to know why she and their four children, their beautiful home and life weren't enough for him.

'It is. I think, for now, I'm happy trying to rebuild my life. I've got four kids at very tricky stages in their lives and a house move coming up. That's what I need to concentrate on.'

'I suppose it's not like Stuart's going anywhere. You can change your mind to visit him whenever you want.'

'Precisely.'

'You're a remarkable woman, Sian, do you know that?'

She looked at him and saw he genuinely meant what he said, by the honest smile in his eyes. He wasn't merely flattering her for information.

'I'm a woman, Danny. We're all remarkable.'

Danny's phone burst into life. It was placed on the dashboard. As he licked his fingers and wiped them on a paper napkin, Sian looked at the display and saw it was someone called Marcus Liversidge calling. She'd heard that name before. He grabbed the phone and swiped to answer.

'Shit. Is that today? Give me ten minutes. I'll be right there.' He ended the call. 'That was a mate of mine. We've got a meet with, erm, someone. Can I give you a call and arrange to meet later?'

'Sure,' she said, trying not to show how relieved she was that he was leaving so soon.

'Thanks,' he said, almost jumping out of her car and running back to his car.

Sian waited until he'd driven off and was out of sight before she abandoned her meal and fired off a text to Christian telling him what she was doing next. Wigtwizzle could wait. She needed to help find Matilda. There couldn't be another night with no answers.

Sian pulled up outside of a twee-looking bungalow in Mexborough. Despite it being the middle of a harsh winter and most people's gardens looking ravaged by the elements, the front garden of Janet Crowther's home was neat. Barren bushes had been clipped back. The edges of the lawn were tidy and straight. The pavement swept of any detritus. This was either the home of a control freak with a serious case of OCD or someone with far too much time on their hands.

Sian pressed the bell and stood back. She looked around at the quiet cul-de-sac. She felt a headache coming on. Her mind was moving quicker than the case was progressing and the lack of information on Matilda's whereabouts was frightening. So much so that she was allowing her over-active imagination to fill in the gaps, and it was seriously warped. The image of finding Matilda in an abandoned building, tied up and dead, was haunting her dreams to the point where she was petrified of falling asleep.

The front door was opened, and Sian felt the warmth from within straightaway.

Janet Crowther had changed a great deal since the last time Sian had seen her on the day of the shooting back in January 2019. Two years later and Janet seemed to have aged ten years. The painful effects of your family being destroyed by one of its own were evident on her grey, lined, thin face.

'Mrs Crowther? I'm not sure if you remember me. DS Sian Robinson. South Yorkshire Police.'

'Yes. Of course I do,' she said softly. She smiled, but it didn't reach her eyes. Her lips were thin and almost blue. 'Is this about Steven? Has he escaped?'

'No. Nothing like that. I was wondering if I could come in for a word?' Sian asked, shivering to hopefully sway Janet into letting her in.

'Of course.' She stepped back. 'Please. Come on in.'

Sian entered the home and stood in the spacious hallway. She looked around at the blank walls. It was tastefully decorated in pastel colours and there was a hint of furniture polish in the air, but there were no photographs or prints on the walls.

'Go on through to the living room. The fire's on.' Janet pointed the way.

Sian went through. The lounge was huge. Floor-to-ceiling double patio doors gave the room plenty of natural light, revealing a back garden just as lovingly cared for as the front. The same colour scheme as the hallway continued into this room with a large sofa in pale pink and matching armchair, both pointed towards a widescreen TV on the wall above the fireplace. The walls in this room, however, were full of photographs depicting people on holiday or standing with a famous landmark in the background. All of them happy and smiling. Sian instantly recognised the faces of Vivien and Malcolm Harrison.

'Take a seat.' Janet pointed to the sofa.

'Thank you,' Sian sat. 'Is Ronald about? I'd like to speak to him, too.'

Janet looked down. 'Ronald died last year.'

'Oh. I'm so sorry.'

'He'd always had a weak heart, ever since he was a child. I think all the doctors were surprised he managed to live to his seventies. He simply went to bed one night, fell asleep and didn't wake up again in the morning. A good death, you might say,' she said, sadness evident in her voice. 'We spent so much time together over the last year. Every day, in fact. We had to be extra careful with the pandemic and Ronald's condition. We couldn't go out or go on holiday, but we did so much at home.' A genuine smile appeared on her face. 'Looking back, I think it was the happiest year of my life.'

'I'm pleased you were able to have so much time together in the end.'

'So am I. Oh my goodness, I haven't offered you a drink. I'll go and put the kettle on.'

'I'm fine. I've not long since had a coffee.'

'It's no trouble. I usually have a cuppa myself at this time. I can't have you going back outside in the cold without anything to eat or drink.' She practically ran out of the room and into the kitchen.

Sian heard the sound of cups and saucers clattering and the kettle boiling. She got up and went to get a better look at the black and white photo showing Janet and her husband on their wedding day. They were the picture of happiness, both standing straight, looking directly at the camera, eyes wide and bright, huge smiles on their lips. Their whole life was ahead of them. They had no inkling of the tragedy they could face all those years later.

Sian hadn't been able to look at her wedding photos since Stuart was sent to prison. Every year on their wedding anniversary, they would sit down together and reminisce, looking through the album, laughing at the fashions and Sian's dated hairdo. She wanted to burn those pictures, but her children wouldn't let her.

'Here we go,' Janet said, coming back into the room carrying a tray with a matching tea service.

Sian jumped and returned to her chair. 'I was just looking at your wedding photo.'

'That's my favourite picture of Ronald. Doesn't he look handsome in his army uniform?'

'He does.'

Janet began to pour the tea. 'You wouldn't think it from looking at that picture, but he was nervous as anything on our wedding day. I'm holding his hand in the photo, but I could feel him physically shaking. Bless him. He was never one for attention. Here you go. Help yourself to milk and sugar. Those muffins are homemade, have as many as you want.'

'Thank you.'

Sian selected the biggest chocolate muffin from the plate. She could never resist anything covered in chocolate.

'Anyway, I'm assuming you're here because of Steven. Am I right?'

There was very little Sian could reveal about the case. The last thing they wanted was the press finding out DCI Matilda Darke had been kidnapped and that one of this country's most violent men, supposedly locked away in one of the UK's most secure prisons, seemed to have found a way to orchestrate it.

Sian cleared her throat. 'We're investigating a crime that has led us to Steve Harrison. We're not sure how he's involved at the moment, but we're pretty certain he's at the heart of it. We're trying to put all the loose ends together. In our investigations, we've discovered your name on a list of official people who have contact with Steve.'

'Yes. I am.' Janet sat back in her seat.

'I hope you don't mind me asking but Steve killed a lot of people. He even manipulated his brother into killing his parents, your sister and brother-in-law. Why would you want to have anything to do with him?'

Sian was asking from a professional and personal point of view. When her husband was exposed as a serial killer of sex workers, she wanted nothing more to do with him. She visited him in his police cell while he was waiting to be charged and stated, categorically, she would no longer be a part of his life. Now, she was being asked to visit him in prison. She knew he had information about the bodies in the woods at Wigtwizzle and he would only speak to her about it. Separating the personal from the professional was not easy. How could Janet Crowther visit Steve, write letters to him, knowing he'd organised the murder of her sister?

'That was a question Ronald asked me on a regular basis, too,' she said, a hint of a smile on her lips and a twinkle in her eyes. Was that a memory of Ronald causing her to briefly soften? 'I think, at first, I visited Steven because I wanted to find out why. Vivien and Malcolm did everything for their boys when they were growing up. They gave them the best life a mother and father could. They weren't particularly strict. They had rules, obviously, but then you have to, don't you?

But there was a lot of love in that house when the boys were young. I couldn't understand how they became what they did. You see, people always say it starts with the family, and it does. But what could Vivien and Malcolm possibly have done to turn Steven into such a disturbed individual? I couldn't answer that. I needed to find out the answer. The only way to do that was to go to the source.'

Sian nodded. She could understand that. To the world, even to Sian, she and Stuart were the perfect couple. They had the perfect life and the perfect family. Four children, all happy in themselves and in their schoolwork. They didn't bring any trouble to their door. They had a wide circle of friends and were popular among their peers. Stuart and Sian weren't rich, but they were comfortable. They had family holidays every year and the kids always got what they wanted for Christmas. There was a great deal of love in their house, too. What had gone so tragically wrong? Would Sian have to go to the source for that answer, too?

Sian swallowed her mouthful of muffin. 'What did Steve say?'

It was a while before Janet answered. Her face was blank. 'I'm still waiting for my answer. Steven doesn't know. I think he's asking the same question himself.'

'So even Steve doesn't know why he committed his crimes?'

'I don't think so.'

'How can he not know?'

Janet shrugged and pulled her woollen cardigan tighter around her, as if a cold breeze had blown through the house. 'I don't know. He's always said he's never known what happened to make him do what he did, but ...' She fell silent.

'But?' Sian prompted.

Janet took a breath. 'He blames DCI Matilda Darke for everything.'

'Everything?'

'He said he changed when he met her.'

'In what way?'

'He doesn't know. He seems to think she had it in for him from the beginning, that she stopped him from getting promotion.'

'But Matilda had nothing to do with Steve. He wasn't in her department. She wouldn't have known about him taking his sergeant's exams or seeking promotion.'

'I'm aware,' Janet said. 'It's what Steven believes. And he's very convincing. There was a time I wondered if he was right. I always said I wouldn't read any of those books written about him, but I read *The Hangman's Hold* by Lionel Miller. I even researched DCI Darke myself and wondered if she and Steven's paths ever crossed. I've no idea what's going on inside his head that's made him latch onto her like he has done.'

'Does he talk about Matilda a lot?'

'The conversation always seems to get around to her at some point.'

'And is he still angry?'

'Oh, undoubtedly. His whole demeanour changes. You can see the anger flowing through his veins.'

A chill went down Sian's spine. 'Has Steve ever said if he's planning on doing anything?'

'Like what?' Janet frowned.

'Revenge. Towards Matilda.'

'I … Has something happened to her?'

'I really can't say. I'm sorry.'

'He's never gone into specifics, but he wants her dead. He's said, many times, that the only time he'll be truly at peace is when she's dead. Then he'll be able to relax.'

The room suddenly felt much colder and smaller.

'And has he ever said how he'd manage to make that happen?'

'Not to me. No.'

'Another name on the list of people Steve has contact with is his cousin, Amy. We don't seem to be able to find her. Can you give me her contact details?'

'I'm sorry? Steven doesn't have a cousin.'

Sian rummaged around in her bag. She brought out her notebook and flicked to the relevant page. 'Amy Monroe.'

'I've never heard of an Amy Monroe.'

'She's listed at Wakefield Prison as being Steve's cousin.'

Janet shook her head. 'Malcolm was an only child, and I was Vivien's only sibling. Ronald and I couldn't have children. Steven doesn't have a cousin.'

Sian's blood ran cold. Who the hell was the person who'd been contacting Steve and posing as his cousin, then? And was she the same woman who tried to run Matilda off the road twice before Christmas and kidnapped her? If she was as dangerous and manipulative as Steve Harrison, then Sian could not see a happy ending to this.

Chapter Twenty-Nine

A dele Kean and Simon Browes stood in the middle of the main autopsy suite and looked at the two tables in front of them. Incomplete skeletons from two bodies had been brought from Wigtwizzle to Watery Street. From the measurement of the bones, they assumed one was male and the other female, but that was only a textbook guess based on the different sizes of the pelvises. There were many tests that needed to be undertaken before they could be more accurate.

'Have you phoned Sian?' Simon asked. He'd been halfway to Nottingham when he'd received Adele's call telling him more bones had been found. He must have broken all records to get back here so quickly. He was red in the face just coming in from the car park.

'Yes. It went straight to voicemail. I left a message,' Adele said. 'What I can't understand is, if Sian's husband is responsible for the bodies at Wigtwizzle, why leave one in the boot of a car and bury two others in shallow graves? And of the two buried in the ground, why leave one clothed and the other naked?'

'Well, they only found partial clothing from one of the skeletons. Maybe they were both fully clothed and animals have carried the clothes away for their dens.'

'Possibly,' Adele thought out loud. 'But that still begs the question about burying two in the ground and leaving one in the back of a car. Why risk a car being found? It would make more sense to bury them all in the ground.'

'Fortunately, we don't need to worry about answering those questions. That's a police matter,' Simon said.

'True.'

After a long moment of silence, they both spoke at once.

'Go on,' Adele prompted.

'I was just going to say, about last night …'

They were interrupted when Donal Youngblood came into the main suite. He'd been assigned the task of removing the clothing from the bones, bagging it and liaising with the team of crime scene investigators, though his mind was still on the recovery of his boyfriend, DS Scott Andrews. He was checking his phone as he came in.

'Donal, how's it going?' Adele asked, taking a step away from Simon. She worried they might be standing inappropriately close.

'Sorry?' He looked up, distracted. 'Oh, Scott's given a full statement and they seem to think the woman they're looking for is the one who crashed into Finn's car around Christmas. They think it's all linked.'

'I meant with the clothes.'

'Oh. Yes. No. I'm sorry. Erm, they've been collected, and I was speaking to … sorry, can't remember her name.' He ran his fingers through his black hair. 'Anyway, they haven't been able to find any hairs on them. Not surprising really. I mean, they've probably been in the ground for a long time. They're not terribly old clothes, by the way. Apparently, the label on the skirt is from a supplier that sells exclusively to Primark in this country. I'm just going to ...' Donal left the sentence hanging in the air, turned on his heel and headed back out of the door, head down, texting rapidly on his phone.

'I don't envy the officer tasked with trying to track that down,' Adele said.

'Thank goodness that's not our job as well,' Simon added. 'Did you manage to extract DNA?'

'Only from one of the skeletons,' Adele said. 'The one we think is female. I was able to extract some from the femur. I can't get anything from the other. The bone is covered in teeth marks and whatever the wildlife didn't get, nature robbed us of the rest. However –' she leaned down and picked up the skull '– there is damage to the skull that has been repaired at some point long ago. There's bound to be a record of that somewhere. Fingers firmly crossed.'

'Any clue as to how our two mystery bodies died?'

'Not from what we've got. The first was strangled, but then we had the hyoid bone to tell us that. With these two, we've only got partial skeletons. Felix Lerego is going to keep me informed to see if they find anything else.'

'Are they widening the search?'

'I believe so. Felix wants the entire wood searched.'

'And has anything else been found yet?'

'I've no idea. I'm sure he'll let us know.'

'Do you think maybe one of us should go out there? I could go. I don't mind.'

'There's no point at the moment, is there? They might not find anything else. To be honest, I really hope they don't find more bodies. The last thing they need right now is a drawn-out case with the press on their backs.'

'I'm sure Sian has a list of missing persons. Between us, we should be able to come up with something,' he said, giving Adele a placatory smile. He placed his hand on her shoulder but quickly removed it. 'How are you today?'

'I'm fine,' she said, looking at him with a smile. 'Thank you. For last night. I'm glad you were with me.'

'You're welcome. I ... It ... Coffee?' he asked, his face reddening slightly with embarrassment.

'Please.' She returned his smile and could feel her face flushing.

Simon went out of the room, leaving Adele with her thoughts. She looked down at the skeletonised bones and her smile faded. She knew of one missing person South Yorkshire Police had on their books: her former technical assistant, Lucy Dauman, who had been missing for over a year. She hoped she wasn't looking at her partial skeleton. The thought of Lucy on one of her slabs was too horrific to comprehend.

Chapter Thirty

M atilda opened her eyes.

It seemed lighter in the small room than it did before. She sat up on the bed and looked over to the door. Above it was a small rectangular window. There must have been something there before, blocking out any light, but now it had been removed and her whole room, her small room, her cell, was visible.

She looked around at the rough walls, the concrete floor, the exposed brickwork. She didn't take any of it in. Her eyes were drawn to the hangman's noose dangling from the ceiling.

Matilda stood up. Every bone in her body seemed to ache. She'd been curled up on her side, holding her body rigid to stave off the cold. But it didn't seem to matter what she did, she couldn't get warm. She walked around her tiny cell to try and get the blood circulating through her legs, relieve some of that muscle tension, but wherever she went, she was always within touching distance of the hangman's noose. The fear and malevolence it radiated scared the living daylights out of her.

She went over to the door and banged on it hard with her fists. The noise resounded off the bare walls.

'Hello. Is there anyone out there? I need to talk to you.'

She pressed her ear against the cold door and listened intently for any sound. Nothing. No muffled conversation, no radio or television, no approaching footsteps.

She banged again. Harder.

'Hello. I really need to talk to you. Please. I ... I take medication. I haven't had any for a while and I'm in some serious pain here.'

It wasn't a complete lie. Matilda was on regular medication following the shooting in 2019 but it was mostly for anxiety and the psychological trauma she was still suffering from. Still, the kidnapper didn't know that.

She was about to bang on the door for a third time when she stopped. She was sure she'd heard something. Her frown deepened as she strained her hearing. There was definitely someone on the other side of the door. She was sure of it.

There was a bang and Matilda jumped back. A rattling noise from above the door made Matilda look up. The small window was opened a crack. Matilda tried to make out who was looking through but all she saw was a silhouette of a person.

'How much pain are you in?'

A female voice. Matilda didn't recognise it.

'It's not pain as such, not at the moment. It's discomfort. But the pain will come if I don't keep moving.'

'What do you take?'

Matilda couldn't tell her what she took as it wasn't pain medication. 'I can't pronounce it,' she said, a half-laugh in her voice. Thank goodness the majority of medications seemed to be a jumble of consonants.

'I can get you some ibuprofen.'

'Thank you.'

Matilda frowned. Why was this woman being kind to her yet keeping her locked up?

'Look, erm, why am I here?' Matilda asked.

'You don't know?'

'No.'

'The noose isn't a big enough hint?' The voice sounded edgier.

Matilda glanced at it over her shoulder. Her heart sank. 'This is to do with Steve Harrison, I get that. I just don't understand why ...'

'This has got *fuck* all to do with Steve Harrison,' she spat, anger evident.

'Then I don't understand.'

'In that case you can whistle for your ibuprofen. If you want to end your pain, use the fucking noose.'

The window slammed closed.

Matilda sat back down on the bed. She could feel the metal frame through the thin mattress. She put her head in her hands. Steve Harrison was known as the Hangman. Every newspaper article he was mentioned in called him by his nickname. The books written about him were all titled with variations of it. The most recent, upon which the number-one Netflix series was based, was called *The Hangman's Hold*. The cover was chilling. The hoop of the noose replaced the 'o' in 'Hold'. Images in newspapers and magazines had the same pictures promoting the documentary. It frightened Matilda; how would the families of his victims feel?

As far as Matilda could think, the noose wasn't symbolic in any other case she'd worked on. So, if she wasn't here for any reason connected to Steve Harrison, why *was* she here?

Chapter Thirty-One

DCs Finn Cotton and Tom Simpson were in the pool car heading for Wakefield Prison. Finn had asked Tom to drive so he could concentrate on what he was going to ask Steve Harrison. He was to be the lead interviewer, after all. The truth was, Finn was nervous. He didn't like going into prisons at the best of times, especially category A prisons that held the most dangerous men in the country, and especially when he was going to be interviewing Steve Harrison who was the most violent man in the UK. He was also the man who had orchestrated the shooting which had left several of Finn's colleagues, his friends, dead. Now Finn was going to be sitting opposite him, and despite there being a glass screen between them, he just knew Steve would pick up on his nerves, his fear, his horror, and use it against him. He needed to channel his inner Sir Kenneth Branagh and put on the performance of a lifetime if he were to have any chance of discovering where Matilda was and who had got her.

Finn's mouth had dried. He rummaged around in his pockets; all he could find was half a tube of Polo mints. He popped two in his mouth and sucked them hard. He offered the packet to Tom who waved them away.

He looked out of the window at the nondescript view. All he saw were industrial units and abandoned factories as they sped along the motorway.

'So,' Finn began, needing something to offer a distraction. 'What's the deal with you and Zofia?'

'What are you talking about?' Tom asked, not taking his eyes off the road ahead.

'You're very close. Always together. Always having a laugh and a joke. And you went home at the same time, very late, last night, and this morning you've come into work wearing the same clothes. Not to mention the fact that I can smell her perfume despite the fact she's never been in this car.'

Tom started to blush. The redness crept up his neck past the collar of his shirt. 'Yes. We're sort of seeing each other.'

'Only sort of?'

'No. Well, we *are* seeing each other.'

'Is it serious?'

It was a long moment of silence before Tom replied. 'I ... I'm not sure. I like her. She likes me, I think. I hope. We're just ... we're taking things slow. She's ... worried.'

'What about?'

'Her mum and dad. They're very protective of her since the accident. They don't want her getting hurt.'

'Understandable.'

'Hmm,' Tom mused.

'What does that mean?'

'They're stifling her. And she has problems saying no to them. It's not my place to say anything, obviously, but they need to let her live her own life. Yes, she's in a wheelchair, but she's fully independent. They can't see that.'

'They're just looking out for her, Tom. She's their only child. She's been through a lot.'

'I know. So have I.'

Finn frowned. He was about to ask Tom to elaborate, but the turn-off for the prison came up and suddenly the huge building came into view. Finn's stomach dropped through the floor. He hadn't even noticed they'd come off the motorway.

'We're here,' Tom said, paraphrasing a quote from *Poltergeist* and doing a chillingly accurate impression of Carol Anne Freeling.

Before they entered the prison, Finn and Tom went over, one last time, how they hoped the interview would play out. Steve was a great manipulator, they both knew that, and they had to be on their A-game and not allow him to get under their skin. Once that happened, they were lost and so was the interview, and so was any chance of finding Matilda.

The interview room was small and stifling. There were no windows and no air conditioning. Finn and Tom sat at a small desk. The limited space meant they were shoulder to shoulder, knee to knee. Finn placed a file and notebook on the table, took a pen from his inside pocket and began making notes. He didn't have anything to write, but he wanted Steve to enter the room and not see two desperate-looking DCs waiting for him.

On the other side of the thick glass, Finn saw movement. A door was opened, a figure walked in. A chair was pulled out and he sat down. Finn continued writing. It was gobbledegook, random words. He clicked off the pen and looked up.

Finn looked into the cold eyes of Steve Harrison. He

remembered him from when he was at South Yorkshire Police. They were both PCs, though Steve had been there longer than Finn, and Finn was on traffic duty at the time of Steve's reign of terror. He knew of him, though. Everyone knew of Steve Harrison. The women loved him, and the men wanted to be him. He seemed happy, confident, full of life. He always had a smile on his face. His eyes were forever twinkling. He had the world at his fingertips, but it wasn't enough.

'Steve, I'm DS Finn Cotton and this is DC Tom Simpson,' Finn began in his most confident tone. It sounded strange to his ears. 'We'd like to ask you a few questions in regard to an investigation.'

Steve didn't say anything. He looked from Finn to Tom and back to Finn. There was a hint of a smile on his lips. He was clearly enjoying himself. This was a change from the norm for a man who spent twenty-three hours a day locked in a prison cell.

'An attempt has been made to kidnap DCI Matilda Darke,' Finn continued.

The smile briefly dropped, but soon returned.

'The woman we apprehended hasn't been very forthcoming with information. However, strangely, she has told us that you were instrumental in the planning of the kidnapping attempt.'

He raised an eyebrow.

'Is there anything you'd like to say?'

Steve looked over to Tom and held his gaze. He turned back to Finn. He cleared his throat.

'DS Finn Cotton. I remember you when you were in uniform. You looked scared of your own shadow.'

'Did I?'

'And now you're a DS on the Homicide and Major Enquiry Team.'

'Homicide and Major Crime Unit,' Finn corrected him.

'How the fuck did that happen? Matilda get desperate?'

'Best man for the job, Steve.'

'Really? Must have been a poor turnout.'

'Steve, you can say what you want about me, I really don't give a toss, but let's not play this game. We're both adults, and I'm very busy. Now, who is this woman who tried to kidnap DCI Darke and how did you contact her?'

Steve made a play of tightening his lips.

Finn sat back in silence and watched him. 'Really? You're not going to answer any of my questions?'

He shook his head.

'We're wasting our time here then,' Finn said to Tom. 'Come on, we may as well go.'

They stood up and made to leave. At the door, Finn turned back.

'Just to let you know, though, Steve. Your attempt to kidnap Matilda was unsuccessful. It was pathetic. I don't know how long you've spent arranging it, but you really should have chosen someone with a bit more brain power, because it was laughable. Now we will be charging her with attempted kidnapping, and she's already named you as an accomplice. It won't be long before we find proof of that somewhere and when we do, you can kiss goodbye to the very few privileges you have left.'

Steve remained seated, his arms folded across his chest. The smile that Finn was itching to slap off his face, seemed to be growing by the second.

'Matilda and Scott arrived at Matilda's house to find there had been a power cut,' Steve said.

Finn turned to look at him. Steve was sitting back in his chair, arms still folded, a smile still on his face.

'What?' Finn asked.

'Scott opened the door, presumably to get a torch from the car or something. But there was someone waiting for him on the doorstep, and he was stabbed in the stomach.'

'How do you know all this?' Tom asked.

'Sit back down.'

They had no option but to follow his instruction. Tentatively, they both retook their seats and stared at Steve in rapt attention.

'Scott was stabbed, twice, I believe. He dropped to the floor, clutching his stomach. The woman stepped over his body and entered the house. Matilda came out of the kitchen and tried to help Scott, but the woman stopped her. She tasered Matilda, injected her with an anaesthetic and dragged her out to her waiting car where she lobbed her in the boot and drove her to a location unknown. The kidnapping was a success because the woman was wearing a camera and it was livestreamed to me in my cell. And you, Finn, are no more a detective sergeant than I'm Scarlett Johansson. Have a pleasant trip back to Sheffield. I'm ready!' Steve called out over his shoulder to the guards waiting outside the interview room.

The door was opened, and Steve walked through. He didn't even look back.

'Well, that didn't go as expected,' Tom said once the door was slammed closed.

'No.'

'What do we do now?'

'I haven't got a clue.'

'We're fucked, aren't we?'

'Something like that, yes.'

Chapter Thirty-Two

'What are you still doing here?' Christian asked DS Scott Andrews when he walked back into the HMCU suite and found the sergeant throwing back a couple of ibuprofen and swallowing them with water from a plastic cup.

'I'm working.'

'You're bloody not. You've discharged yourself, probably against doctor's orders, and you look like you haven't slept in weeks. Go home. Now.'

'How can I go home? Every window I look out of I see Matilda's house. I'd go mad.'

Christian pulled up a chair and sat next to Scott's desk. In the corner, Zofia was sitting behind her bank of computer screens, a pensive look on her face as she studied whatever it was she was doing. Or maybe she was straining to earwig on their conversation.

'Scott, you've done all you can. If we find this woman, you'll be brought back in to try and identify her. Until then, there's nothing you can do. You may as well go home and rest.'

Scott swallowed his emotion. Tears were building in his

eyes. He chewed his bottom lip. 'We're not doing enough. We should be tearing this city apart looking for her.'

The door to the suite opened and Sian came running in. 'I think I might have got her.'

All eyes turned to her.

'You've found Matilda?' Scott asked, almost jumping out of his seat.

'No. I spoke to Janet Crowther. She said Steve doesn't have any cousins. So I called Wakefield Prison back up and asked them to double-check. Amy Monroe is definitely listed as Steve's cousin. Unfortunately, she's never visited so they don't have CCTV footage of her, but she's written and phoned. They've given me the number and they're digging out copies of her letters.'

'Have they sent over copies of any other letters Steve has received?' Christian asked.

'Not that I'm aware of.'

'Why not?' he asked, raising his voice. 'These could be vital documents for finding Matilda. We need them.'

'The guy I was talking to said they're very short-staffed at the moment.'

'Aren't we all, for fuck's sake.' Christian was clearly frustrated.

'Give me the phone numbers, Sian. I'll try and track them down,' Zofia said.

Sian headed over to her desk while scrolling through the pages of her notebook.

'Did Janet Crowther say anything else?' Christian asked as he paced the room, hands on his hips.

'Only that Steve is very angry and blames Matilda for everything.'

'That doesn't bode well,' Scott said.

'Sian, will you come into my office? I need a word.' Christian went to his office. Sian followed.

'Shit, before I forget.' Sian stopped and turned back to Scott. 'Adele left me a message about the bones found out at Wigtwizzle. I tried calling her back, but it went to voicemail. Could you try her for me, Scott?'

'Sure.'

Sian entered Christian's office and closed the door behind her. He was already sitting at his desk, his head down. When he looked up, he had a strained look on his face.

'How did it go with Danny Hanson?'

'Fine. I got the first shot in, and he believed my lies.' She pulled out a chair and sat down. 'The thing about Danny Hanson is that he has a picture in his mind of what the world of journalism and policing is like. He thinks it's all a Hollywood movie. Real life, as we know, is more monotonous. He's just finding that out,' she smiled.

'You didn't take him with you to see Janet Crowther, did you?'

'Of course I didn't. He got a call and was reminded of a meeting he'd forgotten and off he went. I haven't heard from him since.'

'That's good. Just keep on your toes around him.'

There was a tap on the glass and Scott walked in.

'Update from Adele,' he began. 'The body Sian tripped over in the woods at Wigtwizzle has been identified through DNA as Caroline Richardson.'

'Oh my God.' Sian bowed her head. 'She's another of the three missing sex workers.'

'While they were excavating those bones, they found another set, and these belong to a male.'

'A third body?' Christian asked.

Sian's interest was piqued. Stuart didn't kill any men.

'They couldn't get any DNA from his bones as they're too far gone. However, he had an old head injury that they've managed to track down and match with some bridge work done on what was left of his teeth. They've identified him as Duncan McNally.'

Christian frowned. 'That name rings a bell.'

'Funny you should say that,' Scott said with a smile.

'Why?'

'Oh my God!' Sian said, clamping a hand to her mouth. She looked to be on the verge of tears.

'Who is he?' Christian asked.

'He was living homeless in 2019 when Jake Harrison paid him to walk into this station and set off the fire alarm, forcing us all to leave and then allow Jake to open fire.'

'Of course.'

'I feel sick,' Sian said. 'I knew him.' She snatched a tissue from the box on Christian's desk and put it to her mouth.

'Scott, get Sian a drink of water.'

'I'm fine.' She waved him to stay where he was. 'Years ago, I was on a night out with my sister-in-law. We'd been to the City Hall to see a concert. We were walking to the tram stop when these men came from nowhere and started hassling us. Duncan intervened. We treated him to a drink as a thank-you and after that, I kept seeing him around the cathedral. Every time I did, I'd slip him a tenner or whatever I had on me. He used to be in the army but left for whatever reason and found himself unable to cope with life in the real world. I haven't seen him for so long. I've been wrapped up in my own problems with Stuart and everything. I just assumed he'd moved on or he'd made a better life for himself. I didn't think that ...' she trailed off as the tears caught up with her.

'Sian, you weren't to know,' Christian said placatingly.

'Do we know how he died?'

'I don't know,' Scott said. 'Adele didn't say. I don't think they've recovered all the bones.'

'What the hell is going on, Christian?' Sian asked, looking at her DI for help. 'Two sex workers we've been searching for and a homeless man we didn't even realise was missing, but who was known to us. I mean, is this linked to Matilda's disappearance, too? Has Steve been keeping tabs on us all this time and taking people connected to the cases we've been working on and dumping their bodies? Is Matilda going to end up at Wigtwizzle, too?'

'Okay, okay, calm down, Sian. If Ridley sees you like this, he'll definitely take you off the case,' Christian said. He ran his hand over his buzzcut, stood up and paced the tiny room while he thought. 'Scott, here's what I want you to do.'

'I thought you wanted me to go home?'

'You should have done that when I told you to. Now I'm putting you to work. I want you to go over every case we've been working on since Steve started killing in 2017. Then check missing persons and see if any are listed.'

'Wouldn't we have known about it though?' Scott interrupted. 'If someone went missing who was connected to a case, we'd have been told.'

'Not necessarily. And especially not if the case was solved. Get Zofia to help you. Her fingers are like pistons when she's hammering on that keyboard.'

'Will do.' Scott glanced at Sian, saw the distressed look on her face and left.

'What are you thinking?' Christian asked.

'There is an alternative to Steve being involved,' she said, her voice barely above a whisper.

'Go on.'

'Duncan McNally is a skeleton, so he's been dead for some time. It is just possible that Stuart killed him. Maybe Duncan saw him with one of the sex workers and discovered Stuart was the killer, so he was silenced.'

Christian nodded.

'But you'd already thought of that, hadn't you?' Sian asked.

'It had crossed my mind. Sorry.'

Sian sighed. 'I'll go and visit Stuart in prison.'

'Are you sure?'

'No. But there's no alternative.'

Chapter Thirty-Three

As Scott left Christian's office, he almost ran into a PC delivering an Amazon box to Zofia.

'January sales?' he asked.

She set about opening the box. 'I was thinking about Steve Harrison yesterday and all the coverage he's received. There have been so many books written about him already, yet not all of the writers have actually visited him in prison to talk to him. I thought I'd order the books by the writers who haven't just stolen his story from the newspapers, but who have taken the time to visit Wakefield Prison and speak to the source.' She began unloading the paperbacks. 'Maybe there's some clue as to who Steve has had contact with. Or maybe an author has spoken to someone else we don't know about.'

'Good thinking,' he said, going over to her desk and helping her with the contents of the box. '*The Hangman's Hold* by Lionel Miller,' Scott read from the cover.

'That's the most famous one. That's the one that was turned into a Netflix documentary.'

'Did you see it?'

'I've been watching it this morning on one of my screens.' She pointed to the left-hand monitor and a frozen image of a bloodied, handcuffed Steve Harrison being led to a police car. The photo captured the smirk on his face. It was a photo that adorned the majority of the front pages of the nation's newspapers the following day. The journalists knew they were on to something special with a grinning serial killer.

'Every time I see that picture, it brings it all back.'

'You were there, weren't you? When he was arrested.'

'I was unconscious. He pushed me into the side of a speeding tram. How I wasn't killed is anyone's guess.'

Zofia glanced past Scott and into Christian's office where the DI and Sian looked to be having a tense conversation.

'Scott, I don't mean to be negative here, but do you think it would be better if the Chief Constable brought in an outside team to look for Matilda? If Steve is involved ...'

'What do you mean, "if"? He is involved,' Scott almost snapped.

'That's what I'm talking about. You're all too close. You're all angry at Steve Harrison. With emotions running high, that's when mistakes are likely to happen.'

'Zofia, you weren't here when Steve did what he did. You don't know what we're going through. We know him. Inside and out.'

'Which is precisely my point. You know him too much. Maybe someone who doesn't will approach this better.' She held her hands up in submission. 'I'm not saying anything bad about anyone on this team. I care for all of you. I just don't want to see any of you getting hurt. Look at Christian and Sian right now. Go on.' Scott turned around. 'They look like they're at a funeral.'

Scott studied his long-term colleagues. He knew exactly

what Zofia was thinking. This was a personal case and Christian, Sian, himself, Finn, they all had a personal stake in this. They just had to keep reminding themselves not to let their emotions get too intense, which was easier said than done.

'I love Sian to bits,' Zofia said. 'Despite everything. But with Matilda missing and now the bones found at Wigtwizzle being connected to her ex-husband, she's not going to be thinking clearly.'

Scott turned back to Zofia. 'I understand what you're saying, Zofia, I really do. But we've got this. Trust me.'

She looked into his eyes. She did trust him. She was also scared of what any one of them would do to find Matilda and save her.

———————————

Zofia was in prime position in the Homicide and Major Crime Unit. Her desk was at the furthest point in the room from the door. Her back was to the window and the two large twenty-one-inch monitors blocked anyone from seeing what she was doing, though she wasn't doing anything she shouldn't be doing during office hours.

From behind her screens, she could simply look up and see what was going on around her. She looked into Matilda's office. It was sad seeing it empty. It was usually a hive of activity and Sian was always popping in with a packet of Maltesers for her. Zofia hoped it wouldn't be long before normal service was resumed, though the longer Matilda remained missing, the less likely that would be. She looked over to Christian's office and could just about see him behind his desk if she angled her head right. He'd been looking more and more drawn lately, as if the weight of the world was slowly pushing him into the ground. Maybe it was.

After their succinct chat, Christian and Sian left his office. Christian leaned in to Scott, whispered something, to which Scott merely nodded, and they both left together.

'Everything all right?' Zofia asked Scott once they'd left.

'Fine.'

It didn't take a detective to realise that was a lie.

She waited for Scott to elaborate. He didn't. She went back to reading *The Hangman's Hold* by Lionel Miller.

The first few chapters were all about Steve Harrison growing up and how he always wanted to join the police force. It went into great detail about his childhood, his relationship with his brother and parents and his popularity at school with both teachers and fellow pupils. There was nothing significant in his childhood that stood out, nothing that could point to the disturbed killer he was to become. Maybe that was the author's intention. Maybe he was planning to show how Steve changed once he joined the police, and to make them out to be the villain of the story.

Bored of reading about Steve's idyllic childhood, Zofia flicked through the book and looked at the black and white photos on glossy paper. She then went to the end and read the acknowledgements. Her eyes widened.

'I've got something,' she said. She looked up. Scott was intently staring at his screen while jotting something down.

'What?'

'I'm reading the acknowledgements section in the back of the book written by Lionel Miller. Listen to this: "Blah blah blah, *I'd also like to thank the people who took the time to talk to me when it came to understanding the real Steve Harrison, both before and after his crimes. Janet and Ronald Crowther, Rose Osgood, Nina Price and Amy Monroe."'*

'Amy Monroe?' Scott asked.

'She's on Steve's contacts list. Sian gave me her numbers to trace but they don't exist. Well, they did, but they've been disconnected. They were pay-as-you-go anyway. She's down as Steve's cousin but Janet Crowther said he didn't have any cousins.'

'So, who is she?'

'I don't know. But Lionel Miller has spoken to her.'

'Zofia, you're a star,' Scott said, the first genuine smile of the day appearing on his lips.

'I'll contact his publisher, see if they can put me in touch with him. At least we now know she's a real flesh and blood person,' she said, googling HarperCollins and looking up their number.

Scott went over to the murder board and looked at the photofit he and Finn had come up with as an accurate depiction of the woman who'd taken Matilda. Was this Amy Monroe? He doubted it was her real name. He couldn't find anyone with her description anywhere, especially on social media. But then, would someone plotting to kidnap a DCI have a social media presence?

Scott looked up and heard Zofia in conversation with the publisher. He looked past her and out of the window. It was going dark again. Another day nearly over. Matilda was spending her third night away from home, from her friends and her family. Scott had a sick feeling in the pit of his stomach. Had he seen his boss, his friend, for the last time?

Chapter Thirty-Four

Time was getting on and the working day was almost finished. Sian knew she really should think about going home, sorting out the evening meal for the kids, but once she sat down and stopped, her mind would go into overdrive and the dark thoughts about what was happening to Matilda would set in, followed by the tears. It would be best if she kept on working. She checked her phone. There were no missed calls or texts from Danny Hanson, so she assumed he'd been caught up in another story. She gave herself a wry smile. Everyone thought the world of policing was exciting and each day was like an episode of *Line of Duty*. When they saw how mundane it really was, they were disappointed. Hopefully, she'd put Danny off the scent.

'Aren't you going home?' she asked Zofia.

'I'm waiting for Tom,' she said. Her eyes were wide, and she chewed her bottom lip.

'How are things with you two?'

'Fine,' she said, unconvincingly.

Sian returned to looking at her laptop screen.

'Sian,' Zofia eventually said. 'Could I have a private word?'

'Sure.' Sian walked over to Zofia's desk, stretching her aching muscles as she did so. She grabbed Tom's chair and dragged it over to sit next to Zofia.

'I know we're all busy and preoccupied with Matilda and everything, but there's something bugging me, and I need to tell someone.'

'Is it about Matilda?'

'No. Nothing like that,' she answered quickly. 'You know me and Tom have been seeing each other lately?' Sian nodded. 'Last night was the first night that he stayed over and the first night we … you know,' she said, blushing slightly.

'I'm getting the picture,' Sian smiled.

'Don't get me wrong, Tom was lovely. It was my first time since being paralysed and I was nervous, obviously, and Tom was just so tentative. It's just … well, in the early hours of the morning, I woke up and needed the toilet. When I got back to bed, I snuggled into Tom, like you do, and … well, you know his arms are covered in tattoos. I was looking at them and I noticed he's got a scar on his wrist. I looked at his other arm and there's an identical scar there, too.' She lowered her voice. 'I think he's tried to commit suicide at some point. Do you know anything about him?'

Sian took a breath. 'No. I've not been back long myself. Did you ask him about them?'

'No. I mean, they're old scars, so it's probably something going way back, and maybe he's recovered, but what if he's not? What if he's bottling something up?'

'I'm sure anything would have come up in his evaluation.'

Zofia looked down. When she looked back up, there were tears in her eyes. 'I know we've all got a lot going on right now, but do you think you could do some digging for me?'

'I thought you'd be able to find out everything, the way you are with computers.'

She gave a wry smile. 'Normally, yes, but, I'm sort of worried what I'm going to find out. I'd like a trusted friend to drip-feed me information in a painless way.'

Sian smiled. It warmed her that Zofia saw her as a friend rather than a colleague, especially as it was Stuart who was the cause of her paralysis in the first place.

'Of course,' Sian said, placing a hand on top of hers. 'Leave it with me.'

The doors to the suite opened and Tom entered wearing his coat and a beanie hat. 'Ready when you are, Zof.'

'Just coming,' she said, turning off her computers and grabbing her jacket from the seat next to her. 'Thank you so much, Sian,' she said quietly before wheeling herself out of the room.

Sian watched as the young couple left. She couldn't hear what they said to each other at the door but smiled as Tom took over the wheeling of Zofia's chair and headed down the corridor. On the outside, Tom seemed like a regular young man, dedicated to his work, intelligent and happy. What was lying beneath the surface? What demons did he have running through his mind?

'You look deep in thought,' Scott said.

Sian almost jumped. She hadn't noticed Scott come into the suite.

'I thought you'd gone home,' she said, snapping out of her reverie. She put Tom's chair back at his desk and went over to her own.

'No. I'm ... I ... I don't know what I'm doing, to be honest, Sian. I want to go home, but I feel like I'm abandoning Matilda if I do.'

'I know what you mean.'

'Where the bloody hell is she?'

'I'm literally screaming that question inside my head every minute.'

'I'm trying to remain positive but it's not possible, is it?'

Sian looked up at the sound of a crack in Scott's voice. She saw the raw emotion painted on his face. He looked to be in pain, and it wasn't only from the stab wound.

'Fancy driving me to Leeds?'

Scott frowned. 'Late night shopping?'

'That's where Linda Bellamy is.'

'The prison therapist?'

Sian nodded. 'If anyone knows Steve better than we do, it's going to be her.'

'I'll go and see if there are any pool cars available,' he said, suddenly animated.

'Let's use mine,' she said, pulling a face. 'The standard of cleanliness in those lately has gone seriously downhill.' She stood up and grabbed her coat. 'There was a suspicious stain on the front passenger seat that was giving off a nasty smell.'

'Was that the burgundy Astra?'

'Yes.'

'Yeah, I know what that is. Do you want to know?'

'Absolutely not.'

'Sure? It's quite a funny story in a disgusting way.'

'One more word and I'll elbow you where your stitches are.' She pointed at him, a twinkle in her eyes.

Sheffield to Leeds by car should take a little over three-quarters of an hour. Head for the M1 and put your foot down. But with rush-hour traffic and one lane closed due to maintenance, it was over an hour later when Scott turned into the street where the psychologist Linda Bellamy lived. On the journey, Sian quizzed Scott about Tom in a roundabout way. Like her, he knew very little about him, but said he seemed like a sound bloke whose knowledge of Sheffield United ran into the obsessive, his father was drinking buddies with Sean Bean, and he was part of a team who rode on motorbikes from Land's End to John O'Groats raising money for charity.

'What charity?' Sian asked.

'He did say, can't remember,' Scott said as he tried to change lanes in ever-thickening traffic. 'Something to do with mental health, I think.'

That gave Sian pause for thought and she remained quiet for a while. She kept thinking about the face people present to others while privately they're dealing with all kinds of drama and trauma. Matilda was an expert at fooling others into thinking she was fine. Over the years she suffered the grief of losing her husband, the agony over Carl Meagan's disappearance, and Ben Hales taking his own life in her house, yet she was still able to get up in the morning and come to work.

'Everything okay?' Scott asked, glancing across at Sian and noticing her pained expression.

'Fine,' she said, ironically aware that she was hiding her doubts from a trusted friend. 'You missed the turning, by the way.'

———

Scott pulled up just past the drive. The house wasn't visible from the road, surrounded as it was by neatly trimmed evergreens. They climbed out of the car and walked up the driveway, their shoes crunching on the gravel.

It was pitch-dark although it wasn't even six o'clock yet, and the temperature, once again, was below zero.

'Nice house,' Scott said as they approached.

'Hmm. Not cheap.'

'Therapy must pay well.'

Sian had called ahead. Linda was expecting them. Sian had also looked her up on the internet and found that Linda had her own website. As well as visiting prisons she saw clients on a private basis in her own homes, specialising in trauma counselling and rehabilitation.

Sian pushed the bell and stood back. She lowered her voice. 'I don't think I'd like to work from home if I was a therapist and have patients come to my house. What if one of them was a bit ... you know ... psycho? They know where you live, the layout of the house. It's inviting trouble, isn't it?'

'Fingers crossed, she has a good security system.'

'I do. Thank you,' Linda Bellamy said upon opening the door. 'I also have a camera in my front door with a microphone so I can hear what's going on outside, should someone undesirable be lurking around.'

Linda Bellamy stood in the doorway, surrounded by a harsh yellow glow from within. She was tall and athletically built. Her shoulder-length blonde hair was thick and wavy. Her face was lined with a lifetime of experience, and she didn't try to hide it with make-up, apart from a touch of deep red to accentuate her full lips. She was wearing an oversized beige sweater and black trousers with black high-heeled shoes, dressing casual yet smart, despite being in her own home.

'Detective Sergeant Robinson,' Sian said, holding up her ID. 'This is DS Scott Andrews.'

Linda smiled warmly. 'Come on in. I've just brewed a pot of coffee. I thought you might want something to warm you up.'

'Thank you.'

They entered the brightly lit house and allowed the warmth to envelop them. The hallway was vast with a high ceiling and an impressive, and expensive, light fitting that drew the eye. The floor was black and white chequerboard tiles and Linda's heels clacked loudly on them as she led them to a room at the back of the house, passing a snug-looking living room and a brightly lit kitchen along the way.

'Beautiful home,' Sian said, marvelling at the décor.

'Thank you.'

'Have you lived here long?'

'Actually, no.'

The extended lounge had been turned into an office with a large dark oak desk to one side, behind which the wall was fitted with floor-to-ceiling shelves packed with textbooks. There was a burgundy Chesterfield sofa and matching armchair on the other side, an expensive coffee table between them, and more shelving on the opposite wall. Linda poured three coffees from an enamel pot into delicate matching china and asked them to help themselves to cream and sugar.

Linda sat elegantly on the armchair, crossed her legs and flicked back her hair with the back of her hand. She took a sip of her coffee and gave a satisfied smile.

'Before we begin, I'm sure you know, but I do need to say that I am bound by client confidentiality. I can't give you personal information I'm told during my sessions.'

'We're aware of that,' Sian said. 'This is delicious coffee, by the way.'

'Thank you. It's Kenyan. I'm guessing,' Linda said, crossing her legs the other way, 'you want to talk about my work within the prison service.' Sian nodded. 'And as you're from South Yorkshire Police I'm assuming it's about a prisoner from your neck of the woods.' She had a sweet smile on her lips.

'We'd like to talk to you about Steve Harrison,' Scott said.

'I thought it was him.' Her smile grew. 'That Netflix documentary has brought everyone out of the woodwork. You've no idea of the number of emails and phone calls I've received about him since it launched.'

'What have they said?'

She took a deep breath. 'Oh, all kinds of things. I've had women from as far away as South America telling me I need to work harder at getting him released. A woman from Canada asked me if I could arrange for her to be sent a sample of his semen so she could have his baby, and one woman from Spain threatened to set fire to my face if I tried to steal him from her. She was a particularly deluded case.' Linda said all this very matter-of-factly.

'Did you contact the police?' Sian frowned.

'Most of them get deleted. You can spot the rambling emails a mile away. The woman from Spain did cause me to take a step back. I contacted the local police and I'm in the process of taking out an injunction against her.'

'You seem very sanguine about it all,' Sian said.

'I've been in this job far too long to let people get to me in that way,' she smiled. 'Things have worsened since the rise of social media, but I find most people to be harmless in real life. It's easy for people to threaten you via a mobile phone, but meet them face-to-face and they soon crumble.' She smiled again.

'Have you met many of them face-to-face?' Scott asked.

'Oh yes.' She seemed to delight in admitting this. 'Call me a flawed human being if you like, but I do enjoy taking down a keyboard warrior with a few well-chosen words. Now, Steven Harrison,' she said, getting the detectives back to the point.

Sian took another sip of her delicious coffee and placed the cup carefully on the table. 'Obviously, I can't go into detail, but Steve's name has come up in an investigation and we'd like to know your professional opinion on his state of mind.'

'I'm assuming one of his many fans has broken the law,' she said.

'What do you know about his fans?' Scott asked. 'I mean, do any of them particularly stand out as being people we should know about?'

'Not really,' she said, picking a piece of barely visible fluff from her trousers and dropping it to the floor. 'There's an online petition calling for his release set up by a woman in Wyoming. The last time I checked it had more than thirty thousand signatures. I get monthly emails from a young woman in Illinois who writes as if she's his wife, asking what I'm doing to overturn such a scandalous miscarriage of justice.'

'Do you reply to them?'

'Most certainly not. Once you engage them in conversation, it's difficult to get rid of them. As I said, I delete the majority, but I save the odd one just in case they're needed at a later date.'

Sian looked around her. 'Don't you worry about them finding out where you live?'

'I have excellent security. I have a black belt in Brazilian Jiu Jitsu, in which I'm also an instructor. I have a panic button by my bed that goes straight to West Yorkshire Police and a private security firm here in Leeds, and there are cameras in every room recording twenty-four hours a day.'

'Remind me not to go to the toilet,' Scott said.

Linda let out a natural laugh. 'Well, not every room.'

'Tell me about Steve,' Sian said. 'As a professional, what do you make of him?'

Linda uncrossed and crossed her legs again. 'He's angry.'

'What at?'

'Most things. He has a highly inflated sense of self.'

'What does that mean?'

'He believes everyone is out to get him.'

'He's paranoid?'

'No. Sorry, I didn't mean it like that. He seriously objects to being in the Supermax wing, despite what he claims. I know for a fact all prisoners are treated the same, yet he believes that checks, or being forced to change cells, are all personal attacks on him.'

'That sounds like paranoia,' Scott said.

'In his case, he's putting himself at the centre of attention. It's placing himself in the middle of the action, whether he belongs there or not.'

'So he likes the focus to always be on him?'

'Yes.'

'That's dangerous, though, isn't it?'

'Absolutely, especially when the focus isn't on him. Fortunately, at the moment, we're in a period of calm due to the Netflix documentary.'

'And when the attention is off him, how does he react?' Sian asked.

'By doing something to draw the attention to him.'

Sian and Scott exchanged a glance.

'Something has happened, hasn't it?' Linda asked.

'It has. I'm afraid I can't say what at the moment,' Sian replied.

She nodded. 'This is what I don't like about the prison system. It's all wrong.'

'What do you mean?' Sian asked.

'Steven Harrison is in prison for life. He will never be released. Put yourself in that position for a moment. If you have no chance of getting out, what's the point in sticking to the rules of the prison, to the rules of law? He could kill a prison officer, his fellow prisoners, even me on one of my visits, yet nothing more will happen to him, because the maximum penalty has already been administered. If a prisoner has the possibility of being released at some point in the future, he has something to aim for, something to stick to the rules for.'

'Are you saying Steve Harrison should one day be released?' Scott asked.

'Yes. I am,' she stated firmly, looking Scott and Sian directly in the eye in turn. 'If a prisoner knows they will be released, then they will take part in therapy and rehabilitation in order to understand what they did was wrong and atone for their crimes.'

'Some people are plain evil,' Scott said, forcefully. 'Steve Harrison is one of them.'

'You believe in evil?' Linda asked.

'Yes. I've looked it dead in the eye.' Scott's voice was raised.

'Steven Harrison is not evil,' she said, the sweet smile back on her lips.

'He has killed so many people and delighted in it. I saw the look on his face as he tried to push me in the path of a speeding tram. I still have nightmares about it. He wanted to see me destroyed. He orchestrated a day of murder and carnage that Sheffield will forever be synonymous with. He is evil to the core.' Scott spoke with such venom in his voice. Sian held out her hand and placed it on his arm.

'You have a disturbing history with Steven, I'm aware of

that, and I'm sorry for what you've been through, but surely you, as a police officer, can understand the power of the prison service and what it can do for people.'

'Some, yes.'

'Some?'

'Steve Harrison will never atone for his crimes. He literally wants to watch the world burn.'

'If that's the case then what is the point of me?' Linda asked. 'Why do I go and visit him twice a month?'

'You tell me,' Scott said, adjusting himself on the sofa. He was clearly angry with the way this conversation was heading. 'I'm assuming you can't see every prisoner in Wakefield on your visits, so how do they work? Do the prisoners have to make appointments to see you?'

'Yes.'

'And there are a set number of appointments.'

'Yes.'

'And how often do you see Steve? Is it every visit?'

Linda hesitated before answering. 'Yes.'

'How long do these appointments last for?'

'Between forty-five minutes and an hour.'

'So, Steve comes in, sits down and for the best part of an hour he has a captive audience that listens to him talking about his crimes, his life, how he's feeling, what's going on inside his head. To him, that's not therapy, that's feeding his ego. He's loving the rapt attention he's got. He knows, at the back of his mind, that one day you're going to write a book, because people in your profession do, and since he's your most famous client, you'll mention him. That's what he's feeding on.'

Linda swallowed hard. Her face reddened slightly. The room fell silent, and a heavy atmosphere descended.

Sian cleared her throat. 'Can I ask, if your visits are part of the prison service, why is your name on a list of approved visitors? Surely you're not visiting him during regular visiting hours. That would be highly unethical, wouldn't it?'

Linda looked uncomfortable. She did the uncrossing and crossing of legs again. 'I was – "was" being the operative word – writing a book about Steven Harrison.'

'I knew it,' Scott interrupted.

'Why did you stop?'

'Lionel Miller beat me to it.'

'Did Steve tell you he was meeting with Lionel at the time he was meeting with you?' Scott asked.

'No,' she answered, reluctantly.

'So he was playing you off each other, working out which one of you was offering the best deal to write the book.'

'It appeared so.'

'That's exactly what I was talking about. Steve Harrison is rotten to the core. How can you not see that?' Scott exclaimed.

'I believe in the fundamental principle of reform. If Steven knew, when he was first sentenced, that there was a possibility of being released one day, based on his good behaviour while in prison, he would not partake in these mind games he enjoys.'

'Now who's deluded?' Scott said under his breath.

'I beg your pardon?' Linda said, angrily.

'Perhaps we can put aside our own personal views on Steve,' Sian said, holding her hands up as if having to referee between the two. 'Does Steve mention Matilda Darke at all?'

It was a while before Linda answered. She refused to take her steely stare from Scott. 'Yes. She's the main focus of his ire.'

'Why?'

'I'm not at liberty to say.'

'Why not?'

'What we discuss within the confines of our sessions is confidential.'

'If you believe Steve was plotting something, something that could put someone else's life in danger, you'd tell the prison authorities or the police, wouldn't you?' Sian asked.

'Of course.'

'And he hasn't?'

'Well, obviously not or you would know about it.' There was a smile on her lips again.

'You spoke to Lionel Miller when he was writing his book, *The Hangman's Hold*, and you featured in the recent Netflix documentary about him,' Scott said.

'That's correct.'

'Yet you've told us you're not at liberty to answer questions about what you discuss. You seemed more than capable of answering questions from Lionel Miller while he was researching his book, and from the good people at Netflix.'

Linda didn't say anything. She simply stared at Scott, shooting him a daggered look.

'I'm guessing if we offered to pay you for your time, you'd be more open with us,' Scott continued.

'Are you accusing me of compromising my ethics?'

'I'm accusing you of playing fast and loose with the Hippocratic oath when it comes to answering questions you don't want to answer,' Scott said.

'You're asking me to divulge information told to me in confidence. I'm not able to do that. And I have never done that. I helped Lionel Miller when it came to the more intrinsic elements of Steven's make-up, and I more or less repeated it word for word in the Netflix documentary.'

'Steve holds a grudge against Matilda Darke, doesn't he?' Sian asked.

'He does.'

'Has he told you why?'

'He has.'

'Are you allowed to tell us?'

'He blames her for his failings. He believes she stopped him at every turn from achieving his potential.'

'Do you believe that?'

'My beliefs are not important.'

'But surely you can see DCI Darke did not turn Steve Harrison into a killer, that it was his own decision to kill those people,' Sian said.

It was a long moment before Linda replied. 'Yes. Yes, I can.'

'So surely your role is to try to get Steve to see that he alone is to blame for his actions.'

'Blame is not something we discuss.'

'Blame is obvious,' Sian almost snapped.

'Steven's guilt isn't in question here,' Linda said.

'No. It's not. But how can he hold onto a grudge against DCI Darke all this time when there's no reason behind it?'

'To Steven, there is a reason behind it.'

'To everyone else in the world, it's obvious that there isn't. Surely it's your job to make Steve see that, too.'

'My job is to talk to Steven about whatever he wants to talk about.'

'But when he's ranting and raving about Matilda Darke, you should be putting him right, trying to help him to let go of what he's holding onto. He's going to be in prison for a very long time. It won't do him any good keeping everything bottled up.'

'If that's what works for him.'

'But it's not working for him, is it?' Sian spat. 'He's still trying to make Matilda pay for what he believes she's responsible for. Are you sure you're qualified?'

'Sergeant Robinson, I will not sit here …'

'Look,' Scott interrupted, 'I think we're allowing our emotions to get the better of us here. I know I am, and I apologise.' He took a deep breath. 'Linda, DCI Darke has been kidnapped. The woman who took her is working with Steve Harrison. We believe she's called Amy Monroe. Have you heard of her?'

Linda's face blanked. 'No,' she eventually replied.

'Has Steve ever mentioned her?'

'No.'

'Has Steve ever spoken about arranging for DCI Darke to be kidnapped?'

'No.'

'Do you have anything you can tell us that may help us in locating DCI Darke?'

She looked away as she thought. 'I'm sorry, I don't. I only wish I did.'

Scott fished in his pocket for his card. 'If you do think of anything, would you please let me know?' He handed it to her.

'Of course,' she said, taking it from him.

'I know I don't need to tell you this, but I'm going to say it anyway to make it clear. I would very much appreciate it if you didn't tell anyone, and by that I mean Steve, about this conversation.'

Linda pursed her lips as if she was tasting something nasty. 'You're right. You didn't need to tell me that.' She looked at Scott and Sian in turn. 'I am genuinely sorry. I had no idea he was planning anything. If I did, of course I would have told you. I really am genuinely distressed,' she said, a hand on her chest.

'Bollocks she is,' Sian said as they made their way down the drive to the car. 'She's lying.'

'Why do you think that?' Scott asked.

Sian opened the front passenger door and climbed in. 'Everyone called him Steve. We all, at work, called him Steve. Even Faith called him Steve when she was going out with him. Linda called him Steven. The only other person who calls him Steven is his aunt, Janet Crowther. For Linda to call him it as well shows that she has more than a professional connection to him.'

Scott frowned. 'You think she might have feelings for him?'

'Knowing Steve, I think he's allowed her to have feelings for him so he can exploit them.'

'You think she's involved?'

'I'm not sure about that, but she knows far more than she's letting on.'

'So, how do we find out?' Scott asked, starting the car and pulling away from the house.

'By being as devious and as dodgy as she and her beloved Steven are.'

Chapter Thirty-Five

A dele felt drained. She'd had a long day at work performing autopsies on three people who'd died from illnesses relating to Covid-19, she'd written two reports that were long overdue, she'd ignored two emails from her editor asking her, yet again, if she'd managed to go over the proofs of her part of the book she was writing with Simon Browes, and she'd tried to make a complete skeleton out of a selection of bones found at Wigtwizzle. All that while, she was still preoccupied with the whereabouts of her best friend. The last thing she wanted when she pulled up outside the farmhouse she shared with Matilda was more drama, but she hadn't been in the house for a minute before her mobile burst into life. She looked at the screen and saw it was Matilda's mother, Penny, calling.

She swiped to answer and listened as Penny cried and begged to know where her eldest daughter was. There were long, awkward silences when neither of them knew what to say. Penny repeatedly said that she hated her daughter being a detective. It was more than an hour before Adele was able to get her off the phone, promising to call her the second she heard anything.

Sitting in the living room, surrounded by silence, Adele realised she was still wearing her coat and shoes. She kicked off the shoes, threw her coat over the back of the sofa and lit the wood burner.

She was numb. She wasn't cold or warm. She was hungry but couldn't face eating. She was tired but knew she wouldn't sleep. She had to do something.

The silence was disturbing. It seemed strange to be in this house on her own. How Matilda had managed it before Adele moved in was beyond her. She hated the lack of life in the vast house. It was too big for just the two of them. When there was only one of them at home, it was cavernous and frightening.

Adele was in the kitchen, pouring a large glass of white wine, when the doorbell rang.

Her heart sank. Something told her this was going to be bad news. She decided to ignore it, or at least put off answering for as long as possible. It might be avoiding the inevitable, but ignorance was bliss, if only for a few seconds.

The doorbell rang again, followed by a knock on the door.

Adele had no choice but to answer. She hadn't put her Porsche in the garage, so whoever was visiting would know she was in.

She opened the door to find Sian on the doorstep, wrapped up in layers against the harsh January night. Her coat was buttoned up beneath her chin and she had a beanie hat pulled down low.

'Anything?' Adele asked.

Sian shook her head. 'Can I come in?'

Adele stepped back and Sian entered. She headed straight for the living room and stood in front of the roaring fire to try and thaw herself out.

'How's your day been?' Adele asked.

'Pretty shit. It is all connected to Steve. Finn and Tom went out to Wakefield Prison. Steve told them the kidnapper was wearing a camera and he was watching a live feed from his cell.'

'Oh my God.' Adele sank onto the sofa. When she looked up, she had tears in her eyes. 'I thought Steve was in a Supermax wing? How can he have arranged to have Matilda kidnapped? How can he have been watching a live streaming of it, for crying out loud? I don't understand.'

'The prison is investigating, and so are we. Knowing Steve, he'll have managed to get someone on his side. There's a woman we're trying to track down called Amy Monroe, but she doesn't seem to exist.'

'Matilda's dead, isn't she?' Adele asked. 'If Steve's involved then this can only be about killing Matilda.'

Sian's bottom lip began to wobble. Tears fell and she didn't wipe them away. 'Can I have a drink?' she asked once she'd managed to compose herself enough to speak.

'Sorry. Yes. Sure,' Adele said. She pulled herself up from the sofa and went into the kitchen.

Sian followed.

Adele poured a glass of wine for Sian and topped up her own, despite it being still half full. She stopped mid-pour.

'Wait a minute, if Steve was able to watch a live streaming of the kidnapping, he's going to want to see her being killed, too. That's what he'll get his thrill from. Providing he hasn't seen it already, then he's going to want to make sure he's in a position to watch it. Isn't there anything you can do to find out who at the prison is involved? There has to be someone on the inside.' Adele handed Sian her glass of wine.

Sian took a sip, followed by a second larger gulp. 'That's what we are doing. The thing is, he's very clever. And there are very few people around him. I don't know how he's been able to manipulate someone like this.'

'How can someone be so evil?'

'According to Linda Bellamy, evil doesn't exist.'

'Who's she?'

'Trust me, you don't want to know.' Sian pulled out a chair at the table and slumped into it. 'I don't know what's worse, someone who is evil and blatant with it, or someone snide and secretive.' Sian took another large gulp of wine. 'I'm going to see Stuart tomorrow.'

'Really?'

She nodded.

'Is this to do with the bones found at Wigtwizzle?'

She nodded again.

'How do you feel about seeing him?'

Tears rolled down Sian's face. 'I don't want to go.'

'Oh, Sian.' Adele put her glass down on the table and went over to her, pulling her into a tight embrace.

'I promised myself I wouldn't see him. I said I wanted nothing more to do with him.'

'Then don't go. Nobody can make you do anything you don't want to do.'

'I know that. It's just ... this job. You think you're good at what you do, that you can understand the criminal mind and catch the killers, but he lied to me, Adele. He lied and he lied and he lied for our entire married life. I slept with a serial killer for more than twenty-five years and I didn't know about it. And I should have done.'

'Nobody could have known, Sian. You've got to stop blaming yourself.' Adele handed her a sheet of kitchen roll.

She blew her nose. 'I'm trying to move on. I've had my offer accepted on the new house. I've changed my name, for fuck's sake. Yet, it keeps coming back. It will always keep coming back to remind me.'

Adele went around to the opposite side of the table and sat down. She didn't know what to say. The silence was heavy and the sound of a clock ticking in the living room was loud even in the kitchen.

'Do you want to hear something to take your mind off things for a bit?'

Sian looked up. 'Go on.'

'I slept with Simon last night,' Adele said, a smile forming on her lips.

'Really?' Sian's eyes twinkled.

'I thought that would pique your interest.'

'Slept as in slept or …?'

'Let's just say there was very little sleeping involved,' Adele said, almost grinning.

'Was it the first time?'

Adele nodded. 'We've been taking things slow. You know what he's like. He takes shyness and awkwardness to the next level.'

'So, how did it come about then?'

'He came over to see how I was. He stood on the doorstep trying to find the right words and I just thought, screw it. I was numb and wasn't in the mood to talk, I needed to actually feel something. So I grabbed his hand and took him upstairs.'

Sian grinned. 'Adele Kean, you big old tart.'

'Less of the big. And the old.'

'You don't mind being called a tart?'

'Only because it's been such a long time since I had anyone to be a tart with.'

'So, go on then, what's he like in bed?'

Adele picked up the bottle of wine and refilled both their glasses. 'I must admit that I expected him to be a bit ...'

'Boring,' Sian added.

'Yes. I wasn't actually looking forward to our first time together, as I imagined it would be over rather quickly.'

'And it wasn't?'

'Sian, he went on for hours.'

'Really?' she exclaimed.

'I haven't known passion like that since I was eighteen and me and Robson ... well, you don't need to know about that.' Adele blushed. 'He was sensitive, he was rough, he was just a complete animal.'

'We are talking about Simon Browes here, aren't we?' Sian asked.

'I know. I was as surprised as you are. I didn't think he had it in him. He's so meek, but last night ... bloody hell!'

'You'll be repeating the experience then?'

'I bloody hope so.'

Sian drained her glass. 'Is he ... you know ... fully equipped?'

Adele gave her a cheeky smile. 'Let's just say, when I got up this morning, it was an hour before I stopped walking like John Wayne.'

They both burst into laughter. It was what they both needed. For a few minutes they could forget the horror they were living in and relax.

When Sian left, Adele threw something into the microwave and ate it at the kitchen table. It had no taste. She looked down at the plastic tub and couldn't decipher what it was supposed to be. She couldn't finish it so threw it in the bin and went back to the wine.

Everywhere Adele went throughout the house she felt the emptiness left by Matilda. It was the unknown that was the scariest part. Where the bloody hell was she? Was she even still alive?

The pain Adele was feeling was too much. She felt sick. She picked up another bottle of wine and dragged herself upstairs to bed. She knew there was no chance of her falling asleep while her mind was so full, but hopefully she could pass out in a drunken stupor.

Then her phone started ringing. It made her jump. She was struggling to take her jumper off. She looked at the screen and saw it was Pat Campbell calling. She swiped to answer.

'Oh God, I've just realised how late it is. I didn't wake you, did I?' Pat asked by way of a greeting.

'No. I was … I was just getting ready for bed, actually,' Adele said, running her hands through her knotted hair.

'How much have you had to drink?'

'What are you talking about?'

'Your voice is slow and you're slurring your words. Has there been any news?'

'No. Nothing. It's like she's vanished into thin air.'

'Getting pissed won't help, Adele.'

'I know, but it numbs the pain.'

'Only temporarily.'

'Look, I'm sorry, Pat, but I'm not in the mood for a lecture right now. I just want to dive under the duvet and try to blank everything out for a few hours.'

'Sorry. I wanted to see how you were coping. If there was anything I could do.'

Adele swallowed her emotion. She was crying, but so far her tears had fallen in silence. It wouldn't be long before she was audibly sobbing, and she didn't want anyone to hear that.

'I don't think so.'

'How's the investigation going?'

'Slowly. They know Steve is definitely involved, but he's hardly likely to volunteer information to them, is he? Oh, wait, Sian said they're trying to trace someone ... can't remember her name ... I think she said Marilyn Monroe.'

'Wow. You really have had a lot to drink. I think you'll find she's been dead for quite some time,' Pat said, a hint of humour in her voice.

'No. Sorry. It was, urgh, what was it?' Adele pulled at her hair to force herself to focus. 'Amy, I think she said. Amy Monroe.'

'Huh,' Pat said.

'What is it?'

'No. A light went on in my head, momentarily.'

'You know her?'

'I ... the name sounds familiar,' Pat said.

'Who is she?'

'I don't know. I know I've heard that name before, though. Look, Adele, leave it with me. I'll have a think. Promise me you'll stop drinking now and get some sleep.'

'I will.'

'Good. I'll call you tomorrow.'

Adele ended the call. She was sure between them all – Christian, Sian, Scott, Pat – they could get the better of Steve and work out what had happened to Matilda. The only worry was getting to her before it was too late.

Adele reached for the bottle of wine on the bedside table. She might as well finish the bottle, now it was open.

Chapter Thirty-Six

D anny Hanson entered his flat quickly, slammed the door behind him and bolted it at the top and bottom. He'd had a nightmare of an afternoon and having his life threatened was not something he was going to forget in a while. He loved being a journalist, but there were some stories that he simply didn't have the stomach for.

He threw a frozen pizza into the oven and cracked open a can of lager, swigging half of it in a single gulp, then flopped onto the sofa to take stock of the events of the day. He really needed to talk to Matilda Darke. Despite everything they'd been through, he knew she would listen to him. Why couldn't he get to her? There was something else going on here that he wasn't being told, and he had no idea how he could find it out.

He dialled the automated press line at South Yorkshire Police again. There was no mention of the bones being discovered at Wigtwizzle, just a few burglaries, car thefts and drug arrests. None of them interested him. Why were South Yorkshire Police all of a sudden being selective about what they told the media? Surely, after everything regarding the historical child sex abuse, they'd realise they'd eventually be revealed as not having been open with the public? The question was, what were they covering up this time around? Was it connected to the sex abuse scandal? If so, he had a right to know. He was writing a book about it, after all. Or was there more to the bones being discovered at Wigtwizzle than they wanted him to think? As he racked his brain, he still kept going back to Matilda Darke. The unearthing of bones, especially when one of them had been identified as being linked to one of her former cases, was something she'd be involved in.

The oven timer rang. His pizza was ready. He took it out of the oven, cut it into six pieces with a very blunt pizza wheel and took it into the living room. He balanced the plate on his lap and ate with one hand while scrolling through his phone with the other. There had to be someone within his contacts who could give him a more accurate picture of life within South Yorkshire Police right now. He smiled to himself when he reached Scott Andrews's number.

'Scott, it's Danny Hanson. How are you?'

There was a sigh from the other end. A noise Danny was used to hearing.

'I'm fine, thanks, Danny. What can I do for you?'

'I was just wondering how you are?'

'Like I said. I'm fine.'

'Stab wound all healed?'

'What are you talking about?'

'I was told you were admitted to the Northern General with a stab wound.'

'Were you?'

'What happened?'

'Nothing for you to know about, Danny.'

'A domestic?'

'Sorry?'

'Was it a domestic incident between you and … what's he called? Tall bloke who works with Adele. Irish.'

'I know who you mean and no, it wasn't.'

'So, what happened then?'

'That's my business.'

'And Matilda's,' Danny said.

'What?'

'Well, it happened in her house so it's her business too.'

Scott didn't say anything.

'How is Matilda?'

'Why?'

'I haven't been able to get in touch with her. The thing is, Scott, there is something really important I need to talk to her about.'

'Is there?'

'Yes. And she's proving to be very elusive.'

'She's … she's busy. She's very busy, Danny. We're all incredibly busy right now.'

'I was just …'

'I need to go now, Danny. Goodbye,' Scott said, ending the call.

Danny tore another bite out of a slice of pizza and chewed nosily with his mouth open. He thought over the conversation with Scott. He hadn't been able to glean anything from it. Scott was keeping very tight-lipped about the stabbing. He'd seen far too much blood in Matilda's hallway for it to be a simple domestic incident. A crime had been committed at Matilda's house. He was sure of it. Unless … was it Matilda's blood?

He scrolled through his contacts again and selected a number.

'Jason, it's Danny Hanson. How are things?' Danny asked the nurse at the Northern General Hospital.

'Fine, thanks, Danny. Just on my break. How are you?'

'I'm good. Listen, thanks for the information regarding that detective sergeant who was stabbed. Big help.'

'You're welcome.'

'Have you had any more police officers brought in recently?'

'Yes, actually. There was one in tonight. A PC was elbowed in the face. His nose is in a right state.'

'Ouch. I'm looking for someone of a higher rank. And female.'

'Not that I'm aware of.'

'You've not heard of a DCI Matilda Darke?'

'Matilda Darke?' Jason asked. 'Yes, actually, I've heard the name mentioned. When that woman detective was speaking to DS Andrews, the red-haired woman ...'

'DS Sian Robinson.'

'That's her. I was lingering outside the door. She said they needed to find Matilda as quickly as possible, and Scott needed to think long and hard about what happened at her house.'

Danny scratched his forehead. 'They needed to find Matilda?'

'Yes.'

'What does that mean?'

'No idea, mate. You're the journalist.'

'Did you hear anything else?'

'Nothing I could make a coherent sentence out of, but that red-haired detective looked like she had the weight of the world on her shoulders. She was seriously worried about something.'

'Interesting. Thanks, Jason.'

'No worries.'

Danny ended the call. He sat in silence, a slice of pizza in mid-air, halfway to his open mouth. Was it possible? No, it couldn't be. Or could it? Was Matilda Darke a missing person?

Chapter Thirty-Seven

M atilda was lying on the bed. She was so cold, but it wasn't the kind of cold where adding an extra blanket or putting on a thicker jumper would warm her up; this ran deeper. Her bones felt cold. The damp from this subterranean cell had leached into her, mixed with the horror and the fear and the unknown. Matilda was starting to suffer.

She had no idea what time it was, whether it was morning or night. She didn't even know what day it was, or how long she'd been here. Sometimes it felt like only a few hours, other times it felt like she'd been here for weeks. Her mind was playing tricks on her. It was all over the place. Was this a cold turkey effect from her sudden medication withdrawal or was it a psychological effect of all her senses being cut off?

She felt a presence in the room with her.

Her eyes widened.

She wasn't alone.

Slowly, she eased herself further up the bed, the frame creaking under her weight. She sat up and tried to make out the figure by the door in the darkness.

'Dad?' she asked.

He stepped forward into the small chink of light from the tiny window above the door.

Matilda started to cry. During the shooting in 2019, Steve Harrison had manipulated his brother Jake to kill her. When he'd failed and she'd been injured at the police station, she was taken to the hospital for emergency surgery. When news of Matilda's survival hit the media, Jake headed straight for the hospital to finish the job. It ended with her father, Frank, being killed in a stand-off between Jake and armed police. All this happened within a few feet of Matilda lying in a hospital bed in a coma, unaware of her father's murder.

Matilda loved her parents, but she was closer to her dad. He was the one she always turned to, and after the death of her husband he was there for her in a way her mother wasn't. She needed to cry, to scream, to wail, to mourn. Frank allowed her to do all that. Penny was from the school of tough love and urged Matilda to get back on her feet and out into the world. She missed her dad. She missed his hugs.

He sat down on the edge of the bed and took his daughter's hands in his. They felt warm and soft. Matilda began to cry.

'What are you doing here?' she asked.

'I've come for a chat,' he smiled. 'I thought you could do with seeing a friendly face.'

She wiped a tear away. 'I don't know what to do, Dad. I'm scared.'

'That's not like you.'

'I don't know what's going on. I can't ... I can't get my head around any of this.'

'Yes, you can.' He leaned forward, wiped a tear away with his thumb, then ran his hand over her hair, smoothing it down, comforting her. 'You're an intelligent woman. You're a fighter.'

'I used to be.'

'You still are.'

'The more that happens to me, the less fight I have. I cry all the time. I never used to before James died, before the shooting, before I lost … you.'

'There's nothing wrong with crying. It's not a sign of weakness, you know. It's a way of letting out the emotion you're building up inside. Releasing that keeps you alive, keeps you strong. You can still fight and shed a few tears.'

'I really don't think I have any fight left in me,' she said.

'So what's the alternative? You use the noose like she told you to?'

'No,' Matilda replied quickly.

'Then you fight.'

'How?'

'Matilda.' Frank placed his hands on either side of Matilda's face. She smiled at the warmth. 'I've told you this so many times I'm surprised it's not chiselled on my gravestone. You are a fighter. You're the best woman I know, and I'm including your mother in that. You're brave, you're intelligent, you can do literally anything in the world if you put your mind to it. I know you're not in the best situation right now but being in here has limited your options to two – you either use the noose, or you fight. What's it to be?'

'I'm not using the noose,' she said.

'So?'

She looked her dad in the eye. 'I fight.'

'Atta girl.'

'How?'

'You tell me.'

'The only way I can think of is trying to get whoever is on

the other side of the door to talk to me so I can somehow get her to let her guard down.'

'Then that's what you have to do.'

'What if I fail?'

'F... F...' He struggled to say the word, which made Matilda smile. 'That is not a word in the Doyle vocabulary.'

'I'm a Darke.'

'James didn't know the meaning of the word either. Besides, your DNA is Doyle, and Doyles fight back until the bitter end.'

She nodded. 'You're right.'

'Of course I'm right. I'm a Doyle.'

She looked down and thought for a moment. When she looked back up, her father was gone, and a wave of emotion swept over her.

'I miss you so much,' she said to herself, her voice breaking.

She wiped her tears away with the backs of her hands, took a few deep breaths and climbed up off the bed.

'You're right about one thing, though, Dad. I'm a fighter. And there's no way I'm letting that bitch out there think I'm just going to roll over and take the easy way out.'

She grabbed the noose and yanked on it hard. It took a few attempts, but the hook came out of the ceiling and clattered to the floor.

Matilda stood back and smiled. She went over to the door and banged on it hard with her fist.

'I have no intention of using this noose,' she shouted. 'Do you hear me? Are you still out there? If you want me dead, you'll have to do it yourself with your bare hands.'

She went back over to the bed and sat down. 'And the moment you come in,' she said to herself, 'I'm going to fucking kill you first.'

Chapter Thirty-Eight

Friday 22nd January 2021

DS Sian Robinson was sitting on the end of her bed in the master bedroom of her tiny home in Woodseats. 'Master bedroom' was a slight overstatement. There was a double bed in it, a single bedside cabinet and a tallboy. There wasn't room for anything else and if you wanted to get to the window, you had to crawl over the bed. She couldn't wait to leave this shitty house.

A mirror was propped up on the radiator and she was attempting to put on some make-up in the dim light.

There was a tap on the door.

'Are you decent?' Belinda asked from the outside.

'I haven't been decent since before I had Anthony,' Sian said.

Belinda pushed open the door and came in. 'Wow, way to make us wish we'd never been born.'

Sian smiled at her only daughter in the mirror.

'How are you feeling?' Belinda asked, sitting down next to her.

'Nervous. Do I look all right?'

Belinda looked her up and down and took in the navy trousers, white shirt and navy jacket. Her face remained blank. 'You look … fine.'

'Fine?'

Belinda pulled a face. 'Actually, you look like you're going for a job interview as an accountant,' she said.

'These trousers are too tight,' Sian said, pulling at the waistband.

'Here's a question: what do you want Stuart to think when he looks at you? Do you want him to regret what he's done, realise what he's missed? Do you want him to see that you're confident and sexy without him? Do you want to rub his nose in how well you're doing on your own?'

'All of the above,' Sian said after a thought.

'Then change. Because all that outfit says is, "I'm going to be giving you some bad news about your VAT."'

'I don't have anything that says confident and sexy. I dress for comfort.'

'You're a single woman. You're not even fifty yet. You should dress like a cougar.'

'I've had four kids. There's nothing cougar about me.'

'Do you want to borrow my DKNY shirt?'

'Thanks, Belinda, but you're about three foot taller than me.'

'No. Trust me on this. That shirt, a pair of black trousers, those good heels you've got and my padded bra.'

Sian laughed. 'I'm not wearing a padded bra. I think your father knows what my breasts look like.'

'Mum, please, let me dress you.'

Reluctantly, Sian agreed. 'Okay, but please remember I'm going to Wakefield Prison, not an underground nightclub in Amsterdam.'

———————

There were delays on the M1 so it took Sian more than an hour to get to Wakefield Prison. Christian had texted her twice that morning asking if she wanted him to go with her, and he called her while she was halfway up the motorway, repeating his request.

'I'll be fine, Christian, honestly. I'm just visiting a prisoner, that's all.'

'A prisoner you used to be married to.'

'You don't need to remind me of that,' she said, catching a glimpse of the third finger on her left hand, naked since she took off the wedding ring, and seeing the ghost of a dent still there, taunting her.

'Are you all right?'

'I'm ... fine,' she said. A very unconvincing lie. 'Any news?'

'Not yet. I'm going to have a quick chat with Ridley, then we'll begin the briefing. Has Danny Hanson been in touch?'

'Yes. He called before eight o'clock. I let it go to voicemail. He would like an update.'

'I bet he does.'

'I'll come straight back to the station once I'm finished here.'

'Good luck.'

'Thanks.'

I bloody need it, she said to herself.

———————

Belinda was right, the outfit did give Sian confidence. She walked across the car park with her head high and her back straight. That might have had something to do with the tight bra she was wearing, but she felt good, positive, strong, independent. She wondered if this was how Beyoncé felt every day, as she strode along, making sure she didn't trip herself up.

She went through all the security checks, handing over her mobile phone and ID card, which were placed in a locker. She had a security wand waved over her and turned out her pockets. She was informed of all the health and safety procedures and told what to do in the event of a fire alarm. The file she was carrying, containing photographs of the dead she wanted to show Stuart, was scrutinised and verified by a second member of staff before being handed back to her. Then a female officer escorted her from the safety of the office and into the main prison itself. The atmosphere changed in an instant and her stomach fell through the floor.

'How … how is Stuart?' Sian asked, reluctantly.

'He's a model prisoner,' the officer said, not looking back. They were walking in single file along a narrow corridor. 'He takes orders and does his work. Never been any bother.'

'What work does he do?'

'He's in the library.'

This surprised Sian. She'd never known him to read a book except when they went on holiday and that was only to calm his nerves on the plane.

'Does he enjoy it?'

The officer looked back, a questioning look on her face. 'I've no idea. Does it matter?'

'I suppose not.'

They came to the room prisoners used for private conversations with their solicitors.

'Okay, you'll be separated by a screen. There'll be just you and him in the room, but, like I said, there's thick glass between the two of you. He's not dangerous so I don't think you're under any kind of threat, but it's there for your protection.'

Sian looked up at her. 'I was married to the man for more than twenty-five years. I'm pretty sure I can handle him.'

The officer's face dropped. 'Oh my God, you're the wife?'

'In the flesh.'

'He never stops talking about you.'

'Oh.'

'You look loads younger than your photographs.'

Sian smiled and inwardly thanked her daughter for doing her make-up.

'I'll be out here when you've finished to escort you back.'

'Thank you.'

Sian opened the door and went inside. She examined the glass. She'd been in rooms like this many times in her career and had felt no nerves or tension, but this was different. This was new. The man who would be sitting opposite her was her ex-husband. This was a scenario she never thought she'd be in.

The door on the other side of the room opened and Sian's mouth fell open. For some reason, she expected Stuart to look exactly the same as he did the last time she saw him, at the police station on the day he gave his statement. Christian had told her he'd changed, and she was aware of how much people altered in prison, but the transformation in the man she'd loved and adored for more than twenty-five years was shocking. The gentle giant of a man with a rugby player's build, big arms, big legs and friendly smile was gone. He'd lost a great deal of weight, and it wasn't a good look. His head was shaved to the scalp, his eyes had dark circles around them, his cheeks were sunken. He looked ill.

When he saw her, he smiled, and that accentuated the amount of weight he'd lost, as when he smiled he was all teeth. The chubby cheeks were gone. The twinkle in the eyes had died. This was not the Stuart Mills she'd fallen in love with. This was a shadow of a man she thought she knew. This was a complete stranger.

'Hello, Sian. It's good to see you,' he said in his soft voice.

She couldn't speak. She had no idea what to say.

'You look … well, you look good,' he said. 'Very good, in fact.'

She gave him a pained smile.

'How are you?' he asked.

She didn't answer.

'I look a bit different from when you last saw me, don't I?'

She nodded, and bit back the urge to cry.

'It's certainly not a health farm they're running in here. The food's a bit, well, it's not good. Not a patch on anything you made,' he smiled. 'How are the kids?'

Sian looked away. She'd been transfixed by his transformation, and now she remembered why she was here. The man had murdered eight people. Those hands, those once big hands, had stolen the life of eight defenceless people. That was unforgivable. She had nothing to say to this man. She felt so conflicted right now.

Her mouth had dried. She swallowed hard. She opened the file. 'Stuart, you know why I'm here. DI Brady from South Yorkshire Police has told you about the body of a woman found in woods on the outskirts of Sheffield. We've now identified her as Jackie Barclay. She was a known sex worker and disappeared in April 2018—'

'Sian,' Stuart interrupted.

'Since DI Brady came to see you, two further bodies have been found close to where Jackie's body was discovered. They've been identified as Caroline Richardson, also a sex worker, who has been missing since June 2018, and Duncan McNally, a homeless man. We have no record of him as a missing person. Can you tell us anything about these people?' She could feel her words shaking as they left her lips. She looked beyond Stuart, at the wall behind him. 'Do you know these people?' She held up each of the three photographs in turn.

'Sian, can't we talk?'

She swallowed again. She could feel the tears building up inside her. 'I've nothing to say to you,' she said, her voice shaking with emotion.

He placed his hand on the glass. 'Sian, please, I'm sorry. I know it doesn't mean anything, but there isn't a day goes by without me regretting what I did, what I put you and the kids through. I … I can't explain it. I really am so sorry.' A tear rolled down his face.

'Did you kill those people?' she asked, looking him directly in the eye.

'I didn't kill any men. You know that.'

'Dermot Salter,' she said, reminding him of his only male victim. A lonely man who visited the sex workers to keep an eye on them, make sure they were safe and well and provide them with hot drinks during the cold weather.

Stuart looked down. He obviously didn't like to be reminded of his crimes, of the names of the people he killed.

Sian tried to clear her throat. She could really do with a drink of water right now. Or maybe a strong brandy. 'Jackie

Barclay. Caroline Richardson. Do those names ring a bell with you?'

'No.'

'Monica Yates is still missing. Did you kill her, too?'

'No. When I gave my statement to Christian, I told him everything. I told him the truth.'

'You killed so many people,' she said, her voice quiet, struggling to hold onto her emotions.

'I'm sorry,' he cried.

Sian shook her head. 'You have destroyed everything,' she spat. 'How am I supposed to trust anyone now? How am I supposed to believe anything anyone tells me ever again after what you did? You've killed me, Stuart. I'm dead inside. You've done that. You've fucking destroyed me.'

She grabbed the file and stood up.

'Sian, don't. Please. Come back.'

She banged on the door for it to be opened.

'Sian! Please! Don't go!' Stuart screamed. 'I love you, Sian. I love you so much.'

Sian practically fell out of the room into the corridor. The officer pulled the door closed behind her.

'Are you all right?' she asked.

'No. I'm not.'

Stuart wasn't in the mood to go back to work after his meet with Sian. But a job in prison wasn't like on the outside where you could call in sick or with a dodgy excuse if you didn't want to go. You literally had to be dead to get out of work.

He'd been looking forward to seeing Sian again. He didn't expect her to welcome him with open arms, but he didn't think she'd still be so full of vitriol. He knew he'd hurt her and destroyed what they had, but she was genuinely in pain. He'd caused that. He felt sick. Every single night, as he lay on his uncomfortable single bed, his mind went over everything he'd had and how he'd systematically destroyed it. Why? Why had he done that? He'd tried asking Linda Bellamy and she'd offered many reasons why his safe existence hadn't been enough, but they didn't ring true to him. That wasn't the answer. He doubted he'd ever know the truth. All he knew was that he was so very very sorry. For everything.

Stuart was sitting at a table in the library, cataloguing a new delivery of books on to the system, when the door opened and Steve Harrison walked in with a prison guard standing close by. He knew of Steve from the outside. They'd never met, but he'd heard about him through Sian. He'd killed her colleagues, her friends. Steve caused her just as much distress as he did, and he hated him for it. Seeing him on the inside, the swagger, the sneer, he hated him more.

'Good afternoon, Mr Mills,' Steve said in a faux-friendly voice. 'I've brought my books back. How are you today?'

'Fine. Thank you,' Stuart said, not looking up at him. He took the books from him and began to check them back in on the computer.

Steve leaned forward. 'I heard you had a visit from the wife today.' Now Stuart did look up. 'How is Sian? I did enjoy working with her.'

'You never worked with her.'

'No. Not directly, but it was fun seeing the look on her face when I punched her in the mouth.' He laughed. 'My God, she went down like a sack of shit. I hope she didn't suffer any permanent scarring. She's a very good-looking woman. Love a redhead. Love an older woman. I often wondered what it would have been like to fuck her. You know, really fuck her hard.'

Stuart tried not to rise to Steve's bait, but it wasn't easy.

Steve leaned even closer. Their noses almost touching. 'Tell me, Stuart, is Sian a true redhead?'

'I'm not listening to you, Steve.'

'I'm only joking with you, Stuart. Fuck's sake, lighten up. So, what did *ex*-wifey have to say?'

'Nothing.'

'Did she mention Matilda?'

'No. She didn't.' Stuart got up from the desk and went to put Steve's books back on the shelves.

Steve followed. 'Really? She didn't mention me at all?'

'Not everything is about you, Steve.'

'Oh, this is. Believe me.'

Stuart stopped and turned to look at Steve. He towered over him. 'Your name, and Matilda's name, didn't come up once. This was a completely different matter.'

'Huh. Strange.'

'Why?'

Steve lowered his voice. 'Matilda's missing. I'm expecting news of her death any day now. I'm so excited.' He grinned.

'Matilda's missing?'

Steve nodded. His smile was so wide. His excitement was palpable.

'How did you manage that?'

'I have my ways.'

'You're going to have her killed?'

'Oh yes.'

Stuart looked over Steve's head at the guard who brought Steve in. He was by the closed door, staring straight ahead, though it was obvious he was listening to what they were saying.

'How?'

'I won't go into details, obviously,' Steve said. 'But your pretty little wife is going to be searching for her for a very long time. Now, here's the best bit, they're never going to find her.'

'Why not?'

Steve winked. 'Because there'll be nothing left to find.'

Chapter Thirty-Nine

S ian's snack drawer was removed from her desk and a space made for it next to the drinks station, for anyone needing a sugar rush or just something to nibble on as they worked. The only proviso was that you replaced it with something equally calorific. However, during times of crisis or stress or emergency, or simply because it was a workday, the rules went out of the window, and anyone could help themselves.

Finn made the drinks while Tom handed around the drawer for people to take what they wanted. Not much was said, eye contact wasn't made, and the atmosphere was heavy. How was it possible for someone to be missing for three days and there not be a single sighting? The woods behind Matilda's house had been searched and not yielded a hint of her whereabouts. Her house had been searched from top to bottom, her bank records, mobile phone and computer hard drive had all been scrutinised by specialist officers, and nothing of interest was recorded. The houses on Ringinglow Road opposite the turning to Matilda's farmhouse had all been visited. It had been a futile exercise. None had noticed anything untoward and a few of the newer residents didn't even know the turn-off existed.

'Right then, are we all ready?' Christian said, accepting a strong coffee from Finn and taking a deep breath. He felt drained. He'd hardly slept, again. After his wife and kids, Matilda was the person he was fond of the most. She was like family. 'Matilda has been missing for two days and three nights. We know Steve Harrison is involved, from what Scott overheard following his stabbing. We've also heard from Steve that he watched a live feed of the kidnapping taking place. Obviously, we take everything Steve says with a pinch of salt, but he does seem to know a lot of detail about it, so we have to assume, this time, he's telling the truth.'

Scott flicked through his notebook. 'I spoke to the governor of Wakefield Prison again last night. He's looking at the records to see who has had access to Steve over the past few months and they'll all be seriously questioned. He's steaming that someone on his staff could be involved.

'Steve's aunt, Janet Crowther, has stated that Steve was angry about Matilda, but she has no clue as to who he could have asked for help. Also, he has no cousin and there doesn't seem to be anyone called Amy Monroe in existence connected with this.' Christian pointed to the photofit Scott and Finn put together. 'Is this woman going by the name of Amy Monroe? If so, who the bloody hell is she?'

'She could be a fan of Steve's,' Finn said. 'We know he's got a lot of admirers from around the world, the governor told us so. Plus, with the books and the Netflix documentary, he's getting more and more mail by the day. Though of course it doesn't reach him.'

'Did his therapist come up with anything?' Tom asked.

'No. She hid behind client confidentiality,' Scott answered. 'However, we're keeping a close eye on her. She seems ... well, I'm not sure, but there's something not quite right about her.'

'Do you think she could be Amy Monroe?' Tom asked.

Scott turned to look back at the photofit. 'No. Nothing matches. But that doesn't mean to say she hasn't put this woman up to working with her.'

Christian fell silent. He folded his arms tightly across his chest as he studied the image of the alleged Amy Monroe. His breathing grew intense as he thought. He was so frustrated right now at the lack of progress. He felt impotent.

'What aren't we seeing, for fuck's sake?' he asked through gritted teeth.

Scott and Finn exchanged worried glances.

'I've got a zoom call with Lionel Miller at eleven,' Scott said. 'He wrote the book about Steve which was the basis for the Netflix documentary. He also thanked Amy Monroe in the acknowledgements. Maybe he can supply us with a photo or confirm if that image is an accurate representation of her.'

'Ask him about the other people in the acknowledgements, too. If he can't help us, maybe they can,' Christian said. He went over to the snack drawer, picked up a Mars and took a huge bite. He pulled a face. 'I can't stand these,' he said through the mouthful. 'They're too sweet.'

'What are we going to do about Steve Harrison?' Finn asked. 'He saw through my and Tom's act, but we can't just leave him to it, can we? Is there anything we can do to get him to talk?'

Christian swallowed, looked at the remaining Mars and threw it into the bin. 'I think I'll stick to Marathons.' He took a swig of coffee. 'The only thing legally we can do with Steve is talk to him. However, he'll enjoy us asking for help and will clam up. The alternative is torture and, believe me, I'm very close to breaking him out of prison, throwing him in the back of a van and putting a lighter to the soles of his feet.'

'So, we've got nothing to work on then?' Tom asked.

The room fell silent. Even Zofia stopped tapping on her keyboard. They were resting their hopes on Lionel Miller coming up with the goods, but this Amy Monroe, whoever she was, was obviously smart if she had no online presence. Was she simply a fan of Steve Harrison who believed she was in love with him and wanted to hurt Matilda to get close to him, or was she someone else? If so, who?

Christian didn't answer Tom's question. 'Moving on to the bodies found at Wigtwizzle: Jackie Barclay, Caroline Richardson and Duncan McNally. As we know, Jackie Barclay and Caroline Richardson were sex workers before they disappeared in 2018, around the time Stuart Mills was on his killing spree. Duncan McNally was a homeless man, paid by Jake Harrison to come into the station and set off the fire alarm in January 2019.

'Now, Sian texted me about ten minutes ago and said Stuart denies killing them. And she believes him. So that's good enough for me. The question is, why have these three been buried in the same place? What's the connection?'

'They're all in the category of easy victims,' Finn began. 'A serial killer is most likely to choose victims from vulnerable groups – that includes the homeless and sex workers.'

'How did they die, do we know?' Tom asked.

'Jackie Barclay was strangled,' Scott said. 'According to Donal, they don't have a complete skeleton for Caroline Richardson or Duncan McNally so they're unable to tell how they died.'

Christian cleared his throat. 'There is one very obvious link between the two sex workers and Duncan McNally – us.'

'What do you mean?' Finn asked.

'We've been searching for Jackie and Caroline since 2018. Obviously, we didn't know Duncan was missing, but he's connected to us because of the shooting. Is it possible the killer is someone who has been watching us, the team, and killing people connected to the crimes we've been investigating over the years?'

Once again, the room fell silent as they all took in the enormity of what Christian was saying.

'Are you saying the whole team has a stalker?' Tom asked.

'It's not impossible, is it?' Christian answered.

'You mean, someone with a fixation on a specialised unit, someone with an unnatural interest in the police?' Finn asked. 'Someone like Steve Harrison?'

'Is this all connected?' Scott asked. 'The bodies at Wigtwizzle, Matilda going missing?'

'If that really is the case, why kidnap Matilda now?' Zofia asked. 'I'm guessing it's safe to assume Jackie and Caroline have been dead since they were missing in 2018. That's three years. There could be more bodies buried there, going even further back. So, why now? Why is this escalating now?'

'A serial killer will only instigate an endgame when he feels he has no choice,' Finn said. 'He'll believe he's on the cusp of being caught so will want to dictate his own ending. Or there's been a change in his own circumstances. He could be ill or dying and want to go out in a blaze of glory, or maybe he's suddenly lost his job or suffered another huge loss, and the meaning of his life has changed. He's lost control of something, and this game he's playing is the only thing he has control of, so he's taking it by the horns before he loses that, too.'

'You keep saying "he",' Zofia said.

'The majority of serial killers are male. If you want, I can call him Zofia,' Finn smiled.

'No. "He" is perfectly fine. Thanks,' she said nervously.

'What do you think, Christian?' Scott asked, looking at his boss intently, trying to read his pained expression. 'Do you think the bodies at Wigtwizzle are connected to Matilda's disappearance?'

'I want to say no, but I'm fearing yes.'

'So, where do we go from here?'

'I've spoken to the crime scene manager, Felix Lerego. He's getting a complete map of the area at Wigtwizzle and we're going to do a full search. There's a forensic team on standby. If there are more bodies, we need them identified as soon as possible. If they're known to us in some way, we can hopefully find a connection to whoever is doing this.'

'Is there anything we can do in the meantime?' Tom asked.

'Yes. This unit opened in 2010 as the Murder Investigation Team. I want every single case looked into and everyone we came into contact with, for whatever reason, identified, located and questioned.'

'That's a big task,' Scott said. 'None of us were even here at the start.'

'Sian was. She's on her way back. She'll help as much as she can. Now, I've spoken to Chief Constable Ridley,' Christian continued. 'He's going to release a statement later today about bones being found at Wigtwizzle. We can't keep the media blackout going much longer. Now, if Danny Hanson tries to make contact with any of you and asks about Matilda, direct him straight to me. Any questions?'

Nobody answered.

There was a light tap on the glass doors to the suite.

Everyone turned to see who their visitor was. Christian's eyes widened. He did not expect to see this person in a police station ever again.

He ran to the doors and pulled them open.

'What are you doing here?'

'Feeling sick and sweating through three layers of clothing. Am I all right to come in?' Pat Campbell asked.

'Of course.'

She stepped into the suite and looked about her. 'Wow, things have certainly changed since my day.'

'What can I do for you, Pat?'

Pat didn't hear him. She was too busy marvelling at the open-plan suite, the brightness, the technology. Where were the desks with mountains of files and paperwork? Where was the heavy cloud of smoke that hung over the room?

'Sorry? Oh, yes. I was talking to Adele last night and she mentioned that you're looking for someone called Amy Monroe, but you can't seem to find her or anything about her. The name sounded familiar to me, and I've spent most of the night racking my brains, such as they are. I think I know who she is.'

Chapter Forty

Danny Hanson had had a hectic time yesterday. Finally, he'd been granted access to a police investigation, and no sooner had he started than he had to take a step back. He was working on a story with a colleague, a fellow freelancer, and it was a slow burner that had suddenly caught fire. What he discovered, if it panned out, could be massive, and potentially damaging for many people. He had the rumours, but he needed them confirmed before he started to write.

This morning, he woke from a fitful sleep. He usually had a good eight hours, but last night he woke up many times, his dreams dark and upsetting. He showered quickly, read through his emails and social media posts while wolfing down a large bowl of cereal and was almost out of the door of his flat when his phone pinged.

The email was from a Hotmail account. He didn't recognise the sender's name. There was no message, just a link. Normally, he wouldn't press on it, fearing a virus or something that would drain his bank account, not that there was a great deal in there to steal. The subject line, however, was irresistible: 'Matilda Darke's kidnapping'.

He pulled out a chair at the kitchen table, sat down and pressed on the link.

At first, nothing happened as he was re-routed to several sites before a frame of a video appeared. He recognised immediately where the camera was pointing – Matilda Darke's front door. He was almost salivating with excitement. He pressed play.

The door opened and DS Scott Andrews came into view. His smile dropped when he saw something that seemed to frighten him. He staggered backwards, hand clamped to his stomach and looked down to see blood seeping out between his fingers.

There was no sound to the video and Danny leaned in to get a better look at what he was watching. Matilda came into view. She said something, but he couldn't lip read. She was tasered and dropped to the floor. Strangely, Danny was disturbed by what he was seeing. He and Matilda didn't always get on, but he had a grudging respect for her. Watching her on the floor of her hallway, writhing in agony, he felt sad, angry, scared.

His mouth opened as the camera went closer to Matilda and he saw the pained look on her face. She was injected with something, her eyelids fluttered and she slipped into unconsciousness. She was then dragged across the floor by her ankles, past a prostrate Scott, who was bleeding profusely from his stomach.

Outside, Matilda was grabbed, picked up and flung into the back of a car, before the boot was slammed closed. The video ended.

'Oh my God!' Danny said, sitting back in his chair, running

his free hand over his face. The phone was firmly clamped in the other.

If he'd seen this simply on its own, he would have thought it was fake, if that was possible, but put together with his visit to Matilda's house and seeing for himself the blood on the hallway floor, and his contact at the hospital telling him of Scott's stabbing, this was proof that something dark had happened and South Yorkshire Police were covering it up. Why would they do that? Surely the assault and kidnapping of one of their own would be big news and they'd want help from the press and public.

He pressed the link to watch the video again, but it failed. He pressed and pressed, but it was obviously a one-time-only watch.

'Shit,' he said out loud, slamming the phone down on the table. He should have at least taken a few screen shots while watching it.

He wondered why the police had suddenly allowed him access to a criminal investigation. The bones found at Wigtwizzle were a red flag, distracting him from the real focus of Matilda's disappearance. Or kidnapping, as the video attested. *This* was the big story he should be following. The bones had obviously been there for some time; they could wait a little while longer.

He grabbed his satchel and his phone and left the flat, slamming the door behind him. As he headed for his car on the bitterly cold January morning, an idea came to mind. South Yorkshire Police had granted him access to a case; he'd be able to use that to blag his way past reception and into the Homicide and Major Enquiry suite. Once there, he'd reveal what he'd seen, and they wouldn't be able to fob him off with old bones this time.

Chapter Forty-One

S ian wasn't in the mood to go straight back to the station after her meeting with her ex-husband. She drove back to Sheffield in a sort of daze. She wasn't sure how she felt. She was shocked by his transformation. Stuart was never vain. He didn't care about his clothes being designer label, he didn't moisturise, and he never wore a fragrance a day in his life. It took Sian weeks of badgering to get him to clip his toenails. To see what prison had done to him was staggering. He was not the Stuart she knew.

But then, who was the real Stuart? Sitting opposite him, for the first time in more than two years, she expected the dark emotions she felt at the time of his arrest would come back to the surface, that she would vilify herself again because she should have known she was married to a serial killer. It wasn't until she was driving away from Wakefield Prison that she realised she had no feelings whatsoever towards Stuart now. He was a stranger. He was simply another prisoner in a building full of them. If she had to visit him again because of the case she was working on, then so be it. She had no reason to be scared or worried. Stuart Mills meant nothing to her. Her emotions were merely due to her surprise at his change of appearance. That's what she told herself, anyway.

'How did it go?' Adele asked as Sian made her way into the autopsy suite. She'd washed her hands with sanitiser and placed a disposable mask over her nose and mouth.

Sian smiled. 'It went okay.'

'Really?'

'Yes. I was scared to death when I walked into that room. I've heard of people saying their legs felt like jelly, but I've never experienced it. I really did there. I thought they were going to give way beneath me. But when I saw him ... wow, he's changed.'

'Prison pallor?'

'Something like that. I felt like I was talking to a stranger. There was nothing there between us. I told him a few things. I think I allowed the occasion to get the better of me, but now I've had time to think about it, there's nothing anymore. No pain, no horror, just detachment.'

'Is that good?'

'It really is.' She smiled again. 'You know, I was ready to slap Christian when he suggested going to see him, but I'm glad he did. I'm glad I went. I've nothing to worry about anymore. He's a sad individual, and he's never coming out.'

Adele smiled. 'I bet you feel so much lighter now.'

'I do. This is a turning point. I've had an offer accepted on a house. I've changed my name. I'm ... are you looking at my breasts?'

'I'm so sorry, Sian. It's just ... well, they do seem perkier than usual.'

'Belinda lent me one of her bras. It's padded. She said it would give me confidence going to see Stuart.'

'Did it work?'

'A prison officer asked if I wanted to go for a drink after work.'

'Really? Are you going?'

'Adele, he was a child. He couldn't have been much older than my Anthony.'

'Another confidence boost, though.'

'From someone with mother issues? Thanks. Anyway, the reason I've come here rather than go back to the station is because I wanted to have a look at the bones you found.'

'Why?'

Sian's face dropped. 'I had Jackie and Caroline's files on my desk for years. When the murders first began, I made contact with a lot of the sex workers. We were trying to protect them. I just want to see them.'

'They're just bones now, Sian.'

'I know.'

'Come on.'

They walked out into the main suite where Simon Browes was washing down a stainless-steel table following a post-mortem. He watched as Adele and Sian went over to the bank of fridges. Adele pulled one open.

'Are you looking at the bones brought in from Wigtwizzle?' Simon called out.

'Yes. Sian wanted a look.'

'More have come in this morning. You were on the phone at the time, Adele.'

'Right. Thanks.'

Sian's stare lingered on Simon longer than usual as she took in the beige cardigan and the pens in the top pocket of his shirt. 'Are you sure that's the animal you slept with?' she whispered to Adele.

Adele shushed her and gave her a friendly elbow.

The bones collected so far and matched to one victim were laid out in order. There was a skull, a clavicle, part of the sternum with teeth marks imbedded in it, several ribs, the left side of the pelvic girdle missing the pubis and ischium, the left femur, and part of the right tibia.

'Not much, is there?' Sian said.

'I'm afraid not.'

'Are they bite marks?'

'Yes. But they're not human.'

'One saving grace, I suppose. Who is this one?'

'This is Caroline Richardson.'

Sian looked at the remains with a blank expression. 'She was only twenty-eight when she went missing. She wasn't from Sheffield originally. She came from Sunderland. No idea why she ended up here. Her parents didn't know, either.'

'Have they been informed?'

'Yes. Someone from the local police went round.'

'How did they take it?'

'I think they were relieved more than anything. They finally have an answer.'

'Why did she turn to prostitution, do they know?' Adele asked.

'She had a baby when she was twenty-one and it died just after its first birthday. It turned out it had a heart defect that wasn't noticed. Caroline put her to bed one night and woke up the next morning to find her dead. She fell apart. She turned to drink. She lost her job, her flat, her friends. She couldn't cope. Her parents helped as much as they could, but she shut them off. Eventually, they gave her an ultimatum. Whether that was the right thing to do or not, I don't know. They said she needed to sort herself out or they'd have to ask her to leave their home. They were all suffering. The next thing, Caroline was gone.'

'The poor woman,' Adele said, tears in her eyes.

'When I met her,' Sian said, 'there was sadness in her eyes. There was sadness in all of them, but she always had a smile on her face. It was obvious she was hiding something raw and painful, but she was always chatty with me. I just wished she'd opened up to me. I might have been able to help her.'

'Don't blame yourself, Sian.' Adele placed a comforting arm around her.

'They don't trust the police, or any authority figure really. They're never going to accept help from us.'

'Would you like to see Jackie Barclay?'

'Please.'

Sian stood back while Adele closed the door on Caroline and opened another one, revealing the full skeleton of Jackie Barclay.

'I can't look at a skeleton and see a person, can you?' Sian asked.

'Not really. It's like when you go to funerals and see the coffin being brought into the church. I can't get my head around there being a body in there.'

'I know what you mean.'

'Did you know Jackie?'

'A little. She was Sheffield born and bred; had the strongest accent I've ever heard,' Sian said with a smile. 'Her story is more typical. She got into drugs when she was a teenager, became addicted, stole from her family, who then disowned her, and met a bloke who pimped her out for more drugs. She was sad. I mean really sad, like it was deep within her. I remember asking her if she wanted help, wanted to change her life. She just shrugged. She said she'd passed that point years ago; that this was her life now. I knew, there and then, that one day I'd be looking at her in a mortuary. There was nothing I could do for her, though.'

'We had a call from your DI Sharp this morning,' Simon said. He'd been listening in the background. 'She contacted Jackie's family. They don't want her body back. Apparently, to them, she died years ago when she walked out.'

Sian sniffed back her tears. 'I remember speaking to them not long after she went missing. Her mother was just numb. She had no more tears left to cry.'

'We'll pass it on to the coroner. He'll get in touch with the council; they'll sort something out for her.'

Sian turned away.

'Are you all right?' Adele asked her.

'I was going to offer to pay for a funeral for her. But then I thought about Duncan McNally. He was homeless. He'll have nobody to bury him either. I can't pay for them all, can I?'

'No. And that's a slippery slope. You need to switch off at some point. You can't carry every victim with you.'

'I'm aware. I wouldn't be a good detective if I didn't have empathy, though, would I?'

'I suppose not.'

The doors to the suite opened and a trolley was pushed through.

Adele placed a hand on Sian's shoulder and guided her away from the hubbub of mortuary life.

'Is there any news on the search for Matilda?'

'I haven't been back to the station yet, but I don't think so.'

'Shouldn't you be going public or something? Someone may have seen something.'

'I think we may have to.'

'Adele, are you busy?' Simon called out from her office, the phone in his hand.

'I'm always busy.'

'I've got Felix Lerego on the phone at Wigtwizzle. They've found another body.'

Chapter Forty-Two

S unrise in mid-January wasn't until 07:47. Unfortunately, under thick cloud and in the middle of woodland, whatever sun there might be might not penetrate at all and a forensic team would have to struggle with working in darkness, or as far as an arc lamp could reach.

Felix Lerego had spoken to Christian about getting a map of the woods at Wigtwizzle and sending a search team further, deeper, into the undergrowth. Three bodies had been found and they were expecting more. Already this morning more bones had been unearthed around the site where Caroline Richardson's body was discovered. They'd been shipped off to the lab for testing, but Felix needed to know what he was working with here, the terrain, the landscape, the density.

Sitting in the front passenger seat of his battered Land Rover, he watched on a monitor as a fuzzy black and white image appeared. He grabbed his walkie talkie and pressed the button.

'I'm sorry, mate, are you on the moon?'

'What?' the reply came.

'It's breaking up and all I'm seeing is ... well, I've no idea what I'm seeing. I keep expecting to see a space buggy come shooting past any minute.'

'Hold your horses. It's bloody windy this morning. I'm struggling with stability.'

'I don't want to know about your personal life, Barry.'

Barry was standing on the edge of the road leading into the woods. Beside him on the ground was a drone struggling to get off the ground. It was hoped that the cameras attached to the drone could fly over the woodland above and using thermal imaging, Felix and his forensic officers could get a good idea of what they were dealing with and know whether they'd be able to access certain areas using ground-penetrating radar to discover, potentially, more bones or bodies.

'I'm seeing trees and branches, Barry, but it's still in black and white. Are you making a sequel to *The Blair Witch Project*?'

'One's already been made, and it was shite. Just give me a minute,' he said, impatiently.

Felix sat back in his seat and blew out his cheeks. He turned to look out of the window at the thickness of the woodland. In between the trees he could just make out his team of white-suited forensic officers as they began to extend the search. In summer, he could picture this being a beautiful place to bring the family, walk with the dog or have a picnic, but in winter, the gnarled trunks and branches of the trees were bare and reached out like old hands wanting to grab at whatever they could. The cold didn't help either, and he shivered. Was that from the temperature, hovering around zero degrees, or was it a sense of foreboding? These woods had already given up three bodies – how many more were lurking beneath the surface?

There was a bang on the window and Felix jumped.

'Fuck me, Barry, you almost killed me.' He lowered the window.

Barry leaned in, a malevolent grin on his face. 'Ready when you are.'

'I could really go off you,' he said as he turned back to the monitor, which, thankfully, was now in colour.

The drone took off and dipped to one side slightly as the wind picked up. Eventually it steadied as it reached the tops of the trees and travelled further up, taking in the whole of the surrounding area. The wood was smaller than Felix was expecting and soon the trees gave way to fields and open countryside.

Felix took a few screenshots. Later he'd be able to pinpoint where they'd already searched and dug and where he wanted to send his team to look next. Then something caught his eye.

'Barry, come and have a look here a minute.'

Barry leaned into the car. Felix could feel his warm breath on his face as he leaned down. He'd obviously taken up smoking again. Felix leaned slightly away.

'What am I looking at?'

'Can you move the drone a little over to the right? You picked up on something.'

'Where?'

'Just a little more to the right. That's it. Now, can you see that, in between the trees?'

'No. What am I looking at?'

'You're looking at where I'm pointing on the screen.'

'Yes. It's just woods though, isn't it?'

Felix rolled his eyes. 'Can you zoom in, please?'

'Anything you say,' he sighed.

Slowly, the drone descended and hovered over the treetops. As it did so, more of the ground was exposed.

'Is that what I think it is?' Felix asked.

'Huh. It looks like a shed or hut or something.'

'Why would there be a shed in the middle of the woods?'

'Maybe someone's living in there.'

'Are you going all Blair Witch on me again?' Felix asked.

'If you think I'm going in there, you've another think coming. I just operate the drone.'

'Can you get me a clear image of it so we can take a look?'

'I can, but like I said ...'

'Don't worry, Barry, you can stay here and play with your electric kite.'

Felix climbed out of the car into the cold January air and lifted the collar of his jacket. He felt a chill, and he felt frightened. Someone had been using these woods for a purpose, a reason that meant they needed the shelter of a shed. Were they just homeless and living here? Were they turning their back on the twenty-first century to live off the grid? Or was there something else going on in these woods? Something sinister and other-worldly? As much as he loved his job, suddenly, Felix was scared to enter these woods again.

Chapter Forty-Three

S cott went into the toilets and unbuttoned his shirt to check his bandaging. It was still in place and no blood was seeping through, but he was in a great deal of pain. He took the painkillers he'd been prescribed at the hospital and dry-swallowed two of them. He gazed at his reflection. He looked tired. It wasn't easy trying to sleep in the aftermath of an operation, and it didn't help that he was thinking about Matilda all the time.

He kept going over what happened in her house. He was powerless. This woman, whoever she was, stormed in like a hurricane, stabbed him, tasered Matilda, injected her with God knows what and dragged her out of there like a woman on a mission, which, Scott supposed, she obviously was. The whole drama couldn't have taken more than two minutes. It was conducted with military precision. That was the scary part. Nothing was going to stop this woman from kidnapping Matilda. But why?

Scott looked back at his pale reflection. There were tears in his eyes. He had to find Matilda. Alive. Failure was not an option. She'd been so good to him in recent years, helping him come to terms with losing Chris and his best friend Rory, giving him a home in the flat above her garage. She was like a second mother to him. Hopefully this Lionel Miller would have some answers that could point them in the right direction.

Scott made himself a strong black coffee, grabbed a few bars of chocolate from Sian's displaced snack drawer and went into Christian's office, where he closed the door behind him for some privacy. He sat down at his desk, arranged his notepad and pen neatly in front of him and opened the Zoom app.

Scott was surprised by how young Lionel Miller looked. He expected a man called Lionel to be in his seventies, but the man in his computer was probably only in his early forties. He wore round tortoiseshell glasses and had brilliant blue eyes and a wild shock of salt-and-pepper hair that had obviously taken some time to style. An expensive-looking white shirt, open at the neck, revealed a smooth chest. He was a man who looked after his appearance and Scott had to pinch himself to be professional and not ogle the handsome man on the screen.

'Mr Miller, thank you for agreeing to talk to me,' Scott said after clearing his throat.

'You're welcome. I'm sorry we've had to do this via Zoom. I'd have been more than happy to come in to talk to you, but I'm currently acting as a carer for my Aged P in Cornwall.' He smiled, revealing a set of perfectly neat and polished teeth.

Scott smiled back. 'Mr Miller ...'

'Lionel, please.'

'Lionel. As I said in my original email, we're currently

investigating Steve Harrison and I'd like to ask you about him and the book you wrote.'

'Yes,' Miller began, sitting back in his comfortable chair. 'You were deliciously vague in your email. You didn't say why you were investigating Steve.'

'Unfortunately, I'm not at liberty to say right now.'

'I assumed that would be your answer.' He smiled, his eyes twinkling as he did so. 'So, what do you want to know?'

'What I'd really like to talk to you about is the acknowledgements section in the back of your book.'

'Oh. That's not very flattering for a writer. I spent eighteen months writing that, conducted dozens of interviews, was threatened at knife point and you want to talk about the people I thanked for helping me.'

Scott frowned. 'You were threatened at knife point?'

'A slight exaggeration on my part. The life of a writer isn't an exciting one. It was more of a shiv, really. During one particular interview with Steve Harrison, he didn't like the way my line of questioning was going so pulled a plastic toothbrush he'd somehow welded a razorblade to and tried to slice my throat.'

'Oh my God.'

Lionel leaned into the computer, pulled his open shirt down a little and showed off a slight scar. 'It was only a nick, but it drew blood and ruined a perfectly good Paul Smith shirt.'

'Why did he do that? What were you asking him about?'

'As I'm sure you know, Steve's ambition, before he committed his murders, was to quickly climb the ranks of the police force. During my research, I went back to the beginning and to his school. His grades were never good enough. He struggled and was frustrated when he wasn't getting top marks. When I put all this to him, he saw this as my attempt to put the blame on him for his crimes rather than DCI Darke, whom he mentioned at every opportunity for turning him into a killer.'

'So, every time you tried to get him to take responsibility for what he'd done, he turned against you?'

'Correct.'

Scott made a quick note of that. 'What happened to him after he tried to stab you?'

'I've no idea. That was the last time I saw him. I had enough information, and frankly, no story is worth losing your life over.'

'Very sensible.'

Lionel smiled. 'I've been called Mr Sensible a great many times over the years.'

'There are worse nicknames.'

'I'm sure. It's not very exciting, being sensible, punctual, and having everything neat and tidy.'

'Sounds perfect to me,' Scott said with a smile.

'Anally retentive, my last boyfriend called me.'

Scott and Lionel maintained eye contact for a very long minute, before Scott turned away. He could feel himself blushing.

'Going back to your book, Mr Miller. In the acknowledgements section, you mentioned a woman named Amy Monroe. Can you tell me about her?'

'Ah, yes, Steve's cousin.'

Scott didn't correct him.

'A strange woman.'

'In what way was she strange?'

'Well, she's Steve's cousin, a blood relative, so she knows

him, yet there were times where I felt she was interviewing me, wanting to know all about Steve and his life.'

Scott frowned as he made notes. 'Did you ask her why she was asking so many questions?'

'Yes. She said she didn't see that side of the family much so wanted to know why he turned into a killer. I suppose if you find out you have a serial killer in your family you want to know what made them that way, just in case there is such a thing as a killer gene and it's running through your relatives.'

'What did she tell you about Steve during your interviews?'

'To be honest, I knew a lot about Steve by that point so she couldn't give me anything new. She was very vague about his formative years, but, like she said, the two families didn't mix all that often. She knew more about Steve once he was put in prison. She said she took an interest in him, what with him being family. Personally, I'd want to distance myself from a relative who was a killer, wouldn't you?'

'Absolutely. Where did you conduct these interviews?'

'I was living in Birmingham at the time of writing, so I popped up to Sheffield to meet her.'

'Did you go to her house?'

'No. It was always in a coffee shop.'

'How many times did you meet?'

'Three or four, I think. Sorry, forgive me for being nosy, but why all these questions about Amy Monroe?'

'We think she may be involved in something. I shouldn't be telling you this, Lionel, but Steve Harrison doesn't actually have any cousins.'

Miller's mouth dropped open slightly. 'She lied?'

'I'm afraid so.'

'Who the hell is she, then?'

'That's what we want to find out. Do you have a number for her or an address?'

He dipped out of the screen and Scott heard a drawer being opened and files rattling.

'I don't have an address. I remember asking about her own background, merely for context, asking her what she did for a living, that kind of thing, and she never gave me a straight answer. She said she was currently unemployed and looking for work in marketing. When I asked where she lived, she said south Sheffield. There was never a direct reply. I can scan over what information she gave me if you think it'll help.'

'Please.' Scott held up the photofit. 'I'm not sure if you can see this properly, but is this Amy Monroe?'

Lionel leaned into the computer and squinted. 'Yes. That's her. I'd recognise that wig anywhere.'

'It's a wig?'

'To be honest, I didn't realise it was one myself at first. I just thought she had a severe haircut, but one time, we were leaving the coffee shop and this gust of wind came from nowhere and she immediately slapped a hand to her head, and it was obvious then it was a wig. She told me she had alopecia.'

'Did you believe her?'

'I had no reason not to.'

Scott looked down at his notes. He hadn't written much.

'You also mentioned Rose Osgood and Nina Price in your acknowledgements. Who are they?'

'Rose Osgood is my research assistant and Nina Price was a prison officer at Wakefield Prison who talked to me about how Steve was as a prisoner.'

'Why Nina over any other prison officer?'

'She'd spent more time with him than anyone else.'

'Why was that?'

'I'm not sure. I assumed she'd been assigned to him. He's in a Supermax wing, as you know, so he requires more attention.'

Scott wrote down her name and put a question mark next to it.

'One more question. Did you speak to Steve's therapist, Linda Bellamy?'

Lionel's eyes widened. 'I wondered if you'd ask me about her.'

'What do you mean?'

'I looked Linda up after our meeting just to check she was fully qualified.'

'Why did you do that?'

'Because for a therapist, she's far too close to her client.'

'In what way?'

Lionel looked uncomfortable, cleared this throat, and took a swig from a Birmingham City FC mug. 'I'm afraid I'm not going to do my profession much good by telling what I did.' He cleared his throat again. 'I found Linda odd from the moment I met her. I felt she was holding back on what she was saying, so much so that I started paying more attention to what she wasn't saying rather than what she was. Anyway, she offered to make me a coffee and I used the "May I use your bathroom?" line to have a snoop about. Fortunately, the downstairs bathroom had a faulty flush, so I was directed upstairs. Bedside cabinets are a great source of information, so I had a rummage around hers. In the top drawer was a dog-eared photograph of Steve Harrison.'

'She has a photograph of Steve Harrison in her bedside cabinet?' Scott asked, incredulously.

'Indeed. After our interview, I did a little digging and found from a contact of a contact that Linda had left her husband not long after she became Steve's therapist. In fact, you might want to have a chat with Kevan Bellamy. He'll be able to give you more of an insight than I can.'

'Did you tell anyone about this? Anyone at Wakefield Prison, for example?'

'No. I suppose I should have done. Look, has something happened to Linda or anyone?' He frowned.

'No. Nothing like that. Lionel, thank you so much for all your help,' Scott said, trying to change the subject.

'You're very welcome. I'll email the information I have on Amy Monroe, too. If there's anything else you need, you've got my email address and mobile number. I'm available any time. For anything,' he said, giving Scott his sweetest smile.

Scott's mouth dried. 'I'll keep that in mind. Thank you.'

Chapter Forty-Four

Christian took Pat Campbell to the canteen. Scott needed to use his office for his Zoom call with Lionel Miller and, for some reason, he didn't feel right using Matilda's office when she wasn't there.

He bought them both a latte and muffin and they found a quiet corner. Pat had spent most of her time looking around the place, marvelling at how different things were since she was last a serving police officer.

'I never thought I'd see the day when South Yorkshire Police would be serving a latte,' Pat said as Christian brought the drinks over and sat down next to her. 'You had two options when I was here – tea or coffee, and it didn't matter which one you ordered, they both tasted the same.'

'Do you want to hear something even more revelatory?'

'Go on?'

'Mine is made with oat milk,' Christian smiled.

Pat laughed. 'I've bet they've got a gluten-free menu, too.'

'Of course. We had beetroot chocolate cake last week. I was reluctant, but it was delicious.'

Pat's smile quickly dropped.

'Is this really the first time you've been in a police station since you left?'

She nodded and sipped her latte. 'The Billy Latimer case was the biggest of my career and it went on for months. I could see it was destroying the team. Morale was at an all-time low. When he killed DS Whitlock like that, well, it was the beginning of the end for me. I couldn't stand seeing her empty desk every day. I told my Anton that as soon as I arrested Billy, I was handing in my notice. And I did.'

'Do you regret it?'

'Not in the slightest. I didn't like the woman I was turning into. Billy was pure evil.'

'Does he still write to you?'

Pat took a deep breath to steady her emotions. 'Off and on. Adele told me about bones being found at Wigtwizzle. Part of me is hoping that's where Diane Whitlock's buried. I'd like to know what he did with her before I die.'

'Her case is still open, Pat.'

'I know it is. And so are plenty of others. Anyway, I didn't come here to depress you. I've been thinking long and hard about this Amy Monroe character. As soon as Adele mentioned her name a light went on and I know I've heard it before. I mean, it's not a common surname, is it?'

'Only if your first name is Marilyn,' Christian smiled.

'Remember DI Ben Hales?'

'I'd rather not.'

'Well, yes, he wasn't a pleasant man, and he had a fixation on Matilda, too.'

'But he's dead. And he was called Hales.'

'True. But his wife's maiden name was Monroe, and she was the daughter of Chief Superintendent Stanley Monroe.

And Ben and Sara had two daughters. I don't think I ever knew their names, so I don't know if one was Amy or not.'

'Oh my God, of course. Sara actually went back to her maiden name after she split up with Ben. Why didn't I think of that?' He chastised himself. 'I wonder if the daughters changed their name, too.'

'I'm not saying it's definitely connected with them, but it's worth a shot. And the way Ben was with Matilda, maybe either Sara or one of the daughters is angry at Matilda and blames her for Ben killing himself.'

'Pat, you really should be on our team, you know. You'd be brilliant.'

'I saw your team when I came into the office. They all look like they should still be in school. I'd feel like their great-grandmother.'

'Well, thank you, Pat. I really appreciate it.'

'You're welcome. Will you let me know what, or if, anything comes of it?'

'Of course.'

'How is the search for Matilda going?'

'Not fast enough for my liking.'

'You'll find her, Christian. I have every faith in you.'

'I wish I had. Would you like a lift home?'

'No, thanks. I've got my car outside.'

Christian walked Pat out to the car park, gave her a kiss on the cheek and told her to drive home safely.

She climbed into the Fiat Punto and slammed the door behind her. She put on her seatbelt and started the engine but didn't reverse out of the visitors-only space. She looked back at the building she had worked in all of her adult life. If she could go back in time and not sign up to be a policewoman, as they were known back then, she would. She wouldn't recommend this job to anyone. If Matilda was found alive, Pat would do everything in her power to get her to see sense and hand in her resignation. The last thing she wanted was for Matilda to turn into her.

Chapter Forty-Five

'S ian isn't here right now,' Christian said as Danny Hanson was shown into the suite.

'So I see,' he said, looking around him, a satisfied smile on his lips. 'It doesn't matter. It's you I've come to see.'

'Me?'

'Well, I'd prefer to see Matilda, but what with her being kidnapped, you'll have to do.'

A silence descended on the room and all eyes turned to him.

'What makes you think she's been kidnapped?'

'Well, the reaction from your team confirmed it, but I was sent a video this morning showing DS Andrews here receiving a stab wound followed by DCI Darke getting tasered, injected with something to knock her out, then dragged outside to a waiting car.'

Finn and Tom exchanged a worried glance. Danny had repeated everything Steve had told them in prison.

'You've seen a video?' Christian asked.

'Yes.'

'Who sent it to you?'

'I've no idea. It was an anonymous email account.'

'I'd like to see it.'

'I've tried. It was a one-time thing. The link doesn't work anymore.'

'I might be able to try something,' Zofia spoke up from the back of the room. 'Can I have your phone?' She held out her hand.

'I'm not sure about that. I've got some sensitive stuff on there.'

'I just want to see the original email.'

'Danny, give her your phone,' Christian said.

'Hold on a minute.' He held up his hands. 'You've kept this from me. From everyone, in fact. You tried to get me off the scent by giving me all that shite with the bones in the woods. I'm not going to be fobbed off here.'

'I'm not fobbing you off, Danny. Let DC Nowak see your phone and we'll sit down, and I'll tell you everything we know.'

He looked around the room but didn't move.

'You can forward the email to me if you like,' Zofia said.

'I'd prefer that.'

She held out her card. He stepped forward to take it from her and began tapping in the email address on his phone.

'You're very mistrustful of the police, aren't you?' she asked.

'You lie. Constantly. To the press and the public. We used to all trust you. Now you're like a secret organisation. There's no such thing as an honest copper anymore.'

'That's a very cynical view,' Zofia said.

'In my first week as a reporter, I was shadowing an old bloke who'd been a journalist all his life. He gave me a piece of advice I've never forgotten – trust no one, especially if they have a title. I've learned to realise that includes initials before and after a person's name, *DC* Nowak.'

She looked at him, open-mouthed.

'Danny, shall we go into my office?' Christian asked.

Danny followed Christian and the door was closed behind them.

'Wow, he really hates us, doesn't he?' Finn asked.

'The feeling is more than mutual,' Scott said, wincing slightly and placing a hand over his stab wound.

'Are you all right?'

'Fine. Zofia, can you trace it?'

Zofia looked from one computer screen to the other. 'No. There's no IP address attached to the email and anything I try to send it is bouncing back.'

'I thought an email had to have an IP address,' Finn said.

'It does unless you go through something like a tor browser.'

'What about the video itself?'

'The full link is huge and it's bouncing off all kinds of sites until it goes back to the beginning. Whoever created it fitted it with a kill code. Basically, after you've watched it once, it no longer exists. However, you can't completely delete everything online, so it just takes out some vital piece of information, in this case the video, and has the links chasing themselves.'

'So there's nothing you can do?' Scott asked.

'I'm afraid not.'

'When Danny described the video, it did sound very similar to what Steve Harrison told me and Finn in prison,' Tom said. 'I bet the person who sent it to Danny is the person who filmed it.'

'But why get the press involved?' Finn asked.

'Because we haven't,' Scott said. 'I'm guessing Steve will have told whoever he's working with to wait a few days to see if the police put out an appeal. If not, to do it themselves. That's what they've done here.'

'But if that's the case, why make the video a one-time-only viewing? If they want the press involved surely, they'll want the newspapers to show footage from it.'

'Not really,' Scott said. 'It shows them stabbing one police officer and tasering another. That carries a hefty prison sentence. They just want the story of Matilda being kidnapped getting out there.'

'And that's all that Steve wants. More publicity,' Finn said.

Inside Christian's office, Christian and Danny sat at opposite sides of his desk. The door was closed, and the blinds tilted so nobody could see in. Christian told Danny everything, confirming Scott's stabbing and Matilda's kidnapping.

Danny looked visibly shaken. 'And you've had no word about Matilda?'

'None at all.'

'So, it's not like a kidnap for ransom then?'

'No.'

'Do you have any idea who's doing this?'

Christian remained silent. He looked confused as he wrestled with what to tell the journalist.

'Look, Christian, I know I'm a journalist and we're not supposed to get on, but I genuinely like Matilda. I promise, I'm not going to print anything that's going to get her harmed.'

Christian was caught between a rock and a hard place. He had no option but to tell him.

'We believe Steve Harrison is behind it all.'

'The Hangman?'

Christian nodded.

'How? Why?'

'That's what we're trying to work out.'

'Jesus!' Danny exclaimed. He thought for a moment. 'He's going to kill her, isn't he?'

'I think he might.'

'Oh my God! Is there anything you want me to do?'

'Keep it to yourself. At least until we know who is working with Steve on this.'

Danny nodded. 'I will. I promise.'

'Thank you. We're going to release a statement about the bones found at Wigtwizzle this afternoon. I'll send you the press release before it's released to give you a heads-up.'

'I appreciate that.'

'Danny, if you get anything else from the kidnappers, please, let us know before you open any emails or anything.'

'I will. Does this have anything to do with the silent phone calls, the noose and everything?'

'You know about all that?'

'Yes. Matilda told me about it last year. Someone's been stalking her for a while, haven't they?'

'It would appear so.'

'And they've finally struck. Why now?'

'We don't know.'

'I noticed you've got information on your boards out there about the bodies found at Wigtwizzle, which means you're working on that case at the same time as Matilda's kidnapping. Slightly strange. I'd have thought you'd dedicate all your time to finding Matilda and delegate this to another department. Unless there's a connection. Is there?'

'We don't know.'

'You don't know much, do you?'

'Truthfully, Danny? No. We don't.'

'Moving on to these bones, are they more victims of Stuart Mills? Or are you going to say you don't know?'

'I'm afraid so.'

'You really are screwed right now, aren't you?' He thought for a long second. 'Fortunately, I'm not,' he said, standing up.

'What are you talking about?'

'I saw a photo of Duncan McNally on your board, along with the photos of Jackie Barclay and Caroline Richardson. Is Duncan one of the bodies found at Wigtwizzle?'

'Yes.'

'And you're working on the assumption that the same person who killed Jackie and Caroline killed Duncan and buried them all there?'

'It makes sense.'

Danny gave a smile. 'Then Stuart Mills is not your killer.'

'How do you know?'

'Because Duncan and I were in touch. I gave him a few pounds after the shooting, and he gave me chapter and verse of his role in it. I was hoping to write a book one day, but I got sidetracked with my book about the sexual abuse scandal. I met Duncan about a month or so *after* Stuart Mills was arrested. He's not your killer. I'm sorry to say this, Christian, but you've got someone else on your patch who's murdering the homeless and the sex workers of Sheffield. I'll be in touch.'

Danny left the office, and the suite, with a bounce in his step.

Christian remained still behind his desk. He looked ashen. When the first body was identified as Jackie Barclay, he assumed Stuart was the killer. Despite him telling Sian he wasn't and Sian believing him, Christian still expected Stuart to be the killer. Now that theory had been shot down in flames, he had to concede the fact that, once more, there was a serial killer in Sheffield. He put his head in his hands. He wasn't sure how much more horror he could take.

Chapter Forty-Six

There hadn't been much daylight throughout the day. Heavy clouds hung over Sheffield and there was a threat of snow. It was certainly cold enough. By the time Simon Browes pulled up at Wigtwizzle in his Citroen Picasso, Adele's Porsche not being appropriate for the countryside, darkness was already beginning to fall, and it wasn't even three o'clock yet. Sian pulled up behind them in her own car.

Arc lights had been placed at strategic points in the woodland. From the road, they looked ominously like an alien invasion: brilliant white lights casting long shadows of thick branches, and white-suited forensic officers going about their business with precision.

Sian shivered as she buttoned up her coat and joined Simon and Adele, who were staring intently through the trees.

'Do you know what this reminds me of?' Adele began. 'Years ago, I went out to the body farm in Tennessee. You've heard of that, haven't you, Sian?'

She nodded.

'Two acres of woodland with bodies placed in various kinds of states to see how they react to the environment.'

Sian shivered again, though it wasn't from the cold this time.

'I can't understand why people would want to donate their bodies knowing that they're going to be dumped in woodland to rot.'

'They're not dumped,' Simon said. 'They're looked after and carefully monitored. We learn a great deal from what comes out of Tennessee.'

'Have you ever been?' Adele asked.

'Yes. I've been a few times. I'm on good terms with Professor Watson.'

'Did you read his paper last month about how climate change is affecting the decomposition of bodies and how the speed of decomposition is changing the interaction between larvae and maggots? I found it fascinating,' Adele said, rather too eagerly for Sian's liking.

'Me too.'

'Hardly something to read before bedtime. I think I'll stick with Winston Graham,' Sian said. 'Wasn't there talk a while back about having a body farm here in the UK?'

'Yes. I'm against it,' Adele said.

'Why? You've just said how valuable they've been,' Simon said.

'Well, yes, but there's only so much we can get from there, and we've learned a lot from the one at Tennessee. Anything else will just be copying what they've discovered. They're useful for students, I suppose, but as a way of estimating time of death, I think you get a better record from checking when their iPhone was last used,' she said, a wry smile on her face.

Adele spotted Felix up ahead and gave him a wave. He

came towards her, scrambling around in the dusk, taking care not to trip over any exposed roots.

'We've had some excitement,' he said, a smile on his face, slightly out of breath. 'Hello again, Sian. You well?'

'Come on, Felix. Don't keep us in suspense,' Adele said.

'Well, first of all, we've found bones that we believe are from a fourth body. They're not far away from where ... erm, what's she called, the female not found in the car?'

'Caroline Richardson,' Sian offered.

'That's right. We found some more ribs and a femur. At first we thought they could have belonged to, erm, Caroline, and been dragged off by wildlife, but then we also found a third mandible, so we assumed there was a fourth body buried. We started digging further and found more bones. Now, the two sites do overlap at one point, so some bones may belong to Caroline and some to this new one.'

'Male or female?' Sian asked.

'At a guess, female, but only because the pelvis is roughly the same size as Caroline's. Don't hold me to that, though.'

'You have a third missing female, don't you?' Adele asked Sian.

She nodded. 'Monica Yates. We have her DNA on file for a comparison.'

'That's good.'

'Now, here's the exciting part,' Felix said, rubbing his hands together and grinning. He paused, building up the tension.

'You don't get out much, do you, Felix?' Adele asked.

'It's been a while,' he smiled. 'We've found an actual body.'

'A recent body?' Sian asked.

'Well, not that recent. When we sent the drone up earlier, we found a shed, hidden further in the woods. It took a while to get to it and we couldn't see it until we were practically on top of it. It's well disguised. It's not much bigger than your average garden shed. We went in. There's a workbench and a wooden chair, and we found a few empty crisp packets and sandwich wrappers. They've all been bagged and sent for analysis. However, and here's the interesting part—'

'You certainly do love to string out a story, don't you?' Adele smiled.

Felix ignored her. 'The shed is on kind of a raised platform. We began to take up the floor and there's a recess between the shed and the forest floor. That's where we've found the body. I'd estimate she's been there for a couple of years, but you'll know more about that than I do,' he said to both Adele and Simon. 'Follow me.'

Felix headed back into the woods leaving Sian, Simon and Adele no option but to join him as he led the way.

'We haven't found much in the way of gaps for wildlife to get through, so the body looks more or less untouched. She's not visibly recognisable, so her next of kin aren't going to be able to do a formal identification, but she's fully clothed and the clothes haven't been disturbed. I'd say they're the ones she was wearing when she went missing.'

'She?' Sian said, concentrating on where she was walking.

'Oh yes. There's not much hair left, naturally, but it's long. And the clothes are definitely female. A distinctive winter coat, too.'

'Do you have any more missing sex workers, Sian?' Adele asked, looking over her shoulder.

'Not that I'm aware of. But then, Duncan McNally wasn't a sex worker, and he was found here. He wasn't even reported missing.'

'It's bad enough when someone's reported missing, let alone when nobody is missing them,' Adele said.

They reached the shed. Several CSIs were milling around, taking soil samples and photographs.

'We've managed to open up the back of the shed so she can be seen clearly from the back,' Barry told Felix.

'Excellent,' he smiled. 'You won't need to suit up just yet if you fancy a peep.'

'Do you want me to go and have a look?' Simon asked Adele.

'No. I'm fine, thanks.'

'I'll stay up here,' Sian said.

'Squeamish?' Adele asked with a smile.

'Wrong shoes,' Sian remarked.

'How convenient.' Adele winked.

'Listen, I've seen my fair share of gruesome sights over the years, thank you very much. I'm firmly in the camp of if I don't need to see it, I'll save myself the nightmare.'

Adele made her way down the incline. Felix, already at the bottom, held out a hand for her to grab hold of, which she was thankful for. Simon followed.

Felix turned on a torch and led the way around the back of the shed. A white forensic tent had been placed over the body. Eerily, it was perfectly still. Whatever breeze was blowing hadn't penetrated the dense woodland. Felix pulled back the flaps of the tent and allowed Adele to enter.

She looked inside and stopped in her tracks. She clamped her hands to her mouth, eyes wide at the horror she was looking at. The tears fell from her eyes immediately. Emotion rose inside her and a scream started to escape through her fingers. Within seconds, Adele was on her knees, letting out a noise that could wake the dead.

'What's going on?' Felix asked.

Sian, hearing the cry, came charging down the

embankment, almost falling. She saw Adele on the ground, her face contorted in terror. Something was very wrong. She went over to her, dropped to her knees and put her arms around her, holding her tight.

'Adele, what is it?'

She turned, looking to where Adele's gaze was fixed. Her mouth fell open, and she held onto Adele even tighter as she looked at the mummified face of Adele's missing technical assistant, Lucy Dauman.

Chapter Forty-Seven

The look on Chief Constable Ridley's face was not a happy one. The second he heard the news of a fifth body being uncovered at Wigtwizzle, and that it belonged to Lucy Dauman, he stormed out of his office and ran down the stairs to the Homicide and Major Crime Unit on the ground floor. He entered Christian's office and closed the door behind him.

Christian was sitting at his desk, unproductive, head down. When he looked up at the angry face of his boss, he revealed a sad expression and red eyes, evidence he'd been crying.

The sight of a DI in tears made Ridley soften. He pulled out a chair and sat down.

'I'm sorry,' Ridley said. 'I didn't know Lucy. But I'm aware of how close your unit is with Dr Kean and her team.'

'She was thirty years old. She was getting married about a week or so after she went missing. She was so happy. Everything was going right for her. And she was dumped, left to rot beneath a fucking shed in the middle of the woods to just decompose into nothingness,' Christian said, struggling to maintain his emotions.

'Has her fiancé been informed?'

'Sian has sent a couple of DCs and a family liaison officer to her fiancé and her parents.' Christian grabbed a tissue from a packet in his top drawer and blew his nose. 'I remember Lucy telling me once what her parents and teachers said when she wanted to be a pathologist,' he said, a hint of a smile on his face. 'They all wondered how someone so cheerful, so happy, always laughing, joking and bubbly, would possibly want to spend their lives cutting open dead bodies. The job didn't match her personality. She always had a smile on her face. She just loved her work. She loved life so much.'

'I really am sorry, Christian. We're issuing a press release about the bodies being found, but not the identities yet. I believe not all the next of kin have been informed.'

Christian cleared his throat. There was a plastic cup of water on his desk. He picked it up with a shaking hand and took a long sip. 'The third, whom we believe to be Monica Yates, hasn't been ID'd yet. Simon Browes is taking over from Adele, for obvious reasons. He's going to see if DNA can be extracted from any of the bones we've found. We can't actually find a next of kin for Duncan McNally. He was living on the streets of Sheffield when we last had any contact with him. We know he was in the British Army. We may have to contact the MoD and see if they can help.' Christian put his head in his hands. All this, on top of Matilda going missing, was too much for him to cope with on his own.

'Christian, five bodies found in one location – we have to assume the same person is responsible for all five deaths.'

'Stuart Mills has stated he did not kill Jackie Barclay, Caroline Richardson and Monica Yates. Sian believes him. And I believe Sian. Also, Danny Hanson states he saw Duncan

McNally after Stuart was arrested. If the same person has killed them all, which is very likely, Stuart is not the killer.'

'You add Duncan McNally and Lucy Dauman into the mix, and you see there is only one thing all five victims have in common. That's Matilda Darke and her unit.'

'We'd already come up with that.'

'Who has a grudge against this team?'

Christian looked Ridley dead in the eye. 'You know who. The woman who kidnapped Matilda gave a very clear indication Steve Harrison is involved. Scott heard her. And he has no motive for lying. Steve knows far too much about the kidnapping to be making it up. He has to be behind this.'

'And the bodies at Wigtwizzle?'

'He may not have killed them himself. But he's given the order. I know it. I know him. He has no regard for human life. To him, they'll all be collateral damage. He's thinking of the bigger picture.'

'And what is the bigger picture?'

'To kill Matilda Darke.'

Ridley loosened his collar. 'What do you want from me?'

'I want you to allow Sian back onto this. I need her.'

Ridley nodded. 'Anything else?'

'We need to stop pissing about. Matilda has been missing for far too long. We need her found. The only way to do that is to apply pressure on Steve Harrison. I want him brought here and I want him interviewed under caution.'

Ridley stood up. 'I'll put in the call myself and have him brought here tomorrow morning.'

Christian gave a weak smile.

'Christian, send your team home. Have an early finish. Spend the evening with your family and come back to this tomorrow.'

'I … I can't go home,' he said, tears in his voice.

'Why not?'

'I can't rest, not knowing where Matilda is.'

'You'll be no use to anyone if you don't get some rest. I want you out of this station in five minutes,' he said, heading for the door.

Christian watched as his boss left the suite and walked down the corridor. He leaned forward and turned off the desk lamp, plunging his room into darkness. He didn't want Zofia and Tom to see him crying.

When Lucy's car was found abandoned a week after she'd gone missing, and her bank accounts and credit cards hadn't been used, he knew, deep down, that she was dead. Until a body is found, there is always a hint of hope, but the knowledge is there, waiting to be confirmed. Now it had been, he felt devastated. Lucy was more than a technical assistant to the pathologist. She was as much a part of this team as the detectives, and her loss would be felt by everyone who'd come into contact with her. It was unfair. It was cruel.

This team had seen so much heartache over the years and Steve Harrison had been at the centre of most of it. It would end tomorrow. Christian would make sure of that. Steve Harrison was evil. He needed to be destroyed.

Chapter Forty-Eight

S ian had driven Adele home. When they arrived at the
farmhouse, Sian had to coax Adele out of the front
passenger seat. She was numb and in shock. While sitting in
traffic at a red light, Sian had fired off a text message to Pat
Campbell, telling her the news and asking if she was free to
come and sit with Adele. She was waiting by the front door
when Sian pulled up.

'How is she?' Pat asked.

'I can't get anything out of her,' Sian answered, looking
worried.

Sian rummaged in Adele's pockets for the front door keys
and unlocked the door. With her arms tightly around Adele,
she led her into the living room and sat her down on the sofa.
She immediately lit a fire while Pat went into the kitchen to
make a mug of tea for them all.

The room was warming up nicely and Adele was perched
on the edge of the Chesterfield, a blanket around her
shoulders, a blank expression on her pale face, gazing
somewhere off into the distance.

Pat placed a mug in her hands. 'Drink this, Adele. I've put plenty of sugar in. It's good for shock.'

'Is there any brandy or something?' Sian asked.

'I don't think they have anything like that. I think they're mostly wine drinkers.'

'I've never seen her like this. Do you think we should call a doctor?'

'She's shut down. Her brain can't cope with everything she's had thrown at her in the past couple of days – Matilda going missing, and now Lucy being found dead. Her mind can't process it all, so it's switched off.'

'What do we do?'

'We wait,' Pat said, sitting down next to her.

Sian sat on the opposite sofa. She picked up her tea and had a sip. She pulled a face. 'You've put sugar in mine, too.'

'You're also in shock. It'll help.'

A tear rolled down Sian's right cheek. 'When I heard Adele scream like that, I thought it was Matilda they'd found. When I looked … dear God, forgive me … I was relieved it wasn't her. But … straightaway, I knew who it was. I knew,' she cried. 'And then I felt bad for thinking …' She trailed off.

'It's only natural to think like that.'

'Do you think …?' Sian began before stopping herself.

'Go on,' Pat prompted.

Sian shook her head. The look on her face said it all. Whatever she was about to say was too horrific to contemplate.

'You were going to ask if I think Matilda is buried out there.'

Sian nodded and wiped her eyes as the tears continued to fall.

'No, I don't,' Pat said, firmly.

'Why not?'

'Well, for a start, the first body was discovered before Matilda went missing and there's been a police and forensic presence there ever since.'

'That's true. I hadn't thought of that.'

'Also, if this is all connected ... I'm not sure I can answer that. I don't see the point in killing people and hiding their bodies only for Matilda to be kidnapped once they start being discovered. Surely, if Steve is behind this, and he wants to hurt Matilda, it would be better for her to be there when the bodies are found, one by one, so she'll torture herself, wondering if she could have stopped it. Kidnapping her makes no sense.'

'So, you don't think Steve is behind this?'

'I can't see it being anyone else. I just don't understand his rationale behind it.'

'When it comes to Steve, there is no rationale,' Sian said.

Darkness had fallen. The only light in the living room was coming from the roaring fire. Sian didn't feel in a fit state to drive home so called her son, Anthony, to pick her up in the Donnie Barko van. She closed the curtains in the living room just as he was pulling into the driveway.

'Are you sure you'll be all right here on your own?' Sian asked.

'We'll be fine,' Pat said.

Adele hadn't moved. She hadn't touched her tea and she remained in Pat's arms.

'Call me if you need anything. I doubt I'll be getting much sleep tonight.'

Pat nodded and Sian left, reluctantly.

Less than an hour later, Adele was lying down on the sofa,

eyes closed, blanket over her, and Pat was in the kitchen putting together a snack when the doorbell rang. She went into the hall and opened it to find Simon Browes on the doorstep.

'I didn't know if I should bring something. A bunch of flowers or something,' he said. 'How is she?'

Pat stood to one side and allowed him to enter. He went to the doorway of the living room and watched Adele sleeping.

'I'm expecting her to sleep through the night. When she wakes up, she'll need someone here to help her make sense of what's happening,' Pat said. 'Come into the kitchen. I'll make you a drink.'

'Thank you,' he said, pulling himself, reluctantly, from the doorway and following her.

'I'm not very good at this,' Simon said once Pat handed him a mug of tea.

'Sorry?'

'Emotions. I don't know what to say.'

'There's nothing you can say. Adele will want you to just be there.'

'She needs Matilda.'

'She does. But you're a close second.'

'I don't know about that.' He cracked an awkward smile.

'You really like Adele, don't you?' Pat asked, pulling out a chair opposite.

'I do. But I don't think anything will happen between us.'

'What makes you say that?'

'This business with Lucy and Matilda. It's going to take a long time for Adele to come to terms with this, especially if Matilda ... well, I mean, if she's not found quickly. I mean, we don't know how long it's going to go on for, do we? The last thing on Adele's mind right now is going to be going out for a meal with me or a weekend away somewhere.'

'It's a sad fact that when you lose someone close to murder, you do end up losing some of your friends, too. Everyone is in limbo, at first. But it's not long before friends, neighbours, even close family members start to move on. For others, like Adele, losing Lucy like this and not knowing what's happened to Matilda will be with her forever. Her grief will come first.'

'I'm not sure I can deal with all this,' he said, clearly struggling. 'When we started, I didn't foresee anything like this happening.'

'We don't know what's around the corner,' Pat said. 'Which is just as well, really. Or we'd go mad.'

Pat studied Simon. He sat there, rotating his mug in his big fingers, pale blue shirt done up to the top button, but without a tie, the collar neat and crisp. A three-point handkerchief in the top pocket of his jacket, what was left of his hair was sensibly combed. His eyes were wide but not actually looking at anything specific as they darted around the room. His face was unreadable.

'Can I give you some advice?' Pat eventually said.

'Please.'

'You do like Adele, don't you?'

'I do,' he said, looking nonplussed.

'Then just be there for her. Give her a few days, send her a text in the meantime and a bunch of flowers. Let her know you're thinking of her and giving her a bit of space. Then come and visit.'

'You think that'll work?'

'I do. She'll feel better knowing there is someone out there for her when she's ready.'

'You're a good friend to her, Pat.'

'Adele and Matilda have been very good to me, especially

since Anton died. Can I get you another drink or something?' Pat asked, standing up.

'No. I'd better be off,' Simon stood up. 'I just wanted to see how she's doing. I … I have to do the post-mortem … on Lucy,' he suddenly said.

'Is there no one else who can do it?'

'Technically, yes, but I thought that Adele might not want a stranger doing it. Do you know what I mean?'

Pat nodded and gave him a sweet smile. 'I do. That's very thoughtful of you.'

He smiled back. 'This is a very dark time, isn't it?'

'It'll get lighter. It always does.'

Pat showed Simon to the door. When she opened it, a blast of cold air blew in and she shivered.

'Thanks for the tea, Pat,' Simon said, walking past her and out into the darkness.

Pat closed the door behind him and locked it. She went back into the warmth of the living room and sat on the opposite sofa to Adele. She watched as she slept and wondered what darkness was swimming around her mind. It was only two years since her only son was killed. There was only so much heartache a person could endure.

Pat went into Matilda's library, grabbed a paperback from the shelves and went back into the living room. She wasn't tired, and despite it being pitch-dark outside, it was still early. She didn't want to disturb Adele by putting the television on, and she didn't mind missing *EastEnders* anyway. She read the first couple of pages of *The Chameleon's Shadow* by Minette Walters, discovered that she liked it, so made herself comfortable to enjoy a night of reading.

After each chapter, Pat stole a glance at Adele to check she was still sleeping. Her eyes were lightly closed and she looked at peace. She was in the best place.

Halfway through chapter eight, Pat was disturbed by a scream so loud it could have shattered every window in the house. She dropped the book and looked over to Adele to see her face contorted in agony and streaming with tears.

Chapter Forty-Nine

S teve Harrison had been led from his prison cell to the governor's office with a guard on either side. He was told that tomorrow, after breakfast, he was to travel, under armed guard, to South Yorkshire Police Headquarters, where he was to be questioned under caution. He didn't ask why. He merely shrugged.

On his way back to his cell, he had to pass through the main corridor where the prisoners in A block were close to finishing their evening association before being locked in the cells for the night. He broke off from his guards when he saw Stuart Mills sitting alone, reading a battered paperback.

'South Yorkshire Police have requested the pleasure of my company tomorrow,' he said, leaning down and whispering in his ear.

Stuart didn't reply. He continued to read his book and ignore him.

'I wonder if the delectable Sian will be conducting the interview with me.'

Stuart began to blush. His ears started to redden. Around

him, other prisoners had noticed the conversation and edged further away, not wanting to be associated with them should anything happen.

'Is there anything you'd like me to say to her?'

Stuart continued to ignore him.

'Or is there anything you'd like me to *do* to her? I'll be within touching distance. I'll be able to smell her scent, her body odour. I'll be able to lean forward across that table and lick her face. Like this,' he said, and he slowly stuck out his tongue and ran it up Stuart's stubbled cheek.

Stuart had learned not to give in to narcissists like Steve. Years of living with a detective had shown him how to deal with people like the Steve Harrisons of the world. He sat there, rooted to the spot, seething with anger, wanting nothing more than to punch him over and over and over again until he was nothing but pulp. But he wouldn't give Steve the satisfaction.

'Goodnight, Stuart,' Steve said, walking away. 'I'll give Sian your love,' he called out.

Stuart closed his eyes. He could feel Steve's drying saliva on his face. He could smell his scent. He could hear his words ringing in his ears.

Steve had known he would be summoned to South Yorkshire Police. He had something planned. Stuart needed to warn Sian.

Chapter Fifty

S ian and Scott were driving back to Leeds, this time in complete silence. They hadn't called Linda Bellamy to warn her of their visit. This needed to be a surprise.

'I can't believe they found Lucy like that,' Scott finally said. They'd been driving for more than half an hour.

'I know. She was black, practically mummified, but there was no mistaking her. I knew it was her straightaway.'

'How's Adele going to cope with this?'

'I don't know, Scott.'

'Matilda would know what to do.'

Sian looked over to him. She had no idea what to say. She turned back to looking out of the window at the darkened view of the motorway whizzing by.

'Do you get the feeling that we've all died and we're living in some kind of purgatory?' Scott said. 'Ever since the shooting, everything has just … it's all fallen apart. I'm starting to think I died in that school with Rory, and I don't know it yet.'

Sian reached across and placed a hand on top of his. 'You've got Donal.'

He swallowed. He gave her a brief glace. 'He asked me to marry him while I was in hospital.'

'Did he?' she asked, a smile in her voice. 'What did you say?'

'I didn't. I pretended I didn't hear him.'

'Why?'

He wiped away a tear with the back of his hand. 'I don't know. Actually, I do. Sian, I was stabbed. I could have died. Chris *did* die. I went through hell. I still am going through hell. I can't do that to Donal.'

'Do you love him?'

'I do. I really do.'

'Then marry him. None of us know how long we have on this planet. We, more than anyone, know the horror and the violence that are out there, so when you get the chance of happiness, you have to grab it with both hands and keep a tight hold of it.'

'But what if …?' he began, a catch in his throat.

'No what ifs. If you love him, marry him. Make it work. Don't fill your life with regrets.'

Scott inhaled and let out a heavy sigh. Sian was right. He'd turn the tables on Donal and propose to him.

They pulled up outside Linda Bellamy's stylish home. There was a light on in a downstairs room, creeping out from the sides of the curtains. They crunched up the gravel driveway and Sian rang the bell.

'Is it me or is it getting colder?' Scott asked.

'It's not you. It's bloody freezing,' Sian replied.

The door opened, bathing them in a warm glow from within.

Linda was dressed for comfort this time in grey tracksuit bottoms and a navy hooded sweater. Her face was free of make-up and her hair was still damp from a shower.

'I had a feeling you'd return at some point,' she said by way of a greeting. She stepped to one side to let them in.

She closed the front door behind them and led them into her office. At the entrance, she stopped and looked over her shoulder at them.

'I'm assuming this is work-related?'

'Yes,' Sian said.

'Then we'll go in here. I don't allow anything work-related into my private rooms.'

Sian looked at Scott and rolled her eyes.

Linda flicked on the lights and the room lit up, making black mirrors of the windows leading out into the garden. There were no curtains in here.

'Please, take a seat,' Linda instructed, going over to her usual armchair.

'Linda,' Sian began, sitting down and crossing her legs. 'We've been doing some research into Steve Harrison, and we've been led to believe you're more than just his therapist.'

'I don't know where you got that from,' she said, incredulously.

'I spoke to someone who has met Steve Harrison a number of times,' Scott said. 'He's interviewed him, and various people who are close to Steve. He told me to give your ex-husband a call.'

Linda looked uncomfortable. 'You've been speaking to Lionel Miller.'

'I have.'

'I know he went into my bedroom. I could have had him arrested for trespassing.'

'Why didn't you?'

She didn't answer.

'I've also spoken to your ex-husband, Kevan Bellamy,' Scott said. 'He's still very angry about how your marriage ended.'

Again, Linda didn't say anything.

'You have a photograph of Steve Harrison in your bedside cabinet,' Scott said.

'Is that a question?' Linda asked.

'No. It's a statement of fact.'

She shrugged. 'What if I do?'

'Not very professional, is it?' Scott asked.

'Do you have photographs of your other clients in your bedside cabinet?' Sian asked.

Linda remained silent but shot Sian a daggered look.

'I'm guessing the people at Wakefield Prison don't know of your fixation with Steve,' Scott said.

'It's not a fixation,' Linda almost shouted.

'What is it then?'

'It's an … interest. I have an interest in Steven.'

'A personal one?' Sian asked.

'Yes.'

'Why personal?'

'I …' She didn't elaborate.

'You love him, don't you?' Sian asked.

It was a while before Linda replied. 'I do. There's no denying it. Yes, I love Steve Harrison. He's a very beautiful man. A little lost, but beautiful. Inside and out.'

'He's a psychopath,' Scott said.

'Only because that bitch Matilda Darke made him one,' she spat.

Her ugly words shocked Sian and Scott into stony silence.

'Do you genuinely believe that?' Sian eventually asked.

'Of course I do. You only have to look at her.'

'What do you know about Matilda's kidnapping?'

'Nothing.'

'I don't believe you,' Scott said.

'That's not my problem.'

'It bloody is. I can get a warrant to have this house turned upside-down looking for evidence. I can have you arrested for obstructing an investigation. I can also have your licence to practice revoked. Where is Matilda?' Scott asked, firmly.

Linda stared at Scott. Worry appeared on her face. Her bottom lip began to wobble, and tears filled her eyes.

'I don't know,' she said, fighting back the tears. 'I genuinely don't know. That's the truth. I honest to God had no idea he was planning anything. You say I have a fixation on him, but he has one on Matilda. I thought it was love at first, but it's not. He told me how much he blames her. I tried to tell him to get over it. I told him that I loved him, that I'd always be there for him, but he can't let go of Matilda,' she said, the words tripping over each other as she explained.

'Who is Amy Monroe?' Sian asked.

'I've no idea.'

'You've heard of her?'

'Lionel Miller mentioned her a couple of times.'

Sian looked at her phone, found the image of the photofit Scott and Finn had put together and showed it to Linda.

'Do you recognise this woman?'

'No.'

'Are you sure?'

'I'm positive. Who is she?'

'She's the woman we've been led to believe is Amy Monroe.'

'I don't know her. I swear. Look, I'm sorry. I'm really sorry that Matilda Darke is missing, but I have nothing to do with that. I promise.'

'But Steve has.'

'He hasn't told me anything. Look, please, don't tell the prison. I need this job. I need Steve. I love him,' she said, a mixture of a smile and fear on her face.

'He's using you,' Sian said.

'You know nothing.'

'I know Steve more than you. He's using you and when he drops you, it will hurt you so much. You need to get a grip and drop him first.'

'I will fight to get Steven released from prison with my last breath if I have to,' she said with conviction.

Scott stood up, wincing slightly at the pain from his stomach. 'I'm going to be reporting you to the relevant authorities. There is no way you should be a practising therapist.'

Linda jumped up and lunged for Scott. 'You bastard.' She went for his throat, but Sian put herself between them, grabbing Linda by the shoulders and pushing her hard to the floor. 'You should have died in that shooting. Jake should have shot you,' she screamed. 'He should have fucking killed all of you.'

Scott and Sian stood back and watched, open-mouthed, as Linda sat on the floor, tears streaming down her red face, screaming obscenities at them.

'What do we do?' Scott asked.

'I have absolutely no idea.'

Chapter Fifty-One

Saturday 23rd January 2021

Matilda opened her eyes. She was curled up in a corner, facing the wall, her legs pulled up to her chest, her arms wrapped tightly around them to keep her body heat contained. She was so cold. The bare brick walls were damp to the touch, and she could feel their iciness spreading into her. She was literally chilled to the bone.

Matilda's concept of time had vanished. She had no idea what day it was, what time it was or how long she'd been here. Was it daylight, mid-morning or the middle of the night? Was it still even January? Something, however, was different. It seemed lighter in the cell.

Slowly, Matilda pulled herself out of her cocoon. Her body ached as she'd spent a long night tightly curled up. She was stiff and would need to ease herself up gently.

As she turned onto her back, she noticed the door was wide open and a soft light was streaming in. The noose was back dangling from the ceiling, framed in the doorway, taunting her.

'Good morning, Matilda,' a voice called out.

Matilda jumped. She quickly sat up, her back pressed against the metal bed frame.

A figure stepped forward, out of the shadows. It was the woman who'd come to her home, who'd stabbed Scott, who'd tried to run her off the road on two occasions. She was tall and slim with a severe black bob haircut. She didn't look very old – mid-twenties, maybe.

'Who are you?' Matilda asked.

The blank expression on the woman's face dropped to one of disappointment. She walked over to the bed and sat down. As she did, she pulled off the wig to reveal mousy wavy hair. She ran her fingers through it. She gave Matilda an icy smile that didn't reach her eyes.

'Remember me now?'

Matilda didn't. She didn't want to antagonise her any further, but she couldn't lie to her.

'I'm sorry. I don't.'

'Do you know, I didn't think you would. The problem with you, Matilda, is that you enter people's lives, you ruin them, and then you leave, and accept none of the responsibility for the wreckage you've left behind.'

Her accent was pure Sheffield. Matilda tried to place it, to place her, but nothing in her memory jumped to the front. Was she connected to a case she'd worked on in the past? If so, how far back was she going? Matilda had been a detective for more than twenty years. She'd worked on countless investigations. She couldn't be expected to remember them all.

'Look, I'm sorry, I really am,' Matilda said slowly. She hadn't eaten or drunk anything for days. She had very little energy. 'I can't place you. If you tell me … if you tell me what I've done, I may be able to help put things right.'

'Really?' she asked, a sarcastic look on her face. 'Are you any good at raising the dead?'

Matilda frowned.

'You killed my family. My dad. My mum. And my sister. They are all dead because of you.'

Matilda's eyes widened. Why did she have no memory of any of this?

Chapter Fifty-Two

Christian looked at his watch. 'Look, Steve is on his way here to be interviewed under caution. We need to be on our A-game here. He cannot have the upper hand.'

Finn reached for his notebook. 'I called Wakefield Prison first thing,' he began.

'What time did you get in?' Tom asked, going over to the drinks station to make everyone a cuppa.

'I couldn't sleep. Anyway, the governor wouldn't tell me anything about Nina Price. He was very vague and just said she went for another job for more money. However, I called back and chatted to Henry Leech. He was the officer I was chatting to when we visited. He told me, off the record, that Nina was caught in a compromising position with Steve in his cell.'

'A compromising position?' Sian asked.

'Do I really need to spell it out? All I'll say is that she was on her knees, and very quickly fired. However, Nina has a brother, who is still an officer at the prison.'

'Do we know where Nina is now?' Christian asked.

'No. Henry said he doesn't know, but … I think he might do.'

'Why would she help Lionel with research for his book?' Tom asked.

'I'm not sure,' Finn said, frowning as he thought. 'Maybe she's not been able to get another job and Lionel offered her money for information. Or maybe she has feelings for Steve. It would be interesting to see what she helped Lionel with and whether it showed Steve in a good light or not.'

'I could give him another call. He seemed like a helpful bloke,' Scott said.

'It might give him an extra chapter or two for an updated version,' Zofia half-laughed, wheeling herself back to her desk. 'Oh, Sian, before I forget,' she said, picking up a couple of Post-it notes. 'Stuart's called. He really wants to talk to you.'

'Why?'

'I don't know. I spoke to Adam on the front desk this morning and he just said Stuart says it's really urgent you get in touch with him.'

Sian took the notes from Zofia. 'I knew this would happen if I went to see him. I knew he'd see it as some kind of sign to try and worm his way back into my life.'

'Are you going to call him back?'

'No. I'm bloody not. Christian, do you want me to interview Steve when he arrives?' Sian asked, wanting to quickly change the subject.

'I'd love you to, but Ridley doesn't want Steve talking to anyone who knows him. He thinks they'll be easily riled. I think we should send in Zofia and Tom, with you and me observing.'

Tom's face lit up. 'This'll put my psychology degree to good use.'

Christian hitched up a chair and sat opposite Tom. 'I don't want you trying to analyse him or anything. He'll spot it a mile off and play mind games with you. This is a simple question-and-answer session. We need to find out who the woman in the video is and where Matilda is. That's all.'

'No offence, but he's not going to tell us, is he?' Tom asked. 'There's no incentive for him to reveal anything. He'll just sit back and watch us all fumble about in the dark.'

'We offered him a pardon last time,' Sian said. 'We offered him a release from prison and a new identity, and he saw straight through it.'

'Which is why this time we're not going to offer him anything. We'll ask him what he wants in return for information, an arrest and Matilda's safe return.'

'What if it's something we can't give him?' Sian asked.

'He's a bloke who spends twenty-three hours of every day in a cell. There'll be something from the outside world he's missing more than anything. I'm pretty sure we can give him what he wants.'

Sian didn't look convinced. 'Famous last words,' she said to herself.

Chapter Fifty-Three

'**C**an I have something to drink?' Matilda asked.

'You need to understand what you've done, what damage you've caused,' the woman said. The darkness, the sadness, the anger were leaching out of her. Her fingers were clenched, and she was visibly shaking. 'I'd be lying if I said we were a happy family, we weren't. I don't know why. Me and my sister, we didn't want for anything. Mum ... she expected more from Dad, and he couldn't give it to her. I don't know why. Actually, that's a lie. I do know why. You,' she said, looking Matilda firmly in the eye. 'It's all because of you.'

Matilda watched as the pain spread across the woman's face. She was suffering from years' worth of rage which had boiled over and led to her being in this situation. There was nothing Matilda could say to assuage her. She had to sit and listen to her story.

'My grandad – my mum's dad – was a Chief Constable. He had this big house on the south coast overlooking the sea. We'd sometimes go there in the school summer holidays. Me and my sister thought it was great, like something from a film,' she said, a hint of a smile at a happy, distant memory. 'Grandad was very well thought of. Everyone loved him. He was respected. Mum wanted that for us, too. She wanted Dad to be in the same position. But it didn't happen for him. He became a Detective Inspector. He should have gone further, but you stopped him.'

Matilda's mouth fell open. Her eyes widened.

'Remember me now?' The woman asked.

Matilda could hardly bring herself to say the name of the man who had tried his best to get her removed from the force, the man who tried to assault her, the man who hanged himself in her own home, ruining the only place where she had happy memories of her husband.

'Say his name?' the woman said, her voice full of tears.

A tear rolled down Matilda's cheek.

'Don't you fucking dare cry,' she exploded. She jumped up, grabbed Matilda by the collar of her shirt and slammed her against the wall. 'You don't get to cry,' she spat. 'I don't want to hear how sorry you are. Nothing you can say will change anything.' She let her go and Matilda slid to the floor.

Matilda looked up at the noose hanging in the doorway.

'Which one of Ben's daughters are you?' she asked.

The woman wiped her eyes with her sleeve and sniffed hard. 'Lauren. I'm the oldest one. I'm the only one left.'

'What happened?' Matilda asked, struggling to fight back the tears.

'What happened? You really want to know? *You* happened. That's what.'

'Look, Lauren, I was promoted over your father fair and square. There was nothing underhand going on. I don't want to speak ill of your dad, he was a good detective, but he allowed himself to be consumed by bitterness. Instead of getting on with his work, he tried his hardest to destroy my career and hoped to take over. Him getting fired the way he did was of his own making. I know it's not easy to hear, but it's true. He was given plenty of warning to change his ways.'

'When Dad left the force, that's when everything ended for him,' Lauren continued, sitting on the edge of the bed. 'I know I wasn't the best daughter. I know I should have done more, but when I look back, I know it all started with you and that *fucking* promotion you stole from him.'

'I didn't—'

'The force needed a woman,' Lauren interrupted, refusing to listen to anything Matilda said. 'They needed to show a woman in a position of authority. I'm all for equality, but not when it comes at the expense of someone who deserved the job more, and my father really did. He was a better detective than you. Even you have to admit that.'

Matilda said nothing.

'I was doing my A-Levels when Mum and Dad divorced. It was a horrible time. They were always arguing. Mum kept saying how disappointed she was in Dad and the fight had just gone out of him. He let her scream and shout at him. Unfortunately, me and Amy were in the middle of it all. Mum didn't want us spending time with Dad but he really needed us and we wanted to go to see him, but we didn't want to upset Mum. We felt like we were being pulled into all kinds of directions. It was painful.

'The day after my last exam, I just took off. I always said I wanted a gap year before going to university, but at that point I wanted out and I really didn't want to come back. I went as far away as I could go. I went to New Zealand and then Australia. I got drunk. I partied. I took drugs. I slept with anyone and everyone. I literally went off the rails, but I had nobody to stop me. And, do you know something, I fucking loved every minute of it. But there comes a point where you either go down the rabbit hole of becoming an addict or you get out while there's still time. I was on the cusp of falling down that hole and I stopped myself just in time. I wanted a life and a future.

'Fortunately, by then, my A-Level results had come through and they were amazing. I managed to get a job in Thailand teaching English as a foreign language. I was living the dream. The beach was a two-minute walk away from the school. The sea was so clear. I was living in a postcard.

'By then I'd started accepting calls and messages from Amy. She was back at home, and it was her turn to do her exams and she was having to go through what I went through. Mum and Dad were still trying to find any excuse to stab each other in the back and I didn't want any part of it. Then Dad killed himself.'

She stopped talking and turned to Matilda.

'My dad killed himself in your house. I didn't think life could get any worse, but it did. You made it get worse. You killed him.'

'I didn't kill him,' Matilda said, her voice full of emotion.

'He hanged himself because of you. Now, you need to do the same.'

'I'm not going to hang myself.'

'You either hang yourself, or I walk out of this door and never come back. You die a slow, agonising death or you choose the easy way out. You're lucky you get a choice. My dad didn't.'

Chapter Fifty-Four

Christian and Sian were sitting in the observation room next to Interview Room 2. It was a tiny room, no bigger than a storage cupboard. They were close together, legs touching, facing forward and looking through the one-way mirror. The tension increased as they watched Steve Harrison being brought into the interview room, flanked by two prison officers.

The first thing Steve did was look towards them. He gave a sinister smile and winked. He was enjoying himself.

'Whenever I see that man, my blood pressure goes through the roof,' Sian said, not taking her eyes off him. 'I just picture Faith Easter hanging from the banister of that house. Bastard,' she said through gritted teeth.

'If anyone ever doubted there was evil in the world, all they need to do is look in Steve's eyes and there it is,' Christian said. 'I feel sick just looking at him.'

'Did you call Wakefield Prison about Linda Bellamy?'

'Yes. They've suspended her with immediate effect and revoked her visitation rights to see Steve. The governor is also taking it further and launching an enquiry with West Yorkshire Police.'

'Good. There's no way that woman—' She stopped when she saw the door open and Tom and Zofia enter the interview room. 'He flinched,' Sian said. 'Did you see his face when he saw them come in? He doesn't know them. He has no idea what to expect.'

Christian gave a faint smile. 'That's good. He's faced with two fresh-faced DCs. He'd have loved a Chief Constable.'

Tom spoke first, loudly and confidently. He introduced himself and Zofia, told Steve the interview would be recorded and videoed and asked everyone in the room to introduce themselves for the benefit of the recording.

'What do you think of Tom?' Sian asked.

'He seems like a bright lad.'

'Do you know anything about him?'

'Like what?'

'His background.'

He thought for a moment. 'No. Zofia seems to like him.'

'Hmm,' Sian mused.

'Steve, what can you tell us about the kidnapping of DCI Matilda Darke?' Tom asked. He sat, back straight, head held high, hands folded on the table on top of a closed file.

Steve smiled. 'It makes a great film.'

'You know the person who took her?'

'No comment.'

'We know the person who kidnapped DCI Darke is female.' Tom opened the file, took out the photofit Scott and Finn had supplied and placed it on the table in front of Steve. 'Is this her?'

He didn't even look. 'No comment.'

'Did you approach her, or did she approach you?'

'No comment.'

'How did you make contact?'

'No comment.'

'Whose idea was the kidnapping?'

'No comment.'

'Steve,' Zofia began, leaning forward. 'We know you're involved. We also know that you've no reason to help us unless there's something in it for you. Fair enough. I completely understand that. In your position, I wouldn't give away information for free either. So, what do you want from us?'

Steve leaned forward. 'You seriously expect me to do a deal with you? What authority have you two actually got? Fuck all, I'm guessing.'

'So, you'll answer the questions if someone more senior asks them?' Zofia asked.

'I've nothing to say to a college graduate and a cripple,' Steve said, his eyes fixed on Zofia.

Zofia tried not to look hurt, but it wasn't easy. Tom's face reddened as anger rose inside him.

'Bastard!' Sian seethed through gritted teeth.

'Pause the interview and get out of there now,' Christian said into the microphone to Tom and Zofia.

Neither of them in the interview room moved. Steve and Zofia were still locked in a staring contest and Tom looked ready to pounce.

'Shit,' Christian said. He jumped up and stormed out of the room. Sian quickly followed.

He threw open the door and entered the interview room.

'For the benefit of the recording, DI Christian Brady and DS Sian Robinson have entered the room. We'll be taking over the interview from here.'

Slowly, Tom stood up. Zofia, head down, wheeled herself out from behind the desk and out of the room with Tom following closely behind. Sian closed the door and she and Christian took a seat at the table.

'One more negative word about any of my officers, and I'll send you back to Wakefield and I'll make sure any privileges you have left are stripped.'

Steve sat back and smiled. 'You don't have the authority to do that.' He turned to Sian. 'Good morning DS Mills. Lovely to see you again. Your husband says hello, by the way.'

Sian didn't rise to his childishness in purposely getting her name wrong.

'Steve,' Christian began. 'As DC Simpson said, we know of your involvement in the kidnapping of DCI Darke. We want her back. Unharmed. What do you want to make that happen?'

Steve made a play of thinking. 'You know, I wouldn't mind a softer mattress. My back's killing me when I wake up in the morning.'

Christian wasn't expecting such a small condition and it wrongfooted him slightly. 'Okay. That's doable.'

'And I wouldn't say no to a bigger cell. I know there are bigger ones in Wakefield.'

Christian looked to one of the prison officers sitting behind Steve. He gave a single nod.

'Okay. We can do that.'

'Lovely.' Steve smiled.

'Anything else?'

'No. I think that's all I'll require for a more comfortable home.' Steve sounded cheerful and gave his famous smile.

'So, you'll tell us who took Matilda Darke and where she's being kept?' Christian asked.

Steve rolled his eyes. 'Did you honestly think a memory foam mattress and a bigger cell would make me talk? You two are fucking stupid. Jesus Christ, I should have told Jake to kill the bloody lot of you. No wonder the police in this country are a laughing stock if you are the best the force can offer. There is nothing you can give me that will make me tell you where Matilda Darke is. I may not be able to see her die, but I can smile knowing that her death will be lonely, long-drawn-out and painful.'

'You bastard,' Christian said.

'You sound surprised, DI Brady. Surely you've learned by now you can't do deals with me. I just love the violence and the bloodshed and the torment that goes with it. I'll sleep soundly on my wafer-thin mattress knowing you and Sian are going to be kicking yourselves for the rest of your lives because you couldn't save poor Matilda.'

Christian stood up. 'I don't know why we even bothered bringing you here.'

'Neither do I. But thank you. It was a lovely drive over.' Steve turned to Sian. 'Would you like me to give a message to your husband?'

Christian tapped Sian on the shoulder for her to follow him.

'Hold on a minute,' Steve said. 'Calm down, the pair of you. There's no need to go throwing your toys out of the pram and storming out. I'm only having a bit of fun with you.'

'Fun?'

'Come on, I'm locked away for twenty-three hours a day,

you can't blame me for enjoying myself when I get out. Look, sit down, both of you. I'll tell you where Matilda Darke is. I'll tell you who took her, and I'll tell you how you can get her back unharmed.'

'Really?' Christian asked, still not moving from the door.

'Really. And I have just one teeny tiny proviso.'

Christian and Sian exchanged glances and, reluctantly, retook their seats.

'Go on,' Christian said.

Steve left a lengthy silence. He looked at them both in turn. His lips weren't smiling, but his eyes were. The malevolent twinkle was back. They'd both seen it before.

'I want to kill someone,' he said, almost matter-of-factly. 'And I want South Yorkshire Police's approval.'

Chapter Fifty-Five

Pat Campbell had decided to move into Matilda and
Adele's house for a few days, pandemic be damned, and
after an hour of Adele assuring her she was fine to be left on
her own for however long it took Pat to go home and pack a
few belongings, Pat left the farmhouse. The house was
plunged into a dark silence.

It was Saturday morning. Usually, Adele and Matilda
would spend the morning having a lazy breakfast and, if
neither of them was working, they'd think of something to do
together. If they were feeling in an active mood, they'd pop to
Meadowhall, do some shopping and have a light lunch, or
maybe take a trip out into the countryside to have a long walk
and blow away the cobwebs. Or, if they wanted a lazy day,
they'd stay in their pyjamas, order something from Uber Eats
and watch a couple of Marvel films.

There would be none of that today. Adele was alone. The
house felt empty and cold. It was too big for just the two of
them, but there was always something happening.
Occasionally, Harriet would come over for a coffee, or Penny

would call for a flying visit on her way to whichever hobby she was currently immersed in. Scott often popped in from the flat above the garage, sometimes on his own, sometimes with Donal. And Sian was a frequent caller, too, especially when she needed to escape the dramas of her children in that impossibly small house they were all currently crammed into.

But for one person, alone, in a four-bedroom house with huge rooms and high ceilings, it was horrible. There was no noise. There was no conversation. There was no laughter. Adele could feel the silence filling every available space. It was squeezing her. And she hated it.

She sat at the kitchen table in a daze. It would take no effort at all to turn on the radio and have Radio Two blaring throughout, but Adele was drained. All she could think about was her former technical assistant, Lucy Dauman, mummified beneath that shed in those woods. Why? What had she done to deserve such a violent and lonely end? She wanted to call Lucy's fiancé but wouldn't know what to say. She should call her parents too, but, again, there was nothing she could say to make them feel better. Words were meaningless. She looked at her watch. It was almost midday. She wondered if Simon was performing the post-mortem on her yet.

Adele looked down at the table. It was wet. She was crying. Again. Although, had she even stopped crying since she'd woken up this morning? She didn't think so. Matilda was missing. Lucy was dead. She had so much to cry over.

'Come on, Adele, pull yourself together, for fuck's sake,' she chastised herself.

She knew tears solved nothing. She knew, deep down, that in order to survive you had to keep going, be strong, and fight. Matilda was a fighter. Wherever she was right now, Adele knew she'd be fighting to survive. It would be so easy for

Adele to run upstairs, jump into bed, pull the duvet over herself and cry until she faded away. But that was the wrong thing to do. She needed to remain active and positive.

She stood up, pushing back the chair. There was nothing she could do for Lucy, but there were people like Christian, Sian and Scott, committed and dedicated detectives who would find her killer and bring them to justice. She couldn't actively hunt for Matilda, but, again, Christian and Sian and the whole of South Yorkshire Police were looking for her. They'd find her. She knew it.

'So what the hell can I do?' she asked herself.

She walked out of the kitchen, through the hallway and into the living room. Her bag was propped up against one of the sofas where Pat had placed it last night when Adele had been brought home. She opened it, took out her laptop and sat down. Another email was waiting for her from her editor, asking for the final proofs of her chapters for the new book.

All Adele had right now was her work. She couldn't allow that to slip. If Matilda wasn't found … no, she couldn't think like that. Matilda would definitely be found and brought back home. In the meantime, Adele had a great deal of work to do to keep her mind distracted.

Chapter Fifty-Six

C hief Constable Benjamin Ridley didn't usually work at the weekend, but this was no ordinary weekend. He entered his office dressed in jeans and an oversized sweater. Christian was already waiting outside his office when he turned up. He filled him in on the interview with Steve Harrison.

'If there was one person in the world I'd have no qualms over putting a bullet through their head, it would be Steve Harrison,' Ridley said. He stormed over to his desk and slammed his briefcase down on top. He looked into the mini fridge in the corner and saw it stocked with small bottles of water. 'I can understand now why Valerie had an emergency bottle of whisky in her filing cabinet.'

'I don't suppose there's any chance it's still there.'

'No. Like an idiot, I got rid of it.' He slumped into his seat. 'I'm a very sensible man, Christian. I don't drink, I don't smoke, I avoid caffeine and processed foods as much as I can and play squash three times a week. But thanks to Steve fucking Harrison I'm craving a large whisky, a Cuban cigar and the greasiest, fattiest burger imaginable.'

'The best I can offer is a coffee and a Mars bar,' Christian said.

Ridley looked up at him and told him to sit down. 'Does he honestly think we'd give him permission to kill someone?'

'I don't know.'

'And who does he want to kill?'

'I don't know that either. I just stopped the interview. I didn't want to get into any of Steve's mind games. Once he gets in your head, it's a bugger to get him out.'

Ridley nodded. 'You know Steve better than anyone in this station. What would you like to do?'

'Throw him back into his cell and lock the door behind him.'

'Then that's what we'll do. Harrison knows we'd never allow him to kill someone. He's playing with us. The worst thing we can do is enter into a dialogue with him. We send him back to Wakefield, strip him of any contact with the outside world and leave him to rot.'

'But what about Matilda?'

Ridley let out a heavy sigh. 'We get the media involved.'

'Are you all right, Zofia?' Sian asked, handing her a mug of tea.

She nodded. 'Actually, no. I'm not.'

Sian pulled up a chair and sat down. They were in the Homicide and Major Crime Unit. Finn was on the phone, Scott was hammering at his computer and Tom was out somewhere.

'It's the first time I've had a derogatory remark about being disabled. It just hit me,' she said, quietly.

'What you have to remember about the Steve Harrisons of this world is that they're so unhappy with themselves that they like to bring others down to their level. You are no different to anyone else in this room, in this station in fact. You just come with wheels.' Sian smiled.

'Nobody has treated me any different and that's made me feel so much better about being disabled, but what Steve said, well, it was like a knife to my heart. I am a cripple.'

'No. You're not.' Sian dug in her pocket for a tissue and handed it to her. 'You're a human being, you're a detective constable, you're a woman. That's who you are.'

'Will you be honest with me?' Zofia asked, wiping her eyes. 'Has anyone else said anything about me being in a wheelchair?'

'No, they haven't,' she replied firmly. 'And I'm not just saying that, either. Trust me, if they had, I'd have been on them like you wouldn't believe. Steve just enjoys hurting people. Ignore him. You've got a great job, a lovely home and a boyfriend who thinks a lot about you.'

'Does he?'

'Of course he does. I've seen the way Tom looks at you.'

Zofia smiled through her tears. 'Thank you, Sian.'

Sian held out her hands, took Zofia's in hers and squeezed them tight. 'I'm always here for you, Zofia, you know that.'

'Finally!' Scott said, pushing his chair back from his computer.

'What is it?' Sian asked.

'I've gone right round the houses trying to find out who at Wakefield Prison helped Lionel Miller with his book and why.'

'I thought it was that Nina woman.'

'It was. Okay,' he said, pushing himself back to his desk and rifling through his notebook. 'I think I've got this sorted out in my head. So, Nina Price was an officer at Wakefield Prison. She was caught performing a sex act on Steve Harrison and was sacked. It was after she was sacked that she helped Lionel Miller with his research, telling him all about Steve as a person and prisoner. Now, Nina has a brother who is also a prison officer at Wakefield, Ray Clarke. It's taken me a while, but I've found out that Ray can't have any contact with Steve because of the connection with Nina.'

'Where is Nina now? Could she be the woman who kidnapped Matilda?' Finn asked.

'No. Getting sacked was the beginning of the end for Nina. Her husband threw her out, filed for divorce and won custody of their child. Nina is currently living in Rhyl and works as a caretaker at a caravan site.'

'Do we know that for a fact?' Sian asked.

'Yes. I've spoken both to Nina and to the owner of the site. Nina hasn't had any holiday or days off for over eight months. Also, Nina said she'd rather die than set foot back in Wakefield.'

'That seems a tad extreme. It's not that bad in Wakefield,' Finn said, adding a touch of levity to the conversation.

'Also, I've double-checked and triple-checked the people who have contact with Steve Harrison. The rotas of staff on the Supermax wing are changed on a regular basis. There is no one who sees him often enough to be manipulated by him.'

'So how did he manage to see a live feed of Matilda's kidnapping?' Sian asked. 'How does he know all about it? What aren't we seeing here?'

'I really don't know,' Scott said. 'However, Pat Campbell suggested that maybe we should look at Ben Hales's daughters. Ben's ex-wife was Sara Monroe. Now, Pat couldn't remember if one of the daughters was called Amy, but I've been looking them up. Ben and Sara had two daughters, Amy and Lauren.'

'And where are they now?'

'Well, did you know that Sara had died?'

'No, I didn't. When?'

'Hang on,' Scott said, flicking through his notes. 'I haven't got the exact date. It's a few years ago though. She had breast cancer. It spread quite quickly. She was dead within three months of the diagnosis.'

'Good grief. Poor woman. What about her daughters?'

'The news just goes from bad to worse for that family. Amy took her own life a few months after Sara died.'

'Oh my God,' Sian said, sinking further into her chair. 'And Lauren?'

'She's been in Thailand for the last few years teaching English as a foreign language.'

'Do we know if she's still out there?'

'I've looked at her social media feeds and it seems so. She posted a photo to Instagram last week of her on a beach drinking something very delicious-looking and added the caption "Finally living my best life".'

'So, someone used Amy Monroe's name so that we would think this is connected to Ben Hales,' Finn suggested. 'Whoever has kidnapped Matilda wants us to know that this goes back to her past. They've contacted Steve Harrison and got him on board, for some reason we don't yet know, and they've used Amy's name to confuse us.'

'It's worked,' Zofia said.

'If you add the bodies found at Wigtwizzle – the three missing sex workers, Duncan McNally and Lucy Dauman – that's three cases we've worked on in the past few years. Add Ben Hales and that ties in with the unit, too. Someone has been stalking Matilda for a very long time and is using her cases to great effect.'

'But why?' Zofia asked.

'Stalkers are very dangerous people,' Finn continued. 'Whatever reason they have for doing something makes perfect sense to them but will mean nothing to us. They've been following Matilda, getting to know her every move and looking at everything she's been working on – for years. Now, it's all coming to a head, and they've kidnapped Matilda to have control over the endgame.'

'So how do we find them?' Scott asked.

'Hang on.' Finn held up his hand to silence Scott. 'Let me think for a moment. I think Matilda knows who her kidnapper is. In fact, I think we all know who her kidnapper is. We'll have spoken to him at some point. Either we'll have interviewed him in connection with a crime or he'll have inveigled himself in our lives some other way. We'll have laughed and joked with him.'

'You're talking like it's someone we work with,' Zofia said.

Finn turned to look at her. 'Precisely.'

Chapter Fifty-Seven

The human body begins to break down the moment the heart stops beating. As soon as life is extinct, the decomposition process begins. The first signifier is that the body's temperature starts to fall and does so by roughly one degree per hour until it matches the temperature of its surroundings.

With no heart beating, the cells become deprived of oxygen, and their acidity is increased as the toxic by-products of chemical reactions begin to accumulate inside them. Enzymes start to digest cell membranes and then leak out as the cells break down. This process begins in the liver, which is rich in enzymes, followed by the brain, which has a high water content. Eventually, all tissue and organs will break down in this way.

After a couple of hours, calcium will build up in the muscles, causing them to tense. This is called rigor mortis and lasts for roughly thirty-six hours, dependent on the surrounding atmosphere. Eventually, the muscles will relax. Any remaining faeces and urine within the body will start to leak out of every available orifice.

There is a myth that hair and nails continue to grow after death. What happens is that skin loses all moisture and shrinks.

Within a few days of death, the body begins to turn green in places. This is because enzymes in the vital organs have nothing to feed on, so they start digesting themselves, usually with the help of bacteria. It's at this point that the body will start to smell, and it's a disturbing, vomit-inducing stench. The decaying body is releasing chemicals like putrescine. The smell will be caught by local wildlife who will be drawn to it. They'll dig and it won't take them long to find the bloated, rotting corpse. They'll begin to feed. And not just foxes and rats, but bugs will arrive, too. Maggots can digest up to sixty per cent of a human body within a week.

What's left will begin to turn purple, then black as bacteria continue to digest the body. Hair will start to fall out at this stage, too.

Within four months, the soft tissue will have fully decomposed and all that is left will be the skeleton.

Four months, that's all it takes, from life to disintegration.

When determining the cause of death, many factors are taken into account, and, as I will explain throughout this chapter, the smallest detail can change the course of a criminal investigation. A body left in situ, undisturbed, can still reveal the cause of death years later.

Adele was sitting at the dining room table reading the book she and Simon Browes had written together. All she was required to do was read through her chapters to make sure there were no errors, factual or spelling, but her editor had sent the entire manuscript and Adele was curious about Simon's writing style. She'd read his articles and reports in the past and was fascinated by his vocabulary. He was a much more fluid and intelligent writer than she was. Her chapters had a more matter-of-fact, chatty tone and she was jealous of Simon's educated turn of phrase.

This was the final stage in the book. After this, she would not be able to make any more changes. By reading Simon's chapters, she was hoping to steal some of his rich vocabulary and put it among her own words.

She sat back and looked at the words on the screen. A tear fell and landed on the table. She didn't even know she was crying. So much was happening right now. So much was changing, and she was struggling to cope. Her son was dead. Lucy was dead. Matilda was missing. Was she dead, too?

Adele looked around the vast kitchen. She was surrounded by so much death and destruction at work and now it had followed her home. She'd left her house following Chris's death because the memories were too much to live with. Would she have to leave here, too? If so, where would she go? She was already wondering how she was going to return to work, knowing Lucy had been on one of the gurneys and was stored in the fridge.

'Maybe this is where everything changes,' she told herself. 'Maybe I need a complete break. A new job. A new city.'

She pushed her chair back and left the kitchen, walking slowly past Matilda's library. She looked along the shelves until she saw the book she was after. She went through the dining room, running her fingers over the polished oak table, through the double doors and into the living room. The smell from the large Chesterfield sofas mingled with the ash from the fire she'd lit last night. It was homely and comforting. She loved this room. It was perfect to relax in, put her feet up, glass of wine in one hand, the other submerged in a sharing bag of peanut M&Ms which she had no desire to share, a Marvel film on the huge TV, and talking filthy with Matilda about Captain America.

Adele sniggered to herself at the memory. Her life had

settled into a cosy and safe routine. She'd settled for security and lowered her guard. She should have known it would be ruined at some point. Even if Matilda did return home, she would be changed by being kidnapped.

She took a deep breath, and a decision sprang into her mind. She'd wait until Matilda came back and was over the worst of the aftermath, but then she needed to alter her life. Sheffield meant death and horror, tears and destruction. She couldn't live like this anymore. It was time to move on.

Chapter Fifty-Eight

S ian Robinson left the Homicide and Major Crime Unit and released a heavy sigh. She'd watched from a distance as Chief Constable Ridley and DI Brady had led a press conference, detailing the bones found at Wigtwizzle and the kidnapping of Matilda Darke. She'd shed tears, and needed a few minutes to herself.

She walked down the corridor and stopped in her tracks when she saw one of the officers from Wakefield Prison leaving a side room.

'Everything all right?' she asked.

'Fine,' he said. He loomed over Sian, standing well over six feet. 'We'll be setting off soon. Jez has gone to fill up with petrol. You couldn't tell me where the toilets are, could you?'

'End of the corridor, turn left and they're straight ahead.'

'Cheers.'

'Is … is Steve in there on his own?'

'He's handcuffed. Nothing to worry about.'

'Oh good,' she smiled. She watched him walk away and

turn the corner before she opened the door to the interview room and slipped inside.

Steve looked up and smiled when she saw Sian enter. 'Oh, hello, Sian. I wondered if I'd get a chance to see you again before I went home.'

Sian could feel her blood boiling beneath the surface but didn't want him to see how much hatred and loathing she had for him. She pulled out the chair opposite him and sat down. 'So, you want us to give you permission to kill someone?'

He laughed. It was a sound that cut through Sian like a hot knife through a Mars bar.

'I just wanted to see how far you'd go. I knew you'd never grant permission. Doesn't bother me anyway,' he shrugged. 'If I want to kill someone, I will. What can you do to me if I do, slap another twenty years on my life sentence?'

'What would you have done if we'd said yes? Do you have a victim in mind?'

'I've always got a victim in mind.' He leaned forward. 'But I would have loved your permission to kill your husband.'

'Ex-husband,' she corrected him. 'Why Stuart?'

He shrugged. 'Why not?'

'Steve, I'm not going to plead to your better nature, because you don't have one, and I'm certainly not going to beg. I'm going to ask you, one last time, do you know where Matilda Darke is?'

Steve remained impassive, his eyes fixed on Sian. He licked his lips. 'I do, actually.'

'Will you tell me where she is?'

'I could do.' He leaned back in his seat and tried to fold his arms, but the handcuffs wouldn't allow it. 'But you wouldn't find her even if I did.'

Sian frowned. 'Why not?'

'Come on, Sian. There could be a massive neon sign over an abandoned factory saying "Matilda Darke is here" in six-foot letters and you wouldn't see it. I mean, for fuck's sake, you were married to a serial killer for more than twenty-five years and didn't twig on to what your husband was up to.'

Sian balked. She hoped Steve hadn't noticed, but she was sure he had, judging by the twinkle in his eye.

'Whenever there's a serial killer on the loose and the police give a statement appealing for the public's help, they say to look at those around them. Has their husband, brother, father, son changed much over the past few days and weeks? Are they behaving any differently? Your husband killed eight women over God knows how long and you didn't know. You're a trained detective. It's your job to spot killers and you couldn't even find one in your own bed. How do you sleep at night knowing you're partly responsible for all those deaths?'

Sian swallowed. Her mouth was dry. 'I am not responsible ...' she tried to say. She could barely get the words out.

'Of course you are. Have a good long think, Sian. Within an hour of Stuart killing one of those prostitutes, he came home and climbed into bed beside you. He'll have been running on adrenaline. Trust me, I know what that feeling is like. He put his arms around you, arms that were still warm from the touch of one of his victims. He kissed you with lips that had bitten into the flesh of a hooker. When you had sex, his cock had been inside a disease-riddled whore. When you looked into his eyes, those eyes had watched life become extinct. And all you did was lie there and think of England.'

Sian felt sick. She'd been over this so many times. She'd

analysed every memory she had of her home life once Stuart had been arrested, searching for any sign of a change in him, a sign that she should have picked up on. The truth was, she had no idea. Every time she looked at her husband, she saw the man she loved, the father of her children. He was the last person on earth who could have been a killer. He'd lied and manipulated and covered his tracks so well that she didn't see any change in his behaviour.

'You're just as bad when you think about it. I mean, you didn't physically kill them, obviously, but you allowed it to happen by walking around with blinkers on. You must have seen a change in Stuart. There's no way you couldn't have noticed. Yet you ignored it because you didn't want your safe existence ruined. Myra Hindley and Ian Brady, Fred and Rose West, Ian Huntley and Maxine Carr, Stuart and Sian Mills. You're just as complicit in the murder of eight prostitutes as your husband, yet you're walking around a free woman while he's in prison. Where's the justice?'

Sian closed her eyes tight. Steve was saying everything she had been thinking since she discovered what Stuart was really up to. She should have known. She should have seen through his façade.

'Let me ask you a question,' Steve continued. 'When you look back over your time together and you link the dates he committed his murders with what was going on in your own life, did he come home and fuck you after he'd finished fucking those prostitutes?'

It was a while before Sian could compose herself to answer without a torrent of tears. 'I'm not answering your questions, Steve.'

'Answer me one question and I'll tell you where Matilda is.'
Sian eyed him up carefully. She gave him a smile. 'You

almost had me there, Steve. You play a mean game, I'll give you that. You don't know where Matilda is at all. If you did, you'd have given us something, anything so we'd be chasing our tails. The reason you haven't is because you don't know. Nice try.' She stood up and went to leave the room.

'Sian, before you go, is there a message you'd like me to give to your husband?'

'No. There isn't.'

'Really? I know I haven't got your permission, but I will be killing him when I get back. Are you sure you don't have one more thing you'd like to say to him?'

Sian's face dropped. She looked at Steve and couldn't read him. She had no idea if he was trying to rile her again or if he really did plan to kill Stuart.

Steve sat back in his chair and crossed his legs. 'You see, that's the problem with handing out whole-life tariffs, there's no incentive for me to live by the rules of the prison. I could murder someone every week. The government adding more and more years to my sentence means fuck all.'

Sian pushed down the handle of the door and pulled it open.

'Okay, you want a cryptic clue as to where Matilda Darke is, I'll give you one. Firstly, how long has she been missing? Is it two days or three?'

'This is the third day.'

'Oh. In that case it doesn't matter. She's already dead,' he smiled.

Chapter Fifty-Nine

S ian left the station without saying goodbye to anyone. When she went back into the HMCU suite for her bag and coat, it was empty, thankfully, so she grabbed her things and left. Behind the wheel of her car, she fired off a text to Anthony telling him to order a takeaway for them all from whatever app he used, and she'd give him the money when she arrived home. She wanted to be on her own for a while.

She drove through the cold, dark streets of Sheffield, not knowing where she was going. It was only when she indicated right to turn off Ringinglow Road that she realised she'd been heading for Matilda and Adele's house all along.

Adele's Porsche was parked outside the house, a thin layer of frost covering the windows and the bonnet. It was another cold night. Another night with Matilda's whereabouts unknown. Sian wasn't sure how much longer she could cope with all this. She wasn't sleeping, she wasn't eating, and after talking with Steve Harrison her head was heavy with darkness. Why had she walked into that room? She knew what he was like. He used any excuse to try to antagonise people around him, and she'd handed herself to him for him to play with, like a kitten with a ball of wool.

'Stupid bitch,' she said to herself as she tore off the seatbelt and climbed out of the car. She seemed to be devoid of energy.

She rang the doorbell and waited for the door to be opened. She squinted at the brightness from within.

'Sian, is everything all right? Is it Matilda?' Adele asked, concern etched on her face.

'No.'

'You look ... has something happened?'

Sian struggled to hold back the tears. 'Oh God, Adele. I don't know how I can go on with this,' she said, almost collapsing into her arms.

—————

Sian downed a proffered glass of wine in two gulps. They were sitting in the living room, fire blazing, television on mute. She poured out her heart to Adele.

'The thing is,' she said, leaning forward to grab the bottle and pour a second glass, 'Steve's right. I should have known. I should have seen the change in Stuart.'

'Was there a change?'

'I don't know,' she said, frustrated with herself. 'I honestly don't know. There should have been. All the textbooks say that when one person kills another it changes their whole personality. I, as a detective and as Stuart's wife, should have noticed. And I didn't.'

'Maybe Stuart is just a master at manipulation. He fooled everyone around him. Not just you, but your kids, Matilda, his sister, everyone.'

Adele's phone started to ring. She looked at the display, turned the phone to silent and put it back on the coffee table.

'Don't you need to get that?' Sian asked.

'It's Matilda's mum. She's calling me all the time. I've run out of things to say to her.'

'I thought Pat was staying with you?'

'She is. She's just sorting out a few things at home. She'll be over later. Have you eaten?'

'No. I couldn't face anything.'

'You need something to soak up the wine. Come on, I think there's something in the freezer we can have.'

Adele made her way into the kitchen, dragging her feet. Sian followed.

'Have you spoken to Lucy's parents?' Sian asked.

'No. I've dialled their number a few times but never made it to the final digit. I don't know what to say to them.'

'Have *you* heard from anyone?'

'Donal called me about an hour ago,' Adele said, a slight smile on her lips. 'He wanted to see how I was and told me about Lucy's post-mortem results. He said he thought it would be better hearing it from him.'

'Do they know how Lucy died?'

'She was strangled. There's evidence of a thin ligature around her neck.'

'She wasn't …?'

'I don't know,' Adele answered quickly. She knew Sian was going to ask if there was any sign of sexual assault. It was something she didn't want to think about, despite the fact it was her first original thought. 'She was too badly decomposed for us to find out.'

'Why kill her?' Sian asked. 'Was she just in the wrong place at the wrong time?'

Adele's bottom lip began to wobble. She could feel the tears coming on again. She pulled open the freezer and stuck her head inside. 'I've got some fishcakes with a cheesy sauce in them. We can have those with chips.'

Sian nodded. 'I had a sandwich earlier, but I didn't taste it. I've got a permanent nasty taste in my mouth.'

'I know the feeling. This whole thing is a nightmare, isn't it?' Adele asked, turning on the oven to warm up.

Sian pulled out a chair at the table and sat down. 'I feel sick, Adele. I know Steve hasn't physically kidnapped Matilda, but he knows who has. And they'll be just as twisted as he is. What are they doing to her?'

Adele sat down opposite her. 'I'm trying not to think about that.'

'Finn was saying earlier that it's someone we know, someone who's wormed their way into our lives. Then that gets me thinking about Stuart and how I should have noticed what he was up to ... and whoever has got Matilda, I should have noticed that, too.'

Adele's eyes widened. She jumped up from the table, sending the chair crashing to the floor.

'What's the matter?' Sian asked.

Adele didn't reply. She ran out of the kitchen and into the living room. She snatched up her laptop, which was on charge, ripped out the cable and turned it on.

Sian came into the room behind her. 'What is it? What's wrong?'

'Hang on. Let me just make sure I'm not imagining anything here.'

Sian watched with a heavy frown as Adele frantically scrolled through her laptop. On the television, on the wall, the news headlines began. Sian picked up the remote and unmuted the sound.

'*South Yorkshire Police have declared a major incident following the discovery of remains of five bodies in woodland and the kidnapping of a Detective Chief Inspector. We can go live to our North of England correspondent, Danny Hanson, who is at the scene. Danny, first of all, the human remains, how long have they been there?*'

Danny stood at the edge of the woodland at Wigtwizzle. It was dark, but the background was brightly lit by scene-of-crime arc lights. Danny was wearing his trademark blue check shirt and his hair was lifting slightly in the stiff breeze. Sian would bet a full month's wages he was already trending on social media.

'*We don't yet know how long the remains have been here. South Yorkshire Police are playing their cards very close to their chest. However, I've been told there are five bodies, and all the victims are known to the police force.*' He looked down at his iPad. '*Three are former sex workers and one is a homeless man who came into contact with the police during an investigation two years ago. The fifth body is that of a pathology technician who has worked closely with police and has been a missing person for over a year.*'

'*Has the police force said how they died?*'

'*No. We don't have any details at all on the causes of death.*'

'*South Yorkshire Police have also revealed the kidnapping of Detective Chief Inspector Matilda Darke and appealed to the public for information. What do we know of that incident and is it connected to the remains found at Wigtwizzle?*'

'*Again, Fiona, South Yorkshire Police are being very scarce with their details. A source has told me that DCI Darke, an eminent detective within the force, has been missing for more than three days and that a detective sergeant was stabbed during her kidnapping. The Homicide and Major Crime Unit, a unit headed up by DCI Darke, is working round the clock to find her, and one of the lines of enquiry is that the bodies found in the woodland behind me are linked to her kidnapping. Earlier today, serial killer Steve Harrison, currently serving a whole-life tariff in Wakefield Prison, was seen entering South Yorkshire Police Headquarters. We've been told a statement will be released in the morning when, hopefully, more details will be revealed.'*

'Danny Hanson, thank you. The Coronavirus pandemic …'

Sian muted the television. 'I know he's only doing his job, but there are times I really want to smash that bloke's face in.'

'Sian, read this.'

Sian turned to look at Adele, whose face was pale in horror. 'What is it?'

'Please. Just read it and tell me what you think.'

Sian took the laptop and read the highlighted text. She looked back to Adele with a heavy frown. 'I'm not sure what I'm supposed to be reading here.'

'You're reading about Lucy Dauman's murder.'

Chapter Sixty

S cott let out a groan as he adjusted himself on his seat.

'Are you all right?' Zofia asked, looking up from her screens.

'Yes. Fine. It's sitting in one position for so long while recovering from a stab wound. It's a little uncomfortable.'

'Whereas sitting in a wheelchair for the past two years has been a breeze,' she said, a twinkle in her eye.

'Sorry. I'm moaning to the wrong person, aren't I?'

'I'm joking. You should go home.'

'So should you. It's pitch-dark outside.' He nodded towards the window.

Zofia looked over her shoulder. 'I didn't even realise.'

'Where's Tom?'

'I'm not sure,' she said, looking slightly forlorn. 'He popped out a couple of hours ago and I haven't seen him since.'

'Is everything all right between you two?'

Zofia chewed her bottom lip. 'I thought it was.'

'Do you want me to have a word?'

She smiled. 'Not just yet. Thanks, Scott.'

The doors were pushed open, and a shattered-looking Finn entered the suite. His shirt was untucked from his trousers and his usually neat hair was ruffled.

'Remember me telling you about the bloke at Wakefield Prison I was chatting with, the young lad?'

Scott nodded.

'Well, he is Nina Price's brother, Henry Leech. I asked him how he feels about Steve and everything that happened with his sister, and he doesn't blame Steve for Nina getting fired. He said the fault was fifty-fifty. I've also looked at the list of people who have contact with Steve Harrison, and Henry Leech has only been on duty on the Supermax wing twice in the last six months.' Finn went over to the murder board and began updating it. 'Whoever Steve is in cahoots with at the prison, I'm struggling to work out who, why and how.'

'I thought you said Nina's brother couldn't have contact with Steve because of the connection with Nina,' Scott said.

'Officially, he can't, but when you're short-staffed, rules go out of the window.'

'I think I might have something,' Zofia interrupted, glaring at one of her screens. She sat back and looked over the monitors to Scott and Finn. 'I've been going through a lot of social media posts, specifically people who've mentioned Steve Harrison and seem to have a bit of a fixation. Anyway, when you said Lauren Hales had posted that photo of herself on a beach in Australia, something clicked in my brain, but I couldn't work out why. I've just realised what it is.'

'What?' Scott asked.

'Come round here and I'll show you.'

Scott and Finn gathered around Zofia's bank of monitors. Finn took a seat while Scott stretched his aching limbs.

'This is the photo Lauren posted of herself on Burleigh Head beach on the Gold Coast. It was posted last week, and she commented saying she's finally living her best life. Now, look in the background of the photo. What do you see?'

Scott and Finn leaned in and had a good look. The photograph showed Lauren in a swimsuit lounging on the sand, her long mousy hair tied back, wearing sunglasses and smiling at the camera. In the glare of the midday sun, she looked the picture of happiness.

'I'm not seeing anything,' Scott said. 'Mind you, my eyes are that tired at the moment, Blackpool Tower could be in the background, and I'd not notice it.'

'All I'm seeing is a lot of thin happy people having fun,' Finn said. 'Lucky buggers. It's been years since I had a beach holiday.'

'You're missing the point,' Zofia said. 'There are several things wrong with this photo.'

'Has it been photoshopped?'

'No. It's genuine. However, we're in the middle of a pandemic and Australia have some of the toughest lockdown restrictions in the world. They're not allowing foreign tourists into the country. So, how can Lauren have gone there from Thailand for a holiday? Also, and here's the cheat that you can't see, embedded in the meta data of the photo is the GPS of the location. Yes, it was taken on Burleigh Head beach, but it wasn't posted from Burleigh Head beach or anywhere else in Australia. This post was created five days ago right here in Sheffield.'

'Really?' Scott asked.

'I've been looking back over Lauren's posts. She's been on Facebook for well over ten years but in the last few years she's hardly posted anything. In the past month, she's posted more photos and updates than she has in the past two years, giving the illusion she's working hard in Thailand and now holidaying in Australia. Why, all of a sudden, would she want everyone to know what she's up to?'

'To give herself an alibi,' Finn said.

'Exactly. Now, I don't know if you two know about the GPS thing. I don't think a lot do. They just create their posts and press send.'

'I'm too boring to be on social media,' Finn said. 'I created an Instagram page but didn't see the point of it.'

'I've got Facebook,' Scott added. 'But I can't remember the last time I posted anything.'

'Fortunately for you two, I have accounts on all of them. I also have several dummy accounts for emergency purposes.'

'What kind of an emergency would you need to be in to post on Facebook under a different name?' Scott asked.

'It depends what I'm working on at the time. For example, Lauren, unsurprisingly, has her privacy settings switched off so the world can see what she's posted. I commented on her photo saying how gorgeous the beach looked, mentioned I was going there next month and asked if she could recommend any restaurants.'

'Has she?'

'No. She's blocked me. But that in itself is another red flag.'

'So why would Lauren Hales say she's in Australia when she's really in Sheffield?' Scott asked.

'You two tell me,' Zofia said. 'Another question: does she look like the woman who crashed into you, Finn, just before Christmas?'

Again, they both leaned in to the monitor.

'I'm not sure,' Scott said. 'She had dark hair and it was shorter.'

'And she wasn't wearing sunglasses,' Finn added. 'It could be.'

'Zofia, can you get me an address for Lauren Hales?' asked Scott. 'I think we need to talk to her. Her behaviour is very dodgy, and if she's not the one who kidnapped Matilda then she's obviously up to something.'

Chapter Sixty-One

A dele and Sian drove in silence to Watery Street in Adele's Porsche. The journey took longer than usual due to the Saturday evening traffic.

'Do you think I should phone Wakefield Prison?' Sian asked, shattering the silence.

'Why?'

'About what Steve Harrison said. I know he likes to say things to shock people and rile them, but what if he does murder Stuart? I know my feelings towards him are of anger right now, but he is the father to my children. I don't want them discovering their dad was murdered and I could've helped prevent it.'

'I think you should call them. At least inform them of the conversation you had with Steve. They might be able to put measures in place to make sure Steve and Stuart never meet.'

'True.' Sian dug out her phone. 'I'll give Finn a ring. He was quite chatty with someone at the prison.' She looked over to Adele and took in her tense expression. 'Are you all right?'

'I'm fine. Why?'

'You look like you're about to burst into tears.'

'I've just had a dark thought about something. If I'm right … Do you know something, I hope to God I'm wrong.'

'Do you want to share it with me? It might not seem so bad out loud.'

Adele wiped her eye. 'Trust me, it's very bad.'

She swung the car into her parking space and turned off the engine. She whipped off her seatbelt, grabbed her bag from the back seat and climbed out of the car.

It was another cold night. The sky was cloudless, and a full moon shone down on the Steel City. Adele shivered, looked at the building where she worked and headed towards it.

'I'm going to make that phone call,' Sian called out. 'I'll catch you up.'

Adele didn't hear her. With long, determined strides, she tapped in her pass code and entered the building.

Many of the workers at the Medico-Legal Centre hated being in the building after dark, especially when there was a skeleton staff. There was something about being alone among the dead that planted the fear of God in them. Adele had never understood why. She always seemed to get more work done at night when on the graveyard shift. Not that she did that anymore – she had people to delegate that side of the work to. Dead bodies didn't scare her. It was the living that did.

She walked along the narrow, rabbit-warren-like corridors, past darkened offices with their doors closed and their blinds pulled down, and opened the double doors leading into the mortuary suite, where the brilliant white lights seemed to be permanently on. She winced as her eyes adjusted.

Around her, the steel gurneys were empty and spotlessly clean, ready for whatever work tomorrow brought with it. Frightening-looking instruments were put away and worktops were free of clutter. She'd taught her staff well.

Her office in the corner of the suite was lit up and Simon Browes was sitting in Adele's chair, his back to her, glaring at the computer monitor.

She walked slowly over to the office, making sure she made as little sound as possible. Her feelings towards Simon had grown over the last few months, more so since they'd started working closer together and collaborating on their book.

She tapped quietly on the glass, but it resounded in the quiet room. Simon jumped and spun around in his chair.

'Adele,' he said with a smile on his face. 'What are you doing here?'

She tried to smile at him, but her face was frozen. She suddenly felt tired, angry, sad, pained and scared all at once.

'I thought you were going to take some time off?' He came out of the office and stood in front of her. He wasn't a tall man, but he loomed over her. He placed a hand on her shoulder. 'You're shaking. Is everything all right?'

She didn't say anything.

'Adele.' His smile dropped. 'What's happened?' He looked over to the door. 'Are you on your own? Please don't say you drove here in this state.'

'I, er, I had a call. From Donal,' she said, her voice shaking and quiet. 'He told me about Lucy's post-mortem. He said he thought I should hear from him what happened to her rather than read it in a report. I thought that was kind of him.' She gave a slight smile.

'It was. He's a good lad,' Simon said, a frown creasing his forehead.

'She was strangled,' Adele said, a single tear rolling down her left cheek.

'Yes. I'm so sorry, Adele.'

She looked up at him. 'What are you apologising for?'

'I know how much she meant to you.'

Adele swallowed hard. 'Is that all you're apologising for?'

'What do you mean?'

'Aren't you apologising for killing her, too?'

Simon's eyes widened. 'Killing her? You think I killed Lucy? Why? Why would I do that?'

Adele went over to one of the steel-topped tables and placed her bag on it. The thud echoed around the room. She brought out her laptop and turned it on.

'I needed a distraction,' she began. 'I'm all over the place at the moment. With Lucy being found and Matilda going missing, I can't seem to settle. I thought I'd try and do some work to focus my attention, so I've been reading through the proofs of our book.' She looked up at Simon. 'You're a talented writer, Simon. I must admit, I'm very jealous of your prose.'

'Thank you.' He gave a nervous smile.

'Your introduction is to the point yet subtle. You know when to use medical jargon and when to give the facts plainly. That's what I've struggled with in my chapters.'

'Okay,' he said, stretching out the word.

'There's a chapter here where you talk about a body being left for a long time, undisturbed by the elements and wildlife, where, even though the natural process of decomposition has been and gone, we can still determine how a person died. You talk about the almost mummified corpse of a young woman with a ligature mark around her neck.' She looked up at him, tears streaming down her face. 'You're talking about Lucy Dauman, aren't you?'

Simon didn't say anything. His face remained impassive.

'You've even made a typo. Where you should refer to "the body" or "it", you say "her".'

'I ...'

'I commented on it when we were out at Wigtwizzle; how the whole place reminded me of the body farm at Tennessee. I couldn't work it out at first, why there was one body in the boot of a car, two others in shallow graves where one was fully clothed and the other naked, then another buried deeper. But it all fits. You killed them and put them there so you could chart their states of decomposition. You created your own body farm.'

Adele looked up at Simon, stared him straight in the eye. There wasn't a flicker of emotion. He was still and calm.

'Say something, Simon, for fuck's sake,' Adele screamed, her voice bouncing off the walls.

'I genuinely am sorry about Lucy,' he said in a staccato voice.

Outside the Medico-Legal Centre, Sian was on the phone to Finn. She told him everything Steve had said to her about killing Stuart once he was back in Wakefield Prison and he told her he'd give Henry a call and inform them of his plan. When she ended the call, she felt a huge weight lift from her. Despite her feelings towards Stuart, she didn't want to see him murdered.

She went to the entrance where Adele had let herself in. She pulled on the door but it wouldn't open. Adele had closed it behind her, and she needed a security number to gain entry.

'Shit,' she said to herself. She scrolled through her contacts and dialled Adele's mobile. She heard the ringing from the Porsche. 'Oh, well done, Adele,' she said, cancelling the call.

Sian went to the front of the building and cupped her hands around her eyes to look through the window. The reception area was empty and silent. There was a twenty-four-hour access point at the back of the building where blacked-out private ambulances brought dead bodies, she remembered, so she trotted around there and through the iron gates, plunging her cold hands deep into her pockets to keep warm.

Lights were on in several of the rooms in the back of the building, but she couldn't see any members of staff to alert them to her presence.

Her phone started to ring. She took it out and saw Danny Hanson was calling. He was the last person she wanted to talk to, but she swiped to answer anyway as she looked for a way into the building.

'Danny, what can I do for you?'

'Sian, I'm at Wigtwizzle and I've just had a thought. Do you think—?'

'Oh my God!' Sian exclaimed, cutting him off.

Through the window, she saw a door open and Simon Browes wheel a trolley through with Adele Kean, prostrate, on top. She froze, eyes wide, mouth open, and tried to make sense of what she was seeing. Had Adele collapsed or fainted for some reason? She did look ill in the car, but she had been struggling to understand something. Maybe she had asked to see Lucy's body and it was too much for her. But that didn't explain why Simon had blood all over his hands.

Simon stopped in mid-stride, turned and saw Sian. For what seemed like a long time, they remained with their eyes locked. Simon moved first, bolting to the exit.

'Fuck! Danny, help me. I'm at Watery Street. Simon's done something to Adele. He's seen me. You've got to help me.'

Screaming into the phone, she ran and tried to climb over the fence, but she wasn't fast enough. She had one leg over when she was grabbed from behind. Simon placed one hand over her mouth, lifted her up and took her back into the mortuary.

Chapter Sixty-Two

C hristian was brought up to speed by Finn and Scott on developments surrounding Lauren Hales while Zofia found an address for her. Within seconds of her finding it, they grabbed their coats and ran out of the room, leaving Zofia alone with a worried look on her face. She decided she needed a break from the computers and wheeled herself out from behind her desk. The canteen would be closed at this time, but she could get a sandwich from the vending machine outside.

She should have gone home more than three hours ago but felt more useful here than sitting in her bungalow watching mindless shite that passed for Saturday-night entertainment on TV. She had hoped to be spending the night with Tom, but he'd been quiet all day since their failed interview with Steve Harrison.

She turned the corner, stopped at the vending machine and took the money from her purse while eyeing up what was offered. The flavours were always the same – tuna and sweetcorn, tuna and cucumber, egg mayonnaise, coronation chicken. She didn't fancy any of those, but her growling stomach forced her to make a decision.

She looked up and, reflected in the glass of the vending machine, she saw Tom Simpson standing behind her. She wheeled herself around.

'Hello, stranger, where have you been all evening?'

He didn't say anything.

Finn was driving the pool car with Christian in the front passenger seat and Scott in the back watching the satnav as they drove at speed towards Frecheville and the address where Lauren Hales was registered with HMRC as living.

'Do we seriously think Lauren Hales has kidnapped Matilda?' Scott asked. 'If so, why?'

'Maybe she's never gotten over the death of her father and, I don't know, believes Matilda is responsible for him taking his own life,' Christian said.

'She looked perfectly fine and happy in that photo of her in Australia,' Finn said, concentrating on his driving.

'But why now? Ben killed himself four years ago.'

'I don't know, Scott.'

'Has she been stalking Matilda all this time? Is she really responsible for those bodies at Wigtwizzle?'

'I don't know,' Christian said, raising his voice slightly in frustration.

'I just … I can't see it being her.'

'Maybe it's not. But there's something strange about her behaviour and she has a link to Matilda. Tenuous, I know, but what else have we got?' Christian kicked the underside of the glove box in frustration. 'We've got fuck all.'

'Frecheville is a built-up area, too,' Scott said. 'If you're going to kidnap a Detective Chief Inspector, you'd be pretty dumb to take her back to your flat for the neighbours to see.'

'I guess we'll find out when we get there.'

'Turn left here,' Scott told Finn. He winced again, looked down and saw a line of blood on his shirt. His stitches had burst open.

Finn had trouble finding a space so parked on the corner, mostly on the pavement. They walked back to the small apartment block, only three storeys high and containing two flats on each floor. Lauren lived on the first floor in Flat 4.

The entrance to the block of flats was by an intercom door entry system. They didn't want to alert Lauren to their presence by pressing the buzzer for her flat and Finn was just about to ring for the neighbour when Christian tried the handle and it opened.

'I love people who are so security-conscious,' he said with a half-smile.

The foyer was small and there was an underlying smell of damp. They took the stone stairs two at a time and Christian wasted no time in hammering on the door with his gloved fist. He leaned in but couldn't hear any sound from within. He waited a few seconds before banging again.

'She isn't in.'

They all turned to see a middle-aged man in tracksuit bottoms and a stained hoodie in the doorway of the opposite flat.

'Do you know when she'll be back?' Christian asked.

'No. Who are you? Debt collectors?' he asked, looking at each of them in turn.

'Do we look like debt collectors?' Finn asked.

'Why would we be debt collectors? Is Miss Hales in trouble?' Christian asked.

The man shrugged. 'Dunno. I hardly see her.'

'When was the last time you saw her?' Scott asked, trying not to make it obvious he was in pain by holding a hand firmly over his stab wound.

The man looked up as he thought. 'I've no idea. Oh, wait, hang on. It was between Christmas and New Year. I was on a late shift, and we passed on the stairs.'

'You haven't seen her since?'

'No. Who are you guys anyway?'

Christian showed his warrant card. 'We're police.'

'What's she done?'

'We don't know, yet. That's why we need to speak to her. Do you have a contact number or know anywhere else she might be?'

'I don't have her number, but I took a parcel in for her one time last year. Big thing it was. I had it for ages in my hallway taking up space. She was full of apologies saying she'd forgotten she'd ordered it and she'd been staying at her mum's house.'

'Did she say where her mum's house was?' Christian asked.

'No. Why should she?'

Christian dug around in his pocket for his card and handed it over to the man. 'If she comes back, give me a ring straightaway. It's urgent we speak to her.' He headed for the stairs and ran down them.

'What's she done?' The man asked Scott and Finn.

Finn followed Christian while Scott took his time. He looked back at the man over his shoulder. 'Hopefully nothing,' he said.

By the time they were all back outside in the cold and darkness of the evening, Christian was on the phone.

'Why isn't she answering?'

'Who?' Finn asked.

'Zofia. Her phone's just ringing out.'

'Can you remember where Ben Hales lived when he was married?' Scott asked Christian. 'You worked with him.'

'He never shared anything with us. He took privacy to a whole other level,' Christian said, giving up the call and heading back to the car. 'You come into work on a Monday and you spend a good half an hour saying what you did at the weekends and how the family was. Ben just got straight to work. You asked him if he'd had a good weekend and he said "Fine" and that was it. I didn't even know he was married until that time he threatened his wife with a knife.'

'He did what?' Finn asked.

'Long story. He didn't actually threaten her, but he had a knife on him, so it looked bad. That was the beginning of the end for DI Hales.'

'We need to find out where Sara Hales lived,' Scott said as he slowly climbed into the back of the car. 'I know when they split up Ben left, but I'm pretty sure Sara stayed in the house with her daughters. I wonder if Sian'll know?'

'Worth a try,' Christian said, digging out his phone and scrolling through it for Sian's number.

Chapter Sixty-Three

Simon Browes struggled to pick Adele up. She was unconscious and a dead weight. When she asked if he'd killed Lucy and he looked her in the eye, he knew there was no alternative. He lashed out, slapping her across the face with the back of his hand, and she dropped like a stone, cracking her head on the edge of the stainless-steel table as she fell.

He pushed the trolley over to the bank of fridges, opened the door and pushed Adele inside, slamming the door closed behind her.

'Simon, no, she won't be able to breathe,' Sian cried. She was on the floor of the mortuary, arms tied behind her back.

'She doesn't need to breathe,' he said.

'Simon, what have you done? What's happened? Is this about the bodies at Wigtwizzle?'

Slowly, he walked over to Sian and crouched down in front of her.

'I went out to Tennessee, to the body farm, as it's commonly known. The amount of research they can get from one body is immense. I was only out there for two weeks. I didn't want to come home. Seeing the decomposition process right before your eyes, for a pathologist, it's so vital, so important to our research, to understanding what happens to the human body after death.'

'You killed those three women? It wasn't Stuart?'

'No. It was your husband killing them that gave me the idea. The sex workers are on the edges of society, nobody cares for them, nobody would miss them, and they're in a dangerous job, things happen to them all the time. I knew it would be obvious to the police that Stuart was the killer if I just helped myself to one or two.'

Sian tried to stop herself from crying but couldn't. The tears rolled down her cheeks.

'What about Duncan?'

'I needed a man,' he said, simply. 'I wanted to see if there was a difference in the decomposition process of a male and a female. The size of the bones, the density, is so different. I wanted to measure the time difference between the two. I found Duncan around the back of the Cathedral. I told him I was doing research into the homeless and offered him a hot meal in return for him answering a few questions. I drove him out to Wigtwizzle and I hit him over the head with a car jack.'

More tears came. Sian knew Duncan. She liked him. She'd given him money whenever she saw him. The way Simon spoke, so matter-of-fact, about taking a human life, as if it meant nothing, made Sian even more upset for his victims.

'And Lucy?' Sian struggled to say.

Simon stood up. His face paled. 'I didn't mean to kill Lucy. I didn't want to kill her. She saw me picking up one of the prostitutes – no, sorry, you call them sex workers, don't you? She came to talk to me one day, said she knew I was having problems with my marriage, which I was, and that she'd seen me pick up a woman in the red light district and asked if I was taking precautions.' He laughed at the memory. 'She was so forthcoming. She was actually concerned about me picking up an STI. I managed to flannel her, but she kept asking if I was all right. Then, when one of your husband's victims came in, she asked if I knew her, right in front of Adele. I really am so very sorry about Lucy. Do you know, when I strangled her, I cried. I've never cried before. Never.'

Sian took several deep breaths to control her emotions. 'Simon, what are you going to do now?'

'I don't know. I need to think. I'm not a killer, Sian. I'm not like your husband.'

'I know you're not,' she said quickly.

'I haven't killed anyone out of pleasure. This is all about research, about my book, about helping us understand what the human body goes through. It's …'

Sian's phone started ringing.

'What's that? Is that yours?' he asked.

She couldn't speak. Her tears returned. She saw a flash of fear and panic in Simon's eyes. He was unpredictable. That made her fate unknown. She nodded.

'Where is it?'

'Pocket,' she managed to say.

He stormed over to her and lifted her up off the floor with ease as if she was a bag of shopping. He hunted around in her pockets, grabbed the phone and dropped her back on the floor. He looked at the display and showed it to her. Christian was calling.

'Simon, please, if I don't answer it, he'll come looking for me,' she said.

He stared at the phone, allowed it to continue ringing until the voicemail kicked in, then threw it at the wall so hard it broke and landed in several pieces. He began pacing the floor, chewing on a fingernail as he thought.

'Simon, this isn't you. You don't need to do anything drastic. Untie me and we can talk about this, we can find a solution.'

He stopped and looked at her, his face perplexed. 'A solution? To what? I haven't done anything wrong. Have I?'

Chapter Sixty-Four

Z ofia's phone was on silent. It buzzed on her desk, but there was nobody to answer it. The Homicide and Major Crime Unit was empty.

Christian was in the front passenger seat, quietly seething. In the back, Scott was in pain. He opened his jacket and looked down at the blood spreading across his shirt.

'Christian,' he began. 'I think ...'

'Jesus Christ, that's all I need,' Christian said as his phone started ringing. 'Danny cocking Hanson.' He rejected the call.

'Christian,' Scott tried again.

The car door opened, and Finn slipped in behind the wheel, slamming it closed behind him. 'I've got a result,' he said, a grin on his face. 'Remember John Thing, the desk sergeant who took early retirement to look after his wife with Alzheimer's then came back to work in Archive when she went into a home?'

'No,' Christian said.

'It doesn't matter. Anyway, he's been with South Yorkshire Police since the dawn of time. He knows where Ben Hales lived with his wife and he knows where Sara moved to after Ben killed himself. Also, he's done a quick search and the house is still in Sara's name even though she's been dead for a few years. It's never been sold, or the deeds transferred into someone else's name. To all intents and purposes, Sara Hales is still living there.'

'Where is it?'

'You're not going to believe it when I tell you.'

'I'm going to smack you in a minute,' Christian said.

'Ewden Village.'

'Where the fuck's that?'

'About a five-minute walk away from Wigtwizzle.'

'You have got to be shitting me.'

'Nope.'

'Come on then, foot down, Finn.'

Finn put on his seatbelt and started the engine.

'I don't suppose John Thing told you where the hell Sian and Zofia have got to, seeing as neither of them are answering their phones.'

'I didn't ask. Can you find Ewden Village on the satnav for me, please?'

'Scott, are you still with us in the back?' Christian asked as he typed Ewden Village into his phone.

'Yep. I'm here. Taking it all in,' he said with a painful smile.

Danny Hanson drove quickly through the streets of Sheffield, receiving bursts of car horns from other road users as he swerved, ignored changing traffic lights and took the pavement, steering with one hand and scrolling through his phone with the other. He tried calling Sian again, but it kept going straight to voicemail. He called Christian a few times, but it always came back with the busy tone. He was alone in this.

He drove through Upperthorpe and headed for the A61, where he put his foot down and undertook several buses. He ignored the four-word tirades. He missed his turning and had to go to the roundabout before turning back on himself. Once he was off the A-road, he was lost. He'd been to the Medico-Legal Centre so many times he thought he could get there with his eyes closed, but in the dark and in a blind panic, his mind went blank as to which road to turn down. He drove up Malinda Street, looking left and right for the turning onto Watery Street. As soon as he saw the sign, he swung the car left.

'Got you,' he spat through gritted teeth.

'I don't know what to do, Sian,' Simon said. He was back to pacing back and forth.

'You need to untie me. You need to call an ambulance for Adele. You need to let me take you into the police station so we can talk about all this. You're not a violent man, Simon. You're not a killer.'

'I've gone too far, haven't I? It was when Adele asked me to write that book with her. I knew I could put my research to good use, but I wanted to know more. I suddenly started thinking about all the different possibilities of a dead body – clothed, unclothed, buried in a shallow grave of only a few feet compared to a deeper grave of ten feet, trapped in an enclosed space with no air, left to the elements and the wildlife. I was getting so much information. Adele kept saying my writing was beautiful and my insight was incredible. It just made me want to do more.'

His face lit up when he was talking about his work. When the realisation of what he'd done hit him, when he thought of those bodies, the human life he'd destroyed, the light went out and the horror set in.

'I felt bad about Lucy. More than the others,' he said, his voice softer. 'I really liked Lucy. She was fun and happy. She was concerned about my wellbeing. She shouldn't have been so concerned about others. She'd still be alive if she just kept her nose out.'

'Lucy was a caring person,' Sian said. 'But you didn't kill her out of malice. You did it out of fear. That's completely understandable. I understand, Simon. I really do.'

He looked at her and smiled. He walked over and crouched in front of her again. 'You do, don't you? You're surrounded by killers all the time. You've had first-hand experience of what it's like being in the company of a killer. So you know that I'm not like them. I'm not like your Stuart.'

'You're not,' she smiled. 'You're a good man, Simon.'

'Tell me, Sian, what do I do now? How can I get out of this mess I'm in?'

She could feel his eyes burning into her as he looked, hopefully, longingly, at her to come up with a solution. What she wanted was for him to untie her so she could overpower him in some way and call for help. She hoped he didn't see that in her eyes.

'I'll come with you. I'll be with you every step of the way. But we need to do the sensible thing here. The first step is to untie me. I'll call for an ambulance for Adele, then you and I can have a good long chat.'

He nodded. 'You're right. I know you're right.'

He didn't move.

She looked at him and waited for him to do something.

Still he didn't move.

'Simon,' she began. 'Untie me.'

He reached around and began to work at the tight knot.

'Sian, will I go to prison?'

He was so close, she could feel his hot breath on her neck. Of course he would go to prison, but she wasn't in an ideal position to tell him that just yet. She also couldn't lie. She remained silent.

He stopped untying the knot and looked at her. Their noses were almost touching.

'Sian, will I? Will I go to prison?'

She cried.

Chapter Sixty-Five

Zofia and Tom had gone into Christian's office for a heart-to-heart chat. Tom had been thrown when Steve Harrison had called Zofia a cripple and he hated himself for not jumping to her aid. Looking back, there was nothing he could have done. If someone out on the street had said it, he would have punched them in the face, but in a police station, in an interview room, being filmed, he would have been fired on the spot for punching an interviewee, even one as despicable as Steve Harrison.

Tom needed to give his burgeoning relationship with Zofia some serious thought. Romance in the time of Covid was unusual in that they couldn't go out for meals or the cinema for a date. Each time they wanted to be together he'd go over to her bungalow and she'd cook for him, or he'd bring a takeaway. They'd never been anywhere public together. Suddenly, he was worried if people would stare simply because Zofia was in a wheelchair. They shouldn't. But that's what people did. And he didn't want to draw that kind of attention to himself.

'Do you get people calling you names often?' Tom asked, not daring to look Zofia in the eye.

'To be honest with you, Tom, it's the first time anyone has called me anything derogatory. I've never thought of myself as being a cripple. Like Sian said earlier, I'm the same me, I just come with wheels,' she smiled. She looked at his sad face. She knew there was something within his past that was dark, judging by the scars on his wrist, but she didn't want to force him to tell her. He'd explain in his own time. She reached out and took his hand in hers. 'Tom, does it bother you that I'm in a wheelchair?'

He looked up at her. His eyes were wide and filled with tears waiting to fall. 'No,' he said firmly. She believed him.

'It doesn't bother me either. Look, the one person who's said something nasty is Steve Harrison and he's a narcissistic dickhead. I'm not going to be hurt by someone like him.'

The door to Christian's office burst open.

'I know, technically, your shift finished a few hours ago, but if you're staying, you need to be where people can find you,' DI Hilary Sharp from CID said, standing in the doorway, hands on hips, face like thunder. 'Your calls are getting diverted to us.'

'Shit. Sorry,' Zofia said, wheeling herself out of the room.

Hilary stormed out of the suite, her impossibly high heels clacking loudly as she walked.

'Are we okay?' Zofia asked Tom as they headed for their desks.

'Yes. We're fine,' he smiled.

'Good. Do you want to stay over at mine again tonight?' she asked.

'If we ever leave, yes.'

Zofia settled herself in behind her desk and picked up her

phone. 'Why have I had half a dozen missed calls from Danny Hanson?'

Danny pulled up at the side of the road, a little up from the Medico-Legal Centre. He could see Adele's silver Porsche in the car park, a car he could drool over. He was about to climb out of his battered Peugeot when he saw the side door of the building open and Simon Browes exit, dragging Sian with him.

He lowered the window, ignored the icy blast that hit him in the face and sank down in his seat as he strained to listen.

'Simon, you're going about this all wrong. You're just going to get yourself in more trouble.'

Simon said something, but Danny couldn't hear.

He took a set of keys from his back pocket and pointed them at the Porsche. The brake lights flashed as the car unlocked. He pulled Sian around to the front passenger side, opened the door and pushed her in. Danny noticed that Sian's hands were tied behind her back.

'Shit!' he said to himself. 'Shit, shit, shit.' He panicked. He looked around him for something, anything, that would tell him what to do next.

Simon climbed in behind the wheel, started the car, the engine purring, and reversed out of Adele's parking space.

Danny couldn't allow Simon to drive away in Adele's Porsche. His shitty Peugeot was no match for a supercar like that. There was only one thing for it.

As the Porsche left the car park, Danny slammed his foot down on the accelerator and ploughed straight into the back of it. He was thrown forward in his seat and knew by the noise that his car had come off much worse than Adele's, but he kept his foot on the pedal and drove the Porsche into the side of the building.

Danny whipped off his seatbelt and jumped out of the car. He didn't notice Simon was doing exactly the same thing.

'What the fuck …?' Simon called out. He didn't get to finish as, with one punch, Danny felled him to the ground.

Danny ran round to the front passenger door and pulled it open. Sian was inside, her face ashen in shock.

'Are you all right?'

'Yes. I'm fine. Adele's inside. She's going to need an ambulance.'

'Okay.' Danny helped her out of the car and quickly untied her wrists. 'You go, I'll deal with Simon.'

Sian ran back into the mortuary while Danny went around to the driver's side of the Porsche. He had no idea how he was going to secure Simon until police arrived, but it was a moot point anyway because Simon wasn't there.

Sian ran into the mortuary. She was in pain where the rope had cut into her wrists and from Simon's grip as he'd dragged her out to the car. She was crying, and her vision was blurred by tears. She charged through the double doors, ran over to the bank of fridges and pulled open a door. She grabbed the trolley and yanked it out with all the energy she could muster. She looked down at the pale, cold, unresponsive body of Dr Adele Kean and let out a fierce scream from the pit of her stomach.

Chapter Sixty-Six

M atilda and Lauren had been chatting for over an hour. More accurately, Lauren had been talking while Matilda listened. She spoke frankly of her father's suicide and her mother's diagnosis, but her voice took on a sadder tone when she reached the part about her younger sister.

'Amy called me in Thailand to say the doctors had told Mum there was nothing else they could do for her. The only thing left was palliative care. She said I should come home.' She looked at Matilda with tears in her eyes. 'I should have come home.'

Matilda was struggling with the effects of having had no food or drink for the past couple of days. Her energy levels had dropped. She needed to do something to give herself a boost. Lauren's resistance had lowered, and she'd left the door wide open.

'I left it a day. My boyfriend knew something was troubling me. I told him, eventually, and he booked for me to fly straight home. I ... I was in a bit of a mess. I thought I could start afresh in Thailand, that I could leave everything in England behind me. I was wrong. People talk about it being a big world, but it's not. It's so fucking small.

'I landed at Heathrow and took the train up to Sheffield. I was so tired. I kept looking at my phone and because Amy hadn't called me or anything, I assumed Mum was fine. I knocked on the door. Amy opened it and started crying as soon as she saw me. Mum had already died. She'd been taken away and was in the funeral home. I was too late,' she cried. Tears rolled down her face and she didn't wipe them away.

'You weren't to know,' Matilda said softly, one eye on the door.

'If I hadn't waited when Amy called, if I'd got a plane straightaway, I could have said goodbye. I didn't get the chance to say goodbye to my dad and I didn't get to say it to my mum either.'

Matilda didn't know what to say to her. She knew Lauren wouldn't accept anything placatory to try to ease the tension. She remained silent.

'Amy expected me to stay. She didn't say anything, but I know that's what she was thinking. We had the funeral and came back here. I asked if she wanted any help sorting out Mum's things or selling this house, but she just shut down. She wouldn't speak to me. I told her I was going back home. She said I was home. It didn't feel like home. I'd made a new home for myself in Thailand. Amy couldn't see that. She said some horrible things, called me selfish and every other name under the sun. I ... I hit her. I slapped her across the face, told her to grow up, that we all move on, and then I stormed out. That ...' She choked. 'That was the last time I saw her.'

Matilda felt sorry for Lauren but knew that if she offered her apologies, it would enrage Lauren further. She was angry at herself but needed to deflect it onto someone else. She'd chosen Matilda, and if Matilda said anything to cause her to snap, they could both be in serious danger.

'I went back to Thailand. I put my head in the sand, believing everything was going to be all right now. I thought, if I put some space between me and Amy, that after a few weeks, maybe a couple of months, she'd calm down. I lost count of the number of times I wrote an email but never sent it. I wanted her to come out to Thailand with me. I'd made a fresh start. She could as well.

'The local police came to me at work. I was pulled out of the classroom and told that Amy had killed herself. She'd hanged herself, right here in this room. She left a note. The police showed me a copy.' She looked to Matilda. 'Do you want to read it?'

Matilda's eyes widened. 'If you'd like me to.'

Lauren pulled out a crumpled sheet of paper from her back pocket. It was obvious it had been folded and unfolded many times. She handed it to her. Matilda took it with shaking hands.

Lauren,

First of all, I'm not blaming you for my death, so I don't want you to blame yourself either. I wanted you to stay so much with me here in this house, but I couldn't see that you'd made a new life for yourself in Thailand. A life without me. Of course you were going to return. I shouldn't have expected you not to. I said some horrible things to you. I'm so sorry. I didn't mean any of them. I was angry, upset and sad.

The truth is, Lauren, I'm lonely. I always have been ever since I was a teenager. I've never been overly confident and always relied on you or Mum or Dad to be in the background to prop me up. But you've all left me. I'm on my own for the first time in my life and I can't cope. I'm in so much pain. Just waking up in the morning is painful.

In bed last night, I was thinking about when we were growing up and when everything went wrong for this family. I think Mum put a lot of pressure on Dad to get promotion to achieve what Grandad did in his career. She pushed him too hard and when he didn't get that job running the MIT, that's when it started to fall apart. Looking back, when he came home and said the police were going to have a dedicated unit, his face was a picture. He genuinely thought he was going to get the job. He was so happy. I'd never seen him smile so much before. I never saw him smile like that again. I miss Dad so much, Lauren. I miss Mum, too, but I had more in common with Dad.

I think I always knew he was going to kill himself. When he didn't get that job, when it was given to Matilda Darke, I saw his world collapse around him. You could see it in his face. The life just fell out of him. I know how he feels.

Like I said, don't blame yourself for me dying, Lauren. This is all me. Even if you'd said you'd stay in Sheffield, I think I'd still have killed myself. This world isn't for me. It's too dark. Please, do me a favour, and live your life to the fullest. Do all the things I couldn't. I do love you so much, Lauren.

Amy xxx

Matilda handed her back the note. She could feel the emotion rising up inside her.

'I really am sorry, Lauren.'

Lauren took the note back, folded it carefully and placed it in her pocket. She gave her a weak smile through her tears.

'I know you are. The thing is, you are to blame. If it wasn't for you, Dad would have been given that promotion and he and Mum wouldn't have split up. I wouldn't have run away to

Thailand and Amy would have had family around her to help her become more confident and happier. I'm not blaming you for Mum's death. That was unavoidable. But me and Dad would have helped Amy get through it. We'd have banded together. We couldn't do that. *That's* your fault.'

'Lauren, it isn't,' Matilda said. 'I know you're angry and upset. I can feel the pain radiating from you. But you're not angry at me. You're angry at yourself for all the missed opportunities. You're angry you couldn't say goodbye to your mum and dad and your sister. That's understandable. You're full of grief and raw emotion and you don't know what to do with it, but keeping me here like this is not helping either. Do you honestly think you'll feel better if you kill me?'

'I did. That's why I contacted Steve Harrison. He really hates you. I wanted to make you suffer so I asked him what I should do. But then I realised killing you wouldn't help. That's why I tried to run you off the road before Christmas. I wanted us both to go up in a huge fireball. I couldn't even get that right,' she said, looking down at the floor. 'Steve came up with the idea of the kidnapping and as soon as he mentioned it, I knew it was the only solution. I'd kidnap you, bring you here and force you to hang yourself, just like Dad did. Just like Amy did. Then, when you've died, I'll hang myself, too.'

'Lauren, that's not the way out.'

'It really is,' she said with a hint of a smile. 'I've made my peace with it. We're both going to hang.'

Chapter Sixty-Seven

'**W**here's DI Brady?' Chief Constable Ridley asked as he stormed into the HMCU suite and saw only Tom and Zofia.

'He's gone with DS Andrews and DC Cotton, sir,' she said. 'They're following up a lead about DCI Darke.'

'And it takes all three of them?'

'The person of interest is Lauren Hales, the daughter of former Detective Inspector Ben Hales.'

'What?' Ridley asked, eyes widening. Ridley wasn't at South Yorkshire Police at the time of Ben Hales's very public downfall, but he'd made himself familiar with the issues Matilda Darke and the unit had faced since its inception. 'How credible is this?'

'We don't know, sir. That's why DI Brady decided to accompany DS Andrews and DC Cotton. He thought it best to take control of a situation before it developed,' Tom said, making their charge out of the unit sound more plausible.

'Sir, I think you should see this,' Zofia began. She was glaring, mouth open, at one of her computer screens. 'A call has just come through from Danny Hanson at Watery Street. He's asking for police and an ambulance.'

'What's going on?'

'I'm not sure,' she said with a heavy frown as she dialled Danny's number. It was answered on the first ring and Zofia put the phone on loudspeaker. 'Danny, it's DC Zofia Nowak. What's happening?'

'Zofia, I can't get my head around any of this. You need to put out an alert or something for Simon Browes.'

'Who?' Ridley mouthed.

'He's a pathologist,' Tom answered.

'He's responsible for all the bodies found at Wigtwizzle. It's a long story. I tried to stop him, but he's run off. You need to find him.'

'I'll dig out his address and send a team over,' Tom said, hammering at his computer.

'There's something else,' Danny said, his voice dropping. 'He's killed Dr Adele Kean.'

Chapter Sixty-Eight

E wden Village was created to house workers employed to build the two reservoirs in the early 1900s. By the 1970s only fifteen of the seventy houses were occupied, and by the turn of the twenty-first century the village was more or less abandoned. A scattering of stone cottages remained, fewer than a dozen, whose occupants were attracted to the quiet, picturesque surroundings. It offered the isolation of rural life yet was within a thirty-minute drive of the centre of Sheffield and major shopping complexes.

Finn had pulled up next to the first house they'd come to that had a light on inside. He came running back to the car and opened the door, bringing with him a blast of freezing cold air. He slammed the door behind him.

'Lovely old lady, tried to give me her whole life story. Anyway, she told me Sara Hales lived in High Point. It's a cottage just down the way here, turn right, up the incline, right again and apparently I can't miss it.'

'Did she say anything else?' Christian asked as Finn started the engine and began to pull away.

'She's spoken a few times to Sara's daughter Lauren, who comes every now and then to sort out the house. In the last few days, she's seen her car coming more often.'

'I don't like the sound of this,' Scott said from the back.

'Why now? That's what I don't understand,' Christian added.

Finn took the second right turn and they soon saw a single-storey cottage converted from a barn, with green windows and doors. The whole building was in darkness. Parked at an angle at the side, almost tucked away out of view, was a black and grey Suzuki Jimny. Finn pulled up a distance away and turned off the engine and lights.

'How are we going to play this?' he asked.

'Before whoever is in there is alerted to our presence, we need to check the perimeter. Once we've got the entrances covered, we knock and charm our way in,' Christian said. He opened the door and climbed out into the cold, dark night.

Scott and Finn followed.

'Are you all right?' Christian asked Scott.

'Fine. Why?'

'You look pale.'

'I'm from Yorkshire. I'm always pale.'

As silently as they could, Christian walked towards the front door while Finn headed for the rear of the property. Scott went over to the car. He placed his hand on the bonnet. It was stone cold. He quickly turned around when a light lit up the entire surroundings. Either Christian or Finn must have triggered a sensor.

'I saw someone move,' Scott said in a loud whisper, pointing to one of the windows.

Christian looked in time to see someone inside flee from

what he assumed to be a living room. He heard a door slam closed.

He banged on the front door with his gloved fist, the noise echoing around him.

'Finn, call for backup.'

Finn dug his phone out of his pocket and selected Zofia's number.

Scott joined Christian at the front door. Christian banged again.

'You're going to have to break it down.'

'Shit,' Christian said.

He took a step back and raised his right leg, slamming his foot against the lock. They both heard wood cracking, but the door didn't budge. He tried again. Nothing. He tried a third time and the door flew open.

They both stepped inside into the silence. There was an instant smell of a wood burner, coming from the living room. They remained in the doorway and listened intently for any sound. Nothing.

Downstairs in the basement, Matilda was sitting on the floor, her knees drawn up to her chest, her arms wrapped around them. She had no energy left to fight. She knew she was going to die here. There was no reasoning with Lauren at all. Matilda didn't believe in an afterlife, but the closer she came to death the more she thought of her dead husband and the prospect of seeing James again. It was stupid, she knew, but her brain was being starved of what it needed to keep alive, and all manner of thoughts were racing around her mind.

She heard urgent footsteps running down the stairs. Any

hopes that Sian or Scott or Christian would come charging in to save her were lost when she saw Lauren Hales and the dark look on her face. She had a noose around her neck, the rope dangling beside her. There were to be no last-minute saves for Matilda. It was all over.

'Time's up,' Lauren said.

'What?'

'Your mates are persistent, I'll give them that.'

She grabbed Matilda by the arm and pulled her to her feet. Matilda was so weak, it was easy for her to be manhandled. It was only when Lauren picked her up and stood her on the chair and she knew what was going to happen next that Matilda found enough energy to act.

As Lauren grabbed the noose and tried to get it over Matilda's head, Matilda kicked out.

'No! NO!' she screamed.

'Struggle all you want. This is happening,' Lauren said. She put the noose around her neck and tightened it.

Matilda kicked again and kneed Lauren under the jaw. She jumped back in shock and put her hand to her mouth. She spat out blood.

'You bitch!' Lauren hissed. She reached up and slapped Matilda hard in the face. She jumped up onto the chair, held Matilda's face in her hand and squeezed hard. 'I've lost my entire family,' she spat. 'And it's all your fault. I've nothing left to live for. The only thing that's been keeping me going is the thought of taking you with me.'

Matilda cried. Tears rolled down her face.

'Any final words?'

Matilda struggled to catch her breath. 'You don't … you don't need to do this.'

'Fuck you!' Lauren said. She jumped down off the chair and kicked it away.

Matilda felt the noose tighten around her neck. The rope bit into her skin, burning the flesh, her airwaves closing, and she struggled to breathe, choking for air. Her legs flailed as they tried to find something to stand on. Her fingers scratched at her throat as she tried to remove the rope from her neck. It was too tight. There was nothing she could do. Her eyes rolled back, and she could feel the life drain away from her.

Lauren watched as Matilda's body jerked and slowly began to still. The sound of footsteps on the stairs outside the basement forced her into action. She pulled the chair upright and stood on it. With shaking fingers, she wrapped the end of the rope around the beam, secured it in place and jumped off the chair.

The door to the basement opened and Christian rushed in. He stood stock still as he took in the horror in front of him. Lauren was jerking wildly as every instinct in her brain tried to survive. Matilda was almost still, life nearly extinct. He grabbed the chair and pulled it up to Matilda. He wrapped his arms around her legs and took some of the weight off the noose that was squeezing the life out of her.

'Finn! Scott!' Christian screamed.

Finn followed him into the basement. 'Fucking hell!' he exclaimed when he saw the scene.

'I've got her,' Christian said through gritted teeth as he climbed up on the chair with Matilda, unhooked the noose and loosened it around her neck. He lifted her down and placed her on the bed. Her eyes were closed. He felt for a pulse, but there was nothing there.

Finn picked up the chair and put it under Lauren's legs. Copying Christian, he climbed onto it and unhooked her noose. She'd been hanging for less than ten seconds and hadn't lost consciousness. She pushed Finn out of the way, knocking him to the ground, and headed for the door.

'Shit! Scott, she's coming your way,' Finn called out.

Scott was on his phone in the hallway when he heard Finn shout out from downstairs. As he turned, he saw Lauren charging up. He dropped his phone and grabbed her. She looked him in the eye and smiled as she punched him hard, repeatedly, in the stomach, where his stitches were already coming apart.

He screamed out in pain and fell to the floor as Lauren pushed him out of the way. She ran to the front door, pulled it open and went out into the cold, dark night.

Finn charged up the stairs two at a time, saw Scott lying on the floor, his hands clamped to his stomach, blood oozing between his fingers. He felt cold air on his face, looked towards the open doorway and saw Lauren disappear into the darkness. His instinct told him to stay with his friend and colleague and call for an ambulance, but Scott would never forgive him if he let Lauren get away. He charged after her.

He ran down the driveway, looked left and right, but couldn't see her anywhere. He heard the sound of an engine starting and, remembering the parked Suzuki Jimny, he ran back. He couldn't allow Lauren to get out of the drive. Once that happened, she'd be lost. As he headed back, he kept thinking of how Zofia Nowak had thrown herself in front of a Land Rover to stop a killer escaping and had been left paralysed as a result. He looked around him, found a rock at the side of the driveway, picked it up and, as soon as he saw the Jimny in front of him, hurled it at the windscreen. The sound of shattering glass filled the night air and Lauren slammed on the brakes.

Finn went round to the driver's side and opened the door. His quick reflexes caught Lauren's punch before it had time to hit him in the face. He pushed her back, pinning her to the seat, reached inside and turned off the ignition, taking out the keys and throwing them behind him. He reached for his handcuffs in his coat pocket and cuffed her to the steering wheel.

'I'm saying nothing to you,' she spat.

'That's fine. I don't want to hear it anyway.'

Chapter Sixty-Nine

C hristian Brady had lost track of time. He slumped into a seat in a waiting room at the Northern General Hospital and his mind tried to make sense of everything that had happened in the past few days. He felt drained. There were so many unanswered questions, and he didn't have the energy to ask them right now.

'Christian.'

He looked up to see Chief Constable Ridley standing in front of him.

'Oh. Hello, sir,' he said, slightly dazed.

'You look like you were a million miles away.'

'I wish I was.'

He sat down next to him. 'How's Matilda?'

'She's fine. A little dehydrated and she has a bruised larynx, but she'll be fine.'

'You should go home.'

'I know. It's just … three of my friends are in this hospital and two of them might not survive. I'd feel guilty going home to bed.'

'Your wife will be worried.'

'I've called her and told her everything. She understands.'

They fell silent for a while. The sound of the busy hospital filling the void.

'Any news on Simon Browes?' Christian asked.

'Not yet. An alert has been put out to all ports and airports. I'm hoping he'll come to his senses and hand himself in. Why did he do it?'

Christian shook his head. 'I've no idea. Sian said he killed them so he could study their bodies as they decomposed. He'd created his own body farm.'

'Bloody hell. And wasn't he seeing Dr Kean?'

'Yes. They'd not been dating long, though.'

'How is she?'

'Sodding Danny Hanson scared the hell out of us when he said she was dead. In that fridge her heart rate had slowed right down. The next twenty-four hours are crucial. They need to check for brain damage. The doctors seem optimistic, but, well, the way our luck is going at the moment, who knows?'

'Is one of you two Christian Brady?' a tired-looking nurse asked.

'I am,' Christian replied.

'Matilda Darke is asking for you.'

'Is she all right?'

'She needs to rest but she's not listening to a word we're saying.'

Christian chuckled. 'That sounds like Matilda.'

'I've told her you can visit but not for long. She really does need to rest.'

'Thank you.'

The nurse left them. Christian stood up and headed for Matilda's room.

'Christian,' Ridley called. 'I want to thank you.'

'What for?'

'Everything. You've handled this situation so well. You could have fallen apart, but you've been professional and diligent throughout. You're an exceptional detective. There'll be a commendation in this for you.'

Christian gave a wan smile. 'I have a good team. That's how I got through this.'

'A good team needs a good leader. Take the compliment, Christian.'

'I will. Thank you.'

———

Christian entered Matilda's private room. She was propped up in bed by several pillows. She looked shattered, as if she hadn't slept in a week, which she probably hadn't. She was hooked up to several machines monitoring her oxygen levels and blood pressure, and was on saline to increase her hydration levels.

'How are you feeling?' he asked, sitting down on the chair next to her bed.

'Knackered. How's Scott?'

'He *was* fine, until he ran into Lauren Hales again while we tried to rescue you. He's back in theatre. She ripped open his stitches and caused more damage.'

'Jesus. Please tell me you caught her.'

'We did. We have Finn to thank for that. She's at the station. We'll interview her tomorrow.'

'All this time I thought it was Steve Harrison giving the orders to torment me, and it was Lauren Hales all along.'

'What happened between you in that basement?'

'I'll give you chapter and verse in a couple of days.'

He gave her a weak smile and nodded. He leaned forward on the edge of his seat. 'There have been some developments while you've been out of action. The bodies found in woodland at Wigtwizzle. We uncovered five in total.'

'Five?'

'One of them was Lucy Dauman.'

'Oh my God,' Matilda said, putting her head down. 'Where's Adele? Is she all right?'

Christian swallowed hard and ran his hand over his buzzcut. 'In the woods we also found the three remaining missing sex workers and Duncan McNally. Remember him?'

'I do. He set the first alarm off at the station. He's dead?'

'Simon Browes killed them all.'

A look of confusion appeared on Matilda's face. She blinked hard and tried to make sense of what Christian was saying. 'What? Simon Browes killed five people? How? Why?'

'It's a very long story.'

'Bloody hell. Where is Adele?'

'Adele and Sian confronted Simon. Adele was knocked unconscious and placed in one of the fridges at the mortuary.'

'Is she all right?' Matilda asked, fear and worry in her voice.

'We'll know more in a few days.'

'And Sian?'

'Oh, she's fine,' he said with a smile. 'You know Sian.'

'And Simon?'

'On the run.'

'Bloody hell. You get kidnapped for a few days and all hell breaks loose.' She swung back the bed sheets. 'I need to see Adele.'

'No. You need to get some rest,' he said, pushing her back down on the bed.

She sighed and reluctantly relented. 'Okay, but the second I'm told I can leave this place I'm coming straight back to work. In the meantime, I want you to get a search out for Simon Browes. Check his bank accounts and his home address. Take everything apart.'

'Matilda, I know what to do.'

'Also, Steve Harrison may not have been directly involved in my kidnapping, but Lauren Hales approached him. She told me so herself. He needs interviewing.'

'We tried. He refuses to talk to us.'

'Then we strip him of all his privileges.'

'Matilda, that won't work. We've tried. We know Steve isn't directly involved. I think the best thing we can do is ignore him. That will hurt him all the more.'

Matilda slammed herself back against her pillows. She looked angry. 'We need to do something. He's going to continue plotting and scheming until he kills me. I know it.'

Christian leaned forward and took her clammy hand in his. 'Matilda, calm down. We're just going to have to keep an eye on him. As things stand, there is nothing we can do.'

Chapter Seventy

Monday 25th January 2021

The rumour mill had been in full flow since Steve Harrison returned to Wakefield Prison late on Saturday. It wasn't long until the stories reached Stuart about how Steve had taunted his wife, made lewd gestures towards her, cornered her in an interview room when they were alone and put his hand up ... he didn't want to hear any more. He heard the laughs from his fellow inmates as they enjoyed passing on what they heard. It was gossip. A men's prison was as bad as a schoolyard at times.

On Sunday afternoon, Stuart was alone in his cell trying to read but unable to concentrate when the door opened and prison officer Ray Clarke entered. He pushed the door behind him, not fully closing it.

'Why aren't you in the recreation room?' he asked.

Stuart looked up from his paperback. 'I'm not in the mood.'

'You've heard what everyone's saying?'

He nodded.

'Steve Harrison has upset a lot of people in this prison. Someone needs to take him down a peg or two.'

'I'm not that someone,' Stuart said, going back to his paperback.

'You could be. All you need is for someone to turn a blind eye for a few minutes.'

This caught Stuart's interest.

'What are you talking about?'

'If you're the right man for the job, I'll tell you everything you need to know. If not, I'll leave you in peace to read your book.'

Stuart thought for a moment. His mind immediately went to Steve alone in a room with his wife and what he attempted to do to her. The mental image made his flesh crawl. He folded down the corner of the page and closed the paperback.

'I'm all ears.'

———————

Nina Price should never have been a prison officer. She wasn't made of the right material to stand up to a building full of hardened criminals. You needed to switch off, to take everything they told you with a pinch of salt and not get involved with their personal lives. Nina couldn't do that. She believed every sob story going, and when a particular prisoner turned on the waterworks because they were unable to see their child on his or her birthday, Nina stepped in and personally hand-delivered a home-made card or present. On more than one occasion, she sneaked in something from the outside to hand back to the prisoners. It was against every rule in the book, but she thought she was doing the right thing.

When Steve Harrison heard about it, he used it to his

advantage. However, Steve didn't have anyone on the outside to converse privately with and he didn't want anything brought in. He learned very quickly to do without material things. What Steve wanted was sex.

Nina had no choice. Her job was on the line if her bosses found out she was smuggling things in and out of prison, even if it was something banal like a birthday card. It's not like she was bringing in cannabis. But would they believe that?

The first time she had sex with Steve, she had to take a couple of days off work sick, most of which she spent crying in the bath while she tried to scrub herself clean. It wasn't to be a one-off, like she thought, and Steve wasn't a caring and passionate man. Sex with him was hard, raw and painful. She kept what happened between them a secret and painted on a smile for her brother Henry, who was also an officer at the prison. When she became pregnant, and she didn't know if the father of the child was her husband or Steve Harrison, she broke down and told Henry everything. It wasn't long after that Nina was caught on her knees in Steve's cell with tears streaming down her face while she performed oral sex on him. She was suspended pending an investigation, then sacked by the governors.

The prison rota was designed so no officer could get too close to a prisoner on the Supermax wing and risk being compromised, but Henry was sure they could come up with a plan to trap Steve and get their revenge.

Henry's boyfriend was Ray Clarke, another officer at the prison. Between them, they played the long game. They needed to get close to Steve, but Steve had to think he was the one with the upper hand, and he was a very mistrustful person. It was a long time before Steve asked for something.

Ray smuggled in a mobile phone. They had no idea he was

using it to watch a live feed of the kidnapping of a Detective Chief Inspector. When they found out what had happened, they instigated a random security check of his cell. The mobile phone wasn't there. Ray had tried recording Steve's phone conversation with Amy Monroe, but he was never able to get close enough to plant a device. It was looking hopeless.

In the background, Henry and Ray watched as Steve focused his taunts on Stuart Mills. Steve and Stuart's ex-wife had history and Steve loved playing with Stuart's mind. They could see Stuart was seething and wanted nothing more than to rip Steve's head off and use it as a football. He just needed a little push, a little incentive.

'The thing is, Stuart,' Ray began, 'Steve's right. He's in a Supermax wing. He's never getting out of this place, so there's no reason for him to stick to the rules of the prison. He can do anything he wants and there's nothing we can do to punish him further. The same could be said for you, too. You might not be on a secure wing, but you're on the never-never list. You could get your revenge on Steve Harrison for whatever he may or may not have done to your wife, and all you'd get is a couple of weeks in solitary.'

'What do you want me to do?'

Ray smiled.

On Monday morning, after breakfast, Stuart Mills headed, as usual, to the prison library to begin his job. He turned on the computer, checked in a couple of books and went about neatening up the shelves. He made himself a mug of tea, nibbled on a finger of KitKat and went back to his desk as prisoners filed in and out.

At eleven o'clock, the room was cleared as prisoners from the Supermax wing were brought in to exchange their books.

First, Ray Clarke brought Graham Appleby in. Graham was in his late sixties and had been in Wakefield Prison for more than thirty years, having tortured and murdered six women in London over a period of eighteen months. To look at him, he seemed like a mild-mannered grandad as he entered the library wearing an oversized navy cardigan and walking with a slight limp. He always had a friendly smile on his face, and he enjoyed reading the novels of John Grisham and Michael Connelly. He selected three, had a brief chat with Stuart about how his bunions were causing him gyp, then left.

Stuart was putting Graham's returned books back on the shelves when Ray came back with Steve Harrison.

'Just popping to the toilet. I won't be long,' Ray said, giving an almost invisible wink to Stuart. He left the library and locked the door behind him.

Stuart and Steve were alone.

'Leave your books on the table, Steve,' Stuart instructed. 'Just going to flick the kettle on.' He headed into the small kitchenette.

'Saw your wife at the weekend,' Steve called out.

'Ex-wife,' Stuart said, wanting to show Steve's words couldn't hurt him. He hated calling Sian his ex-wife. He loved her so much.

'She's looking good for a woman her age. Doesn't look like she's missing you at all. She's lost weight, looks toned, breasts are still holding up, too. I had a feel.'

Stuart closed his eyes and tried to block out Steve's words. He knew he was lying. He knew it.

'I mean, she was a cow, don't get me wrong. She wanted to think she could be everyone's shoulder to cry on, a friendly face to chat to. I can't stand do-gooders like that, but there was something about her that whenever I saw her, I wanted to bend her over—'

'Steve,' Stuart interrupted. He needed him to shut up talking. He popped his head around the corner to look at him. 'While we're on our own, fancy a cheeky cuppa?' He gave him his best smile.

'Okay.'

The kettle boiled. Stuart took the lid off and poured in the half bag of sugar that was on the tabletop.

'I don't suppose there's any biscuits I can nick,' Steve said.

Quick like a cat, Stuart turned on Steve. He grabbed him by the throat, slammed him against the wall, kicked the back of his knees and watched as he fell to the floor. He turned him over onto his back and straddled him.

'Fuck's sake, Stuart, I'm only having a laugh with you,' Steve grinned, looking up at him with that smile he thought made him so good-looking.

Stuart gripped Steve by the throat with his right hand, reached for the kettle with his left and tipped the contents over his face. Steve's cries were heard throughout the prison.

Epilogue

Friday 29th January 2021

Matilda read through the report from Wakefield Prison. Steve Harrison had suffered severe burns to his face and neck and lost the sight in his left eye. Some of the boiling water had gone into his mouth and burnt his throat. His recovery would be long and painful. He would be scarred for life. Stuart Mills had suffered scalding to his hands and was currently in the prison hospital until charges were brought against him. She looked up from the laptop screen at Christian Brady sitting opposite her desk. She wasn't officially back at work yet, but nothing would keep her away.

'Have you told Sian?' she asked.

'No. Not yet. I thought we could do that together.'

Matilda nodded. 'Not here, though. We'll take her out somewhere quiet for a drink.'

'I hear Scott was discharged from hospital this morning,' Christian said.

'Yes,' Matilda smiled. 'He's staying with Donal for a few

days before coming back to the flat. Did you know they're getting married?'

'No.'

Matilda's smile grew. 'Scott proposed almost as soon as he woke up, and Donal said yes.'

'A good news story.'

'I know. About time we had some good news around here.'

'I'm afraid I'm going to bring the mood down now,' Christian said.

'You couldn't let us have a minute of happiness, could you?' She gave him a wry grin. 'Go on.'

'Lauren Hales has been detained under the mental health act. She tried to kill herself again last night in the remand centre.'

'Jesus,' Matilda sighed, putting her head down. It was a while before she looked up. 'I want to hate her, but I can't. Do you think I should go and see her?'

'No, I don't,' Christian replied firmly. 'Concentrate on the good people you have around you. Look after them.'

Matilda looked past Christian and out into the main suite. Tom and Zofia were sharing a desk, looking at something on one of Zofia's screens. From where Matilda was sitting, she could see below the desk; they were holding hands. That made her smile. At the next desk, Finn Cotton was reading from his tablet, dunking a biscuit in his tea and looking engrossed. Dismissing his heroics, he had simply returned to work as if nothing had happened.

'What are you thinking?' Christian asked.

'I'm thinking I want to go home.'

'Then go home. You're still on compassionate leave, yet you've been in here every day since you were discharged from hospital.'

'Pat Campbell said I should resign and put my mental health first.'

'Maybe she's right.'

'You just want my office,' she smiled.

He chuckled. 'Don't listen to Pat, or to me. For once, listen to yourself and do what you want to do.'

She stood up and grabbed her coat from the back of her chair. 'I'm taking a week off. I'm going to do nothing but sit at home, eat biscuits and read. Then I'll decide what to do.'

There was a knock on the glass door. They both turned as Finn opened the door.

'Danny Hanson's on line one. Who wants to talk to him?'

'And that's my cue to leave,' Matilda said with a smile.

Adele was home alone, sitting at the dining room table, laptop open in front of her. She'd just hit send on an email to her publishers, filling them in on everything Simon Browes had been up to and telling them that their co-authored book was tainted. She doubted they would go ahead with publication, but if they did, her name must be removed from the cover. She wanted nothing more to do with it.

The second email was more personal, and she could feel tears welling up in her eyes as she composed it. It was only a couple of lines long. There was no need for waffle when you were handing in your resignation. How could she continue being a pathologist now, after all this? Simon Browes had stood back and watched as his own victims had been wheeled in, and they'd performed the autopsies together to discover how they died, and he knew all along. And then there was Lucy

Dauman. Every time Adele thought about her, she cried. She was sad and angry in equal measure.

She hit send and leaned back on her chair. Her career was over. She had no idea about her future. The first thing on her to-do list was her recovery. She had returned home from hospital only yesterday afternoon, after being given the all-clear. The scans had come back normal, and she'd suffered no brain damage from being knocked unconscious and locked in a mortuary fridge. Physically, she was fine; mentally and psychologically, she was not. Matilda told her to delay resigning until she was fit and well, but at present it was the only clear thought she had in her head. Now her recovery could fully begin.

It had taken a long time, after Robson had abandoned her, to trust men again. She finally thought she'd found someone worthy of developing a relationship with and he turned out to be a psychopath. How could Simon Browes have killed all those people and not realise what he was doing was wrong? When she confronted him with what he'd done, he'd said it was all for research. He couldn't see the immorality of his actions. That's what was so frightening.

Adele stood up and went into the kitchen. She supposed it was too early for a vodka so she settled for a strong coffee instead. Matilda had stocked the cupboards with chocolate and biscuits. She didn't care if she ballooned. She needed comfort right now and that comfort could only come from Cadbury's, McVitie's and Tunnock's.

Her phone pinged an incoming email. She dug it out of her pocket and read it while the coffee was brewing. It was from Lucy Dauman's mother, telling her the funeral was next Wednesday. Adele didn't feel up to going out at the moment, but it was an event she refused to miss. She needed to say goodbye.

Coffee made, she took it through to the living room. It wasn't even lunchtime yet, but she supposed she could find some mindless crap on television to sit in front of and ignore for a few hours.

The doorbell rang, making her jump. She wasn't in the mood for visitors but could hardly pretend she was out when she only came home from hospital yesterday.

She dragged her feet through the hallway, pulled open the door and shivered as a blast of cold air hit her.

'Hello, Adele.'

'Simon!'

Acknowledgments

I am forever grateful to all the people who help turn my ideas into the finished book. There may only be one name on the front cover but without the expertise of some amazing people, there wouldn't be a book at all. So, many thanks to everyone at Harper Collins and One More Chapter, specifically my editor, Jennie Rothwell, who knows her job inside and out and gives me so much encouragement. Lucy Bennett for the amazing cover design, Tony Russell for copy editing, Simon Fox for proofreading, and Arsalan Isa helping with editing.

My agent, Jamie Cowen at The Ampersand Agency, is a wonderful sounding board. He leaves me alone to get on with the business of writing yet he's always in the background to whisper advice whenever I need it.

For all the technical information that goes into this book, I thank Philip Lumb for his expertise in pathology and post mortems. Simon Browes for his encyclopaedic knowledge of all things medical. "Mr Tidd" for his insight into police procedure. Andy Barrett for his detailed emails about crime scene investigation. I cannot thank you all enough for your help. I apologise if there are any errors. I sometimes have to bend the truth to match the fiction.

Those closest to me who support me in my work every single day include my mum who has encouraged me my whole life and continues to do so to this day. Chris Schofield and Kevin Embleton are always there for me when I need them. Jonas Alexander, who I don't see as much of anymore, but is just a text message away (Dental plan). Chris Simmons, for the fun chats and the boosts of morale.

A massive thank you to all the readers. Whether you listen to the audiobooks, read the ebooks or the paperbacks, I want you to know how much your support of my work means to me. I literally wouldn't still be writing if it wasn't for you.

Finally, and one last time, I'd like to thank Maxwell. This is the last book I wrote with him listening to me reading sections out to make sure the dialogue flowed. He ignored me every time, but his company was invaluable. Sleep well, Max. Look after him, Woody.

ONE MORE CHAPTER

The author and One More Chapter would like to thank everyone who contributed to the publication of this story...

Analytics
Emma Harvey
Maria Osa

Audio
Fionnuala Barrett
Ciara Briggs

Contracts
Georgina Hoffman
Florence Shepherd

Design
Lucy Bennett
Fiona Greenway
Holly Macdonald
Liane Payne
Dean Russell

Digital Sales
Laura Daley
Michael Davies
Georgina Ugen

Editorial
Simon Fox
Arsalan Isa
Charlotte Ledger
Lydia Mason
Jennie Rothwell
Tony Russell
Kimberley Young

International Sales
Bethan Moore

Marketing & Publicity
Chloe Cummings
Emma Petfield

Operations
Melissa Okusanya
Hannah Stamp

Production
Emily Chan
Denis Manson
Francesca Tuzzeo

Rights
Lana Beckwith
Rachel McCarron
Agnes Rigou
Hany Sheikh
Mohamed
Zoe Shine
Aisling Smyth

The HarperCollins Distribution Team

The HarperCollins Finance & Royalties Team

The HarperCollins Legal Team

The HarperCollins Technology Team

Trade Marketing
Ben Hurd

UK Sales
Yazmeen Akhtar
Laura Carpenter
Isabel Coburn
Jay Cochrane
Alice Gomer
Gemma Rayner
Erin White
Harriet Williams
Leah Woods

And every other essential link in the chain from delivery drivers to booksellers to librarians and beyond!

YOUR NUMBER ONE STOP

ONE MORE CHAPTER

FOR PAGETURNING BOOKS

One More Chapter is an
award-winning global
division of HarperCollins.

Sign up to our newsletter to get our
latest eBook deals and stay up to date
with our weekly Book Club!
<u>Subscribe here.</u>

Meet the team at
<u>www.onemorechapter.com</u>

Follow us!

 @OneMoreChapter_

@OneMoreChapter

@onemorechapterhc

Do you write unputdownable fiction?
We love to hear from new voices.
Find out how to submit your novel at
<u>www.onemorechapter.com/submissions</u>

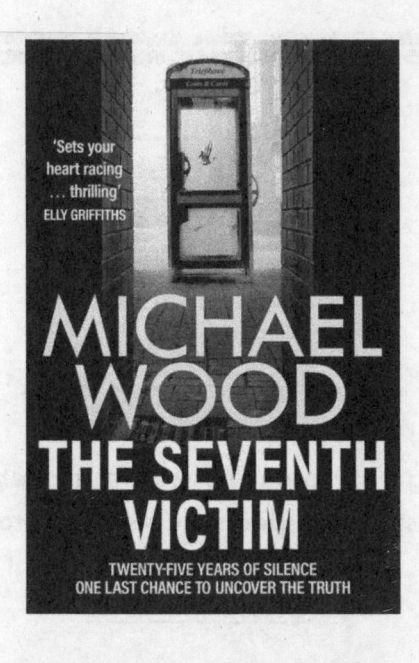

From the bestselling author of the DCI Matilda Darke series comes a standalone thriller that will keep you on the edge of your seat until the very last page...

Available in eBook and paperback now

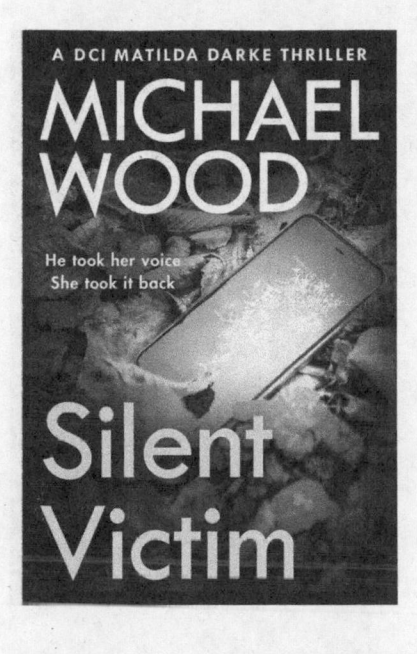

A DCI MATILDA DARKE THRILLER

MICHAEL WOOD

He took her voice
She took it back

Silent Victim

DCI Matilda Darke and her team have been restricted under special measures after a series of calamitous scandals nearly brought down the South Yorkshire police force.

Now Matilda is on the trail of another murderer, an expert in avoiding detection with no obvious motive but one obvious method.

Available in eBook, audio and paperback now

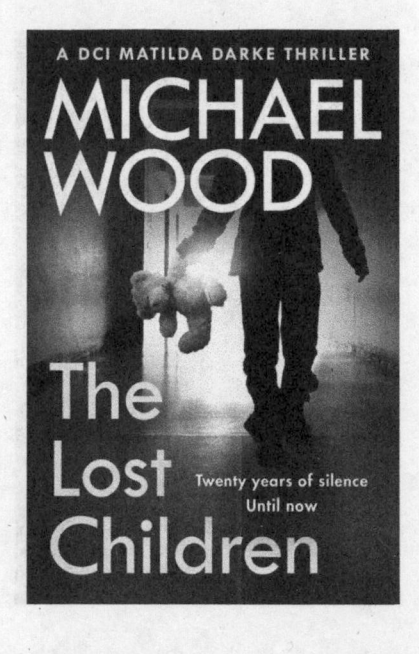

The Lost Children is an utterly gripping crime thriller weaving a breakneck tale of a vast network of secrets and lies, a relentless detective determined to sabotage it, and a murder that shatters two decades of silence.

Available in eBook, audio and paperback now

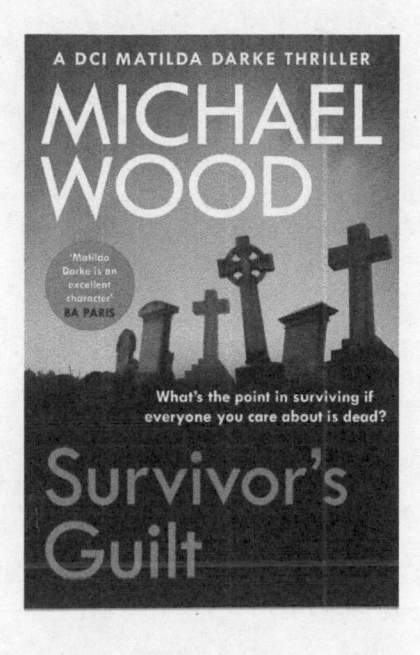

Nine months ago DCI Matilda Darke survived a bullet to the head. The brutal attack claimed dozens of lives, including those she loved most, and the nightmares still plague her every waking thought.

Now, she's ready to get back on the job. But a new terror awaits. A woman is found murdered and her wounds look eerily similar to several cold cases. Desperate to find a lead, DCI Darke and her team must face a terrifying truth: a serial killer is on the loose in Sheffield.

Available in eBook, audio and paperback now